Tales of Eleusia

Shadow of the Spider

(Revised)

A Quest To Save A Queen

M. E. Burgess

2023

ISBN: 978-1-962204-06-4 (ebook)

ISBN: 978-1-962204-05-7 (Paperback)

ISBN: 978-1-962204-07-1 (Hardcover)

Printed in the United States of America

Main Characters

(The characters are not listed in order of appearance.)

Olympian Council

Hera – Queen of the Gods, wife of Zeus
Zeus – King of the Gods, husband of Hera
Mercury – Messenger of Zeus
Rudana – Enchantress and Queen of the Sirens

Glockamarians

Azmodeus – Wizard
Sharra – Queen of Draukenberg
Nikolai – King of Draukenberg
Spider – potential destroyer of Eleusia
Yonnus – blacksmith and father of Mikel
Talman dan Vay – father of Tovan
Drogo – brother of Portia
Phineas – father of Portia
Mikel – member of the riddle quest
Jamie – member of the riddle quest
Jeremiah – member of the riddle quest
Portia – member of the riddle quest
Melisande – member of the riddle quest
Tovan – member of the riddle quest
Petre – member of the seed of life quest
Kara – captured by Spider

Other Members of Quests

Crutchin – a Wildenchin, child of the earth
Bandiloimaa (Bandi) – Mikel's Wickersnit assistant
Crooks – a mountain pixie and assistant to Azmodeus

Elves of Donagal

The Willik – the Lady Queen
Collpepper – gryphon rider
Arynn – gryphon rider
Erisan – handmaiden to The Willik

Dwarves

Maxim – escort out of Glockamar
Reygould – dwarf king
Calliotrope – who was once Kartoudik

Aradell – Home of the Riddle Quest

Sphinx – holder of the first riddle
Brutus – the sea monster that supposedly has the second riddle
Brax – dragon from the Crystal Spire Mountains
Crill – son of Brax
The Songmaster – father of Crill and dragon leader
The Snake Turtles – holder of the third riddle
Rosamund – Queen of the Sprites and Fairies
King Hagmar Sylxidor (Rumplestiltskin) – holder of the fourth riddle
Cerce – enchantress and holder of the fifth riddle
King Friere – sorcerer and holder of the sixth riddle

The Hollows – Place of Evil

Minotaur – a boy named Adonis transformed
Corilla – witch sent to assist Spider
Zorna – witch sent to assist Spider
Druet – witch sent to assist Spider
Kartoudik (Calliotrope) – King of Hag's Breath Forest
Alecto, Tisiphone, Magaera – the Furies
Clotho, Lachesis, Atropos – the Fates

Chapter Titles

Eleven Years Ago In Draukenberg, Eleusia…

The rooftop garden was one of Sharra's favorite spots. Her husband, King Nikolai, had it built as a wedding gift for her when he had brought her to Magnigona Castle as his bride five years before. From here, she had an excellent view of the countryside that surrounded them, which was mainly miles of forest dotted with villages and hamlets. The Gillian River, which began its journey in the rugged Zagoroth Mountains in the west, passed them by with swift determination on its way to the Mogell Sea in the north. She had grown quite used to the soothing sounds of the river. There had been many nights when she had gone to bed, her head filled with the concerns and problems that needed to be solved for the diverse inhabitants of Draukenberg, only to be lulled to sleep by the sounds of the river.

She watched with pride as her two-year-old triplets scampered in and around the trees and bushes, playing a noisy game of tag. She would have enjoyed it more if the feeling of foreboding that had been with her since early morning was not starting to increase. Sharra glanced once again at the sky. It was probably her imagination, but she was certain that it had darkened slightly in the east. Something was wrong, and she had a terrible feeling that she knew exactly what it was. She quickly sent out a mind-link to the only one who would know what to do.

Azmodeus. Come quickly.

The air rippled around her, and seconds later, an elderly man dressed in a tunic and sandals stepped out from behind one of the trees. His once red hair and beard were streaked with grey, the lines of experience on his face telling of a man who had lived long and seen much. However, there was nothing weak or frail about the man. He strode forward like a warrior, emanating power and strength with every step.

Eyes angry and wary, he demanded, "Has he shown himself again?"

Sharra shook her head as she gestured to the startled maid to move away.

"No. The sensation I am feeling is not of him. There is another coming, Azmodeus. This one hates and wants revenge. It's her. I know it's her! You must take the children and hide them! She mustn't find them!"

With every word, Sharra became more and more frantic.

Azmodeus called out to the maid. "Lucilla, take the children to their father as fast as you can. Do not stop for anything."

He turned back to Sharra and, taking her hands, pulled her to her feet.

"Do not be afraid, Highness. You must go into hiding with your husband as we planned, and I will look after the children. Everything has been arranged."

"Why are the others allowing this?" she cried. "They promised us. They promised to leave us alone."

"I don't know. But as soon as you are all in places of safety, I intend to find out. Now come."

He turned and began to stride quickly toward the door that led into the castle.

"Wait!" called out Sharra as she turned and ran back to fetch her cape that she had left under a tree.

"No," cried Azmodeus. "You don't dare be alone...."

It happened quickly. Sharra snatched up her cape and took two steps toward him just as an impenetrable mist settled on the garden. He saw her turn and look over her shoulder, and then she disappeared from sight. When the mist lifted seconds later, the Queen of Draukenberg had vanished, her cape left forgotten on the ground.

Chapter One
A Day Like Any Other…Almost

Jeremiah

Jeremiah knew that he was being reckless…reckless and stupid. But he didn't care. His anger at his foster brother had escalated into an unimaginable rage, making him forget everything he had ever learned about descending the mountain safely. He shot over the moguls like a daredevil, narrowly missing trees and bushes that appeared out of nowhere and passed by in a blur.

"I hate him! I hate him!" he shouted into the snowflakes that were getting thicker by the minute.

Deep down, he knew that he shouldn't have taken the ski-out to the parking lot in the first place, and certainly not alone. He'd overhead other skiers talking about the blizzard that was beginning to blanket the upper runs. It wouldn't be long before the entire mountain would be engulfed.

"I am not an idiot!" he continued to yell into the bleak surroundings. "Just because he gets sports scholarships…just because he's the captain of this stupid team and that stupid team…just because…."

He punctuated each word with alternating stabs of his pole into the snow beneath as he carved his way down the slope. At the top of a particularly steep section, Jeremiah's sanity finally returned. He slid to a stop and leaned over his ski poles to catch his breath.

Nothing he did had ever pleased his foster brother. Harry and Grace Billins, Bill's parents and his foster parents, had always been kind to him – although, at times, they tended to look at him with vacant expressions as if wondering why he was there. He had always found that odd. Bill, on the other hand, had always been aware of his presence and took advantage of every opportunity to make his life a misery. Jeremiah sighed. Killing himself on the mountain was not going to solve his problem. At thirteen years of age, he should have known better.

Straightening up, he realized that he was looking into a total whiteout. An undulating wall of white, stinging particles surrounded him, and every breath he took seemed to freeze a bit more of his lungs. The wind was increasing in strength, and even in the minute that it took him to realize that he was in serious trouble, the freezing cold began to make its presence felt.

Jeremiah had a good idea of where he was on the ski-out despite the lack of visibility. Angling his body toward the downward slope, he began to traverse across the incline. When he reached the trees at the edge of the run, he turned and traversed across to the other side. It was a slow, tedious process, but he knew that it was the only way that he would get down in one piece. The cold was beginning to severely affect his fingers, toes and face, and the jacket that was supposed to protect against temperatures found in the Arctic was beginning to feel like a summer vest. When Jeremiah finally stopped at what he hoped was close to the bottom of the slope, he knew that his chance of reaching the parking lot at the end of the ski-out was slim.

At first, he thought that the shadows drifting in and out of the blizzard on either side of him were clumps of thicker, drifting snow. As they began to take on the shape of animals, he closed his eyes, convinced that his imagination was getting the better of him. However, when he opened them, the shapes became even more distinct. Wolves! He was being stalked by a pack of wolves! For a second, he froze. Waves of panic rolling over him, his heart pounding in his ears. Stories of a pack of overly large wolves hunting in the area had been tossed around back up in the ski lodge that afternoon. Most had scoffed at the idea. There hadn't been a wolf seen in this area in years. Well, he could certainly prove the scoffers wrong if he lived to tell the tale. He choked on the thought that the living part was highly doubtful.

How was he to escape? Where was he to go? A dim memory poked its way through his panicked mind. Wolverine Gorge was at the foot of this particular slope. If he could get to it, he could make a stand just inside its narrow entrance and fend off the creatures with his ski poles. Part of him laughed uproariously at the preposterous idea. The other half mentally shouted back that it was his only chance.

Without further thought, he jumped straight into the air, turned his skis to face down the fall line and shoved off, all in one smooth movement. He knew he had startled the animals left behind judging by the snaps and snarls that converged on the spot where he had been. Flying blind, Jeremiah prayed that he was heading in the right direction and that if he were, he wouldn't end up mangled on the rocks at the foot of the trail leading up into the gorge. Suddenly, the boulders he had seen in his mind loomed up through the snow ahead.

Swooshing to a halt, he clicked out of his bindings and, carrying his ski poles, struggled through the snow to the path that was only an indent in the drifts ahead of him. His boots made the climb treacherous, the soles slipping on the incline and failing to grip the rocks that protruded through the snow. Panting from desperation and near exhaustion, he finally reached the top of the path and the narrow entrance to the gorge. As quickly as he could, he turned back to face the animals, holding out two shaking ski poles as a threat.

The creatures were panting as hard as he was, and he realized that the only thing that had saved him up until now had been timing. He had been able to slide across the surface of the snow while the wolves had had to plunge through growing drifts. That was one point in his favor. Quickly sizing up the situation, he didn't feel he had much else going for himself. Niggling at him through his panic was the thought that these were something more than wolves. They were twice the size of the ones he had seen in the zoo. The heads resembled those of horses, and their shoulders would have been level with his had they been standing side-by-side. The thought made him almost laugh out loud. Standing beside one of these monsters comparing heights? The creature would rip him to pieces before he got within arm's length.

Yes, laugh, young human. Laugh, for soon you will be dead.

Jeremiah stopped waving his poles around and took a startled step backward. Had one of them said that to him…inside his head? Madness. He was beginning to hallucinate. He was beginning to lose it completely. The creatures even looked as if they were grinning at him.

One of the wolves growled and put an enormous paw on the path. Three pairs of slanted yellow eyes focused on Jeremiah's face and never glanced away as they all began to move forward. He shouted and gestured with his poles, but apart from hesitating for only a moment, the three continued to stalk up the path toward him.

Jeremiah's nerves finally got the better of him. Yelling like a madman, he turned and struggled up the narrow pathway behind, conscious of the fact that if he made one wrong step, he would plummet over the edge and land in the gorge a hundred feet down on his right. He would never survive the fall. All at once, a wall of snow engulfed him, and his ability to see anything vanished. He felt for the cliff wall on his left and found a small outcrop of rock. He stood for a moment, trying to listen through the wailing of the wind that twisted around him. Were the wolves behind him? What if they grabbed a leg and pulled? Trying to control his harsh, raspy breathing, he moved his hand along the wall and then cautiously stepped forward with his right foot, releasing the grip he had had on the rock. Without thinking, he took a second and then a third step. He suddenly realized that he had completely lost his sense of direction. A wrong step at this point could be his last. Beads of perspiration broke out across his forehead. Trying to control the panic that was building up inside, he held out one of the ski poles and stretched it around his body, trying to connect once again with the wall. At one point he thought he had made contact but he never had a chance to find out.

At first, he thought his eyes were playing tricks on him. The snow in front of him began to swirl in a circular formation, slowly at first and then faster and faster until it took the shape of a vortex similar to the satellite pictures he had seen of bird's-eye views of hurricanes. A growling sound, like that of some predatory animal, emanated from the center and as the maelstrom increased in speed, the roar grew to deafening proportions.

"What the…" he whispered.

Two things happened in quick succession. The ski poles were wrenched from his hand and went flying as straight as arrows into the center of the rotating mass. Before he could defend himself, he was jerked off his feet like a puppet on strings and yanked forward. He had time for one frantic, horrified shout before the vortex closed in around him.

Jamie

The Morrison girl had humiliated Jamie again, and everyone knew it and seemed to be enjoying her embarrassment. Snorts and snide comments seemed to be everywhere throughout the classroom, and some of the students were even flapping their hands at her from behind their ears. Jamie hunkered down into the seat and pulled her backpack onto the desk. The fish girl had done it again. During swim class, Jamie had managed to go the length of the pool on a single breath underwater. She had done it many times before, but this time, Marilyn had gone after her in the changing room. She and two of her friends had held Jamie down while Marilyn had attached plastic, rippled ears to her own. Before Jamie had had a chance to react, the three girls had dragged her out into the pool area shouting, "It's true! Fish girl has gills!"

She tried to ignore the others as she pulled out her laptop to get ready for class. The Morrison girl would pay dearly for this humiliation. Revenge would be hers. The fact that she had never yet followed through with one of her threats of revenge was irrelevant.

"Can we begin class now, or do you need a few more minutes to prepare yourself?"

Jamie knew before glancing up who belonged to the voice. Although she loved math, the teacher in question would never have believed her despite her solid marks. Grant Barker was convinced that somehow Jamie was cheating and refused to believe otherwise. She looked up at the portly figure now glaring down at her from beneath a pair of bushy brows, the weight of which could have sunk a small ship.

"Well?" he continued. "Are you going to join us anytime soon?" He ran his middle finger and thumb down the opposite sides of his mustache, his eyes clearly showing his dislike for her.

"Yes, sir," she whispered, shoving her pack under the desk and opening up her laptop.

She knew why he tried to make her life a misery. Her father had refused to support Mr. Barker's plan to cut out the fine arts options to save money. Her father had a tremendous impact on the final decision since his wife had been an internationally famous portrait artist prior to her death. Old mustache face was also on Jamie's list. Someday she would have her revenge. Images of shaving off his precious mustache almost had her breaking into giggles. Imagination, Jamie did not lack.

She took several deep breaths and plowed determinedly through her afternoon. When the dismissal bell finally put an end to her misery, she was out the door and down to the parking lot, where Andrew waited patiently beside the limo in order to drive her home. This hadn't helped her either. Money was not an issue in the Whitmore family and being a rich kid had not done anything to help her reputation. As soon as she got through the front door, she raced up to the study on the second floor of the two-story home that her father had purchased in North Vancouver. It was a comfortable room with furniture and furnishings that had been lovingly transferred from home to home. Her only regret was that they never seemed to stay in one place long enough to get used to it. The saving grace was that her mother's paintings were always the first things to be placed on the walls, which made each house feel like home.

Her cat, Sparkles, sidled up to her, crawled onto her lap and waited for her tummy rub. Jamie laughed.

"I haven't forgotten you, spoiled creature. After all, you are…"

And then she remembered. *They* were coming home today.

She leaped to her feet, suddenly filled with what she would have described as righteous anger. Sparkles was sent flying, landing unceremoniously on the floor with an angry yowl and a spitting hiss. Jamie knew she was being irrational, but she couldn't help feeling the way she did. Luckily, her love for adding dramatic flair in coping with problematic situations saved her from trampling her phone and tablet into fragments.

"I will not tolerate that woman in my house. I will ignore her like so…."

She struck a pose for her audience of one, tilted her head back, closed her eyes and pursed her lips. It would have had a much more dramatic effect had she not looked like she smelled something disgustingly vile.

"…and if I have to speak to her, my words will simply drip with sarcasm like this."

Slanted green eyes blinked lazily back at her as she stretched an arm above her head, the attached hand arching in a regal pose. She placed the other hand on her hip. Jamie had never seen a regal pose but felt that this was close enough.

"Marla. If you ceased your ludicrous giggles long enough to become cognizant of your surroundings and those within it…"

Sparkles yawned.

"…you would realize that no one is at all inquisitive enough to be the slightest bit intrigued by what you have to communicate, articulate, express, verbalize or state."

Sparkle rolled over on her side, stretched her feline form to the limit of its elastic length and closed her eyes.

"And then I would…oh, you silly cat. You're supposed to be watching. That was my best Harriet Clarkson impersonation yet."

Sparkles didn't bother to open an eye. The mention of the fictional teenage detective so admired by her mistress that she had watched every episode at least five times didn't even elicit a twitch of an ear.

Jamie flounced down on the window seat and, picking up the cat, dumped the now protesting creature back onto her lap. She turned a pouting face to the view outside the window. It was raining again. When did it not rain in Vancouver? They had been in their new home for one month, and all it had done was pour with buckets of the stuff.

From her position on the window seat, Jamie had an excellent view of the driveway that wound its way down from the house to the main gates of the estate. Their new home was halfway up the mountain to Whistler Resort, and the fact that she was so close to a ski hill should have had her bursting with excitement. At the moment, it didn't. *They* were coming home today, which was one of the reasons she had raced up to the study when she got home. As soon as the car came into view, she was going to lose herself in this ancient mausoleum she now had to call home.

"I'll bet he proposed to that witch," she muttered.

Sparkle gave her an inquisitive glance and then returned to dozing on her lap. Jake Whitmore's supposed relationship with his secretary was of no interest to the cat. The fact that Jamie's father had taken Marla on a business trip to Hawaii and might have proposed to her there was the furthest thing from her sleepy mind. She yawned without opening her eyes.

Jamie sighed. Her mother had passed away from cancer five years before. She had been eight at the time, and the loss had been almost too much to bear. She loved her parents dearly, but after the death of his beloved Amy, Jake Whitmore had spent more and more time away from home on business. He barely acknowledged his daughter, leaving her in the care of the housekeeper even when he was home. Mrs. Watson had done her best to take the place of a parent, but it wasn't the same, and as time went on, Jamie became more and more lonely and less secure in what was left of her family.

Marla was the final straw. She would become totally invisible to her father if that woman became Mrs. Whitmore. Mind you, she mused, what would be so different? Lately, her father often looked at her as if wondering who she was.

Mrs. Watson had broken it gently to Jamie one afternoon that she had been adopted when she was three. She didn't know very much about it as the family hadn't hired her as a housekeeper until after Jamie had arrived. At first, Jamie had been quite upset.

"Why didn't they tell me?" she had asked, her eyes filled with tears. "I deserved to know."

Mrs. Watson had taken her hand gently in her own. "Amy would have told you had she lived. But you mustn't go on so. They loved you as their own, and you've wanted for nothing. Is that not true?"

Jamie had to admit that as far as she was concerned, Jake and Amy couldn't have been better parents to her. However, ever since she had found out about her beginnings, the desire to find her real parents had taken root in her thoughts. She hoped her father would not feel hurt by her wanting to find them.

The front door of their home suddenly exploded open with a tremendous bang. A movement at the gate caused her to glance out the window. Her father's car had just turned into the long driveway that ran up to the house. If it wasn't him, then who had had the nerve to slam their way into their house? She crept out of the room and crossed the landing to the balcony that overlooked the main floor. She reached the banister just as Mrs. Watson came through the kitchen door into the main foyer.

"Who are you?" Mrs. Watson demanded harshly. "What do you think you…"

Suddenly a scream rent the air, followed by the sound of a body hitting the floor. Horrified, Jamie backed away from the banister and looked frantically around. What had happened to Mrs. Watson? Something evil was in the house. She had to hide. Was Mrs. Watson all right? Where could she go?

Her thoughts in a jumble, Jamie crept along the landing to the hall that ran the length of the house at the back. Sounds of breaking objects and heavy items hitting walls told her that the intruder was looking for something. She picked up her pace, moving as stealthily as possible to the cobweb-infested stairs that would take her up to the attic. She had used the space often, and no one bothered her up there. In fact, she was convinced that no one knew the attic actually existed. The trunks and old furniture scattered throughout its immense space held the memories of previous owners, and she'd spent several afternoons exploring the contents and pieces.

Sparkle bounded into the room ahead of her. As she closed and locked the door behind her, a terrible thought struck her. What of her father and Marla? What would happen to them if they walked in on this? But what was *this*?

Light from the grimy windows provided enough illumination for her to see, and she rushed unerringly down the room, stopping in front of a full-length, freestanding mirror that had obviously seen better days. It was a rectangular, gilt-edged monster, much taller than her own five-foot, four-inch frame. At the moment, it was reflecting back a frightened girl with huge, terrified eyes.

It was subtle at first. The edges of her reflection began to blur and a mist drifted gently across her image. She stepped forward and cautiously touched the glass. Instead of the hard, slick surface that she had expected, it gave beneath her fingers like soft rubber. It resembled the surface of a bowl of jelly.

"Wow," she whispered. "What is going on?"

The pounding of feet and guttural shouts now coming from the second floor sent her heart into her throat. There was more than one intruder. Sparkle wound around her legs and she had the strangest feeling that the cat was pushing her toward the mirror. She suddenly realized that the intruders had found the stairs to the attic. She knew the old door would not keep them out for long and within seconds, it began to buckle inwards as if a strong force was pressing into it from the other side.

"What am I to do?" she whispered, crossing her arms in front of her and squeezing tight to keep from screaming. She turned back to the mirror, hoping that somewhere in the attic was something that would save her.

She choked at what she saw. The glass in the mirror had vanished completely. The mist that had been seeping gently into the reflection when she had first looked was now a swirling mass of storm clouds. The shrieks and wails of an angry wind began to fill the attic, whipping her hair past her face. She realized with horror that she was being pulled into the vortex of the storm. The door crashed open behind her and she spun around to face her attacker. Before she had a chance to see what was there, Sparkle leaped at her and hit her with such a force that it sent her into the swirling void behind. Jamie had time for one horrified shriek, and then she was gone.

Chapter Two
Trouble In The Valley

Mikel

On the same day that Jeremiah and Jamie were experiencing frightening events in different places in their world, the young people sitting under a tree in Glockamar Valley in the dimension of Eleusia, far from that of Earth, were having their own troubles. Each day, they attended lessons provided by the old master Azmodeus, which had always been something to look forward to. But during the last few weeks, the conversation had focused on why the children had been disappearing from the village.

"But where has she gone, sir?" whispered Tovan's sister, little Annmarie. "Katta is my friend…my very best friend."

Mikel, one of the boys sitting in the back, watched Azmodeus mentally wrestle with how he was going to answer this question. He was also wondering the same thing. Two months ago, there had been thirty children who attended the class, but today, there were only twenty. How many would there be tomorrow?

"It's because she could heal others, isn't it?" blurted out Damiette, who was sitting in front of him. "She could heal with her hands."

The Master sighed.

"Yes. She has been taken to the Sanctuary in Toria."

Mikel shook his head. None of the other children who had been taken there had returned. No one, including their parents, had heard from them again. He raised his hand.

"Master, why just young ones like us? Everyone knows it's against the law to do magic, but it used to be that if children forgot or did it by accident, they'd always just get a harsh talking to by an

Elder, not be taken away to Toria or any other place. Why is this happening?"

"I do not yet know the answer to your question, Mikel, but I intend to find out. Many of the valley folk no longer possess magical abilities of any kind, so it is also not possible that all of the children who have been taken do either. So why so many?"

"Well, my father believes that it's a contagious affliction and that the families of those individuals who have it should also be sent to Toria."

Mikel didn't need to turn around to know who had spoken. Portia was the daughter of the Head Man of the village, who was now also running the Valley Council in Toria. She constantly made certain, as a result, that everyone knew that that made her one social step above them. Tugging at the stole of her city-bought robe, the only city-bought robe in the village area, Portia raised her nose even further into the air and looked pointedly over at Tovan. There were mixed grumbles from most of the other children, but no one ever challenged her except Mikel, who couldn't be bothered to do so on this occasion. Portia's father was only too quick to come to his daughter's defense by way of inflicting pressure one way or another on the family of the child who did so.

"Now, Portia," admonished the master, his voice calm and kind. "We all know that just because one member of the family displays abilities doesn't mean that others in the same family are capable. It is quite normal for people to worry about what is happening right now in the valley, but quite another to jump to conclusions."

"My father does not jump to conclusions!" shouted Portia.

This time Mikel did turn around. The girl had leaped up from her stool during her outburst and was now glaring red-faced at Azmodeus, her hands clenched at the sides.

"If it's not contagious," spat out Portia, "then why have both Tovan's brother and sister been sent to the Sanctuary?"

Mikel glanced over at Tovan, who was trying desperately not to cry. Her brother and sister had been taken because it was discovered that they could mind-link with one another. What nobody knew was that he, Tovan, and three other friends could do the same thing. But they were keeping that information to themselves. If others found out…he didn't want to think about that.

Azmodeus lost the complacent, almost absent-minded expression usually to be found on his face.

"Portia. You are behaving without respect or manners. "Sit down, please."

"I will not! And you are going to be sorry for embarrassing me."

With that, Portia turned and stomped away from the little classroom in the meadow, followed by her brother, Drogo, who kept throwing menacing looks back over his shoulder at the group. It would have been suitably dramatic had Portia not tripped on a root and stumbled clumsily into the trunk of the tree under which they were all seated. Roars of laughter erupted from the group until she turned to glare at them. All laughter stopped in an instant except for Mikel's hearty guffaws. He was not afraid of Portia or her father. No one messed with the village blacksmith, who took absolutely no nonsense from anyone and who happened to be his father.

Azmodeus shook his head and pulled himself stiffly to his feet. "That will be all for today, young ones. Be off with you now. I know there are chores to be done at home before the sun sets."

Mikel approached Tovan and helped her lift Anmarie to her feet. Each of the young people were dressed the same in cotton robes that covered them to their knees, dark pants, rawhide boots and colored sashes tied around each waist. Although the colors of the clothes were of personal choice, the sashes were not. Each of the jobs in the village and on the surrounding farms was communicated to others through the color of the sashes they wore. Mikel's was black, to communicate that he was the son of the blacksmith, while those of Tovan and Anmarie were white, announcing that they were the daughters of the dairy farmer down the road.

"Come on," he whispered. "We'll talk on the way home and ignore Portia. The girl is just plain bad."

Tovan gave a watery smile, took hold of Anmarie's hand and followed Mikel to the road. He didn't have to look around to know that Melisande, Petre and Kara were right on their heels.

Tonight? asked a voice into his mind from someone behind.

Both Mikel and Tovan subtly nodded their heads. The group had agreed when the disappearances of their friends and family members had begun that it was safer if they were seldom seen actually talking together. More and more city spies were moving out into the countryside, making it harder for the locals to know whom to trust. They were even beginning to mistrust members of families who had been friends for generations.

The five were strong examples of the physical diversity to be seen in the residents of Glockamar, diverse differences brought to Eleusia from Earth by their ancestors. Melisande, at fourteen, was the oldest. Her school days were coming to an end, and she would shortly be joining her family in their clothing business. Her dark complexion and the rich chestnut color of her hair with its streaks of copper tones gave her an exotic look that Mikel, at thirteen, couldn't help but notice. He knew deep down that Melisande was out of his league, but that didn't stop him from trying. His green eyes lit up whenever he saw her. Mikel's dusky skin had a lighter tone than hers, and his hair had a distinct dark red caste to it. Red hair was common within the community, but what he hated most was the dusting of freckles across his nose and cheeks. He thought they made him look like a child. Tovan, at twelve, was a mix of several cultures. Her hair, which she often stated was her greatest flaw, was actually several interesting shades of brown, with a mass of curls that never seemed to stay in the spots where they were placed. Her complexion had an olive tone to it, and her large hazel eyes had an upward tilt at the corners giving her a slightly elfish appearance. Black-eyed Petre was twelve with lighter skin, and hair almost white blond. Never afraid of a good adventure, he was often up to his elbows in trouble, always looking for great adventures.

Eleven-year-old Kara, on the other hand, had hair the color of ebony, a light copper-colored complexion and was the only one in the group to have blue eyes. The five were very different in appearance, age and personality but were the best of friends.

Tovan, Mikel and Anmarie continued on through the village as the others dropped off one at a time to travel to their own homes. The village of Torsvale was a collection of a dozen cottages, each of which housed a family that was responsible for providing one resource to the other families in the area, such as woven cloth, bread or footwear. Surrounding the village were a number of farms, each one specializing in one item of produce such as fruit, vegetables, milk or meat. The village was only one of many scattered throughout the vast expanse of the mountain-encased Glockamar Valley, deep within the Zagoroth Mountains on the west side of the country of Draukenberg. The Glockamarians had no contact with those who lived on the outside of the valley out of choice. Their ancestors had moved into the mountain basin when they first arrived on Eleusia, sealed it off from the rest of the country and banned the use of magic in any form, severely punishing those caught using it. The Magi were the only ones who had permission to use spells but only in extreme emergencies. Now, hundreds of years later, no one remembered the real reasons for the ban but continued to follow the laws as they had been originally set down.

"Someone's been watching our house," said Tovan in a low voice.

"How do you know?"

"Last night when I went out to milk the cows, I spotted someone behind one of the trees beside the barn. I could see the sleeve of their tunic, but I pretended not to notice and walked casually into the barn. When I came out, whoever it was, was gone. I made certain of that, but when I came back to the house, my parents were arguing."

"What about?"

"My father said that the situation in the valley is getting worse and that more and more children are being taken to Toria. He said that people are afraid to talk to anyone about it in case that person is an agent or a spy."

"I know," replied Mikel, grimacing. "Yonnus said that there is an evil in the city and that the members of the council are refusing to listen to anyone who protests."

They were silent for a few moments as they walked through the center of the village. As they passed the local inn, the hair on Mikel's neck stood up as a wave of vile evil swept over him. He had never had this feeling before and, as a result, almost panicked. He turned his head and caught the movement of something pulling back into the shadow of the building. It was a figure disguised in a wide-brimmed hat pulled low over the face and a cloak that hung from the neck to booted ankles. Whoever the person was, Mikel was not going to hang around to find out. He sped up, forcing Anmarie and Tovan to run to keep up with him.

"Slow down," panted Tovan as they reached the edge of the village center. "Why did you run like that?"

"Have to get home," he lied, having no intentions of scaring her. This was something he had to share with his father. "Hey, you said your parents were arguing, but so far, you haven't told me why."

"Oh, dad wants us to move up into the caves in the mountains to be safe from whatever is causing all of this, but my mother doesn't want to. He says he and some of the others have been moving supplies into them for a while. I agree with my mother. I don't want to go either. You can get lost in those caves, and there's stories about horrific monsters that troll the tunnels looking for an easy meal."

"I don' like momsters," wailed Anmarie.

"There aren't any monsters," chuckled Mikel, patting her gently on the shoulder and getting a small smile in return. "I've been all through those tunnels, and I've seen nothing. Don't worry, Anmarie."

At the gate to the farm, the girls turned off, and he continued on up the road. It would be another quarter of an hour before he reached his home partway up the mountain. Mikel knew his father would not be home for several hours, which meant that he had time to try out his latest invention. When he arrived at their cabin, he tossed his school sack inside and got to work in the smithy. It wasn't long, however, before he knew he had a problem, the remains of which were hanging from the two wooden handles in his hands. Unfortunately for Mikel, he had a bad habit of trying to make things better, but more often than not, he made them worse. As a result, his father had often warned him to touch nothing in the smithy when he was away, or there would be horrible consequences. Such threats seldom stopped him from experimenting, and today had been no exception. He had been working on a plan to make the bellows more effective, and today, he had put it into action. His theory was that by making the valve for the air to enter and the nozzle that let the air out larger, the force would result in a better and hotter fire. On the first attempt, too much air had been sucked in, and when he had pulled the handles together to expel the air, the leather on the sides had burst. Yonnus was going to have his head.

All at once, he felt an abrupt change in the air as if something had been ripped open and then closed again…like the abrupt opening and closing of a door. He dropped the now useless bellows, his eyes never leaving the entrance to the cave that was situated at the top of the path behind the cottage. The disturbance had come from deep inside the mountain, possibly as far as The Cave of Winds. He wiped his hands on a cloth and then picked up a lantern in one hand and an axe in the other. Climbing the path with practiced ease, he entered the mouth of the cave.

He crept down the tunnel, carefully placing one foot in front of the other and listening to any sound that came to him from the dark space ahead. Mikel had traveled this particular tunnel many times before and knew each twist and turn by heart. The Cave of Winds was not far ahead, but he stopped and then moved slowly forward when a light suddenly flickered in the darkness ahead. At the final turn, he was able to see into the space and was completely startled by what he saw.

A strangely dressed figure was kneeling on the ground holding up a flickering light. A close-fitting hat made of something shiny hid the face, and fuzzy-looking material was wrapped around the lower part of the head. Only the eyes were visible. He assumed the person was male, but it was difficult to determine with all the material that was draped over his body. He didn't feel that the stranger would cause him any harm, as he appeared to have only one hand. The other arm ended in a green, fingerless stump. Where had this creature come from?

Chapter Three
Sudden Arrivals

Jeremiah

Jeremiah lay face down on the ground gasping painfully, blood pounding in his ears. He was dead. He was certain. It was disconcerting, however, to feel his scarf rubbing against the skin of his right cheek and to smell the musky dampness of his mittens. If this was death, he'd brought along his body complete with its senses.

Pulling himself to his knees, he was suddenly aware that nothing appeared to be broken or bruised, which was a tremendous surprise considering how he had landed. He sat back on his heels and looked around at his surroundings. Where on earth was he? This was definitely not the place he had left. A faint light from above showed that he was inside what appeared to be a massive cave stretching into the gloom in all directions. The silence was eerie, his breathing sounding loud and shallow in the unmoving air. Shadows rose from the floor, some reaching to where his shoulders would have been had he been standing. They resembled ghosts, and he shivered.

As he rose unsteadily to his feet, he unzipped the waist pouch in which he carried survival essentials. Rummaging through the contents, he pulled out a package of matches, removed one and struck it on the side of the box. He was totally unprepared for what happened next.

Beams of light, every color of the rainbow, exploded in shocking waves around him. They burned his eyes, slashed across his clothes and dropped like bolts of lightning from the ceiling. In his shock and confusion, Jeremiah fell to his knees, the match slipping from his fingers to sizzle on the ground beneath. As the match went out, so did the incredible light display.

"Holy smokes!" he whispered.

All was still and quiet. There was no further evidence of the balls of light that had attacked him so suddenly and silently a short time before. Groping around in the dark, his fingers curled around the matchbox that he'd dropped in his shock. Once again, he struck a match and held it high above his head. The light show began again, but this time, he held his ground. What he saw was magnificent.

Ice of incredible purity surrounded him on all sides. The walls of the cavern reflected his image back to him from thousands of varying angles and in as many shades and tones of color. It was breathtakingly beautiful, and he found himself gaping stupidly as his eyes moved slowly across the polished surfaces. Crystal clear stalactites and stalagmites hung from the ceiling and rose majestically from the floor. He smiled.

"My ghosts."

"Who are you?"

The harsh demand shot across the silence like a bullet being ejected from a gun. Jeremiah froze, the match flickering for a moment before blinking out. Light continued to reflect off the cavern walls as he slowly turned to face the speaker.

Dressed in a tunic, a black sash wrapped around the waist, and pants tucked into knee-high leather boots, the figure staring back at him had shoulder-length hair, which in the glow of the lantern he carried, appeared to have a slight red cast to it. The tunic had strange black markings all over it, as did the boy's face, leaving Jeremiah with the impression that he either belonged to a band or was a member of a cult. It was the axe clutched in one hand that bothered him the most.

"Who are you?" came the question a second time.

Jeremiah guessed that the boy was close to his own age and relaxed slightly.

"Jeremiah Billins," he replied, removing his helmet, hat and scarf. "Who are you?"

The boy seemed to be taken aback slightly when Jeremiah revealed a head of light red hair, and his grip seemed to tighten on the axe he was carrying when he removed his other green mitten. Jeremiah found that a bit unnerving, to say the least. He had the feeling that the boy knew exactly how to use it.

"My name is Mikel dan Jorin. Where are you from?"

Jeremiah found himself curious about Mikel's accent. He held the vowels longer than was necessary and clipped through the consonants.

"Calgary, but we're staying in Banff for spring break."

The boy's brow furrowed slightly.

"How did you get here?"

Jeremiah shrugged his shoulders.

"I don't know. I got caught in a blizzard and was chased by wolves into Wolverine Gorge. Partway up, I got attacked by a swirling vortex, and here I am."

The boy, Mikel, stared at Jeremiah for several seconds, his expression one of complete confusion.

"I don't understand your words, Jeremiah Billins. What is this 'blizzard' or 'spring break'? Is 'Baniff' a place?"

"It is pronounced 'Banff,'" replied a deep voice from the shadows.

Both boys turned to face the figure that moved into the circle of light.

"Azmodeus," sighed an obviously relieved Mikel, loosening his grip on the axe as the old school master stopped and leaned on his staff. "I was beginning to wonder what to do with him."

He jerked his head toward Jeremiah, who was staring at the old man with his mouth hanging open. Jeremiah was totally stupefied, and his thoughts were in no better shape. The old man looked exactly like the wizards that he had read about in books, two of which had come alive for him in movies over the past few years. Hair more white than red flowed over his shoulders, and a beard hung down to his belted waist. His robe was similar to Mikel's but, in this light, looked almost black. Dark pants were tucked into knee-high boots that had obviously seen some wear. His hat resembled a cake folding over on itself several times, topped with a peak that would not stand up so flopped over to one side. At the moment, he was resting on his staff.

"Welcome, young Jeremiah," chuckled Azmodeus, appearing to thoroughly enjoy the look of amazement on his face. "I hope the trip here was not too hard on you. I'm afraid it was the only way I could get you here in the time allotted."

Jeremiah had enough wherewithal to at least nod.

"But where is our other young friend?" asked the old man, walking further into the chamber. He peered into the gloom behind Jeremiah and then cocked an ear as if listening for something.

"Pardon me?" croaked Jeremiah.

His voice came out in an embarrassing squeak. He stopped and cleared his throat, this time purposefully lowering his voice, which in the end, was almost as comical as the squeak.

"Pardon me, sir, but could you please explain to me how I got here? There must have been some scientific phenomenon at work for me to travel from one place to another in the manner in which I did. Was it perhaps a wormhole?"

The old man peered intently at Jeremiah, then suddenly threw back his head and roared with laughter.

"You, young man, are just like your grandfather," he finally sputtered, wiping tears away from his eyes with the back of one gnarled hand. "Jaxom would have loved you."

Jeremiah's eyes moved to Mikel, who was glaring at him and then back to the old man. He shook his head. He'd landed in a loony bin, or then again, maybe he really had died, and this was some kind of crazy afterlife.

A soft thud sounded beside Jeremiah, and he took a startled step backward. A cat dropped out of thin air and bounded over to Azmodeus, stopping at his feet. It meowed loudly, and the man's expression changed from one of pleasure to one, both thoughtful and worried. Jeremiah shook his head again. Surely the cat was not communicating with the man. Animals could not communicate with people. There was simply no way that this old man was getting a message from a cat.

"This is not good," mused Azmodeus, tapping his upper lip with a boney forefinger.

"What's wrong?" asked Mikel.

Jeremiah stared at the boy. A cat appears out of nowhere, gives the impression of communicating with this ancient nutcase, and this Mikel kid doesn't ask what's wrong until the old curmudgeon appears to be distressed? What kind of place was this?

A whoosh sounded beside him, and he leaped back again as something landed with a loud thud.

"Don't people use doors around here?" he croaked when he saw what it was.

The girl was on her back in the dirt, arms and legs sprawled out in a manner that gave the impression of a beached starfish. She was wearing jeans and a T-shirt, so he assumed she hadn't been plucked off a mountain like he had. The look on her face was one of shocked disbelief, and he immediately felt a kinship toward her. He wasn't the only one now who appeared to be stranded in a madhouse. He bent down, grabbed a hand and helped her get groggily to her feet. He was slightly taller, but both seemed to have the same color of hair. When she raised her face to his, he was startled to see how much they resembled one another.

"They look alike," gasped Mikel. "They're almost identical."

"Not quite," chuckled the Azmodeus, obviously enjoying the reaction of the newcomers. "Similar but not identical. This is the first time they have met in many years."

Jeremiah stared at the confused girl. What was the old man talking about? They had never met before. He would certainly have remembered it if they had.

"Why, they look just like…just like," mumbled Mikel.

"Yes, I know. They resemble Portia."

Mikel shook his head, his expression twisting into one of utter disgust.

"They'd better not resemble her in personality, or I'll have to do something about it…something they won't like."

He hoisted his axe for emphasis, but Azmodeus held up his hand and shook his head. The boy lowered it with a reluctance that was not lost on Jeremiah.

"Where are they?" cried the girl, looking anxiously around. "They were breaking into my house."

The old man nodded as if he already knew what she was going to say.

"What happened, Jamie?"

Jeremiah's eyes narrowed. How had the old man known her name? But then he suddenly realized that Azmodeus had also known his name when he'd arrived.

"Someone broke into our house, and I think they hurt Mrs. Wilson," she gulped, tears rolling down her cheeks. "My father was just driving down the lane… I hid in the attic, but something broke down the door and…and if Sparkle hadn't knocked me into that…that wind thing…."

She stopped for breath, panting and sobbing all at once.

"…and here you are," he finished for her.

Jamie nodded.

"Hmmm," mused Azmodeus. "It appears that I got both of you out of your dimension in time."

"Is someone after them?" asked Mikel.

"We will discuss this later," muttered the old man. "Mikel, escort our guests to your home. I will be there shortly, but there is a task I must complete first."

Azmodeus stepped forward into the cave and, with Sparkle in his wake, quickly vanished into the darkness beyond. Without a word to the other two, the boy turned back into the tunnel, leaving Jeremiah and the girl to fend for themselves. Jeremiah looked over at Jamie. He grabbed her arm and propelled her forward, muttering under his breath at the same time that there were no such things as magic or talking cats.

"Science," he grumbled. "Now that's the ticket. Scientific logic is what is needed here."

Chapter Four
Explanations And Betrayal

Mikel

The girl Jamie appeared to be in shock. She was slumped in a chair and stared as if in a trance at Azmodeus seated on the other side of the table. Beside her was the boy Jeremiah who looked like he could have been her brother. Yonnus, his father, was leaning against the wall with his huge arms crossed while Mikel glared at the two strangers from the window alcove. Why were they here?

"I want to reassure both of you," began Azmodeus, "that all members of your previous families are safe. Your home will require a bit of a cleanup, Jamie, but Mrs. Watson is safe and unharmed, as are your father and his new wife. I took a quick trip to your homes last night just to be certain."

"Thank you," she whispered shakily, too shocked to even feel slightly annoyed about the 'new wife.' "But where are we, and how did we get here and why?"

"Let me explain," he replied. "There are many realities other than the one that you know, all of which exist side by side and, on occasion, overlap. Time is an interesting phenomenon. It twists and warps in quite wonderful ways. A great deal of money has been spent in your dimension attempting to find the existence of life on other planets, when in reality, life exists all around us. Quite close, actually, in hundreds of different worlds and dimensions."

"But how did we get here?" asked Jeremiah, his eyes wide with curiosity. "You still have not explained that."

"There are points that can be maneuvered in space that can allow for entries into and departures from different worlds. In both your cases, I used the vortex, which is fast and relatively painless."

"A vortex," whispered Jeremiah. "So I did see a vortex just before I fell into the gorge. What world are we in then?"

Azmodeus leaned forward, resting his elbows on the tabletop, and tented his fingers in front of his long bony nose.

"Jeremiah, you have always been an avid reader of books that depict elves and magic folk disappearing into the west at the end of the stories, have you not?"

"How did you know?" asked Jeremiah, narrowing his eyes slightly.

"I've been watching over you for years."

Jeremiah gulped, opened his mouth to speak and then closed it. It didn't take long for curiosity to get the better of him.

"Are you saying that you brought us to this 'west'?" he asked in bolder tones. "That you brought us to the world of elves and magic folk?"

"Excellent," smiled the old man. "I knew you were a quick study. Yes, I did, to answer your question. There is magic folk here and so much more."

"I don't believe in any of this. Fairy tales don't exist. Those were just stories I read. They aren't real."

Mikel snorted and rolled his eyes in disgust. Jeremiah pointedly ignored him, and Mikel grinned, finding his reaction amusing.

"Tell me, children," smiled Azmodeus. "What language are you speaking?"

Jamie glanced over at Jeremiah, who simply shrugged his shoulders.

"English, of course," he replied.

Azmodeus shook his head.

"I'm afraid not. You have been speaking the language of Draukenberg, the language of your birth, ever since you arrived. Neither of you realized it because it came to you so naturally – although I must admit, both of you are speaking it with an accent."

"That's impossible," cried Jeremiah, pounding the tabletop with a closed fist. "I don't believe any of this."

Mikel snorted again and gave them a look that clearly informed them he thought they were idiots. This time, Jamie glared back at him, angry tears filling her eyes. She suddenly stood up so quickly that her chair fell over backward.

"I want to go home," she demanded, her voice shaking. "My father must be missing me by now. Someone has to tell him where I am."

"Calm down, my dear," soothed Azmodeus, his expression gentle. "I know that this is difficult for you, but you must sit down and listen."

He crooked a finger, and the chair righted itself, slipped forward against the backs of her knees, and Jamie collapsed with a thump into the seat. She looked at Jeremiah in astonishment, the color draining from her face. His expression matched her own as he looked down at the chair and back at her. They turned in unison to gaze in wonder at this strange person.

Mikel had grown bored listening to the two strangers who held no interest for him. Several times, he looked away and stared intently out the window, not bothering to disguise his impatience to be off to meet his friends at the creek. He was already late for their meeting. There was no reason why his father and Azmodeus couldn't deal with the newcomers without him, although he couldn't figure out why the wizard had brought them to Eleusia in the first place. He had quickly recovered from the shock of realizing that the two strangers had come from another world, brought to Glockamar Valley by the power of magic. He and his father were two of a very small group who knew that the old teaching master was a wizard, and a powerful one at that. The old man had encouraged him to develop his ability to mind link but to never reveal this skill to anyone except Yonnus. He had always revered the old wizard's judgment, but in this case, he felt Azmodeus had made a mistake. Of what use were these two off-worlders going to be to anyone?

"That's better," continued Azmodeus, his dark eyes twinkling. "I do so hate to talk to a distracted audience. Now, where was I?"

Yonnus moved forward and sat down beside Azmodeus. He was a big man with powerful arms, shoulders and chest. A beard of the same color as his black, unreadable eyes covered his face, and the hair that reached to his shoulders was a great curly mass. Although he wore a tunic similar in style to those worn by Mikel and Azmodeus, the sleeves had been torn off at the shoulders to allow for more freedom of movement.

"Should you be telling them all this, Azmodeus?" asked Yonnus in a deep, rumbling voice coming from the depths of his massive chest.

"They need to know," replied the old man. "It is expected that they would be confused in the beginning."

He looked back at Jamie and Jeremiah. "I cannot explain everything you need to know tonight, young ones. It is more important that you rest in preparation for what is to come."

Jeremiah shook his head. "I want you to tell me what's going on," he demanded. "Why are we here?"

"I don't want to rest," joined Jamie, trying to be brave through her tears. "As far as I'm concerned, you have some explaining to do."

"You are both tired," crooned Azmodeus, pointing his right forefinger first at Jeremiah and then at Jamie. "You can't wait to lie down, and you will remain asleep until the morning sun rises. When you awaken, you will both be calm and relaxed, more accepting of what has happened."

All at once, the two appeared to be having trouble keeping their eyes open.

"Mikel, be so kind as to show each of these young persons to a place where they may sleep."

Without a word of protest, Jeremiah and Jamie rose from their chairs, yawning and stretching. Staggering into each other, they followed Mikel out of the room and down the hall into one of the rooms at the end. Without a word, each climbed into one of the two beds available and dropped into a dreamless sleep.

As soon as he had deposited them into their beds, Mikel slipped out to join his friends at the brook and a short time later, stopped at the edge of the forest and tried to mind-link with his friends. Moments before, he had suddenly lost all contact with them and was totally confused by the mental cries filled with horror and panic that had filled his thoughts before the links had been severed. He continued to move through the trees but with more stealth and caution. Something was terribly wrong. When he reached the bank overlooking the brook, Mikel got down on his hands and knees and then onto his stomach, sliding forward in order to see over the edge.

"Wha…?" he began and then clamped a hand over his mouth.

Horrific creatures were lifting his four friends, who appeared to be unconscious, into an enclosed black wagon which he recognized as the one from the Sanctuary. The bodies of the monsters were covered with thick, dark hides resembling the bark of trees. Muscular arms hung down to their knees, and the thick legs were covered in pointed, needle-sharp thorns. Their heads were distended forward, resembling those of pigs complete with snouty noses, sharp pointed ears and small circular black eyes. Their enormous hands were clawed, which at the moment were being used effectively to toss their victims unceremoniously into the wagon. Beasts such as these did not exist in Glockamar, but something about them pulled at the back of his mind. He should know what they were but why and how? Other thoughts crowded out those ones for the moment. Someone had betrayed them. Why hadn't the group known that these monsters were in the vicinity? Then again, he hadn't picked up on their thoughts either. Didn't they have any?

As he watched, something clambered down from the top of the wagon and ambled to the back. It moved in a lurching manner, a tightly fitting black suit covering its long, spindly arms and legs. Its head was bald; huge round eyes stared out from beneath bushy brows, and its mouth was one long thin line that stretched from ear to ear. It looked like something that had not seen the sun in a long time.

Three figures emerged from the bushes, two smaller ones and one adult whose rotund body strained at the seams of his robe. Mikel peered closely at the three. It was Portia, her brother and her father. What were they doing here? Portia's father handed something to the skinny lurching creature, and the three moved back into the trees. Had he given the creature something in the form of payment? They certainly hadn't come to rescue his friends, and with that thought, Mikel had to stop himself from leaping up and shouting at them. They had turned them in! They had reported them to these fiends! Wait until Yonnus and Azmodeus heard about this. Heads would roll!

A twig snapped behind him, and he glanced back. Standing above him, aiming a black cylinder directly at his face, was one of the nightmarish creatures. He had time to shout out the name "Azmodeus" once before the mist coming out of the tube the monster held rendered him as unconscious as his friends.

Chapter Five
Evil Doings In The Dark

Spider

The cell was typical of most that can be found in castle dungeons. It was small, dark and smelled of many lifetimes of stale water, garbage and creatures best left undescribed. Light hadn't penetrated the interior since the days of the original construction, but no one remembered that particular date. The castle had been there since before time itself. Water ran down the inside walls, ranging in quantity from droplets to narrow rivulets and was only of benefit to the moss and fungi that clung to the stony surfaces. Apart from the dripping and running of the water, the only other sound was that of the scurrying feet of rodents that had provided generation after generation of occupants. It was a strange place to house a statue of such beauty and quality of workmanship.

The young woman had been caught in the act of turning to face whoever or whatever was approaching from behind. One hand was raised as if to ward off the intruder, although she seemed to be more startled than frightened. Every detail from her facial expression and each fold and crease in her clothing gave the impression that this had been a real person frozen in the moment and transformed into alabaster of the finest quality. Gazing upon her, one could almost feel the air move as her hair swung across her shoulders as she turned or heard her slight exclamation, looking upon who or what approached. It was difficult to imagine why such beauty and perfection was being housed in the most despicable of holes.

Something within the shadows moved. A shape encased in a cape that covered it from head to foot emerged from the deep darkness. If there had been light, it would have been impossible to see the face, so deeply was it buried within the massive folds of the cowl. Spider sighed with frustration. The statue could not be destroyed until the time was right. To do so would destroy her own powers and send her soul screaming with horror into the Seventh Realm…at least, that had been the warning she had received from the other one.

"Let them search," she muttered. "They will never find the queen in time, and Draukenberg will be mine and mine alone."

Something that might have been a laugh but sounded more like a venomous hiss hung on the air for a moment and then, like wisps of smoke, faded away. She turned and walked to the door, pulling it closed behind her without looking back. The lock squealed as the key was turned in the rusty mechanism. At the sound of the satisfying click, the key was removed and pocketed within the recesses of her cape. Only one other person knew of the location of the statue, which, as far as she was concerned, was one too many. How she hated being this one's servant. She was used to making her own evil and devious plans and had been quite content to do so in The Hollows before the other had tricked her into following through with her own plans. She did have to admit, however, that she was getting great pleasure out of the experience.

Spider glided up the three sets of stairs leading to the chamber on the main level, her feet touching neither steps nor landings. The other would be waiting for her now, and it never boded well for anyone to be late for an appointment with her.

The chamber was not much brighter than the dungeon cell. Spider preferred the dark. Heavy drapes covered the windows, the only light being that which crept in around the edges during the day. At night, the room was darker than the outside world, no starlight or moonlight making its way into this lair.

Spider entered the main room and paused. She was there, draped in a cape and cowl designed to hide her identity, but Spider knew her name. The other turned with a flourish to face her.

"You are late," the other snapped. "Is it still safe?"

Spider moved toward the woman, in the faint light exposing the twisted hunch of her back and the awkward shambling gait she used when she walked.

"She is safe," she hissed back.

"And what of the task I gave you in Glockamar? Is that moving along at a fast pace? Have you yet found any of the three?"

"We have captured and tested many but have not found any of the ones you seek," Spider replied coolly. "And you. Have you done what was expected?"

The woman became quite still and then suddenly expanded to twice her size.

"Do not question me," she bellowed, her projected voice booming through the room. "You forget who I am."

Spider remained unmoved by the woman's threatening size and attitude. She knew that no harm could come to her.

"And you must not threaten me," replied Spider, incapable of keeping a sneer out of her voice. "If the others were to know what you have done, Hera, they would have you flogged or worse."

The woman gave a knowing chuckle, returning to her regular size. "No one will ever find out…especially from you. I am handing Draukenberg to you on a silver platter when this unfortunate episode comes to an end. Why would you want to hinder the process now?"

Spider had to agree but would never admit that to her. "And what of the children in the different dimensions?"

The woman appeared to be thoughtfully considering Spider's question. "The rumors from my spies are that two were spirited off into the same dimension. I know now which one, and have already sent emissaries to try and grab them before Azmodeus gets his hands back on them. However, they may be red herrings put there to confuse me. The real triplets may have been in Glockamar all this time, disguised and in hiding. I want you to speed up the process of searching for any children who possess talents. You will know the strength of their powers as soon as you lay your hands on them. The royal triplets possess powers much stronger than the skills currently shown by any of the Glockamarians. Most of the adults have probably lost their powers through lack of use, which bodes well for me. However, if they escape us, I have a cunning plan to bring them to me instead. In the meantime, I want to personally see every child that you find with talent. If they are not the right ones, you may dispose of them as you wish."

Spider hissed slightly. "Azmodeus is not going to sit back and let you do all this without a fight."

The woman threw back her head with a laugh, giving Spider a glimpse of pearly white teeth and skin that was smooth and unmarked. "He will be kept so busy that he won't have time to come after me. With everything that I am planning, he won't know where to begin."

Her amusement suddenly ceased. "I will have those children, Spider," she whispered menacingly. "Nothing evades me for long if I am determined to find it. You must find them for me, and what you do with the rest is up to you."

From the depths of her cowl, two orbs burned red as Spider stared back at her nemesis.

"You will not fail me," threatened the woman. "There are ways you can be punished if you fail."

Her outline wavered and began to shrink in size. In an instant, she was gone. Spider stared at the spot where the other had been for several moments. She was suddenly filled with a strong desire to get the job done as quickly as possible. Although she hated the other, what was being offered in exchange for her part in the deed was most certainly her heart's desire, and she relished the thought of all the evil she would inflict on the unsuspecting Glockamarians in the days to come. Dark thoughts and plans coursed through her mind, and she hissed with pleasure. She would find those children, and oh, she did so enjoy transforming the others after she had examined them. It gave her such a feeling of satisfaction.

Filled with renewed vigor and purpose, Spider ambled as quickly as she could to the entrance of the balcony outside the chamber and prepared herself for the flight to Toria. Her form began to shimmer and change like a piece of wax that was melting and molding itself into a completely different shape. The squawks, groans, and curses that were emitted during the procedure made it obvious that Spider did not like to shape-change. Nor did she do it often. Due to the number of shapes that emerged and were then discarded, she also didn't appear to be very good at it. She finally settled for the shape of a large, ungainly crow, leaped off the edge and wobbled skyward, barely missing the cliff walls on either side.

Within the shadows, the real caretaker of Mohandas Keep gave a cruel smile. He knew of the plan and hoped that the hags would be successful in their quest. New additions to his collection of the living dead would be welcome…most welcome indeed. It would be some time before he could play his part in this most insidious plot, but he could wait. He had all the time in the world.

Chapter Six
Chickens Don't Have Wings

Jamie

Jamie yawned and stretched. She'd had an excellent sleep, and she smiled contentedly as she opened her eyes. The first thing she noticed was the wooden ceiling with its darker beams striping the surface from one side to the other. This was not her bedroom ceiling. She sat up and looked around. She was lying fully clothed on an odd bed that was simply a mattress supported by ropes tied to side rails. In an identical bed beside her, was the strange boy she'd met the night before. The room was small, the walls made of wooden logs lashed together with what looked like strips of strange heavy cloth resembling a leather hide of some kind. There was one window open to the outside air and one wooden chair in the corner. She concluded that they were in a cabin of sorts. But where?

She leaped off the bed, staggering slightly from the suddenness of the motion. Yesterday's events came back to her in a rush, and her stomach knotted with the realization that she was still trapped within this horrifying nightmare. Like Dorothy who went to OZ, she would surely have to wake up sometime. This situation couldn't possibly be real.

"I was hoping I would wake up somewhere else," moaned a voice from the other bed.

"Me too," sighed Jamie, her voice shaking slightly. "Like back in my own bed."

She glanced over at the boy, who was now pulling himself up into a sitting position. In the light of day, he looked less like a copy of herself, especially with his hair standing up like the spines of a hedgehog all over his head. Both had a similar shade of red hair, green eyes and a dusky tone to their skin. Jeremiah's nose was wider and his face rounder than hers, but there was no mistaking the strong resemblance.

"This can't be happening," moaned the boy. "If I'm dead and this is my afterlife, I must have made some monstrous mistakes in my previous life."

"Do you have any idea where we might be?" she asked, the reality of their situation beginning to sink in.

"How would I know that?" he replied grumpily. "Another question is, why are we here? And exactly where is 'here'? Who are these weird people, and why do we look sort of alike?"

"That's a bunch of questions," replied Jamie glumly, plunking herself back down on the bed. "I don't have an answer or even a decent guess for any of them."

"What's your whole name anyway?"

Jamie paused for a moment and found herself struggling as she tried to introduce herself.

"Jeremiah...I can't seem to remember my last name."

The boy looked at her, a look of confusion on his face.

"I'm Jeremiah...wow, I can't remember mine."

They stared back at each other, identical expressions of puzzlement on their faces. The situation was becoming more frightening by the minute.

"I…I can't even remember where I lived," added the boy in a small voice. "Have our memories been wiped out?"

"Jeremiah," whispered Jamie. "I'm really scared."

Both were silent for a few moments, and then Jeremiah sighed.

"I think we have to try and make the best of it. We have no idea what to expect here, so although it's hard, let's size things up before we do anything stupid."

Jamie nodded. If Harriet could go with the flow in her adventures, she could too.

"Azmodeus said last night that he'd used the vortex because it was fast and painless," said Jeremiah. "He gave the impression that there were other ways to cross from one dimension to another…that is, if his story about dimensions is true. Fascinating."

Jamie snorted. "One would think that you were enjoying the situation."

"Well, it is incredible," grinned Jeremiah, "and that was some form of telekinesis that he used on your chair."

"It was magic, silly boy, but I'll bet you don't believe in that stuff. Now, how are we going to get out of here?"

She stood up and walked over to the window. The soft aroma of flowers covered with dew wafted over her as she leaned on the windowsill. She was startled to see that they were at the edge of a forest, thick evergreen trees almost hiding the mountain peaks the rose behind them.

"How can we get out of here when we don't know where 'here' is?" argued Jeremiah coming up behind her.

She turned back to look at him.

"When we go back to sleep and don't end up waking up where we came from, but end up 'here' again instead, then 'here' is what we have to get used to. So we keep our eyes and ears open, investigate and at the first opportunity…run!"

Jeremiah shook his head and groaned. "Do you always talk like this? Fast and totally incomprehensible?"

"I always make sense," she snorted and turned back to the scene outside the window. "All we have to do is climb out this window. We're on the ground level and…holy smokes!"

"What?"

"L…look over by those t…trees," she pointed, her hand shaking with excitement. "Do you see it?"

"Where? Cripes! What is that?"

"A satyr," whispered Jamie, totally entranced by her discovery.

The object of their attention was gazing back at them from the edge of a forested grove. It was about the size of a skinny ten-year-old boy, but that's where the resemblance ended. Pointed ears stuck out on either side of a sharp-featured face, and two small horns sprouted from the forehead just below a mop of thick black hair. The creature was bare to the waist, but the rest of his body was covered with thick, bristly fur or hair. His legs were shaped like the back legs of a goat ending in small pointed hooves. As soon as it realized it had been noticed, it turned and vanished into the woods.

"What kind of thing was that?" sputtered Jeremiah.

"A satyr," repeated Jamie, her eyes glowing with excitement. "Greek and Roman myths are full of stories about them."

"That can't be right," argued Jeremiah. "I mean, I like to read books like that too, but none of it is true. Myths are fairy tales. They never happened, so how can this sartar thing be real?"

"A lot, you know," replied Jamie loftily, turning away from the window. "I suppose you're one of those people who doesn't believe in anything that you can't prove yourself. And it's a satyr, by the way, not sartar."

Jeremiah planted his fists on his hips and glared at her.

"And I'll bet you grew up believing in Tinker Bell and Peter Pan."

"So, what if I did? At least I know my myths, and that was a satyr."

"Hah!" scoffed Jeremiah. "It was a trick of the light. It was probably some old goat that wandered away from its pasture."

Jamie could feel her temperature rising. What an absolute idiot, and she was stuck with him for the moment. The argument would probably have continued and become quite aggressive if it hadn't been for the muffled sound of someone shouting at the top of their lungs somewhere beyond the door.

"Now what?" groaned Jeremiah. "We're going from bad to worse. Someone's being tortured."

"Come on," whispered Jamie, moving cautiously to the door and opening it carefully. "Be quiet."

Someone was definitely in the room down the hall, shrieking horrible curses and threats at someone else.

"You rotten scum of a cow's turd! If my father gets his hands on you, he'll hang you from the tallest tree and gouge out your eyes and wrap your entrails around the trunk and…"

The curses continued.

"She sounds pleasant," snickered Jeremiah. It was obvious to Jamie that the screamer was a female and not a happy one at that.

"Come on," she whispered, taking a deep breath. "It's time we got out of here anyway."

They crept down the short hallway that led to the room that they had been sitting in the night before and cautiously peered around the doorjamb. What they saw startled both of them. Tied to a chair in the middle of the room, her face flushed and furious, was a girl who resembled the two of them. Her hair was a darker red, her eyes more brown than green, and her skin tone lighter but there could be no mistaking the similarity in facial features. They fell over one another, getting into the room.

The girl stopped her ranting at a very nonplussed Yonnus and stared back at the pair in astonishment.

"Does everyone in this place look like us?" gulped Jamie.

"No," rumbled Yonnus getting up from his chair and moving over to the stove. "And thank the rocks," he jerked his head in Portia's direction, "there's only one of this one."

"Who is she, and why is she tied up?" asked Jeremiah.

"Her name is Portia, and she's tied up so she won't go running to her father and get others sent off to Toria."

"They deserved to be sent there," shouted Portia. "And for your information, Mikel was the worst. Your precious son turned the others against me…he and that horrible Tovan…."

"Enough!" bellowed Yonnus. "I've had just about enough of your ear splittin' bellyachin', and if anything happens to my son before Azmodeus can get to Toria, you'll be the one hangin' from the tree."

Jamie had no idea what the two had been going on about, but one thing was certain. She was not going to mess with Yonnus. Even Portia gulped and silenced her tongue, although hatred and anger still blazed from her flashing eyes.

"Now, that's better," drawled Yonnus, bending down and removing toast and eggs from the oven. "We're going to have a nice breakfast in silence…."

He stopped and glared pointedly at Portia before continuing.

"…and then we'll get ready for our journey."

"What journey?" asked Jamie and Jeremiah in unison.

"The only journey I'm going to make is to go home," spat out Portia between gritted teeth.

Yonnus continued as if none of them had spoken. "Our friends should be here soon, so we don't have much time. Come on, you two. Sit down and get busy."

Jamie took her place at the table, feeling very confused. What journey? What had happened to Mikel? And how could Yonnus get away with keeping this girl as a captive and tied up in a chair? Surely someone was missing her and had contacted the police.

The big man stomped over, picked up Portia and the chair together and plopped them down in front of the table. His big fingers deftly untied the ropes that held her arms.

"Now eat, you wild pox on my life. It will be some time before you can eat again."

He turned to Jamie and Jeremiah, who were staring at him in bewilderment.

"Eat!" he bellowed.

Afraid to anger him further, they dove toward the food and shoveled helpings onto their plates. Portia, however, simply crossed her arms and glared.

"Suit yourself," shrugged Yonnus, sitting down to his own meal. "It's your stomach."

The three ate in silence under the critical gaze of a very angry Portia. Jamie empathized with the girl. She would have been just as angry had she been in the other girl's situation. She paused, her fork halfway to her mouth. But she was in that situation, and so was Jeremiah. They had also been wrenched out of their lives and had ended up here but for what reason?

She glanced over at Yonnus, dying to ask him a question but afraid he would take her head off. Finally, she couldn't resist.

"Mr. Yonnus, sir," her voice came out in a squeak.

"Yonnus will do," he replied gruffly.

"Yes, sir," she swallowed. "I saw a satyr outside our...."

Yonnus stopped and frowned at her from beneath black bushy brows.

"You saw a what?"

"A satyr…sir…Yonnus…outside our…"

"I knew we had delayed too long," he muttered.

He shoved his chair back, stood up and hurried to the open door of the cabin, mumbling something about sinking someone into quagmire. Pulling a small brown whistle from his pocket, he took a deep breath and blew. A high-pitched note echoed back and forth throughout the room and then escaped into the morning air. At the same moment, a small, feathery creature waddled in, stopped and peered at them through beady eyes and clucked.

"What is that?" asked a startled Jeremiah.

Portia glanced at the creature. "It's a chicken, you idiot."

"But it doesn't have any wings," gaped Jamie.

Portia rolled her eyes. "Chickens don't have any wings. Under what mushroom were you born?"

Jamie gave her a questioning look. Portia's face was twisted into an ugly expression of disgust, and for one brief moment, Jamie wondered if that was the way she looked when she was angry. It made the other girl look very unattractive, and Jamie was vain enough to think that she would have to remember that in the future. Harriet Clarkson would never be caught looking like that.

"Eat!" bellowed Yonnus again, moving around the room, pulling out knapsacks, cloaks with hoods and other odds and ends that he seemed to consider important. "And then get yerselves washed and ready."

"What are those?" asked Portia, pointing to the pile of cloaks.

It gave Jamie a moment of pleasure to see the confusion on the other girl's face. "Cloaks with hoods," she replied.

"What do you do with them?"

"Wear them," chuckled Jeremiah. "What mushroom were you born under?"

Jamie giggled as Jeremiah nudged her with his elbow. When she glanced over at Portia, the look on the girl's face almost made her choke on her toast. They might all look similar, but she was certain that she and Jeremiah had just made one nasty enemy. All of them lost their desire to argue when at that moment, a dwarf right out of a fairy tale or legend, complete with a sword strapped over his shoulder, appeared at the door and sauntered into the cabin. Within minutes they were dressed, outfitted for a trek and deep within the mountains behind the cabin.

"Do you have any idea where we're going?" whispered Jamie to Jeremiah, who was plodding along beside her.

"Not a clue," he muttered back. "No one said anything back there."

Ahead of them was Maxim, the dwarf who had appeared at the cabin several hours before. Slightly ahead of him was Portia. Yonnus had removed the ropes that had bound her hands and feet, but she had been doing everything possible to slow them down, and the big man was beginning to openly show his frustration. He was striding purposefully ahead of all of them, and behind Jamie and Jeremiah were two of Maxim's friends. Everyone except Portia carried lanterns in order to see as they wound their way through mile after mile of mountain tunnels.

Earlier that morning, when they had emerged from the cabin in order to start their trek into the mountain behind, Jamie was taken aback by the view and the strangeness of the sky. A huge valley stretched out in front of them, surrounded by the most rugged and incredible mountains she had ever seen. They were literally sheer cliffs, the tops disappearing thousands of feet above.

"This looks like an enormous room complete with a strange roof."

"You have a good eye, girl," Yonnus had responded. "That is a most appropriate description of Glockamar Valley, for the community exists inside a range of impenetrable mountains. The ceiling is actually a shield made by magic to protect the inhabitants from the outside world. No one can get in or out except those of us who know of the secret tunnels."

For the first time since meeting her, Jamie found Portia at a loss for words. She had simply stared at Yonnus as if he had grown a second head.

"Something tells me that she didn't know," Jamie had grinned.

"Few of them do. The inhabitants have been warned for so many generations not to go beyond Glockamar's boundaries that they have forgotten that they live inside the mountains, not outside."

"Why do they live inside?" Jamie had asked.

For a moment, it had appeared that Yonnus would answer her question, but then he suddenly changed his mind. The expression on his face gave the impression that he had felt he had said too much.

"All will be answered soon," came the curt reply.

Despite the fact that their three bearded companions were a quiet lot, Jamie couldn't help but wonder why the dwarves were so heavily armed. Each had a sword strapped diagonally across his back and carried a metal mallet. Smaller throwing knives were tucked into belts, boots and pockets of the hooded capes they all wore to keep out the mountain chill. Despite the fact that Jamie didn't feel threatened, she couldn't help but ask herself: Were they prisoners, or were they being protected? And if protected, protected from what?

They continued to move through the mountain for another hour before they noticed the darkness begin to soften. As they rounded a sharp bend, a ragged circle of light greeted them at the far end. Without a word, the two dwarves moved up from behind and took the lanterns from Jamie and Jeremiah.

"Thank you," said Jamie, smiling politely.

The dwarf simply grunted.

At the tunnel entrance, Yonnus stopped and waited for the rest to join him. Piles of rubble were heaped on either side, but a clear path could be seen leading away from the mountain and down.

Yonnus turned to the three dwarves and bowed from the waist.

"Grudran bay flayman," he rumbled.

The three returned the bow.

"Grudran fin wazin," they replied in unison.

They conversed in this strange language for several minutes, and then the four bowed to each other once again, and the dwarves vanished back into the tunnel.

"No wonder they never spoke to us," exclaimed Jamie, her eyes shining. "Were they speaking dwarfin?"

Jeremiah didn't reply. His eyes were focused on something beyond the cave entrance, and judging from his now colorless face and gaping mouth, Jamie figured that it had to be something extraordinary. She wasn't wrong.

Two huge creatures were perched on the ground in front of the tunnel entrance. Their bodies were equal in size to those of elephants and she could only guess at the length of the wingspans when the magnificent appendages were fully extended. The heads were those of eagles, but the bodies belonged to the lion family and were covered with fur except for the backs, which sprouted layers of golden feathers. The four heavily muscled legs on each creature ended in taloned claws like those of large birds of prey. They were both magnificent and terrifying at the same time.

"Gryphons," breathed Jamie, excited beyond her wildest dreams. "They're gryphons."

"S...something else from your myths?" stammered Jeremiah, his voice ending in an embarrassing squeak.

"You bet," grinned the girl.

Standing in front of each of the creatures were tall, slightly built individuals dressed in fur tunics and brown leggings. Long hair was pulled back into a single braid which hung down the back of one and draped over the shoulder of the other. It was, however, their pointed ears that caused Jamie to giggle.

"I think you'd better take back your remarks about Tinker Bell and Peter Pan, Jeremiah," she teased. "Those are elves."

Jeremiah was stupefied.

"What has happened to sanity and rationality?" he muttered.

Suddenly Portia screamed. They whipped around and saw her clinging to the rock wall just inside the tunnel entrance. She was staring at the gryphons and their riders, her expression one of sheer horror. Yonnus looked up at the sky and shook his head. Turning and marching resolutely past them, Jamie heard him mutter something about where was Azmodeus when he needed him. Just as he reached Portia, she fainted. Catching her easily before she hit the ground, he scooped her up and strode back toward them.

"Are you two going to come without a fuss?" he muttered.

"Do you mind telling us where we're going?" asked Jeremiah in what he hoped was a respectful manner.

"To Donagal," replied Yonnus. "Home of the elves."

Jamie had to cover her mouth to stop herself from shouting with excitement, ignoring the fact that Jeremiah looked as if he was going to be sick, and Portia, in her current state, couldn't have cared less.

The trip from Grumbletops, which was the name the elves had given to the range of mountains that housed Glockamar, to the elfin city of Donagal, was proving to be the ride of Jamie's life. They had flown for miles over the most amazing country that she had ever seen and at a height from which she would never have imagined flying without the aid of an airplane. She was squeezed between the elf rider, Collpepper, and Yonnus on the gryphon Fernwing. Straps circled her waist and were attached to cleats on the animal's harness. If she slipped, it would be a wicked wrench, but she wouldn't fall from her mount. She tried not to think of that as they sped over what looked like a living map. After all, her heroine, Harriet Clarkson, girl detective, would have taken this in stride.

Jeremiah was strapped in behind an unconscious Portia, who sat propped up between him and the elfin rider Arynn. Jamie suspected heights terrified him, judging from his bloodless skin and tightly shut eyes. As a result of his refusal to observe what was going on, Jeremiah was the last to realize that something was wrong. Jamie saw Collpepper signal to Arynn, and all at once, both gryphons banked steeply toward the ground. If she hadn't been strapped on, she would have fallen for sure. As the other gryphon passed Fernwing, she caught Arynn looking behind them and straining around, she tried to peer beyond Yonnus, who was also glancing back. Without the wind blasting into her face, she could see further and with clearer vision.

At first, she didn't see anything out of the ordinary. There were a few clouds in the sky but nothing that warranted fear of a storm. A flock of birds was trailing them at a distance. She looked closer. Funny…they were flying through the air like snakes would look swimming through water. As she watched them approach, a cold knot began to form in her stomach. They definitely did resemble snakes, and they were heading straight toward them. Fast!

"What are those?" she called back to Yonnus.

"Rogue worms!" he shouted. "Hang on!"

His answer didn't explain anything, but she was not going to argue with his instructions. Hanging on for dear life, she willed the gryphons to fly faster. Their mounts streaked toward a forest, and the rogue worms followed. Images of gigantic trees streaked past as the elves guided the gryphons in and around massive trunks at tremendous speeds in an attempt to dodge their pursuers. The worms followed close behind and although Jamie didn't dare let go of the harness to look back, their high-pitched screams made her long to cover her ears. At one point, flames appeared beside them. Were the creatures belching fire at them? Like dragons? The sudden erratic changes in direction were making her feel nauseous, but she preferred that sensation to being engulfed in flames.

Suddenly it was over. With hideous shrieks, the rogue worms pulled back and left them to continue on unhindered.

"What happened?" cried Jamie, suddenly aware that tears were running down her cheeks.

"Donagal," shouted Yonnus, pointing ahead.

Jamie hurriedly brushed the tears from her cheeks. Harriet Clarkson had never cried during a death-defying adventure, and neither would she. The thought did not stop the panicked shaking that rocked her frame and caused her hands to tremble so violently that she had difficulty holding on to the harness. She tried to look ahead at the elfin city, but without goggles, facing into the wind only made her eyes water more.

They landed in a large meadow, and Yonnus helped her down from Fernwing. Collpepper had leaped off his mount as soon as they had touched down in order to make certain that his gryphon had come through the ordeal unscathed. Arynn was doing the same with his own beast. From all parts of the meadow, elves were rushing forward to help. As Jamie's feet touched the grass, her body kept on going, and she landed with a thud on her bottom. Her legs felt like sponge. Yonnus reached down and helped her back to her feet.

"What are rogue worms?" she stammered.

"The scum of the animal world," muttered Yonnus. "You probably know them as dragons, but those rotten devils don't live in the Crystal Mountains with the others. They wouldn't be welcome."

"Dragons," breathed Jamie. They had actual dragons in this world. "But what did they want with us?"

"They wanted to kill us," snorted the big man. "Or should I say, they wanted to get rid of you children."

"But who…" gulped the girl.

"All will be revealed," smiled Yonnus, resting his hand gently on her shoulder. "Think positively, little one. She didn't succeed this time, now did she?"

"Not this time," whispered Jamie. But what about next time? And who was *she?*

Chapter Seven
Five Little Birds In A Cage

Mikel

Mikel felt violently ill, and the lurching of the wagon was not helping. He was lying on the floor in one corner, Tovan beside him, and Kara in the other corner. Melisande and Petre occupied the opposite end. There was enough light coming in through the bars at the top to allow him to see that the others appeared to be in a similar condition. Judging from the quantity of light, he guessed it to be early morning.

"Would you stop your blubbering, Kara," he moaned. "We can't do anything about this for the moment, and I feel too sick to care."

Petre groaned and tried to sit up. "What was in that stick they pointed at us? I feel as if I'm going to die."

"What were those monsters?" came the muffled voice of Melisande, who had barely moved since regaining consciousness. "I've never been more terrified in my life...except for now."

"Trolls," grumbled Mikel, having finally remembered why they were familiar to him.

"How do you know that?" asked Tovan, trying not to move her head.

"I read about them in Azmodeus's notes. They live in the deep part of the mountains and usually want nothing to do with us. Kara, stop snivelling."

"I...I can't," wailed the girl. "I'm not supposed to be here."

"What do you mean by that?" asked Tovan, trying to sound more interested than she felt.

"Sh...she promised," sobbed Kara. "She promised I w...wouldn't be taken."

"Who promised?" sighed Melisande.

"P...Portia."

For several seconds, no one moved or said a word, and then slowly, the four of them pulled themselves to sitting positions and looked at the girl cowering in the corner.

"What do you mean, 'Portia promised'?" demanded Tovan.

"She overheard us talking about m...meeting a few weeks ago and threatened to do terrible things to me and my f...family if I didn't tell her where and when. Drogo even h...hit me a couple of times."

"Why didn't you tell us?" snapped Petre. "I would have sorted out those two."

"But that doesn't mean that these trolls would have had a reason to pick us up," said Melisande, clutching her head. "What else did you tell her?"

"I t...told them that you all had afflictions. Portia didn't believe me, but it didn't matter. She told her father anyway."

"I was right," snapped Mikel. "That was Portia, her brother and father back there, and they were paying to have us all taken. And then she told you that you wouldn't be put in here with us? You silly idiot. Do you think for one minute that she would have left you behind as a witness?"

"I didn't think of that," whispered Kara, rubbing the heels of her hands into her eyes.

"It doesn't appear to me that you thought at all," sighed Melisande. "We're in a nice mess now."

Mikel stared at her for several minutes, incapable of commenting further. He was furious. He'd always argued that Kara had been too young to have been one of the 'Eagles,' the name of their group, and this had just proven his point. With a snort of disgust, he turned away, ignoring the whispered "I'm sorry" from the corner.

That was when he spotted it. The back door of the wagon was loose, and one of the bolts holding it closed had almost shaken itself out of its fitting. Swallowing hard and trying to keep his head steady, he crawled toward the back of the wagon.

"Move, Petre."

He pushed the other boy aside in order to get a better look.

"What is it?" asked Tovan.

"I don't know," he replied. "Just give me a minute."

At that moment, the lurching stopped, and the wagon moved forward on more even ground.

"We've reached the main road into Toria," explained Melisande, who, of the five, had been the only one to have ever visited the city. "We'll be there soon."

Kara's sobs increased.

"Stop it, Kara," grunted Mikel. "Give me a chance to concentrate."

He examined the bolt and looked around for something he could use for leverage. There was nothing on the floor, nor was there anything that he could pull off the walls. Taking off his boot, he used it as a lever to try and push the bolt up through its casing.

"Petre, hold the door steady, would you?"

The boy groaned. "What are you trying to do, Mikel? Even if you get the thing open, we've nowhere to go."

Mikel glared back at him. "If you want to stay in here, that's your business. But I'd rather do something than go meekly to whatever fate is waiting for me in that place. Now, hold the door."

"Alright, alright," moaned Petre, wincing as he got to his feet.

"There are no trolls behind the wagon," came Tovan's voice from the front. She had pulled herself up and was peering through the bars that ran around the top of their enclosure. "They're all walking beside the cows at the front."

"Good," replied Mikel.

He doubled his efforts. Putting everything he had into it, which wasn't great considering his wretched physical condition, he pushed and wiggled the bolt upward. When he had finally reached the conclusion that nothing was going to budge it, it popped out into his hands, and the door gave a sudden lurch, banging loudly against the metal bottom of the wagon.

"Hang onto the door," hissed Tovan. "One of the trolls is coming back. It heard the noise."

Petre and Mikel held the door tight against the frame with every ounce of strength they possessed. It seemed to take forever before Tovan finally gave them the 'all clear' signal.

"He's moved back to the front."

"I'm going to try and get the other bolt out," said Mikel, straining to keep the door in place. "Melisande, can you help Petre hold this thing? If it works, this whole door is going to go and we have to be ready to jump out and run for it."

"They'll catch us," argued the girl moving forward to help.

"No, they won't," said Tovan from her lookout spot. "From what I can see, they don't move quickly."

"Plus," grinned Petre, "we'll have the element of surprise on our side."

Tovan glanced back out through the bars.

"Well, we'd better hurry. I can see Toria just ahead of us."

Mikel got to work, tugging and pushing with every ounce of strength he possessed. The second bolt wasn't as loose as the first, but his determination seemed to be no match for the piece of metal. Slowly it inched upwards.

"We've entered the city," whispered Tovan harshly. "Hurry!"

They could hear sounds of activity outside the wagon. Voices called out to one another, but as the wagon came level with the voices, they appeared to drop to whispers or go silent altogether.

"Get ready," hissed Mikel. "It's now or never." With a last mighty effort, he gave the bolt a final smack, and the door fell off into the dirt behind. "Move!" he shouted, grabbing his boot.

Everything happened at once. They scrambled out the back, the trolls barked orders at one another, and people began to yell and shout on either side of the wagon.

"Run!" screamed Tovan.

People parted on either side of them and then closed ranks. It took them a moment to realize that they were being helped, not hindered. Panting for breath, they raced deeper into the city, winding around objects in their path and darting between the individuals standing in their way.

"Up there!" yelled Melisande, pointing to a flight of steps carved out of rock.

They flew up the stairway and followed a path that led between two rows of houses. They felt like they'd been running forever when Tovan finally stopped and bent over, barely able to catch her breath.

"We can't stop," gasped Mikel, "but we have to move slower and quieter, so we don't draw any more attention to ourselves than we already have."

"Where's Petre and Kara?" asked Melisande looking around.

For the first time, they realized that there were only three of them.

"Let's get off the road and wait," suggested Mikel.

They moved into a dark alley between two of the houses and crouched down. Toria was a city of stone carved out of a natural valley basin in the mountainside. The houses were in a dozen raised tiers; individual homes carved into the rock like elaborate caves. Each housefront was different from the others, uniquely carved by the original inhabitants to show ownership. At the end of each alley between the houses was a wall of rock. The three were trapped in the alley they had selected, but the thought never crossed their minds. They waited in the shadows, watching the road for their friends.

"Something has happened to them," whispered Melisande finally. "They would have been here by now."

The other two nodded.

"What should we do?" asked Tovan.

Mikel thought for a moment. "Maybe there's someone here who would be willing to give us shelter. We need to figure out where we can go because we sure can't go home. That's the first place they'd look."

"Well, we can't stay here," said Melisande. "Another thing is our clothes. As soon as anyone sees us, they're going to know we're from the country. The inhabitants usually wear leggings and jerkins in Toria. Robes, which look a lot better than ours, are only worn on formal occasions."

"Great," mumbled Tovan. "If they put out some sort of description, it won't take much to spot us."

"Let's get out of here," said Mikel. "Their chances of finding us are going to grow the longer we wait."

A shadow crossed their line of vision, blocking out what little light was trying to flicker into the alley. The three looked up, their hearts in their throats and eyes circles of fear.

"You are not going anywhere," whispered the grey apparition looming above them.

"Azmodeus!" Mikel went from fear to relief so quickly he thought he would be sick. "How did you know we were here?"

"Master?" gasped Tovan and Melisande almost in unison.

"Ah, my senses did not lead me astray," chuckled the old man, moving deeper into the shadows of the alley. "That happens the odd time, you know. You shouted my name, which instantly connected with me through a mind link, and then it was just a case of following it's trail to you. But where are Petre and Kara?"

"We don't know," replied Tovan, still shaking in reaction to seeing this hooded figure suddenly loom over them. "We've been waiting for them, but so far, there's been no sign."

"Maybe they didn't escape from that wagon," muttered Melisande.

"Yes, the wagon," murmured the wizard. "How did you manage to get yourselves in there in the first place?"

In a matter of minutes, he had heard the whole story from three very angry young people.

"Ah, that Portia," sighed Azmodeus. "Well, there is not much we can do about her for the moment. Let's see if I can find Kara and Petre. Hmm...I can still sense Petre, so that must mean that he has not yet entered the monster's lair but of Kara …alas, she is in the wagon that is entering it as we speak."

Mikel looked at the other two, their faces expressing the same feeling of confusion. The monster's lair? What was that?

"Why is the schoolmaster's beard only a few inches long?" whispered Tovan to Mikel. "And how can he sense Kara and Petre from here? And how did he find us?"

"No questions right now," said Azmodeus, holding up his hand. "I have to move you to a safer place, as trolls will already have been dispatched to hunt you down."

He poked his nose out from the alley and surveyed the street from one end to the other.

"Follow closely and say nothing. We don't have far to go."

The three didn't argue. Mikel knew what Azmodeus was capable of doing, but the other two only saw him as the old master and trusted him as such. There were few people in this upper back street, but no one paid any attention to them as they passed. Mikel had a feeling that Azmodeus might have had a hand in ensuring that they went unnoticed. After all, they were still wearing country robes that should have caused some interest or curiosity on the part of the Torians.

He led them down to the end of the street and up a set of stairs to the top level of the city. The houses here were much smaller than those below and had a seedy, unkempt look about them. He turned into an alley a short distance beyond what appeared to be a theatre and gestured for them to go first while he remained on the lookout. With a last cautious glance at the street, he followed them. At first, the three could not understand why he had brought them to the end of a dark alley facing a wall of rock. Azmodeus didn't explain. He simply knocked a code on the wall with the end of his staff, and the outline of a door appeared in the rocks.

"Inside quickly," he whispered, jerking it open.

They stepped into the darkness, the door swung back into position with a soft thump, and they found themselves in a fairly narrow tunnel that was dimly lit by torches in sconces scattered down the walls on either side. Following Azmodeus down the incline for a short distance, they emerged into a large cavern that was a whirlwind of activity. Parcels of food and bags of clothing were piled up against one wall while swords and other weapons dotted the floor. Dozens of humans, dwarves and, to the astonishment of all three, elves were busy packing a variety of these items into carry sacks.

Mikel had met the dwarf friends of his father before, and although he had never met one, he also knew about the elves. He found it amusing when he looked at the faces of Tovan and Melisande, who had never met or known about either race. They stared at the scene in shocked amazement. One of the dwarves bowed and greeted Azmodeus in the same strange language that Jamie, Portia and Jeremiah had heard at the exit of their tunnel. The old man returned the greeting, and the two conversed for several minutes before the dwarf called to one of the women, who hurried over.

"This is Sophie, young ones," said Azmodeus, introducing a beaming woman who could, except for the deadly-looking sword strapped to her side, have been anyone's grandmother. "She is going to get you something to eat, some more appropriate clothing and show you where you can rest a bit. I will be back as soon as I can find out what has happened to Kara and Petre."

"Let me go with you," protested Mikel, stepping in front of the wizard. "I'm more than old enough to help."

Azmodeus chuckled and shook his head. "No one can keep up with a wizard, Mikel. Besides, you have a job to do here by looking after these young ladies. I'm placing their welfare in your hands."

With that, he turned on his heel and strode back up the tunnel, soon disappearing from sight. When Mikel looked back at the girls, he saw two different expressions. Melisande had her hands on her hips and was glaring at him, and Tovan looked puzzled.

"I do not need a boy still wet behind the ears looking after me," snapped Melisande.

"Did he say 'wizard'?" asked Tovan.

Mikel snorted as he pushed past them to follow Sophie into the cavern. If Azmodeus thought for one moment that he was going to waste his time worrying about females, the old man had another thing coming. As far as he was concerned, all they did was take up valuable space!

Chapter Eight
Into The Lair

Kara

Kara was pushed through what felt like miles of hallway past dark, dank-looking rooms toward a set of enormous doors at the end. The chamber they entered was so huge she could barely make out the two figures at the far end. The strange little creature behind gave her a rough shove that forced her to stumble forward. The troll had referred to it as a goblin, and apart from the trolls and the strangely dressed soldiers, the goblins were the only other creatures she had seen since leaving the wagon. They were ugly shrunken little things with long arms, short bodies and wizened hairless heads. Their eyes were round pale globes that never seemed to blink, and they terrified her. She was shaking so hard that she could barely walk, but every time she slowed down, the creature would shove her forward again. The two figures at the end had not yet seen her and were in the middle of a disturbing conversation. The black-cloaked creature sitting in a grand throne on top of a circular platform was yelling at someone facing her from the floor below.

"None of the brats from the wagon have been found, and Hera will be furious when she arrives!"

Her voice grated through the air, the added hiss giving depth to its already nightmarish quality. Kara's shaking increased, and she thought she was going to be sick.

"There is only a short time left according to the Prophecy, and there has been no indication that Azmodeus has succeeded in any area. This is good, but we will not wait. You will move Hera's soldiers and my trolls out at first light tomorrow and bring in all the Glockamarians you can find."

"And the parents?"

"To be transported here along with their children. I have no time for further testing, so will transform them all. We must move quickly or face the wrath of the goddess."

"We will begin in the outlying districts. By working back toward the city, we will tighten the net, allowing few to escape."

"None to escape!" she bellowed, glaring down at him. "I want every man, woman and child of Glockamar, and for every single one that is missing, I will remove as many pieces from your hide!"

"Yes, your worship…your highness…your…"

"Enough!" she shot back at the groveling figure whose nose was now on the ground in front of her. Suddenly she noticed Kara and the group with her.

"What is it?" she bellowed and then pulled herself out of the chair, her face twisting into a truly frightening semblance of a smile. "A child. How wonderful. Is she from the wagon?"

"Yes," grunted the troll from behind.

Kara was now close enough to the platform to actually see her, and what she saw made her gasp with horror. Only the face was visible, but it was enough to bring terror to the stoutest of hearts. It resembled a skull with white skin pulled taut over sharp bones. The slanted cats eyes were red, standing out in sharp contrast to the pale face, and her lipless mouth was drawn back in an ugly grin. Small pointed teeth glinted in the dim light. Kara dropped to her knees, put her hands to her ears and began to scream.

"Stop that noise!" shrieked Spider.

Kara was beyond caring. One scream followed another, echoing back and forth across the room. Spider eyed her with disgust. Raising her hand and pointing a gloved forefinger at her, she muttered some words under her breath and closed her eyes. Kara opened her mouth to scream again. Suddenly, she was filled with a pain so wrenching, she felt she'd been split in two. And then she felt nothing.

Nothing at all.

Chapter Nine
Petre Gets A Change Of Clothes

Petre

Petre tried to shrink into an even smaller shape as another quad of trolls passed by on the road. He had taken refuge behind an outcrop of rocks down one of the alleys and was terrified to move away from what little safety and security it provided. He had no idea where to go or what to do. Every time he thought of Kara and what she had done for him, sorrow and rage coursed through his whole being. Somehow, he had to try and help her and hiding here was not going to resolve anything. However, every time he thought of moving, his body refused to respond. Fear kept him rooted to the spot.

Petre knew by observing the occupants of Toria that he was going to have to find a change of clothes before he did anything else. His robe made him stand out, and people would remember him passing and tell one of those monsters. Not everyone would be willing to risk their necks for some country kid, of that, he was quite certain. It was also obvious from the reactions of the Torians that the trolls terrified them as much as they terrified him. Not many would take the chance of protecting him for fear of retaliation. The boy had never felt so alone in his life.

He peeked out into the roadway once again and choked. Strangely garbed soldiers were checking the alleyway across from his own, and if he didn't make a move soon, it would only be a matter of time before they found him. Taking a deep but shaky breath, he glanced back into the alley in which he was hiding. Each of the buildings on either side had back entrances, and if one was open, he might be safe for at least the moment.

Scuttling away from his hiding place, Petre cautiously descended the alley to the closest door. The shadows grew deeper the further in he went, which provided some consolation as he would be harder to see from the roadway. He approached the first door and tried the latch. It was locked. Panic set in. He could hear the heavy tread of the soldiers coming closer, and without bothering to be cautious or quiet, he rushed across to the door in the other building and pressed the latch. To his relief, it gave. He slipped inside, closing the door gently behind him. For several moments, he leaned back against the door and tried to calm his thudding heart and shaking limbs. His breath was erupting in short, noisy gasps, and if there was anyone around, he was certain that they would hear him.

Petre quickly took stock of his surroundings. He was on a dark narrow landing with stairs going up on his right and down on his left. He moved to the left and down as quickly and quietly as he could. At first, he could make out very little. As his eyes became adjusted to the dim light coming through a small opening that had been carved through the rock wall to the outside, he could make out piles of objects that filled the space from floor to ceiling. An aisle had been created to allow individuals to pass through unhindered, and he did just that.

He spotted mirrors, fake plants and painted scenes of odd and bizarre landscapes. Several times, he jumped away from objects only to discover that they were costume headpieces of strange people or creatures. It struck him that this lower level might be the storage area for the thespian group that traveled through Glockamar every so often, putting on plays and musical acts. If he was right, the upstairs of this building would be a theatre and inside the bins might be costumes. He rummaged through the closest container and eventually had a small pile of clothes at his feet of what he thought might be acceptable.

"No, those won't do," chuckled a voice behind him.

Petre almost jumped out of his robe. He hadn't heard anyone come down the steps, but then again, he'd been making quite a bit of noise. He turned and saw the outline of a slightly built man standing with hands on his hips, and if the outline of the shape was accurate, the stranger had short spiky hair sticking out all over his head.

"You're one of the fugitives, aren't you? One of the kids who escaped from the wagon?"

Petre didn't reply. He looked around frantically for something to use to defend himself.

"I'm not going to hurt you, boy. By accident or design, you've landed yourself in a safe house. Azmodeus sent out a message to keep a lookout for you, and here you are."

"Azmodeus?" questioned Petre, his voice cracking in a most embarrassing manner.

"Don't worry," continued the stranger. "He's a friend. You know him as the schoolmaster, but he's more than that. My name is Crutchin, by the way."

Petre simply stared at him.

"You must be Petre."

"How do you know?"

"Simple deduction," laughed Crutchin. "There were two boys in that wagon, and Azmodeus has rescued Mikel, so unless they're making girls differently these days...."

"I'm Petre," he grumbled.

"Excellent," replied Crutchin rolling backwards and forwards on the balls of his feet. "Now, let's get you outfitted."

He darted forward and pulled a few more items from the bin, including a cape and an idiotic hat.

"You're about to become an actor, Petre."

"An actor?"

"Well, you can't hang around with me and pretend to be my nephew if you're not. Azmodeus tried to find you, but I sent a message telling him you're safe and he can leave. He's going to get the other three out of here and then come back for you."

"Only three?" queried Petre. "Don't you mean four?"

"Three. One, it appears, did not escape the trolls."

Petre's shoulders slumped. Kara didn't make it then.

Throughout this exchange, Crutchin continued to rummage through the bin. Petre was to discover that the strange little man could never simply stand and talk. He was constantly active and busy.

"But how could you have sent him a message?" asked Petre suspiciously. "You only just found me."

At that, Crutchin did stop and look at him. *The same way you communicate.*

The words rang clear as a bell into Petre's mind.

"You see?" chuckled Crutchin. "You are not alone."

He went back to his scavenging and finally found all the items he wanted. Pushing Petre behind a screen, he heaved clothes over the top for him to try on, rejecting the first few attempts and finally settling on one mismatched and, as far as Petre was concerned, totally unsuitable collection. He wore long boots, a pair of pants that belled out from the waist and gathered at the knees, some kind of shirt with wide sleeves and ruffles down the front, a cape that felt slippery and a hat that stood up in a point and from which feathers had been stuck around the band on the outside. He had no idea what the colors were because the light was too dim, but he had a feeling that he was going to like them less than the outfit.

Crutchin stuck Petre's robe deep down in the bin and piled mounds of other clothing on top.

"Now, we'll feed you, and no, you are not going to try and find this girl Kara…yet."

Petre's eyebrows shot up. "How did you know?"

"Your thoughts are pretty transparent, and my skills in reading are absolutely phenomenal if I do say so myself. I'm going to have to teach you how to block off your thoughts. You'll be too vulnerable to others if you keep being that open. Getting back to Kara, the only way you can help this girl is to help yourself first."

"But I have to help her," protested Petre. "If it hadn't been for her, I would never have been able to escape."

"Yes, yes, a veritable heroine."

"But she was."

When the door to the wagon had fallen off, Kara had been the last to tumble out the back, only to fall flat on her face after a few running steps. Petre had glanced back, but before he could try to return to get her, she had shouted at him to run, scrambled to her feet and had run back to the slow, lumbering trolls, darting in and around their large legs like a bee in the middle of a herd of cows. When one large clawed hand had finally snagged her robe and tossed her into the back of the wagon, he knew that she had sacrificed herself in order to give the others time to escape. She had indeed been a heroine.

"All in good time, boy, but first things first. Come with me."

Another thing that Petre was to learn about Crutchin was the fact that the man never walked anywhere. He bounced. Every time he took a step, it was as if a spring were in each shoe. When they entered the upstairs level, Petre was to discover something else. Crutchin looked like something rejected from a nightmare. His hair consisted of blue spikes, his cape was pink, the shirt was yellow with orange stripes, the pants bright green, and the boots purple.

Petre looked down at his own outfit with great trepidation. It was almost identical.

"I can't wear this," he spluttered.

"Of course, you can, dear boy," came Crutchin's quick, nonchalant reply. "What better way to blend in than to stand out. No one bothers to really look at us because they're so used to our bizarre presence. Besides, not just anyone is accepted into our company, and the general populace knows that. Everyone will think that you've been with us for ages and they just haven't noticed. Now come. We're off for food and drink."

He turned with a flourish and led the way through the small theatre to the front door. Throwing it open, he paused dramatically on the outer porch, gestured to Petre and swept down the steps to the road. If Petre hadn't been so frightened, he would have laughed out loud at the spectacle. Reluctantly, he followed Crutchin down the steps, feeling like an idiot in his new attire.

They had not gone far when a quad of trolls emerged at the end of the street. Petre stopped and stared, his whole being frozen with terror. Barely breaking stride, Crutchin placed an arm stronger than it looked around his shoulders and propelled him forward, speaking both out loud and into Petre's mind.

"Now we must discuss that last performance of yours. *Look at me, Petre.* You need to watch your timing in that last scene. *Look at me, Petre! That's better.* As soon as the first line of Domondo's is finished, *breathe! Breathe!* You must sweep in as if you own the stage, *smile and nod,* and move over to the tree before saying your line. *Smile and nod.* As soon as you are finished, *they've passed us by but keep nodding,* sweep back out and don't look back as you exit. *Turn with me.* Now, let's get something to eat."

Petre found himself stumbling into what appeared to be an eating establishment. It took several minutes for the shock to wear off, but when it did, he looked around curiously. He had heard of places where you could go to pay for cooked food, but there were none in his village. Crutchin pushed him toward a bench and table in the corner, boisterously placing the food and drink order as they went. Once seated, Petre looked over at his companion.

"Does nothing frighten you?" he asked.

Crutchin threw back his head and laughed.

"Looking in the mirror usually does it."

Petre burst into laughter as well and, for the first time, momentarily forgot his troubles and concerns for Kara.

Chapter Ten
The Monster Revealed

Phineas

The members of the Valley Council were meeting in the main chambers of Government House on the east side of Toria Square, next door to the Sanctuary. It wasn't a large building, having been carved out of solid rock the same way that all the buildings had been made in Toria, but the furnishings were most impressive and the statues imposing. The room in which they were meeting held a large mahogany-colored marble table around which all twenty members representing the near and far corners of Glockamar could be comfortably seated. On this occasion, however, most of the dignitaries were too agitated to enjoy the comfort of the stuffed couches or the numerous plates of appetizers generously scattered across the table surface.

"I want to know where my son is," yelled a large man with a florid complexion. "He went out last night to meet up with friends and has not returned."

"Where is my daughter?" cried another.

Phineas dan Yoro smiled with pleasure as voices were raised around the table demanding to know one thing and then another. Deep in the shadows behind a half-open door, a slight figure wrapped in a cape pushed the hood off his face revealing a few spikes of blue hair and strained forward in order to hear what was being said. However, in his enjoyment of knowing what had happened to the missing sons and daughters and the predictable reactions of the parents, Phineas failed to notice.

Banging his gavel on the table, he brought a reluctant silence to the room. Sitting back in his chair, he templed his ringed fingers over his rotund stomach and smiled patiently at what he considered to be a group of morons, the smile never reaching his eyes. He knew he was considered a pompous man, and he reveled in the reputation that his acts of cruelty were well known throughout Glockamar. He had never allowed an investigation to be made into his wife's sudden death, which had left more than the members of the council suspicious, but Phineas was a powerful man and to anger him meant reprisals of a nasty sort, so no one had ever had the courage to confront him on the topic. His small army of dangerous reprobates who had never done a day's work in their lives but who he paid handsomely, made certain of that. The fact that many despised him did not bother him. As far as he was concerned, a man in his position had to expect opposition and even dislike from others. Jealousy always stirred up unacceptable emotions.

"I'm sure there's a reasonable explanation, my friends," drawled Phineas. "Your children will turn up eventually. They are probably off somewhere and up to no good as usual."

Ignoring the shouts of protest, he turned his attention to the council member whose son had not returned the night before. It gave him tremendous internal satisfaction to know exactly what had happened to the boy. The fact that his own daughter was missing was irrelevant. He had never been that fond of Portia, if truth be known, and so far, no one knew of her disappearance. He intended to keep it that way. He hated expressions of fake concern.

"You know that Petre is unreliable, Hugo. We all know that Petre is unreliable. He's obviously got himself involved with some hotheads and has taken off with them. He'll be back when the thrill is gone."

"How dare you!" shouted Petre's father. "How dare you talk like that about my son. If anyone's son needs discipline, it's yours!"

Voices were raised once again, but this time, no amount of hammering on Phineas' part was having any effect on silencing them. He suddenly spotted the figure in the shadows who was about to close the door and slip into the hall behind, but before he could do anything about it, the main doors to the chamber were opened with such force that the thunderous bang that reverberated through the chamber succeeded where Phineas had failed. All conversation stopped, and eyes reflecting a variety of emotions from surprise to annoyance at being disturbed turned toward the door. The figure in the shadows stopped and turned back to look.

Soldiers marched into the room in a two-row formation that split at the door, one row marching around the perimeter in one direction, the second doing the same in the opposite direction. When the two rows met, they had effectively surrounded the members of the Council, cutting off their ability to leave the room.

"What is the meaning of this?" shouted Phineas, leaping to his feet.

The others demanded to know the same. Glockamar didn't have any soldiers. Where had these men come from with their vacant stares, drawn swords and outlandish uniforms? Why did they have such dead-looking eyes?

A figure draped in black from head to toe, shambled through the doorway and paused, providing time for several creatures to move in behind her.

"Trolls," Phineas whispered to himself. "She's got the trolls. That means the Laurel Tree is dead or dying. What is going on here?"

He leaned forward to get a better look.

The figure shuffled forward into the chamber, her appearance and that of the creatures who followed her effectively stifling any further protests on the part of the council members. The temperature in the room appeared to drop, and the aura that permeated the space was one of evil oppressiveness.

"Who are you, and what do you want?" demanded Phineas, the quake in his voice audible to all despite his attempts to sound powerful and authoritative.

The figure stopped halfway to the table.

"I am Spider," came the harsh reply. "I am the one who has been testing your children."

Blank and confused looks were exchanged between the council members.

"I have grown bored with you," continued the intruder. *"Glockamar no longer needs you or your supposed guidance. There is a new ruler here, and you have become baggage. You will serve me now."*

There was a strained silence for a moment, and then first one, and then another began to shout in protest. Spider raised both arms toward the group, muttered several unintelligible words, and a white flash and horrific crack filled the chamber. When the light returned to normal, the men who had previously been seated around the table had been changed into creatures quite unimaginable... except for Phineas.

"Take these new members of our goblin troupe back to the Sanctuary," she instructed the trolls. "The others will teach them their duties. Leave me that one."

She gestured to Phineas.

"I know him, and he has a wicked mind, one who wants to feather his own nest. I have need of such creatures."

Phineas gave a slight self-satisfied smirk. Sometimes, it paid to be the evil, nasty one.

As the trolls herded the newly formed goblins out of the chamber, the figure hiding in the shadows quietly closed the door and slipped into the dark hall behind. Crutchin took off at a brisk walk, trying to keep as quiet as possible until he reached the first bend. Taking a quick look behind, he noted that the door was still shut, indicating that no one had seen him or was following. At that point, he began to run, his heart pounding in his chest and his soul thankful that the circle of ensorcelling light that had changed the rest to goblins had missed him by inches. Azmodeus had to be told about this, and quickly.

Chapter Eleven
Into The Unknown

Petre

"Unhand her, you paltry sop!"

Even to Petre's untrained ear, the words sounded silly.

"Take your hands off of her, you swine!"

Now that sounded better, but he would never suggest that change to Crutchin. The funny little man would just ignore him.

Petre was practicing his lines for their next show. The troupe had performed twice since his arrival in Toria, and although he had only been given walk-on parts, he had enjoyed being in the spotlight, if only for brief appearances. In their new show, he was actually going to have three lines. However, his newfound interest in the theatre had not detracted from his goal of trying to rescue Kara. Each day, he had taken to walking past the Sanctuary whenever he had a spare moment. To the casual observer, he appeared to be a young man idling away his time by strolling through the neighborhood, but under the brim of his hat, his eyes were flicking back and forth over the structure in order to spot something that would assist him in his search for her. So far, he had not seen anything that would help.

The front door of the theatre suddenly banged open and closed with such ferocity, Petre shot to his feet, the script slipping off his lap and landing on the floor. Crutchin's blue hair looked more frantic and spikier than ever, but it was the expression on his face that stopped Petre from making any flippant remarks.

"What's wrong?" he called out.

"Grab your stuff," yelled Crutchin, running down the aisle. "Spider is making her move, and we've got to get out of here. She's just taken over the council and changed all the members into goblins!"

"What are you talking about?" asked Petre, snatching his belongings off the table and following Crutchin to the stairs that led to the back landing and the basement.

"The trolls, goblins and those zombie soldiers are in the process of catching and herding all the Torians to the Sanctuary. Spider will transform them all into goblins like she's done with the others. Her intention is to transform all the inhabitants of Glockamar. We knew it would happen, but none of us expected the creature to play her hand this soon."

"I still don't know what you're talking about," cried Petre, following Crutchin down the steps to the basement. As they reached the foot of the stairs, a thudding and pounding on the front door of the theatre halted them for only a moment.

"That will be them now," said Crutchin, giving an odd chuckle. "Stupid creatures. They don't even realize that the door's unlocked. Come on. I'll answer your questions later."

Confused and frightened, Petre followed Crutchin through the rows of theatre paraphernalia to a corner that would have been directly under the stage. The little man shoved a box aside and pulled a latch attached to the brick wall behind. A small door opened, exposing a dark hole.

"We'll have to crawl for a distance," whispered Crutchin, "but at least the trolls won't be able to follow us. They're too big."

Petre could hear heavy footsteps thudding across the floor above.

"Quickly!" commanded Crutchin.

Petre didn't need to be told twice. He went through first, and Crutchin followed, pulling the door shut behind them. For several minutes, they crawled through a space so black Petre couldn't see a hand in front of his face. When he reached the point of beginning to panic, a pale light filtered through the tunnel exposing a small door in the wall ahead. Crutchin squeezed past Petre and, upon reaching the door, pushed gently down on the latch and opened it just enough to peek out. He pulled back quickly.

"Trolls!" he hissed.

The two remained motionless and tried to calm their erratic breathing. Petre's heart was pounding so loudly; it was the only thing he could hear. Finally, Crutchin pushed on the door, peeked out and then opened it further. Gesturing to Petre to follow, he moved quietly out into the alley between the theatre and the next building. It was the same little alley that Petre had hidden in just a few days before. Crutchin led him to the back of the building across the alley. Between the rock wall of the walkway that passed at a level equal to the height of the theatre and the back wall of the building was a narrow walkway that anyone of regular height and weight would have had difficulty passing through. Neither Petre nor Crutchin found it taxing. When they reached the other side, Crutchin looked out and then gestured to Petre.

"We don't have much time before another quad searches this section again. Stay close, boy. We're only steps away from safety."

He moved along the wall that formed the side of the walkway until he reached the mid-point between the buildings on either side. Tapping out a signal on the surface of the rocks, identical to the one Azmodeus had used several days before, the outline of a door formed, and he pushed it open. Pulling an astonished Petre through the opening before the door closed, he sighed with relief. They both were safe.

The spy who watched them from the walkway above, however, would not have agreed with them. Phineas had spotted the two when they had emerged from the theatre and, recognizing Petre, had quietly tracked them along the walkway above as they had moved from building to building. Not only had he seen them vanish through the door in the rock, but he had also memorized the coded knock. He grinned wickedly as he turned and hustled down the roadway toward the Sanctuary. He would go directly to his mistress with this news. Oh, wouldn't she be pleased with him! He rubbed his hands together in glee at the thought of the honors and rewards she would bestow upon him.

Crutchin guided Petre through an enormous cave filled with a bustling group of people filling carrying packs with supplies. Like the girls who had arrived several days before him, he had never seen dwarves or some of the other communities represented in the group. He looked around in amazement.

"Haven't you ever seen a dwarf before?" asked Crutchin sometime later, passing Petre another boiled tuber as they sat companionably together in a back section of the cave.

"No," replied the boy, surveying the scene around him. From what he could determine, the occupants were preparing to vacate the cave.

"Why are they leaving?" he asked.

"It's no longer safe," shrugged Crutchin. "Up until now, this cavern was used to smuggle children out to safe places in the tunnels before they could come in contact with Spider. It has also been used as a meeting place for conspirators."

Crutchin had already explained to Petre about Hera's curse and the fate of those brought into the presence of the evil monster that occupied the Sanctuary.

"With that old creature thing now going after everyone, we need to get as many outside the mountain as possible. It won't take her long to transform the inhabitants of Glockamar– not with the help of the trolls and goblins who are under her control and those strange soldiers that have shown up."

"Why are the trolls working for this spider thing?"

Crutchin sighed. "The Laurel Tree in Toria is critical to all of Eleusia for one main important reason. It guides the trolls in their role as tree-keepers. They make certain that all trees on Eleusia survive. If the Laurel Tree dies, the trolls leave their jobs, causing the deaths of all trees. Unfortunately, we hadn't expected Hera to move so quickly."

"We?" questioned Petre.

"Those of us on the inside and on the outside of the mountain who were working against her. Part of the plan, which involves some of your friends, is already underway…. I hope."

Petre shook his head. Up until a couple of days ago, he hadn't been aware that he lived inside a mountain with a roof or that there were other races of people, such as dwarves and elves, most of whom lived on the outside. The story of Hera's curse and this Spider creature, he had found completely unbelievable, and as for magical gods and goddesses, Crutchin had obviously had too much ale in the pub the night before. Creatures like that couldn't possibly exist. However, until now, he would never have been able to conjure up an image of an elf or dwarf. And what about the trolls? Until recently, he wouldn't have believed in them either. His mind was in a complete muddle.

"Are you saying that my father will be transformed into one of these goblin creatures?" he asked.

"That's right," nodded Crutchin.

A look of pain crossed Petre's features.

"I'm sorry," said Crutchin in gentler tones. "If it's any consolation, Azmodeus believes that the goblins will revert back to their natural forms if we can find Sharra and break the curse. Just stick with me and-"

A shriek at the other end of the cavern startled both of them into leaping to their feet.

"Trolls! Goblins!"

The far end of the cavern was suddenly swarming with the horrible creatures; the trolls pointing the ends of the tubes they were carrying into as many faces as possible. Petre knew what would happen if he came into contact with those again.

"Come on!" shouted Crutchin.

He grabbed Petre by the front of his shirt and dragged him toward a tunnel that led away from the cavern. He was so shocked he couldn't seem to get his legs to move.

"Get going!" shouted Crutchin again. "Do you want to end up a goblin?"

That prompted Petre into action. He raced behind Crutchin into the tunnel and along its length as fast as his now energy-charged legs would take him. Torches had been placed at even lengths down the walls allowing them to see clearly as they pounded on. They could hear shouts and running feet behind them as those goblins that had spotted them gave chase. The tunnel seemed to go on forever. Petre's sides began to ache, and his knees felt like jelly. They weren't going to be able to keep up this pace much longer. Crutchin, however, seemed to be tireless and kept shouting encouragement over his shoulder, but Petre knew that if something didn't happen soon, they'd be caught by their pursuers.

Suddenly, the tunnel ended, and they emerged outside the mountain onto a large flat shelf. They raced to the edge. If it hadn't been for Crutchin grabbing him, Petre would have catapulted over the precipice and landed on a rocky riverbed several hundred feet below. They turned to face the goblins that had stopped at the cave entrance and were now eyeing them maliciously.

"There's nowhere to go," gasped Petre, bending over slightly in an attempt to catch his breath.

Crutchin reached under his cape and drew out a sword from a scabbard strapped to his waist. Petre's eyes widened in shock. He had never known that Crutchin carried a sword, let alone knew how to use one. Were they going to have to try and fight their way out? With one sword?

Crutchin waved the sword menacingly at the goblins that were now creeping toward them.

"Listen carefully, Petre," he hissed. "What I'm going to say is going to sound positively insane, but you must trust me. When I give the word, we are going to turn, you are going to grab my arm, and we're going to step off the cliff."

"What?" cried Petre. "That is definitely insane!"

"You have to trust me," snapped Crutchin. "There is no time."

"But…" gasped the boy.

"Don't argue!" shouted Crutchin. "On a count of three. One…two…three!"

Petre turned and, because he didn't know what to do, grabbed for Crutchin's arm with two hands. Together they stepped off the cliff into empty space.

Chapter Twelve
A Meeting In Donegal

Jamie

Jamie burst through the door into the suite of rooms she shared with Portia and Jeremiah to find the boy prancing around the room, poking at the empty air with a stick.

"Are we being attacked by invisibles?" she chortled, throwing her cape and hood onto a nearby stool.

Jeremiah stumbled to a halt and turned to her, grinning sheepishly.

"Yonnus told me that he's going to be teaching us to use a sword this afternoon. He wants to wait until the others get here, whoever 'the others' are, so I thought I'd give it a try first."

"I don't think I like the sound of that. I don't know if I could ever attack someone. What if I hurt them?"

"It's better than someone hurting you back," was Jeremiah's staunch response.

Jamie flopped into the nearest chair, and Jeremiah took one of the others. They were dressed in identical brown jerkins and leggings given to them by the elves, although Jamie had not yet taken off the fur vest that covered her from neck to knees. She had worn it under a long cape to stay warm on her trip with Collpepper and Fernwing. As she pulled off the knee-high boots, she told him about her flight.

"I wish you weren't so afraid of heights, Jeremiah. Donagal is the most amazing city I have ever seen."

Nothing had prepared her for the elfin city. It was built into the tops of trees that made the largest redwood back in her world look like a mere sapling. The only way to reach the place was to fly in, and then, it was important to know which tree you were visiting. An intricate pattern of roadways and bridges connected the trees together, and it was difficult to comprehend at times that the wide streets, large homes and shops were actually built on the tops of tree branches. What startled her was the actual color and shape of the trees. They were a dark purplish blue with long spikey leaves that could easily have cut through metal. She learned very quickly not to touch them. They had been beautifully designed for protection.

From high above, the forest resembled the outline of a fortress. Thickly foliaged lines of enormous trees formed a massive outer wall shaped as a square, with circles of trees at each corner resembling the bastions of a castle. Collpepper had told her that there were elfin soldiers guarding the entire rim of Donagal because the city was so close to The Hollows. She had no idea what that was, so simply nodded. The city itself could be seen within the protective wall, and as they dropped down to return, she noticed that the main roadways appeared to spiral out from the central tree, which was the largest.

"Home of the Willik," shouted Collpepper.

That hadn't helped either, but she assumed that she would find out soon enough.

"I got quite good at hanging on with my knees and letting go of the harness," she grinned as she came to the end of her story.

"Oh sure," snickered Jeremiah. "The last time I looked out the window, you were in the process of almost doing a backflip off of Fernwing. Practicing for the circus, were you?"

Jamie laughed and threw a boot at him, which he was able to catch and return. The fight was on! He grabbed his stick and began an attack which she thwarted with her boot. Hooting with laughter and shouting out atrocious threats, the two battled their way around the room, climbing over chairs and ducking behind tables.

"Stop it!"

The two ceased their battle and turned to the furious red-faced girl standing in the doorway to the bedroom she had selected as her own upon her arrival.

"What's your problem?" asked Jamie.

"Some of us refuse to behave like idiots," snapped Portia. "However, why should I expect anything but stupidity from you two."

"Miss Congeniality is present, I see," drawled Jeremiah. "But then again, she's so brave. She hasn't left this room for three days."

"She's still wearing her robe," said Jamie, shaking her head. "At least some of us like to have baths and change our clothes, Portia. You should come outside with us to get some fresh air. This is the most wonderful place I have ever seen."

Portia turned her back on them and looked out the main window.

"These creatures are disgusting, and as soon as I get the chance, I'm going home. At least there, I'll be appreciated."

"You have to be the nastiest, most mean-spirited creep I have ever met," snapped Jeremiah.

"That's enough," interceded Jamie quickly. "Maybe Portia misses her family more than we know."

The boy slumped back into a chair. "You know, I haven't missed my family once. In fact, it's a terrible thing to say, but I can't even remember them or the place I came from. I remember other things like video games and books but not family."

"Neither can I," confessed Jamie. "Every so often, something niggles at the corner of my mind, like I should remember, but then it's gone."

"Well, I can certainly remember my family," spat out Portia, giving them a withering look. "My father is probably frantic with worry. If I don't get home soon, who knows how it will affect him."

In the three days they had been in Donagal, Portia had refused to leave their rooms and had actually thrown objects at the elves who had brought her trays of food. Her robe was beginning to show signs of wear and tear, and her physical appearance had noticeably deteriorated. Hair hung in dirty, lank strands, and Jamie had begun to detect an unpleasant odor when she got too close. The girl and her clothes needed a good scrubbing.

A sharp knock at the door halted further conversation, and Jeremiah got up to open it. A young female elf stood in the hall, her arms piled high with towels. Behind her was a line of others: two struggling with a copper tub, others with kettles of steaming water and still others with soap and clean clothes.

"Excuse me, Master Jer, but we are here to give Lady Porteea her bath. You and Lady Jam are requested to go to the others who are waiting in the meeting room."

They had stopped trying to correct the strange names that had been given to them shortly after their arrival. Despite their best efforts, "Jer," "Jam," and "Porteea" had remained.

"The others?" asked Jamie.

"The Revered One has arrived and insists on meeting with you as soon as possible."

"I am not having a bath, and I am not going to any meeting," shrieked Portia, stamping her feet and shaking a closed fist at them.

"I am sorry, Lady Porteea," continued the elf calmly. "But the one named Yonnus said that if you didn't take a bath willingly, he was going to throw you into the water, clothes and all."

She smiled shyly at Jamie and Jeremiah as Portia began to howl with rage.

"I apologize for the bluntness, but Master Yonnus told me to tell her those exact words. However, I assured him that we had our own ways of dealing with problem children. Would you two be so kind as to leave?"

"Not a problem," grinned Jamie as she and Jeremiah stepped aside to let them enter.

One elf remained in the hall, and as they closed the door behind them, Jamie asked, "Are you certain that your friends can handle her? She's a nasty piece of work, you know."

The elf, who didn't look much older than either of them, grinned and nodded.

"Don't worry," the young elf replied. "They're stronger than they look."

He turned, and laughing, the two followed him down the hall. Jamie hoped Portia would drown.

The inn in which Yonnus and his charges had been housed had been built on top of one of the larger branches, where it joined with the trunk of the tree. Part of the building had actually been carved into the trunk. Pausing at the top of a wide set of stairs and examining the tavern area beneath, Jamie spotted Azmodeus sitting at a table facing them with three smaller individuals sitting in chairs at the same table with their backs to the stairs. Yonnus was leaning against the wall. Jamie and Jeremiah descended together, and at the bottom, the elf gave a quick nod to them and then to Azmodeus before departing.

"Thanks," mumbled Jamie. She could sense Jeremiah also pulling back slightly.

Yonnus, she'd come to know, but the strange old man whom she'd only met once made her very nervous.

Azmodeus stood up, beaming happily. "Come and join us, young people," he called out boisterously, gesturing to them to come and sit down. "I want you to meet your new traveling companions."

Wondering what he had meant by 'traveling companions,' she followed Jeremiah around the table to the side opposite the three strangers and was quite startled to discover that they were young people close to her own age.

"Mikel, you have already met," said Azmodeus. "This is Tovan, and the other young lady is Melisande. Girls, meet Jamie and Jeremiah."

Mikel looked at her through narrowed eyes and then glanced away. Jamie had the distinct impression that he'd written her and Jeremiah off at their first meeting, and nothing was going to change his mind. In this light, she noticed that the boy's hair was actually a dark red, his eyes a deep shade of green similar to her own and a skin tone slightly lighter. Tovan was the smallest of the three. She had a more olive complexion than the others, with curly reddish-brown hair and incredibly large hazel eyes. She was gazing up at

Jeremiah with the strangest expression on her face, and Jamie squelched a giggle when she realized that Jeremiah had suddenly gained an admirer.

Melisande had coffee-colored skin and long, thick hair, the color of dark copper that flowed down her back. She was beautiful and exotic, with the longest eyelashes Jamie had ever seen. From the look on Jeremiah's face, Jamie got the impression that the young beauty had equally impressed him. At that moment, she noticed the look on Mikel's face when he saw Jeremiah staring with great interest at Melisande. If looks could kill, Jeremiah was a dead man. Mikel was jealous!

'So,' thought Jamie. 'That's how it works. Poor Jeremiah. I wonder if Melisande knows how Mikel feels?'

The girl in question was, in turn, looking at her with great interest. They shared a smile.

"Now, young people," smiled Azmodeus, rubbing his hands together. "As soon as Portia joins us, we can begin our business."

Angry shouts and retorts greeted this news, causing Jamie to take several startled steps backward. Mikel leaped from his chair, his expression one of outrage.

"She got us into this mess in the first place," he shouted. "I certainly won't be having anything to do with her."

"Neither will I," joined in Tovan. "Thanks to her, my parents are probably frantic with worry."

"Why is she here?" asked Melisande.

"Because she's related to them, somehow," replied Mikel, pointing accusingly at Jamie and Jeremiah.

Jeremiah banged his hand on the table, surprising everyone except Azmodeus, who simply smiled and gave the impression that he was thoroughly enjoying himself.

"We are not related. I will not be compared to that spoiled, sniveling female that I've had to put up with for the past four days."

"Neither will I," joined Jamie, equally angry. "She's a very nasty piece of work."

For the first time, she noticed that Mikel looked at both of them with some interest.

"Well, it's obvious that none of us are enamored by the presence of Portia," said Melisande, her voice calm, her hands folded demurely in her lap. She appeared to be completely unflustered by Jeremiah's outburst. "I would like to know why we are all here."

Before Azmodeus had a chance to answer, what had appeared to be a fur scarf unfolded itself from around the old man's neck, yawned loudly and dropped to the table.

"Sparkle!" cried Jamie, holding her hands out to her pet.

The cat gave an affectionate meow and then transformed into something quite alien to Jamie's memories of anything. She pulled away from it in shock. The completed transformation stood about two feet tall with a pale blue face, arched brows, slanted gold eyes, a blunt nose, and a wide mouth filled with dazzling white teeth. The ears were peaked like those of an elf and poked out from beneath fine white hair that covered the head and body; long and curling on the head, short and thick on the body. The creature stood upright on slim bare legs and feet as blue as its face. The arms were also slender and blue, the long fingers on the hands tipped with claw-like nails. The creature turned slightly, revealing a luxurious white tail that, at the moment, was casually flicking back and forth like that of a contented cat.

"What is it?" asked Tovan, her expression one of puzzlement.

"A mountain pixie," chuckled Azmodeus. "They're very mischievous and cunning and will tend to trick you instead of helping you if they get the chance. However, if they like you, they do make good and loyal friends, and if you are ever in a position to save their lives, they will bond with you for life. Crooks has been with me for a long time now."

"But where is Sparkle?" asked Jamie.

"Crooks is Sparkle, or was, I guess you would have to say," explained the wizard. "She is a 'malleable,' which means that she can change her shape and was actually your Sparkle cat when she wasn't with me. I sent her to guard you when I didn't need her here."

"To guard me?" asked Jamie, staring at the creature. "It was Sparkle who sent me into…into what…a mirror! I remember now. She pushed me into a mirror and…"

"Ah, Portia," smiled Azmodeus, getting to his feet. "Your timing is perfect."

Jamie turned in time to see a much cleaner Portia stomping toward the table, looking as if she were ready for battle when she suddenly spotted Tovan, Melisande, and Mikel. Her whole demeanor changed in an instant as she hurriedly looked around for an escape route. When Jamie, whose attention had been diverted by Portia's arrival, looked back at Crooks, the pixie was gone.

"Yah, it's different now, isn't it?" sneered Mikel. "You were full of confidence the night you, your father, and your brother handed us over to the trolls. Now how do you feel?"

Portia looked at the other two girls, whose expressions were also far from welcoming. Straightening her shoulders, she tossed back her wet hair and stuck her nose in the air. Jamie looked over at Jeremiah, who shrugged his shoulders, looking as confused as she felt. What had happened to cause so much dislike between Portia and the others?

"That didn't take you long," continued Azmodeus pleasantly, ignoring the fact that Mikel had spoken.

"I was not going to put up with those horrid creatures any longer than I had to," Portia retorted.

The old man shook his head. "You are going to be faced with much unpleasantness in your future, Portia," he said softly.

"You really must do something about your attitude."

"I don't care," she snapped.

"Sit down, please," he said crisply.

Portia hesitated.

"Now!" he commanded.

She reluctantly did as she was told, sliding in beside Melisande, who moved as far away from her as was physically possible. Mikel had remained standing, which allowed for a good-sized space to exist between them. At the wizard's bidding, Jamie sat down on one side of him and Jeremiah took a seat on the other.

Azmodeus smiled. The time had come.

"Now, young ones," he began, "I realize that you all have many questions, but bear with me as I tell you a story. The tale might confuse you, but then perhaps it might not. When the time of man came to Earth's dimension, those of the magical and mythical realm chose to move here to Eleusia. Some of the folks came because no one believed in them any longer. The ancient Greek, Roman and Norse gods and goddesses were in that group. Some came because they were being persecuted, like the wizards and sorceresses and some because they no longer had a space in which to live. The elves, dwarves, and fairies experienced that situation. The gods and goddesses settled in the realm of the sky, while other races either moved into the ample forests, mountains, or meadows or created areas that suited them best. The characters of fairy tales and myths created Aradell in which to dwell, while the dragons, at least the good ones, settled in the Crystal Spires."

"Where do the bad ones come from?" asked Jamie.

Azmodeus quirked an eyebrow. "You're thinking of the rogue worms who attacked you on the way to Donagal, aren't you?"

She nodded, still getting shivers down her spine whenever she thought of the monsters.

"Unfortunately, not all the creatures of magic and myth are good. Those with evil in their hearts settled in an area of bogs and swamps, treeless hills, and mountains. They surrounded it with fog and mist and called it The Hollows. If one is unlucky enough to wander into it, he or she will find a grey world full of danger, monstrous creatures, and sorrow. Few who ever enter are seen again."

Jamie wasn't the only one to gulp at this news.

"What about us?" whispered Melisande. "What about the Glockamarians?"

"We are all Draukenbergians," continued Azmodeus, stopping the protests from Jamie and Jeremiah by raising his hand. "Thousands of years ago, our people lived in the dimension of Marcialla, but when that world began to deteriorate, they were transported to the island of Atlantis in Earth's dimension. Atlantis, in time, was also destroyed by earthquakes, so they chose Eleusia and were allowed to come by the immortals because of their magic. They settled in this part of the world and called it Draukenberg."

"Their magic?" gasped Tovan. Jamie noted the meaningful look she gave Mikel.

"The people of Glockamar are also descendants of those who lived in Atlantis?" asked Jamie. "But why do they live inside that mountain valley and the rest live outside?"

"Some of our forefathers felt that Atlantis had been destroyed by magic and so when they arrived here and discovered a huge valley gorge in the Zagoroth Mountains, they used their magic for the last time to create a bubble over the valley so that nothing could get in or out. They named it Glockamar, which in the ancient language of the Atlantians means 'solitary.' They made certain that the rain would fall each night on the fields and forests and that the climate and temperature would never change. They cut it off from the rest of Draukenberg so that magic from the outside could not creep in and then forbade the use of magic by any of their people."

"That explains everything," cried Tovan clasping Melisande's hand. "That's the reason why we have always been forbidden to use any magic."

Again, Jamie sensed that she had missed out on a very large something. A whole group of magic people had been transported from Earth to Eleusia? How? She felt as if she had been dropped into a situation so confusing, it was beyond her understanding. Empathizing briefly with Portia, she too, wanted to go home, wherever that was.

"That's only part of it, I'm afraid," replied Azmodeus. "There's a great deal more, and it affects all of you."

The old wizard emitted a deep sigh. "Eleven years ago, there was a young woman named Sharra, the Queen of Draukenberg, who lived in Magnigona Castle in the north with her husband and three young children. She unfortunately, caught the eye of the god Zeus, who was convinced that she was the reincarnation of a mortal river nymph who he had fallen in love with thousands of years before in Earth's dimension. Zeus had worshipped young Io, but when his jealous wife, Hera, found out and began to search the countryside in order to find and destroy the little river nymph, Zeus relented and promised he would have nothing more to do with her."

"Hera," whispered Jamie. Was he talking about the wife of Zeus? Was that the person who was chasing them and wanted them dead…the one that Yonnus had referred to as 'she'? She gave an involuntary shiver.

"Unfortunately," continued Azmodeus, "Zeus never forgot Io, and when he first saw Sharra, he was convinced that Io had been born to him again and began to pursue her. Hera found out, and eleven years ago, Sharra disappeared in front of my own eyes. It was a moment I will never forget."

He stopped to take a sip of water. His audience sat with their mouths open and their eyes as round as saucers. Only Yonnus appeared to be quite relaxed and unaffected by the tale.

"This missing woman is a queen?" asked a dumbfounded Jamie.

"She is the Queen of Draukenberg," replied Azmodeus. "Tovan, Melisande, Portia, and Mikel would not have heard of her as they were in Glockamar and cut off from the rest of the country. Now, where was I?"

"There's more?" choked Tovan.

"Oh, my goodness, yes. Now, Hera didn't want to stop there. She wanted to find Sharra's three children and destroy them. In the old days, goddesses were quite renowned for killing off the offspring of people they didn't like. However, the father of the triplets and I were way ahead of her. We placed one of the triplets in Glockamar to be raised there, and the other two were placed in

Earth's dimension. Each child was raised not knowing that the other two existed or knowing who they were."

His words hung on the air for several long minutes before Jamie had the courage to speak.

"Are you talking about us?" she finally asked.

Azmodeus nodded.

"You stayed with one family and Jeremiah was sent to a family in Calgary, who since his disappearance, has no recollection of him. Your foster father has ceased to think of you, Jamie. All records of both of you have disappeared in Earth's time. The third triplet remained in Glockamar."

Jeremiah sighed and shook his head. "If all of this is true…" he said.

Azmodeus drew his brows sharply together.

"If this is true," he repeated in a stronger voice, "then this Hera will be after us as soon as she knows we're all here."

"The satyr," said Yonnus, matter-of-factly. "We moved out of the mountain earlier than planned because you spotted one, Jamie. Satyrs are Hera's spies. And there was the chase by the rogue worms. Hera sent them; that's a certainty."

"Portia is the third triplet," stated Mikel, "which is why we're going to have to tolerate her presence. That means that this Hera wants to destroy Portia, Jamie, and Jeremiah."

Azmodeus made no comment on Mikel's assumption but continued on.

"Actually, Hera has changed her original plan. She grew bored with the game of just trying to find and eliminate the three and decided to spice it up a bit. She came up with a prophecy. If the prophecy is fulfilled several weeks from now, the curse on Draukenberg will be lifted. If the prophecy is not fulfilled, the creature named Spider, who now rules in Glockamar, will unleash evil and war throughout the country and beyond into others. She has the ability to turn individuals into creatures called goblins who become her slaves."

"What?" gasped Jeremiah. "Goblins? There are goblins here?"

"Is that what happened to my sister and brother?" cried Tovan. "They were turned into goblins?"

Azmodeus nodded. "Up until now, she has only brought those children to the Sanctuary that might have been suspected of having magical talents. Unfortunately, she is now in the process of rounding up all Glockamarians, both children and adults, and transforming them into goblins. If she is not stopped, all the realms of Draukenberg will be at war with those supporting Spider and Hera, including those creatures from The Hollows. It wouldn't surprise me if our enemies in Hvedrung, the country north of us, were in league with her. I believe that Hera has been planning this for a long time."

"What about Sharra?" asked Jamie, her voice shaking, "How do we find her?"

"Supposedly, when you complete the quest, we will know," replied Azmodeus.

Jamie was in total shock. She was being pursued by a goddess who wanted her dead? Her mother was a queen? A kidnapped queen? The whole thing was ridiculous and impossible. Even Harriet would have scoffed at this mystery plot.

"I'm very confused, Master," stated Melisande. "I don't know what you mean by 'Atlantis' or these gods and goddesses. I have now seen elves and dwarves, but I still don't understand why we are all here in this place. And what do you mean by 'a quest'?"

"I agree," said Mikel. "I want to know what the prophecy is and what it has to do with the three of us. If Hera is after the triplets, then why are the rest of us here?"

"I want to know where Portia is," broke in Tovan.

Everyone's attention was immediately diverted to the empty space beside Melisande.

"I never saw her leave," said Mikel, with a look of surprise.

Yonnus stood up. "I did, but she'll be back soon. No worries."

He walked toward the door, which opened before he reached it. An angry Portia stomped through, flanked on either side by elves.

"We found her on the stairs, Yonnus," said the one who appeared to be in charge. "I'm not sure how she was going to get back to Glockamar from here."

"I felt that a short walk would do her good," chuckled Yonnus. "After all, she hasn't been out of her room for several days. Thank you, gentlemen."

The elves nodded and retreated back through the doors, leaving a fuming Portia glaring at the big man.

"I want to go home," she spat out. "I want to go home now."

"Oh, you wouldn't like it, my dear," said Azmodeus, standing up and walking around to the other side of the table. "I'm certain that Spider has already begun her takeover of Glockamar and you wouldn't like what she is doing."

"I don't care!" shouted Portia. "I will not stay here with this lot. I will…"

Suddenly Portia's mouth was moving, but there were no words coming out.

"I really wish you would control yourself," sighed Azmodeus. "The elves of Donagal are a gentle race of folk and do not need to be abused by your temper. Now, if you stop shouting, I will give you back your voice."

Portia stared at him, her face drained of color. Tovan and Melisande's expressions mirrored that of Portia's and even though Jamie had seen the old man work his magic once, she was as stunned as the others. As the wizard bent his head down to have a quiet word with Portia, Jamie suddenly noticed that Azmodeus' beard had changed shape.

"His beard got shorter," she whispered to Tovan. "Can beards actually change lengths?"

"I saw that happen before," the girl replied softly. "It was short when he rescued us and longer when we met him again a short time ago."

Mikel, overhearing them, laughed.

"He's a wizard," he explained. "Every time he casts a spell, he loses some of his beard. It grows back quickly after he's finished."

"A wizard?" gasped Tovan and Melisande in unison.

"He can really do magic?" asked Jamie thinking back to the chair in the kitchen at Mikel's home. She had been right.

Mikel nodded, giving a smug smile that bothered Jamie slightly. He appeared to be proud of knowing more than the others. Was he a bit of a pompous know-it-all?

"Well?" demanded Azmodeus of Portia.

The girl nodded, and the old man lowered the hand that had been aimed in her direction.

"I…" began Portia.

Azmodeus quickly raised his hand, and she clamped her mouth shut.

At that moment, a young elf woman entered the room. "Old master," she said in a voice that tinkled like bells, "The Willik will see you now."

"Thank you," replied Azmodeus with a bow. "Come everyone. We have been granted an audience with one of the wisest sages in the land. It is a high honor, and you will all behave in a respectful and humble manner at all times."

"Why are we going to see this person?" asked Melisande.

"The prophecy, little one. You are about to hear the prophecy and receive advice as to how to proceed. Hopefully, you will receive answers to the many questions going through your minds."

Chapter Thirteen
Evil Plans Afoot

Spider

"My spy tells me he has them all in Donagal. The game is about to begin."

Hera's expression was one of absolute triumph. Spider remained silent and continued to stand unmoving by the podium while Hera perched on the chair in its center. It wasn't necessary for her to comment. Hera was only boasting to indulge her own ego.

"I have placed six riddles in Aradell, home of the fairy tales and myths, which sits right beside The Hollows."

Spider snorted.

"Devious. Whenever the land changes shape in Aradell, they must choose the right door to take them to safety. The wrong door will take them to The Hollows. Being mortal, they will not be safe from the land changes, as only the residents of Aradell have that privilege. Very cunning indeed."

Hera preened at the unexpected praise from her minion, which only disgusted Spider.

"Yes. He will have to send six of his precious children off by themselves to find and answer them. Each child will have to answer one of the six riddles. Sharra's three despicable creatures will be the ones I destroy last, so they can watch their friends die first. It is such a wonderful quest...one outlined beautifully in a prophecy."

"More like a curse," cackled Spider.

Hera laughed again before continuing.

"But it is a curse. I have cursed Draukenberg and only by fulfilling the prophecy can it be saved. I sent it to the old elf woman twelve days ago. It was quite dramatic, I must say. I had a raven fly

into her chamber through an upper window and drop it into her lap. I'm certain that set her old heart racing. Oh, I would have given anything to have seen the look on her face."

Spider snorted. "It's amazing the evil plans one can come up with when one is bored."

Ignoring the comment, Hera stood and began to pace back and forth, gleefully rubbing her hands together as she walked.

"The problem for them is that they won't know where to go when they get in there. I have provided no guiding instructions or a route map to follow from one location to the next...only strange images. They are doomed! They will never finish by the deadline I have set. In twenty days, they will have had to have correctly answered the six riddles using only hints of location instructions and have found the seed for the Laurel Tree in order to get the trolls back to work. If they do not succeed, Draukenberg will become a land of darkness, desolation, and death and the New Olympian Council will not approve, of course, and..."

Hera quickly broke off from revealing her next thought, leaving Spider wondering. What had the goddess meant by the New Olympian Council not approving? Of what? Did Hera have more secrets than she had shared with her? It left Spider feeling slightly uneasy.

"What about Sharra?" asked Spider, refusing to give Hera the satisfaction of inquiring about what she was going to say. "What plans do you have for her?"

"A very special one," smirked Hera, a strange glint in her eyes as she stared back at Spider.

Spider made no comment, although she had to agree that the woman had developed a masterful plan. Hera had thought of everything. She tried to control the shiver of excitement that raced through her body at the thought of being involved in such a marvelous scheme.

Hera's demeanor suddenly turned dark and frightening.

"However, I don't want any surprises. I don't trust Azmodeus or that ancient bag of elf bones. I have a plan."

"Another one?" rasped the Spider sarcastically.

Hera's mood changed abruptly.

"Where is my little treasure?" she called out sweetly. "Show yourself."

Spider took a step back as a shimmering creature rose from the floor in front of Hera. It took a lot to unnerve her, but this certainly had. She realized at once that this was a creature referred to as a chameleon, a creature that could blend into the background and never be seen. It was difficult to decide what the actual shape of the creature was as it was constantly flickering with colors that allowed it to blend into the background of the chamber.

Hera pulled a small black bottle from a pocket in her cloak and held it up.

"Yes, I have a very important task for this creature, and he'd better be successful. He knows the consequences if he fails."

The colors rippled slightly as if the chameleon had shivered.

Spider simply stood quietly, staring hard at the goddess. She knew that Hera wanted to tell her more of her plan, but Spider refused to ask, which angered the goddess.

"Don't play the superior role with me, you wretched creature," she snapped. "You will never win. How is your work going here?"

"I have transformed a large number of the Glockamarians. Phineas keeps them coming in on a regular basis and all the trolls are now under my control. Your soldiers have been of some help, but they are more of a hindrance because they cannot think for themselves."

"Are you criticizing my decision to use them?" snapped the woman, bending threateningly toward her.

Spider did not step away from her but simply held her ground. "They were helpful in taking over the Council, but they are no longer needed."

"They will be for what is to come," replied Hera. "In the meantime, I will transport them back to Olympia and restore their minds. They will not remember being here. At the right time, I will

return them to you. It is time for me to go. I have been in this realm too long. Come, chameleon."

As her shape began to shimmer, she threw out one more bit of news. "I have summoned the three sisters from The Hollows to be of assistance to you."

Spider lurched forward in protest. "I don't need any assistance," she growled low, her stance threatening.

"You will," came the laughing reply just before she disappeared.

In her anger, Spider transformed over twenty Glockamarians that afternoon before she could think rationally about all that Hera had revealed.

Chapter Fourteen
The Prophecy

Mikel

The small group followed the young woman down a long hallway that abruptly turned into a circular wooden passageway. The Willik's chamber was carved into the actual tree, and as they entered the wooden grotto, all talking and whispering stopped. Mikel felt that he had walked into a sacred place, one that smelled of fresh wood and damp earth. The space was full of candles floating above them in the air, and small glittering objects crisscrossed the ceiling in random patterns like lightening bugs flying slightly out of control.

"Come forward, everyone."

The voice came from a chair that had been placed in the center of the room. Their guide joined several other elf maidens grouped loosely behind it and gestured to Azmodeus and the others to come forward. From the folds of the dark material draped over the piece of furniture emerged the outline of an elfin woman dressed in a dark robe that covered her from neck to ankles. Her hair was white but that was the only obvious indication of age. Her bearing was erect and the skin on her face and hands was as unlined as that of a young girl. It was her eyes that were the most startling. They were a deep shade of violet and when she looked at Mikel, it was as if she possessed the wisdom of the ages and could see into the depths of his soul. The Willik was blind, but few were aware of that fact for her ability to see was on a much deeper level. Mikel had never met the Willik but had heard a great deal about her from Azmodeus. He couldn't resist feeling excited and privileged at meeting her now, even though he was working hard at the moment to control it. He never revealed his true feelings to anyone and would be caught dead before showing sappy, girly emotions.

Azmodeus bowed deeply when he stopped in front of the Willik and the others followed suit.

"Thank you for meeting with us," he said. "We are honored."

"It is good to have you all here at last, Azmodeus," she replied with a smile. "Welcome, Yonnus. But I have not met the young ones, although I know them all."

This comment startled Mikel, but he clearly stated his name as she looked in his direction. He detected a slight pause and a frown when Portia's turn arrived, but it was so quick that later he felt that he had imagined it and gave it no further thought.

"Azmodeus has told you the story of Sharra and her family?" asked the Willik. "Of Hera's jealousy? And the prophecy that is actually a curse?"

He, along with the others, responded with a verbal "yes" or nod of the head, except for Portia, as she had left in the middle of the wizard's tale and was completely in the dark as to what the Willik was talking about. She looked around in confusion but had the grace to remain silent when everyone ignored her. Mikel frowned in her direction. Nothing would ever convince him to give her the time of day. His dislike of her bordered on hatred.

"He did not tell you the prophecy?"

"No, he didn't, ma'am," replied Mikel as the rest shook their heads.

"Good. That is as it should be, for there is more to the prophecy than its words."

She extended her hand and a weathered scroll suddenly materialized out of the air. Unrolling it with care, she handed the parchment to Azmodeus and began to recite the contents of the document from memory.

It shall be
When Callisto and her hunting son
Revolve in a triad with the Serpent,

Mikel cast an uneasy look around and noticed that the others appeared to have the same thought. First of all, the document didn't make any sense at all except for the phrase "but for death." He had flinched when those lines had been recited.

"As I'm certain Azmodeus told you," began the Willik, "Hera captured Sharra and has hidden her in a place we have not yet found. Having grown tired of hunting down the triplets, she decided to make the game more interesting and exciting and bring the triplets to her. The challenge is for the six of you to enter Aradell to find and solve the six riddles. A different person must answer each riddle. At each location, you will find a clue to the next riddle location that you will have to figure out."

"What if we are not successful?" asked Melisande.

The Willik sighed. "Then you will die."

There was a collective, horrified gasp.

"There is more," continued the elf.

"Another, who is not here, will be given the task of finding the seed to save the Laurel Tree that controls the trolls. All tasks must be completed when the stars are in alignment in seventeen days."

"I can't do this," whispered Portia. "I just can't."

For the first time, Mikel found himself reluctantly agreeing with Portia. She had voiced what he was sure all of them were feeling.

"It is a gigantic task," said the Willik, the sightless eyes that passed over them filled with compassion. "If you fail, the evil that will envelop Draukenberg will turn it into a place of horror in which only those who follow Spider will survive. Those creatures in The Hollows would rule and the rest of us would be destroyed. Hera is going against the promise made by the other gods and goddesses of New Olympus. They had agreed to leave us alone in this part of the world and allow our people, even those in The Hollows, to flourish in our chosen realms as long as we lived in peace with one another."

"Someone must inform them that she has broken the promise they gave," snapped Azmodeus.

The Willik smiled and held up her hand. "Don't worry, my old friend. I have sent out three draycona, traveling three separate routes. Hopefully, one of them will bypass her traps and arrive safely at New Olympus."

She turned her attention back to Mikel and the other five equally confused and quite terrified young people standing in front of her. "Hera is a master of deceit and if you accept this quest, you will have her to worry about along with everything else. I cannot force you to go, but I must know each of your individual decisions. What Hera is doing is against our laws. She has hired others to do her dirty work and that alone will get her banished if we can get word to New Olympus."

Mikel stood in shocked silence. The stories told by both Azmodeus and the ancient elf were almost unbelievable. If the two were telling the truth, the fate of Draukenberg rested on six pairs of ignorant and inexperienced shoulders.

"I will go," said Tovan startling them all. "My brother and sister are most likely these goblin things by now and I can't have the rest of my family hurt any more than they are at this moment."

Her eyes filled with tears and she looked away.

Mikel looked over at Tovan. She was the smallest and the youngest in the group, but she was willing to go without knowing anything about it.

"I will too," Jeremiah stated firmly, although his voice cracked. "After all, this Sharra is supposed to be my mother."

Jamie nodded in agreement, obviously not trusting herself to speak.

"There was never going to be an argument from me," stated Mikel, his words of bravado sounding a bit false and shaky. "No one destroys my home for any reason."

"Of course," said Melisande, "although I have never been very good at solving puzzles."

"I'll help you" and "Don't worry" came out of him and Jeremiah in unison. His face as well as Jeremiah's, turned bright red, but theirs were not as scarlet as Melisande's.

"I did not say that in order to seek help from anyone," she snapped as Mikel glared at Jeremiah, who was doing the same back to him. "I was only giving you ample warning."

Mikel became even more embarrassed when he noticed the Willik fighting to keep a smile from her face and Azmodeus turning away so that none would see his mouth curve up at the corners. He was losing his cool, tough guy image quickly.

All eyes now turned to Portia, who stuck her nose in the air when she noted the expressions on all their faces. Mikel couldn't understand why the girl was coming along, even if she were one of the triplets. She was their weakest link, the one who couldn't be trusted and the one who would most likely do anything to ruin their chance of success.

"I'm going as well," she replied haughtily. "I, at least, have the ability to think intelligently…more than I can say for the rest."

Mikel felt his anger explode and opened his mouth to throw out a very inappropriate retort but was interrupted by the Willik, who pointedly ignored Portia's comment and the expressions of fury on the faces of the others.

"Good," she replied. "We have our six."

"B…but," stammered Jamie, "how can we defend ourselves? If there are going to be things out there that will want to stop us…"

The old woman smiled. "Before you leave, you will receive instruction in how to use a sword and a staff. The young people from Glockamar have already had that training as part of their schooling and, from all reports, are quite good at defending themselves. Unfortunately, one never knows when an enemy may strike. Each of you also possesses strong gifts of magic that you will have to discover as you go. Those of you from Glockamar were selected for those reasons. You all have strong magical talent potential, which is needed on this journey. I cannot explain what they are to you or warn you of the repercussions of using them unwisely, for that is part of your natural growth and evolvement in our world. We must all travel that path alone. However, one of you has a gift that requires something from me."

She gestured to Erisan, one of the handmaidens, who moved forward and held out a delicate chain with a glittering crystal hanging from one end. The white light caught within radiated such a glow that the others had to avert their eyes.

"This is for you, Portia," said the Willik, Mikel noting the violet of her eyes darkening. "You are the one I fear the most, for your emotions are the most unstable and jealousy and selfishness dominate your soul. You are the one that can be the most easily led down the dark paths."

The girl blushed scarlet and opened her mouth to obviously make a defiant retort. However, something in the Willik's expression appeared to stop her.

"And yet," continued the woman, "you are the one who has the capability to save us all in the end. The ability that you will discover about yourself on this quest is one that shows itself only once in many generations. This bracelet, my gift to you, is the Megreykin Crystal and has a unique and special purpose that is linked to your heart. By giving it to another, by allowing another to live at the risk of losing your own life, you will discover the true Portia. Only you have the talent to be linked to the power that exists in this crystal."

Erisan clasped the bracelet onto Portia's wrist and the light inside the ball dimmed to a mere flicker. The girl made an attempt to remove it.

"I wouldn't do that, my dear," warned the woman. "If you remove it for any reason other than for what it was intended, you shall forfeit your life. You will die within minutes."

Mikel's eyebrows shot up. That was certainly not a gift that he would have wanted. Portia dropped her hands to her sides and the color that had suffused her cheeks only moments before drained away. The Willik turned her attention back to all of them.

"I am tired and must now leave you. Beware of Hera, her spies, gifts found in strange places and imposters. The satyrs, centaurs, and a host of other mythical beasts obey her. I leave them in your most capable hands, Azmodeus."

The wizard bowed to her, and suddenly, The Willik was gone. The elf maidens stood behind an empty chair and none of them appeared to be startled or concerned about the manner of the elf's departure.

"Wow," whispered Jeremiah. "I am never going to get used to this place."

"Come, my young friends," said Azmodeus. "We have much to do and very little time."

A very quiet group followed him out of the chamber and into the hallway, each with their own thoughts about what they had heard. Now that they had committed themselves to a quest they knew nothing about and to a place that at the moment was a mystery, any confidence and determination that had been shown in the Willik's chamber vanished as quickly as she had.

Mikel was deep in thought but not about what they had just learned. He was actually very concerned. He had been uncomfortable throughout the whole conversation with the Willik and it had had nothing to do with what the elf woman had told them. He turned to his father, who was walking behind him.

"Yonnus, can I speak with you before we get back to the main level?"

The big man grunted.

Quickly Mikel related what he had sensed in the chamber and Yonnus wasted no time in gesturing to Azmodeus. After a quick conversation, the wizard instructed the others to go to their chambers and then quickly led the two up a second set of stairs to an upper level. They entered her private chambers just as the Willik was raising a cup to her lips. She stopped and placed it back down on the table beside her and turned to greet the visitors.

"Forgive us for intruding," said Azmodeus bowing solemnly. "But Mikel has something to tell you that is of great importance."

He looked down at Mikel and gestured to him to speak.

"When we were in the big chamber, there was something else there apart from us. It was…" he paused, his voice cracking slightly, "it was evil and dangerous."

The Willik raised an eyebrow.

"Is that evil with us now in this chamber?" asked Azmodeus, looking around. It was a small room with very few places to hide.

"Yes," Mikel replied, pointing a shaking finger at the darkest corner. "There."

Azmodeus raised his arms and a sound similar to that of a cracking whip filled the chamber and shook everything in the room that had not been nailed down. Vibrating waves of air rolled over everything in its path.

The outline of a strange misshapen creature attempting to flee but frozen in mid-step was visible through the waves. With a flick of his hand, the vibrations ceased and two elfin guards moved in, grabbed it by its arms and carried it effortlessly to Azmodeus. It began to change its shape into that of a wild cat, but the guards held tight to their captive. Even its attempt to shock with the shape of a snake twisting and turning in their grasp, did not faze the two elves. Reluctantly, it resumed its original form.

"What is it?" asked the Willik, standing in order to attempt to penetrate the mind of the creature.

It was not much taller than she was, but although it had a humanoid shape, it had longer arms and short, stumpy legs. It was covered from head to toe in a shimmering material of mottled colors that kept shifting and changing. There didn't appear to be a mouth, but two little green eyes could be seen angrily glaring at them through the undulating patterns.

"A chameleon," stated Azmodeus, eyeing it carefully. "They are the nastiest little creatures to inhabit The Hollows. Why are you here?"

The creature struggled slightly, growling and spitting from what definitely now looked like a mouth. It also appeared to possess an ample number of ferocious-looking teeth, but that could have been an illusion.

"He's here to poison the Willik," said Mikel coming up from behind. "It was a potion that is meant to kill instantly. He put it in your tea, mistress."

The Willik gasped and fell back into her chair.

"How do you know that Mikel?" whispered the elf, her hand at her throat.

"I can read his thoughts. There are several of us in our group who can mind link."

"He is correct," responded Azmodeus. "But can our friend here, mind link as well, I wonder. If you don't want to see a bad end, chameleon, tell us who was behind this plot."

The creature gave him a sly, crafty look but remained silent.

"It was Hera," volunteered Mikel.

The chameleon shot him a malicious glare, its green eyes flashing with anger.

"Why?" asked the wizard, undeterred by the creature's threatening expression.

They waited for several moments, but there was no response. Once again, Mikel provided the information. "She wanted the Willik out of the way."

"Rotten, little scum," growled Yonnus. "It needs to go back into The Hollows where it belongs. Chameleons are related to the spider gnomes and they cause problems wherever you go in that cursed land. Anyone who goes into the forests in that place does not come out alive because of them. I'll drop him in if you like. We'll hang him on a rope under a griffin and at the right time, I'll cut the rope. Should be quite entertaining."

A horrible moan emerged from the creature as it struggled desperately to escape the grip of its captors.

Mikel grabbed Azmodeus' sleeve and tugged hard. "Hera will kill him. Because it failed, she will hunt him down and destroy him."

"Serves it right," muttered Yonnus.

Azmodeus glanced over at the Willik, who was studying the creature with great interest.

"Strange," she mused almost to herself. "Chameleons are not able to shape-change, only blend in with the background and yet this one can. I wonder what it really is."

Azmodeus looked back at the creature and then shook his head. "We'll keep him here for the time being," he said, turning to Yonnus, who was smiling happily at the thought of his plan. "I don't have the time to deal with it and no, we are not dropping him back into The Hollows…at least not for the moment."

The grin on Yonnus' face grew wider, much to the horror of the chameleon.

"Put him in a holding cell," Azmodeus directed the guards, "and give him some food and water."

"Don't hurt it," called out Mikel as they dragged it away.

"I'll do more than hurt it if I ever get my hands on it," growled Yonnus.

"I agree with Mikel," the Willik thoughtfully remarked. "He might prove to be important to us one day."

The strange thing was that the creature did not struggle as it was marched away by the guards. In fact, it looked almost happy, to everyone's surprise.

"I would like to thank you, Azmodeus," said the Willik, directing her comments to the wizard. "You brought us a wonderful talent. Mikel, we would never have discovered this heinous plot if it hadn't been for you. Now, if I may ask the two of you to leave, I need to speak to Azmodeus alone and would someone please take away this horrible cup."

Yonnus obliged and both he and Mikel bowed to the Willik before leaving the chamber. Mikel, however, left feeling very disturbed. There was a lot more to that chameleon than he had told the others. Somehow in their exchanges, a bond had formed. He made up his mind to try and see the creature alone.

Later that night, he pulled himself into the shadows at the top of the ramp that sloped down to the section containing the holding cells. He had earlier struck up a conversation with one of the elfin soldiers and had casually asked where the holding cells could be found. All but one of the cells faced the outer edge of the tree, with bars on the inside but none on the outer wall, which opened to the air hundreds of feet above the ground. As far as the elves were concerned, there was nowhere to go if a prisoner escaped short of jumping out of the tree into thin air, which would obviously have resulted in a bad ending for the person concerned. The one enclosed cell was for those who did have the ability to leave through an open door.

He peeked around the corner of the doorway. There were two guards, one close to the entrance and a second halfway down. How was he to get past them without being seen?

"I wish you would go for a walk or fall asleep or something," he muttered under his breath.

To his surprise, the two guards emerged from the grotto, walked over to a bench nearby, sat down and went straight to sleep. He stepped out of the shadows, absolutely stunned by what had just happened. They had done exactly what he had absently wished for. What an amazing coincidence. He hurried down the ramp to the cell at the end, determined to take advantage of the situation. It was the enclosed one warded with spells so that nothing could escape.

"I know that you are there, chameleon," he whispered. "I have come to talk to you. I promise that I did not tell the others that you could mind-link."

A shape began to slowly form in front of him.

"You are not a Hollow's chameleon. Who are you and what are you, and why am I the only one who can read your thoughts?"

The creature simply stared at hm.

"Come on, chameleon, or whatever you are, I don't have much time."

You do have time. Your spell will long last.

I didn't cast a spell, scoffed Mikel, through the link.

Who did? Not was I the one.

That's ridiculous. I cannot cast spells.

Something resembling a laugh rumbled out of the creature.

I don't have time for this nonsense. You are not from The Hollows. Where are you from? What are you? And what is your name?

The creature laughed again. *That be questions many. Hvedrung. Wickersnit. Bandiloimaa.*

Mikel stared at the creature in confusion as he tried to sort out what he had said.

Alright. Let's see if I understood all that. You are from Hvedrung? You are a Wickersnit, whatever that is, and your name is Bandi something? Is that right?

Name me is Bandiloimaa. The name you is Mikel. You from Glockamar. You be a wizard. I be your assistant. Yes?

Mikel stared at the creature in complete shock. What in all of Eleusia was he talking about? And what did he mean by being his assistant? Deep down inside, a strange sensation was beginning to form in the pit of his stomach.

"I don't understand," he whispered out loud.

I explain. You put on the elves a spell. They out went and sleeped. You a wizard be. I knew in first moment. We bonded are.

"I did as well," said a voice behind him. "In fact, I have known about you, Mikel, for a very long time."

With a startled yelp, Mikel spun around and took several steps backward. Standing in front of him was a grinning Azmodeus.

"The Willik also sensed it when you came to see her tonight, which is why she put the chameleon…I mean Bandiloimaa in the cell with orders not to hurt him. You are indeed a young wizard, Mikel, and this Wickersnit is going to be your assistant, just as Crooks is mine. All wizards have assistants.”

Mikel backed up a few steps. “No,” he groaned. “This is impossible.”

“I’m afraid it is possible. When we finish with this terrible mess, you will come to me for training. In the meantime, you must be careful what you wish for. Your skills are new and vulnerable to harsh magic.”

Azmodeus turned back to Bandiloimaa and opened the cell. He gestured to the creature to come out, which Bandiloimaa did without hesitation.

“I know this has been an incredible shock to you,” he began but paused when Mikel blurted out, “Shocked? How I feel goes so far beyond shock.”

Azmodeus smiled. “Mikel, you will be alright. You have a strong personality and have never turned down a challenge. Once you get the hang of it, your doubts and concerns will vanish. Join the others before you go back to your room. They are discussing the plans for tomorrow. However, before you go, I must tell you about Bandiloimaa. He will stay with me tonight for his own safety. He must be under the protection of a wizard or sorceress at all times or Hera will destroy him. You were correct earlier. He has failed her and so is at terrible risk. Tomorrow will be soon enough to begin your friendship and learn about one another.”

Mikel turned a very pale face up to Azmodeus, the expression on his face one of anger. “I don’t like this, Azmodeus,” he snapped, as he turned to leave. “I feel as if I’m in a nightmare. I didn’t ask for this and I don’t want it. And I certainly don’t want anything to do with him.”

The Wickersnit received his second glare.

“I am so sorry, Mikel,” sighed the wizard “I had wanted so very much to prepare you for this but knew that you had to discover your skills for yourself. For you to have discovered this on the night before you were to leave is most distressing. Simply be careful how you use your magic for the sake of all of you. Now let us go. Bandiloimaa, you must come with me. Can you please change into a more palpable shape? One that doesn't scare the wits out of anyone we meet?"

The Wickersnit's shape solidified and then molded into one that did not impress the wizard, although it did bring a gasp from Mikel.

"A spider that big is not appropriate. Try something else."

The spider immediately transformed into a pink bat, which immediately flew up and attached itself upside down to the underside of the brim of the wizard's hat. Each time the wizard moved his head, the creature swung back and forth, giggling merrily at his funny trick. Azmodeus shook his head and for a brief second, Mikel almost chuckled.

"Now I know how Hera caught him," said Azmodeus. "Bandiloimaa is young and inexperienced and probably fell easily into her trap. You're going to have your hands full with this creature, Mikel."

"Great," he mumbled, walking ahead of the two.

"Stop laughing, you twit of a thing," snapped the wizard. "You have a difficult task ahead of you and Mikel will need you. You must be more serious if you are going to help protect him."

"He's the last thing I need," whispered Mikel under his breath.

The bat turned a sickly shade of purple and silently dropped to the wizard's shoulder, where it crawled meekly under the edge of the wizard's cape.

"That's better," he chuckled, following Mikel up the ramp. He casually waved at the two guards who were returning to their stations, confused as to why they had found themselves outside on a bench, waking up from what had been a very pleasant asleep.

Chapter Fifteen
Into Aradell

Jeremiah

"I can understand why you, Portia and I were selected to go," whispered Jeremiah to Jamie as they entered the chamber with the rest. "Supposedly, we're Sharra's kids. But why, out of all the kids in Glockamar, were the other three chosen? Because of these magic powers they all supposedly have? Just to answer riddles? And what is draycona?"

Jamie shrugged her shoulders. "What I'd like to know is where our father is, who he is and why no one talks about him being missing. And how can kids get rid of an angry goddess, something called a spider and goblins and trolls? Where are the magic swords and shields that always protect heroes when they go on quests?"

Jeremiah shook his head. "I don't know, but why do prophecies always talk about death?" was all he could muster.

A short time later, five young heads and a grey one bent over the piece of parchment. Portia was slumped in a chair on the other side of the room, her facial expression one of utter disgust.

"But what is a Callisto and her hunting son?" asked Melisande. "I've never heard of them."

"They are stars in the sky," explained Azmodeus.

Several confused faces turned to look at him.

"They are planets and suns that you can see at night. They twinkle and sparkle like little white lights."

Jeremiah and Jamie were the only ones who didn't look confused.

"Are the stars in the same configurations here as they are on Earth?" he asked.

Mikel snorted. "What difference does that make? This is Eleusia."

"On Earth, if you join the stars together with imaginary lines, some of them make the shapes of people or animals or things," he explained, ignoring Mikel. "I think we call 'the serpent' Draco the dragon, but I don't know the others."

"Callisto is the Big Bear," chimed in Jamie, "and her hunting son is the Little Bear. I can tell you the story if you want to hear it. It's really a fascinating one all about…"

"Not right now," muttered Mikel. "We don't have time."

Jamie glared up at him for so rudely interrupting, but he took no notice, although Jeremiah did. One of these days, he was going to have to teach Mikel some manners.

"The constellations are not the same," replied Azmodeus. "However, there are configurations that resemble those in Earth's dimension, so our forefathers simply labeled similar ones with names that were familiar to them."

"So, does the prophecy mean something about three groups of stars coming together?" asked Melisande.

Jeremiah realized that this was the first time the Glockamarians had ever heard of constellations, but after all, they had experienced in the past few days, he could understand their confusion. He wasn't much better off about a lot of other things. Anything, it seemed, was possible.

"You are correct, Melisande. Once every century on Eleusia, these three constellations come together and rotate in a circular fashion around our north pole. When they next come into alignment, your quest must be finished or Draukenberg as we now know it will cease to exist."

"When will that happen?" asked Tovan.

"In seventeen days."

"Seventeen days," whispered Melisande as the others groaned. "That's not enough time."

"It will have to be," sighed the old man.

"And we have to solve six riddles," sighed Melisande. "Oh, I'm not good with riddles."

This time, both Mikel and Jeremiah restrained themselves from offering to help the girl, although they both turned and glared at one another.

Tovan read the next section of the prophecy out loud.

"On a quest that once begun, cannot but for death be undone…"

"I think we all get that part," shivered Jeremiah, suddenly wishing he hadn't gone skiing that day.

"Only then may the trident stand between that which is good and that which is evil…"

No one spoke this time. They simply exchanged confused and puzzled looks.

"Well, that's great," sighed Jamie. "All we have to do is go into this place called Aradell, answer six riddles, and get back to Toria…all within seventeen days. Sounds like a piece of cake to me. No problem."

Jeremiah picked up the parchment and looked at it more carefully. "What is this in the corner?"

He handed the parchment to Azmodeus, who peered down at it with great interest.

"I do believe that this is your first clue. This small drawing resembles a large cave. Once you are into Aradell, search for something that looks like this."

"Caves," moaned Tovan. "I hate caves."

"Well," smiled the wizard. "From the looks of it, it's a big one, which might help."

He handed the parchment back to him. "Put this in your pouch. You will need to take the prophecy with you. Trust your own intuitions. Each of you has magical talents and capabilities that you will discover on this journey. I cannot come with you, but I can tell you about Aradell. It has many different terrains and weather patterns. One moment, you might find yourself in a desert, and in the next, a tropical forest. The land has a habit of changing by flipping over, so you must be cautious. To be caught in a land change would be most unwise. There are doors that will appear out of nowhere at various times and some will lead you to safety, but others will lead you into greater danger. The Hollows is linked to Aradell and some of those doors will lead you into that shadowed land. Hopefully, you encounter few land shifts but be prepared for them. Also, some of the fairy tales, myths and legends have mutated over the years, so beware of surprises. Do not always trust what you see."

"It seems that a lot of things can bring our quest to an end," muttered Jeremiah, not feeling at all brave. "But how will we know where to go once we get into Aradell?"

"The first location should show itself as soon as you enter Aradell. If you are successful, you will receive a clue that will direct you to the next location. At each riddle location, there will be a door that will take you close to the location of the next riddle. You must use those but be cautious."

Jeremiah shook his head. "It sounds more like we're going to be going from one trap to the next."

"It does indeed," agreed Azmodeus. "However, you have a secret weapon. Mikel has the ability to sense danger, evil, and discord. Listen to him."

Jeremiah looked at the boy in surprise. The way Mikel was scowling, he was obviously not comfortable with this information being revealed. Turning beet red with embarrassment, he looked angrily over at Azmodeus, but the wizard simply responded with a pleasant grin. Jeremiah couldn't figure out why Mikel was so angry. As far as he was concerned, that would be a great gift to have. The girls appeared to be equally impressed, which seemed to embarrass Mikel even more.

"How will we get from Aradell to the Sanctuary if we make it?" asked Melisande.

"Yonnus and I will be waiting to transport all of us to Toria, where we will face the final confrontation. You have many puzzles and riddles to solve before then."

Jeremiah looked around at the group and sensed the same growing apprehension and fear that he was feeling.

"We can't do this," whispered Tovan.

"Yes, we can," snapped a voice from the shadows. "What a bunch of pathetic whiners."

Portia stepped forward into the light, her arms crossed over her chest and her expression one of defiance.

"Gad," grumbled Mikel. "I'd forgotten all about you. It was actually pleasant, now that I think of it. Perhaps I could forget about you permanently."

"Enough, you two," chuckled the wizard. "One would get the impression you didn't like one another and that simply won't do."

Jeremiah didn't smile. He was concerned. It had been obvious from the start that Mikel and Portia detested each other. He also noticed that both were impatient and quick to anger, and a combination such as that was not going to bode well on such a dangerous mission.

The following morning, he found himself standing with the small group on the misty border of Aradell. He was dressed like the others in elfin leggings and a jerkin, leather boots laced to his knees and a cloak that covered him to his ankles. His hat was pulled down over his ears and a pack containing food, water, and other essentials was strapped to his back. The Glockamarians had swords in scabbards at their waists and all carried staffs. He and Jamie had both refused to even practice with swords. After his initial excitement at the thought of learning how to use one, rational thought set in. He had felt that in the short time they had had to train, he'd probably be better off swinging a stick at their enemies as opposed to a blade that would probably end up chopping himself or one of the others into pieces.

Tovan shook her head, her face pale in the morning light.

"We're never going to get through this," she whispered.

Part of him had to agree. This had the earmarks of some sort of suicide mission. Just keeping track of everything they should or shouldn't do, the enemies they might face in Aradell and the fact that they only had sixteen days left to succeed made him feel sick to his stomach.

"We have to try," he whispered back.

May the Fates protect you.

Jeremiah glanced back at Snippen and his rider, Arynn, who had flown Azmodeus, Tovan and himself from Donagal. Ever since his arrival in the elfin city, someone had been speaking into his mind at the oddest times. At first, he'd ignored it, thinking the thoughts to be figments of his own imagination, but lately, he'd felt that there was more to it than that. The only common factor had been the presence of the griffin and the elf whenever this strange event occurred, and he was convinced that it was tied to one or both of them. He bowed respectfully and then turned back to face the valley.

Be watchful and listen. There are others with whom you may speak.

Jeremiah tripped as he started to follow the others down the hill. The message had been so clear; its owner could have been standing right next to him. He glanced back over his shoulder just as the mists of Aradell engulfed him, his last vision being that of the wizard waving encouragingly.   Within minutes, the group of six was facing their first obstacle. They had become separated from one another in the mist.

"Stop and stay where you are," called out Melisande. "I've got some rope, and if each of you calls out your name one at a time, I'll find the first one and the next and so on. Grab on to the rope when we reach you, and then we can all keep together."

The next few minutes proved to be a bit of mayhem as they sought each other out and attached themselves to the rope. Melisande carried on in the lead, and Jeremiah brought up the rear. In this manner, they continued down the hill, eventually emerging below the mist into what appeared to be a desert.

"Wow, it's warm here," said Jamie, letting go of the rope and dropping her pack to the ground. As she slipped off her cape, hat, and fleece vest, attaching them to her pack, the others followed suit.

"That's better," sighed Tovan readjusting her pack. "The temperature changed quickly enough. One minute we were freezing and a few moments later…this." She gestured to the panorama in front of them.

"It's not just the temperature or the landscape," added Melisande. "When we started down the path, it was early morning. Now, it appears to be late afternoon. What is that powdery stuff lying all over the ground that looks like brown flour?"

"Sand," replied Jeremiah, throwing in what he hoped was a casual smile that gave a hint of 'I'm interested in you'. Melisande ignored him completely. Shrugging his shoulders and feeling a bit put out, he finished his explanation. "If this is a typical desert, it will be hot, dry and full of sand. We must save our water."

He looked around, taking in the view. Apart from a canyon directly in front of them, rolling sand dunes faced them wherever they looked. It was a horrible, desolate place in which to start their journey.

"I think the only place we should go is into that canyon," he suggested.

"What's a canyon?" asked Melisande.

"It's like a tunnel in the ground but with no ceiling," explained Jeremiah. "I'll have to wait and show you," he added when he saw her blank look.

"Where's Portia?" asked Melisande, glancing around.

"Well, I know she came through with us," said Mikel. "She was holding the rope in front of me."

"Let's carry on," muttered Melisande, picking up her rope. "Knowing Portia, she's probably rushed off to be the first one to whatever is coming up next."

"Stupid idiot," muttered Mikel in disgust. "Only a fool would rush off into a dangerous situation without thinking."

"Well, we are talking about Portia," said Jamie.

"You can say that again," replied Jeremiah.

"Well, we are talking about Portia," quipped Tovan.

That brought a smile from everyone. They continued down the path, walls of rock gradually building up on either side of them. By the time they reached level ground, the tops of the walls were a hundred feet above them.

"This is your canyon?" asked Melisande, and Jeremiah nodded.

"How could she have moved so far ahead of us?" asked Jamie. "She must have been running."

"Wait," said Melisande, stopping and holding up her hand. "Listen."

In the silence that followed, each of them heard a voice up ahead, calling out a name that the three of them hated.

"Drogo! Drogo!"

"What would Portia's brother be doing here?" asked a puzzled Tovan.

The five raced along the canyon floor following the sound of Portia's voice. As they came barrelling around a bend in the canyon wall, they pulled up short at the scene that greeted them. Portia was surrounded by a large group of fierce-looking men, most still seated on powerfully built horses. Several were standing beside Portia: two were holding her arms so that she could not run away, and others were rummaging through her pack. The five instinctively moved further back into the shadows so as not to be seen.

"They look like they belong in the 'Arabian Nights' stories," whispered Jeremiah.

Most wore cloth turbans while others sported fezzes with tassels. They wore either long satin jackets split up the sides and pulled in at the waists with elaborately tied sashes or rough cloth robes cut in a similar style wrapped with sashes of poor quality material. All wore wide pantaloons pulled in at their knees by long boots. Their tough, bearded faces matched the fierce demeanor of their horses. Eyes flashed, nostrils flared and none stood placidly waiting for instructions from their riders. They pranced, eager to be off and nipped at others that got too close. The saddles were decorated with exotic designs and tassels and colored strips of material were wrapped around the reigns and bridles. However, it was the abundance of knives and swords that was of major concern to the five in the shadows.

"Who are you?" demanded the man dressed in the finest apparel, wearing the largest turban. "Where have you come from?"

Portia didn't answer him. She appeared to be too terrified to open her mouth.

"Speak up, girl!" he shouted, threatening her with his sword.

Portia began to shake so hard that her legs began to give way.

"Your radiance," interjected a young man stepping nervously forward. "If I may be so bold, this female looks to be well-fed and cared for. She might be someone worth ransoming."

The leader paused and lowered his sword. "That is good thinking, my son."

"We have enough money, father," said another. "The female will just be a burden on our next raid."

"That is even better thinking, other son. I will decide her fate inside. Bring her."

He turned away from Portia, who was now sobbing openly and faced the bare rock wall of the canyon. Raising his arms, he bellowed out the words that Jeremiah instantly recognized.

"Open Sesame!"

"Holy smokes," he whispered. "It's 'Ali Baba and the Forty Thieves'. Those are the forty thieves. And there's our cave!"

"I gather that the forty thieves are not pleasant fellows," came the quiet tones of Melisande's voice over his shoulder.

"Not at all. Azmodeus said that Aradell was the home of myths and legends, but I never imagined this."

"I hope they don't harm Portia," whispered Tovan.

"Are you developing a soft spot for her?" asked Mikel with a sneer.

"We need her for the quest," she snapped back.

They watched as the rock wall in front of the thief ground back, revealing a large opening to what appeared to be a cavern. The thieves wasted no time in entering the cave, dragging Portia along with them. As soon as they were inside, the leader shouted, "Close

Sesame," and the entrance reverted back to its original state. It was now impossible to see where the entrance had been.

"Now what do we do," sighed Melisande. "We can't leave Portia inside with those ruffians."

Mikel snorted. "Well, if it were up to me, I would just leave."

"Well, it's not up to you, thank goodness," grumbled Jeremiah. "Without Portia, we're finished before we begin."

"Look buddy," snarled Mikel, his face flushed with anger. "I didn't ask to come on this idiotic trip. I was practically told to come. Remember?"

"We all agreed to come, Mikel," said Melisande, attempting to calm him down. "None of us had much choice, so we have to make the best of it."

"I'm not going to listen to you," shouted the boy. "And I don't have to do anything you say."

Jeremiah was about to yell back at him when he noticed the confusion on Mikel's face.

"What is it?" he asked.

"I don't know," Mikel replied," but it hasn't been me speaking for the last few minutes. I got mad because you were all yelling at me."

"We weren't yelling at you, Mikel," exclaimed Jamie, looking around cautiously. "You were doing all the yelling."

"What is going on here?" asked Melisande, taking several steps back into the canyon to look around.

Suddenly Mikel cried out. "Stop! Come back!"

The others turned in time to see a shadowed creature scuttle back through the canyon.

"What was that?" cried Tovan.

No one had an answer.

"Something was speaking in your voice," shuddered Melisande. "Something was trying to pitch us against each other…"

"…in order to split up the quest," finished Jamie.

Melisande nodded her head in agreement. "We are going to have to be more careful. There are evil creatures out there that want to end this quest and getting us to argue is a great way of splitting us up. Dissention in the ranks, so to speak."

A noise drew their attention back to the cave wall. The rock was grinding back once more to expose the space concealed behind. The thieves thundered out, horses snorting and dust flying, making it difficult for the group to make out any details. The leader was the last to exit, and as he did so, he turned in his saddle and raised his arms.

"Close Sesame," he bellowed.

He then followed his companions around the curve of the canyon and was lost in sight.

"Don't say anything," whispered Jeremiah. "They might come back."

He was grateful for once that Mikel didn't argue with him. The five waited quietly until they could no longer hear the horses.

Melisande was the first to break the silence. "Was Portia with them?"

"I couldn't tell," replied Jamie. "There was too much dust."

There was murmured agreement from the others.

"Well, come on then," said Tovan, squaring her shoulders and walking forward.

The rest followed, flinching at each strange sound. When they reached the wall, Jamie turned and faced them.

"Who should make the command?" she asked.

"What do you mean?" asked Melisande.

"Well, the leader of the thieves had a great booming voice. Maybe it won't open for us."

"I'll try," said Jeremiah, about to stride forward, believing that he had the most knowledge of the situation.

Jamie crossed her arms over her chest. "What makes you think that you will be successful?" she asked, a touch of sarcasm in her voice.

"And why didn't any of you bother to ask me?" demanded Mikel, glaring at all of them.

"Why don't we all shout it out," suggested Melisande, holding up her hands for peace. "All of us together should be able to do it."

It suddenly hit Jeremiah that they didn't need anyone else to cause dissension in the ranks. They were doing it themselves. He immediately backed down and let Melisande continue.

"Okay, let's try it. On the count of three: One. Two. Three."

"Open Sesame!" they shouted.

At first, nothing happened. Just as they were about to try again, a grinding noise filled the silence, and the entrance to the cavern opened up before them. They all had to fight hard to stifle a cheer.

"Well done, everyone," whispered Jamie, peering into the dark depths. "Do you think they've left a guard?"

"Only one way to find out," whispered Jeremiah, moving cautiously forward.

The rest followed him, pausing just inside the entrance to allow their eyes to become adjusted to the darkness. Openings in the cavern ceiling allowed shafts of dull, grey light to enter, which provided them with an opportunity to take in their surroundings. The cavern was quite large and appeared to narrow down into a tunnel at the far end. Piles of coins and golden objects littered the floor, and priceless silks and furs filled every available nook and cranny. It truly was a treasure trove. Of Portia, there was no sign.

"This is amazing," laughed Jeremiah. "I have read this story many times, but you have to actually see a treasure trove to believe it."

Tovan shook her head. "I could never have imagined anything like this. My parents have never had more than a few coins at a time and gold objects are only found in the Sanctuary."

Mikel bent down to pick up one of the objects, but Jeremiah stopped him. "I wouldn't touch anything in here. I wouldn't be a bit surprised if those thieves know where everything has been placed and have set traps."

The boy jerked his hand away and stepped back.

Melisande ran her hand across her forehead and sighed. "They must have taken Portia. There's no sign of her."

A sudden, piercing scream coming from the tunnel jolted them all into action. As a group, they raced into the entrance, which after a short distance, opened up into a brightly lit courtyard. It was circular in shape and open to the sky. The tunnel they had raced through was also the only entrance in or exit out, but no one, including Jeremiah, noticed that at the time.

Portia was sitting in a chair, her arms and legs tied to the furniture so that she couldn't move. The chair had been placed in front of a massive statue and she was looking up at a female face that was both magnificently beautiful and wickedly sinister at the same time. The rest of the body was that of a lion with large curved wings that started on her back and came to points above her head. Jeremiah knew that he and Jamie were the only ones who knew what it was. He was about to rush forward when suddenly Jamie dropped her pack and took off at a run toward Portia. As the huge face began to arch down toward Portia, Jamie began to yell. The face turned toward her and Portia shook her head as if suddenly released from a strong grip. Jeremiah watched in horror as Jamie confronted the monster.

"Who interrupts me?" boomed the creature, its question ricocheting off the canyon walls and sounding more like multiple voices rather than one. "I have not yet asked my riddle."

"Then ask me," shouted Jamie. "Let me answer your riddle."

For a moment, the grey rock eyes simply stared at her. Suddenly the face took on a hideous expression. The light darkened and a powerful roar preceded a wind that sent Jeremiah flying, stinging particles of sand raking across his face and hands. As suddenly as it appeared, the wind was gone. He dragged himself to his feet, noting that the others hadn't fared any better.

"Very well," replied the monster. "I will ask you the riddle, but if you are wrong, all six of you will belong to me."

Jamie nodded.

"What walks on four legs in the morning, two legs in the afternoon, and three in the evening?"

Jamie's face broke into a broad grin. "You have asked this riddle many times before, Sphinx The answer is 'man'."

"Explain your answer!" demanded the Sphinx.

"In the beginning, man crawls on all four legs. When he gets older, he walks on two, and when he is old, he uses a cane."

The Sphinx was silent for several terrifying moments and then nodded. "You may pass," was all she said, pulling her massive head up and resuming her stone-like pose.

Everyone rushed forward to help release Portia, Jeremiah swooping up Jamie's belongings on the way. When he got there, he was concerned to see Jamie shaking like a leaf and her face the color of chalk. She had sounded so confident and sure of herself, but she had probably been terrified. If Jamie really was his sister, she was a great addition to his family of one as far as he was concerned.

"What is that creature?" asked Melisande, trying to keep her eyes from straying to the monster's face.

"A Sphinx," explained Jamie. "It's a creature out of Greek and Roman myths in our dimension. If travelers had the misfortune of running into her and couldn't answer her riddle, they would die."

The older girl shivered and then turned to Portia. "Why did you run ahead of us?" she asked.

"I saw our garden at home," was her sullen reply. "My brother was in the middle of it calling out to me, but when I ran toward him, he moved further away. No matter how fast I ran, I couldn't reach him."

Dark expressions passed between the others. Twice in a very short time, members of the group had been deceived.

"I could have handled that old Sphinx," snorted Portia.

"Oh really," replied Jamie. "For your information, she was about to suck out your soul. You'd be dead right now if I hadn't stopped her."

For a moment, all were quiet. The severity of the dangerous situation they now found themselves in was beginning to really hit home.

"Thank goodness, you stopped her, Jamie," said Melisande in an almost hushed whisper. "You should be grateful, Portia. She saved your life."

"We're all going to have to be careful," cautioned Jeremiah. "We've got to be constantly on the look-out for danger and protect each other."

Except for Portia, the others nodded in agreement. Portia simply scowled down at her feet, anger tinting her cheeks an obvious pink.

Suddenly Melisande gave a start. "What is that noise?" she asked.

As one, they turned toward the tunnel entrance and listened. Shouting could be heard coming from the cavern and a horrible reality made its presence known. Jeremiah felt the bottom of his stomach clench into a knot.

"So little people," hissed the Sphinx from above. "The robbers have returned and are now searching for you. They will of course, capture you because you are trapped in here with no way out."

She began to laugh. The harsh, bitter sound echoed and re-echoed off the cavern walls around them.

"We forgot to close the door to the cave," shouted Jeremiah over the noise. "They knew as soon as they returned that there was someone in here."

"What are we going to do?" wailed Tovan. "We have to get out of here!"

Even above the laughter of the Sphinx, they could hear the shouts and threats of the robbers as they roared into the tunnel.

"A door!" cried Portia. "Look! A door!"

Standing by itself in the middle of the sand was an ordinary door. It was as if someone had just stuck a doorframe upright in the sand.

"It might lead us to the wrong place!" shouted Melisande.

"If we stay here, we die!" howled Portia.

Tovan stared at the door in horror. "Wait! What if it's the wrong doorway?"

Ignoring her completely, Portia yanked the door open and leaped through, followed by Mikel and Melisande. Between them, Jeremiah and Jamie dragged a protesting Tovan through and slammed the door behind them just as the robbers exploded out of the tunnel.

Chapter Sixteen
Darkvale

Petre

"Who and what are you?" asked Petre, still in shock from their strange departure from the cliff top. He was sitting on a rock a few steps away from where they had landed after literally floating down through the air.

"A Wildenchin," stated Crutchin grinning from ear to ear. "And if you had kept your eyes open, you might, possibly, have enjoyed the view on our interesting descent."

"A Wildenchin?"

"I would tend to think that the closest translation would be 'wild child'. We are the children of the earth, those who protect plants and trees and the creatures who inhabit those environments. There are others who protect water and still others who look after the creatures of the air."

"But how is it connected to what you did up there?"

Crutchin chuckled, appearing to be thoroughly enjoying his confusion.

"I draw my power from the earth. In our case, I simply pulled up enough force to slow us down and cushion our fall. I must only use my powers for good. If I used them against anyone or anything, I would lose them."

"Then what about that sword? Would you have used it against the goblins?"

At that question, Crutchin laughed and bent the sword easily in half.

"This is a prop I grabbed when we left the theatre. It wouldn't have inflicted even a bruise. We must move on. This is not a good spot in which to linger."

Petre pulled himself up on shaking legs and stumbled across the riverbed following Crutchin into the trees. He kept looking at the little man in wonder. What else was the Wildenchin capable of doing?

They had not walked very far when something invisible swished past Petre's head, lifting his hair and causing his cape to flap. He stopped and looked around. It happened again and this time, whatever it was, lifted his hat right off his head.

"Crutchin!" he shouted. "I think we're being attacked!"

The little man turned and watched as Petre swatted frantically at something he couldn't see. He was beginning to panic.

"Stop, Petre. It's just the wind."

"What's a wind?" he cried, only cutting his efforts back by a fraction.

"It's just moving air. You didn't have any winds in Glockamar, Petre. Stop. It's alright."

Crutchin was still chuckling as he ceased his frantic movements.

"You probably think I'm an idiot," Petre muttered, feeling stupid.

"Of course not," replied Crutchin, obviously forcing his expression into one of a more serious nature. "I would have reacted in exactly the same way had I grown up inside a mountain. Now come. We have a long way to go before we can rest."

They walked for quite a distance in silence through a forest that left Petre quaking with fear. Huge trees, gnarled and knotted with age, rose up all around them, their branches overlapping and forming an intricate, interlaced pattern overhead. It was getting late and the setting sun, which seemed much brighter outside the mountain, was having difficulty, penetrating through the branches to touch the ground beneath. It was shadowed and dark and Petre heard strange noises all around him, something he had never experienced in Glockamar. He also noticed that it was turning cool, almost chilly, and pulled his cape tighter around his thin body.

They eventually emerged from the forest into a meadow, sparsely dotted with clumps of trees. It was dark now, and when Petre looked up, he gasped. "There are lights in the sky!"

"Stars," replied Crutchin. "I keep forgetting that this is your first trip outside the mountain. Oh, there is going to be much for you to learn but wait until we camp for the night before I explain. We are not far from the rendezvous point and the others will be there shortly."

Petre followed him as if in a trance, tripping over his feet as he tried to walk and peer up at the sky at the same time. At last, they came to a small knoll on which Crutchin sat himself down and gestured to Petre to do the same.

"Sit boy, and I'll explain about the stars and constellations while we wait."

And he did just that. Petre absorbed the information like a sponge, completely forgetting all the questions he had had about Crutchin and the thing called wind in his attempt to learn more about the fascinating sparkles in the massive sky.

"When your people arrived in Eleusia and chose to live inside the mountain range that we call the Zagoroth Mountains, they did their best to mimic life as it was on the outside."

"But why did they choose to live inside, instead of outside?"

"Magic," stated the little man. "They felt that magic had destroyed their civilization in Earth's dimension and they wanted nothing to do with it here, so they cut themselves off from the outside. The use of magic was banned inside Glockamar which was why Spider, Hera's minion, didn't have any trouble bringing children who might have gifts of magic to Toria. All the occupants had had it so ingrained in them over the generations that magic was wrong that they didn't fight it when their children started being taken away to be cured."

"But none of them got cured," argued Petre. "None of the children ever came back."

Crutchin nodded. "By the time people began to realize that, it was too late. Spider was in control. She was trying to find the six children of the prophecy. She didn't care about anyone using magic. After all, she was using it herself."

"But how would she know when she had the right six?"

"I'm not quite certain, but three of them belong to Sharra and her husband, King Nikolai. The other three supposedly have special magical gifts necessary for the quest that Spider would recognize. I don't really know all the details. Ah, here they are."

With a terrified shout, Petre fell forward and flattened himself on the ground when he caught sight of what was landing. Three massive creatures with heads and bodies out of nightmares were landing on the ground in front of them. Even his experience on the cliff top had not been as terrifying as this. He covered his face with his hands and tried desperately to control his shaking limbs which felt impossible, considering he only had seconds to live.

"Petre dan Coro," boomed a familiar voice. "Is that you, I see? Groveling in the dirt?"

He peeked up through his fingers and instantly recognized the two figures striding toward him.

"Yonnus? Master?"

He got to his knees and then slowly dragged himself to his feet. The sight of the creatures standing calmly behind them was not comforting but if Yonnus and the master were not concerned, then he shouldn't be either…or so he hoped. Mikel's father greeted Crutchin with an enthusiastic pounding on his back and then strode over to Petre and ruffed up his hair.

"I'm glad to see that all went well," said Azmodeus, sitting down on the rock that Crutchin had so recently vacated. "You gave me a moment of concern."

"Ah," scoffed Crutchin. "It was nothing. My only fear was that Petre wouldn't hang on."

Petre was about to ask how Azmodeus had known about their adventure when he remembered how well Crutchin could mind link.

That was probably how he knew where the party was going to land as well.

"We need to set up camp for the night," said Azmodeus. "You two young ones go and help our friends while Yonnus and I get a fire going."

Petre hesitated.

"They're only gryphons, boy," chuckled Yonnus. "Besides, they've already eaten."

Petre swallowed hard and walked hesitantly toward the elves and the flying monsters, trying to ignore Yonnus' chuckles that followed.

A short time later, with the three elf riders joining them, the group sat companionably around a fire eating baked vegetables and bread. There was a slight breeze but between the fire and a cloak Azmodeus had given him, Petre was quite comfortable.

"When do we begin?" asked Collpepper.

"Tomorrow," replied Azmodeus. "I would ask that you and your riders take the four of us to Darkvale. We will land far enough away so that neither you nor your mounts will be affected. From there, we will make it down on our own."

"Agreed," replied Arynn. "Our beasts especially could not handle the sound of the voices. It would drive them mad."

"I apologize for interrupting," said Petre humbly. "If I am not being too bold, could someone please explain to me what this is all about?"

Azmodeus gave Crutchin a meaningful look. "It's time to educate the boy."

Crutchin nodded and turned to Petre. "Come with me, young one. I want to show you something."

Petre got up and followed Crutchin away from the fire and in the opposite direction from the gryphons, much to his relief. He stopped at the edge of the meadow, facing the trees, and Petre stopped right beside him. Stretching out both hands toward the trees, Crutchin whispered softly into the night and to the boy's amazement, a strange mellow light seeped up from the ground below, illuminating the trees above.

"What do you see?" asked Crutchin.

Petre looked into the forest. "Some of the trees are very much alive but others are dead or dying. Why is that?"

"The trolls," replied Crutchin.

"The trolls? Those monsters that captured us and took us to Toria?"

Crutchin nodded. "As I told you, the trolls are the tree keepers of Eleusia, nurturing the roots and providing them with what is needed. When Spider took control of Toria, Hera told her how to destroy the Laurel Tree in the garden of the Sanctuary."

"That let this Spider creature control the trolls?" asked Petre.

"That's right. The trolls have been forced to become her servants and have left their jobs as tree keepers behind. If we don't bring life back to that tree, the trolls may never return to their natural tasks, and the trees throughout Draukenberg will wither and die."

"But how do we do that?"

"Tomorrow, the elves and gryphons will take us to a place called the Darkvale. It is inhabited by the sorceress Rudana and her followers, the sirens. Their songs and her voice have the ability to drive most people mad, but Azmodeus will protect us from them. At least, I hope he will be able to do that. Anyway, we want her to tell us what to do in order to bring the tree back to life."

"And then the trolls will go back to their tree keeping," concluded Petre.

"Exactly. However, the six traveling through Aradell must be successful. If they are not, then we will fail as well for Spider will simply destroy the tree again. She is very strong with all her powers."

As Crutchin turned to walk back to the fire, the glow beneath the trees vanished. Petre strode beside him. "Crutchin," he asked. "What happens if the sorceress does not give us the information?"

"Well," shrugged the little man. "We won't really be in a position to care."

"Why not?"

"We'll be dead."

The following morning, the four stood on the edge of a valley, examining the view below and contemplating the dangers.

"It looks peaceful enough," said Petre, barely controlling the shiver that crawled up his back.

Yonnus grunted.

"Looks can be deceiving boy, especially when you're dealing with someone like Rudana."

Petre didn't bother to explain that he had made the remark facetiously.

It did look peaceful, but it certainly didn't look safe. The lake was in a valley shaped like a bowl. The sides of the bowl ranged from steep rocky cliffs and inclines covered with dead bits of brown grass. The trees that grew in the valley, if you could call them growing, were all leafless with huge roots that spiraled out from the trunks in great hummocks, each space underneath large enough for all of them to take shelter from a storm, should that happen. The bushes were oversized, but they too were leafless and dead looking. Petre surmised that they were far from dead and possibly as dangerous as anything else that might lurk here. He glanced back at the elves and gryphons that had stopped in a meadow much further back, well beyond the voices of the sorceress and her sirens. For a moment, he wished he were there and then Crutchin asked an innocent question and his feelings on the subject made an abrupt about-face.

"Is it necessary to take the boy?"

"You can't leave me behind," protested Petre indignantly.

Azmodeus chuckled. "No, I would never leave you behind. Everyone has to visit Darkvale once in his or her life so don't worry, young master. You are coming with us."

Petre smiled smugly at Crutchin.

"Hopefully, you will not live to regret it," added Azmodeus.

His moment of glory burst like a bubble as the wizard moved forward into the valley. Crutchin followed, and Yonnus gently pushed him in behind the Wildenchin. Silently, they descended toward the lake.

The silence was eerie. There were no sounds of animal or insect life, only the gentle lapping of the waves against the rocky shore of the lake. At one point, Petre thought that one of the trees within his peripheral vision moved but when he looked, the tree in question was as motionless as the rest. It happened again just moments later, but once again, when he looked, not a branch of the tree was moving. He shivered and kept his eyes on Crutchin's back. Halfway down the hill, the sky darkened and ripples began to appear in the water. A cold wind picked up and the ripples developed into waves that grew in height and force the closer the four came to the shoreline. Azmodeus stopped and raised his arms. Petre felt as if a wad of material had been stuffed into each ear and the sensation was far from pleasant. The old man's voice was audible but muffled as if coming from a great distance and his beard had shortened by half.

"Let us be off to meet Rudana," he cheerfully threw over his shoulder as he continued down the hill.

Petre began to notice the heads of strange water creatures dotting the crests of the waves. They seemed to ride the undulating water with ease, their plant-like hair catching in the wind or floating in the water around them. The hands that emerged were clawed, the teeth sharp and pointed, and the faces were a nightmarish green with the most evil-looking eyes Petre had ever seen, sitting on either side of long angular features. If he didn't know better, he would have thought of them to be strange horses if there were such things as water horses. The creatures appeared to be singing although he could hear nothing and concluded that these must be the sirens.

Azmodeus stopped at the shore facing the lake.

"Rudana," he called. "I request your presence."

For a few moments, there was nothing but green flashes of lightening and the grumble of thunder overhead. And then she was there at the shoreline, hovering directly in front of them.

Petre gasped. Her skin was the color of milk, but her eyes and the hair that hung to her waist were pitch black, like a starless night.

Her slight figure was clothed in shimmering seaweed and everything about her glowed softly as if she were illuminated from within.

"Azmodeus," she smiled, revealing little pointed teeth. "It has been a very long time."

The old man nodded. "You look as lovely as ever, Rudana."

"And you have aged like an old tuber," laughed the sorceress. "Where did my handsome young suitor go?"

"Now Rudana," grinned Azmodeus. "I was never your suitor as you well know. Your idea of courtship is to eat the poor unlucky soul as soon as you get your hands on him and I chose not to meet such a fate."

"True," she sighed. "I really do have trouble controlling myself in that regard. Why have you sought me out this time?"

"I have come to ask a favor. Eleusia has been placed in danger and…"

She waved her hand at him. "I have no interest in what goes on in the mortal world. You should know that. Now tell me what you want before I grow impatient."

"I want to know how to bring the Laurel Tree in Toria back to life."

Rudana threw back her head and laughed. Even through the padding in his ears, Petre winced. Something moved and he quickly looked around. The trees had crept closer to them. Of that he was certain.

"Yonnus," he whispered. "The trees…"

"Sh!" replied the big man, turning his attention back to the sorceress.

"So, you silly wizard," continued Rudana, "someone has killed off the Laurel Tree which means the trolls have left their job as tree keepers. Who has them under their control, I wonder? Oh, this is too wonderful."

"It is not wonderful," snapped Petre. "It is very serious."

Azmodeus turned and gave him a sharp look and Crutchin placed a restraining hand on his shoulder. Rudana looked down at him as if noticing him for the first time. Amusement and something else flickered across her features as she suddenly regarded him with interest.

"Ah, how fascinating," she mused.

Without taking her eyes from Petre, she responded to the wizard's concern.

"You want to bring the Laurel Tree back to life and for that, you will need its seed."

She turned her attention back to the three men. Petre took a step backward, feeling as if he'd suddenly been released from a powerful grip. He also stepped back on a tree root that had not been there a few moments before.

"Thank you, Rudana," responded Azmodeus, "but where do we find such a seed?"

"I don't know the answer to your question, old man, but I do know who does."

"Yonnus," hissed Petre, tugging on the big man's sleeve. "The trees are coming closer."

This time both Yonnus and Crutchin looked around. The trees had indeed moved and were now clustered around the four. Azmodeus glanced briefly over his shoulder before looking back at the sorceress and gestured to the trees surrounding them.

"Are you trying to tell us that you won't release us after you provide an answer?"

Rudana laughed again. "We shall see, we shall see," she replied, smiling widely at the expressions of unease on the faces in front of her. "As I said before, I do not know where such a seed exists, but I can send you to those who do."

"Thank you," replied the wizard in his most humble voice.

"However, you should know that there will be a price to pay, both now and later, for my sisters will exact a payment even more costly."

"We must go to the Furies?" he asked, frowning.

Petre heard Yonnus take in a sharp breath.

"Of course," she laughed. "My sisters know everything. Now for my price as temporary as it may be."

Azmodeus put up a hand. "It will not involve harming any of us."

"Only if you have grown slow-witted with age," she cried, extending her hand.

In an instant, the wizard's beard had vanished and the trees surrounding them began to moan. Branches in the shape of huge clawed hands tore at their clothes and began to encircle bodies. The padding was gone from Petre's ears and in its place was the most horrid wailing noise he had ever heard. It was enough to make his head explode.

"Grab hands!" shouted Azmodeus. "Crutchin!"

Petre felt his hands grabbed, and in a twinkling instant, the four were on their faces in the meadow where they had left their friends. The elves ran toward them as they struggled to their feet.

"Sorry about the landing," apologized Crutchin. "When you draw that much power from the earth so quickly, it becomes a bit unwieldy."

"I thank you anyway," chuckled Azmodeus, brushing the grass from his robe. "Ah, that woman is invigorating. I do enjoy having her as an adversary."

"I don't understand what happened," said Petre, shaking his head to get rid of the remnants of the wailing sirens.

"My beard," laughed the wizard. "She knew that I was protecting all of you with my magic and a wizard's magic is found in his beard. Every time I cast a spell, it shrinks depending upon the amount of magic needed. However, it always grows back. By taking my beard, she knew we would be vulnerable to the sirens, but she also knew that Crutchin was a Wildenchin and could get us out of there. Wonderful woman. Ah, there we go."

Petre's eyes grew round with amazement as, in the blink of an eye, the missing beard on the old man's face grew back to its former luxurious length.

He winked at him. "As Rudana said, the payment would only be temporary."

"So, she only wanted to scare us?" asked Yonnus.

"Of course," chuckled Azmodeus. "Today was obviously one of her better days. You wouldn't want to meet her on a bad one."

"Master," asked Petre, "What happens if you can't grow your beard back?"

"Then I have no magic left," replied Azmodeus. "But that has never happened and let us hope that it never does."

"Do we know where we must go to find the Furies?" asked Crutchin.

The wizard's face lost its humor. "Unfortunately, yes. But before we continue on, we're going back to Donagal. I must speak with the Willik."

He turned and walked toward the gryphons, with elf riders accompanying him.

"What's wrong with the Furies?" asked Petre, walking beside Yonnus and Crutchin.

"Well, you know how I told you before that if Rudana didn't give us the information we would probably be dead?" asked Crutchin.

Petre nodded.

"Even if the Furies give us the information we need," continued Yonnus, "we will probably end up dead."

"That's the difference," grinned Crutchin.

"Great," mumbled Petre.

Maybe this was one adventure he should have missed.

Be brave, young Petre, be brave.

The boy turned and looked back in the direction of the lake. He was certain that the voice in his mind had been that of Rudana. Now, what had she meant by that? Shaking his head, he turned and followed the others.

Chapter Seventeen
The Trouble With Centaurs

Mikel

When Mikel had entered Aradell, Bandi had come with him but out of sight from the others. The Wickersnit, whose long name Mikel had shortened to Bandi, had been riding comfortably on the back of his pack, disguised as a fly. The two had agreed that no one would know of the chameleon's presence for as long as possible. He was not in the mood to explain to anyone that he was a wizard or why he had a Wickersnit with him. Despite his reluctance to have the creature come along, a strange bond had formed between them, the night before in the cell. He couldn't describe it, but he knew that each had an obligation to look after and protect the other.

'It's hogwash anyway,' he thought. 'It was just a coincidence.' *Not be washhog. You be wizard. Not coincidence. Bandi know. Oh, be quiet, fly, or I'll smack you.*

Mutterings and one nasty oath had come back to him, but then Bandi had remained silent and had not moved until they reached the end of the canyon, outside the cave. Mikel had not called out 'stop' to the strange creature running away from them but to Bandi who with a '*Follow I*' had taken off after it. Before Mikel could stop him, the Wickersnit was gone. Despite the severity of the situation that had waited for them in the cave of the thieves, Mikel couldn't stop worrying about Bandi who had not yet returned from wherever the creature had taken him. Hera had certainly been behind the attempt to cause dissension by using him and with Bandi away from his protection, the Wickersnit was vulnerable to Hera catching him.

Bandi! he had shouted as the door in the chamber of the Sphinx had closed behind them and with a second to spare, he had heard, *I here! I here! And we in trouble big.*

Now he was sitting beneath an overhanging ledge just off the path that they had been following and although not great, would have to do for the moment. Not feeling comfortable lighting a fire, the six were crouched together beneath it eating some of the dried rations provided for them by the elves. It was deathly quiet which didn't help calm anyone's nerves in the slightest and kept their voices to mere whispers. They had arrived in a place that seemed to be in permanent twilight and completely devoid of color. Everything was in varying shades of grey and black, and from what they could see, the landscape was made up of hills of rock. No one said it, but they knew this was The Hollows.

"Well, you have to admit," whispered Jeremiah. "We couldn't have been more wrong. Azmodeus did warn us to be careful."

"But where could we have gone except through the door," shrugged Tovan. "We would have been killed if we'd stayed there. This had to be Hera's doing."

No one spoke for a moment.

Portia, who was sitting apart from the group, pulled her knees up and rested her chin on them, looking away from the rest as she did so and sullenly examined her surroundings. Mikel selected a spot as far away from her as possible and not simply because of his dislike for her. Unknown to the other five, Mikel was carrying on a conversation with Bandi and he was getting more and more disturbed by what he heard.

The creature I not know. Small, green, fast runs.

Where did it run to?

Into desert. Strange lady in cape him meet. Disappear they did.

You mean they took off very fast?

No. Poofle they went. Not there. There. Not there.

They disappeared into thin air?

Did not I say? came a disgruntled response.

Did she see you?

Not I. Change to rock very small.

Well, don't go off like that again, Bandi. You know what she'll do to you if she catches you.

The Wickersnit didn't respond, but his mental shiver said it all.

Mikel shook his head. The woman must have been Hera. This quest was becoming more and more dangerous. The boy turned his attention back to the group.

"I just wish I didn't feel so alone," said Melisande. "I know we have each other, but most of us are strangers and none of us really knows what we're doing."

Jeremiah nodded. "You've got that right," he replied.

"The other thing is that this world is new to all of us," said Jamie. "You four didn't even know that you lived inside a mountain until the other day and the world that Jeremiah and I come from is about as regular as it gets. There are no such things as trolls or elves or even magic."

"We didn't think there was either," sighed Melisande. "I still don't know why we six were chosen. I can understand you two and Portia, but why the three of us? There are many young people our age in Glockamar."

A snort came from Portia.

"The Willik said that we had strong gifts and that was why we were chosen. Don't any of you ever listen?"

"Jamie and I asked the same question when we were coming out of the mountain," said Jeremiah, ignoring Portia. "You must have very powerful talents waiting to be discovered."

Again, there was silence.

"What do we do now?" asked Tovan. "Somehow we've got to get back to that desert place or we won't be able to carry on."

"In this light, we'll be lucky to find anything at all," muttered Jamie. "We don't dare make a fire or anything. We'd be spotted from miles away."

Melisande shivered. "I'll bet there are lots of creatures who'd love to spot us and more."

Jeremiah looked over at Mikel. "When all these different people and creatures came to the West, why were the evil ones allowed to come as well?"

He shrugged his shoulders. "Azmodeus said that everyone who possessed magical abilities was allowed to come, the rotten evil ones as well as the good ones. However, supposedly there were evil humans and creatures already here in the other two kingdoms. The soldiers of Draukenberg constantly patrol the borders to keep them out and so far, it has worked. There hasn't been a battle in a long time."

"Battles," whispered Jeremiah. "That's all we need to make this a more exciting. A battle."

Mikel nodded in agreement. He tried to squelch the thought that a good battle would be just the thing. But then again, the girls wouldn't be able to handle it.

"There are other kingdoms?" asked Jamie.

Mikel nodded.

"Chatra-Mando is in the south and we trade with them but we have nothing to do with those in Hvedrung across the Faldor Passage in the northeast.

"Like that's true," broke in Portia sarcastically. "What do you really know about anything? You've been stuck inside a mountain all your life."

Mikel looked over at her and felt his face twisting into an expression of disgust. Portia was the total outcast of the group and she deserved it as far as he was concerned. She had never had a close friend because of her horrible attitude and the nasty tricks she and her brother had always pulled on the others in Glockamar. He felt himself getting unreasonably angry again.

"Well, at least my father didn't murder…"

Tovan and Melisande gasped.

"Mikel!" snapped Melisande angrily. "That wasn't…what's wrong?"

He leaped to his feet, a feeling of great evil suddenly enveloping him. He raised his head and looked around. The feeling was becoming more intense and he had the sensation that his insides were squeezing together to the point that he could barely breathe. Being able to sense the approach of others had always been a skill of his, but to feel such evil was new. This was similar to the horrible feelings of evil that he had felt when the stranger had ducked into the shadows of the village and when the trolls had attacked them at the stream.

I too feel it, came a message from frightened Bandi.

"I wish to know who is coming," Mikel whispered to himself.

Suddenly a clear picture formed in his mind and he gasped out loud.

"What is it, Mikel?" asked Jamie nervously.

"We have to hide," he whispered. "Quickly. Something evil…there's something evil coming."

"I don't see anyone," said Portia, looking around.

"You must believe me," he stated firmly. "We must get away from this path."

He bent down and hurriedly threw his belongings into his pack. Jamie looked over at Jeremiah, her expression one of uneasiness. They all glanced nervously at one another and then as one, began to pack their own satchels.

"Hurry!" he pleaded. "Please hurry!"

The urgency in his voice affected them all. Within seconds packs had been filled and the six were scrambling up the incline above the ledge, Bandi clinging to Mikel's vest. Further up was a dark shadow that proved to be a small cave. They would be hidden from the path but would still be in a position to observe. They fell to the ground, pushing their packs behind them and peered over the edge.

All was quiet. They waited for such a long time, Jamie finally whispered, "Maybe you overreacted, Mikel. Your nerves got the better of you."

Muttered mumblings began to quietly emerge from the others. Jamie was not the only one to start to push up from the ground.

Suddenly he grabbed her hand. "There!" he hissed.

Several creatures came into view along the path just beyond the ledge where the six had so recently been sitting. Each half-man, half-horse creature trotted slowly toward the ledge, a large ugly tipped spear in one hand and a shield in the other. There were at least a dozen of the warriors.

"Centaurs!" gasped Jamie.

"We don't have a chance against them," groaned Jeremiah. "Look at the size of them. Look at their weapons."

Mikel slid his sword partway out of its sheath. "Quit being such a weakling, stupid. If we have to fight, we fight."

No! cried Bandi. *No chance! No chance!*

"Only if we have to," retorted Jeremiah. "You just make sure you don't do anything dumb enough to get us into a fight."

"Stop it you two," hissed Jamie. "This is not the time nor the place."

She glared at both of them. Mikel gave the same look back to her and then to Jeremiah who angrily turned his head away from him.

Why behave you this way?

Mikel shook his head as if clearing it.

I don't know. Something is not right.

As the leader of the centaurs reached the ledge, he stopped and began to sniff the air around him.

"Can he smell us?" choked Tovan.

No one answered. They were all too terrified. The centaur leader looked up the hillside, and his eyes seemed to bore into their own. Had he found them? As he moved off the path and began a slow traverse up the hill, they knew he had.

"Move back into the cave," hissed Mikel. "Come on."

The centaur stopped for a moment as if he had heard him and then continued at a faster pace.

"Hurry," insisted Jeremiah.

Without stopping to argue, they pulled back from the edge, grabbed their packs, and scurried into the small space provided by the cave. Each pushed back against the rock wall and held their breath. A moment later, the centaur appeared over the edge and stood peering into the darkness of the cave.

Mikel tried not to gasp out loud. The creature was huge. Where a horse's head and neck would normally be, emerged the upper half of a human male. He was covered in thick fur down to his waist, and muscles rippled through his massive arms and chest. The hair on his head was long, almost like that of a mane, and the eyes were close together on either side of a long aquiline nose. The body of the horse was also strong and muscular with tufts of thick fur hanging down the backs of each leg to the hoofs. He moved closer to the entrance, his nose working overtime to catch the scents that came his way. He sniffed around the edges and then stepped back to get a better look.

Melisande, who was beside Mikel, began to move slowly along the wall that slanted to the right.

"Tunnel," she whispered when she slid back.

The centaur stopped moving and appeared to be listening. He sniffed again and moved closer to the entrance. Mikel's heart began to pound in his chest and he found it hard to breathe. The only thing saving them for the moment was that this particular centaur was too big to get into the cave. He hadn't, however, missed the fact that there had been much smaller centaurs in the group. They couldn't wait any longer.

"Run!" shouted Melisande. "There's a tunnel here. Follow me."

The centaur gave an angry shriek and hurtled his spear into the darkness of the cave. There was a startled yelp and then the six were thundering down the dark tunnel, running blindly as fast as they could. Those trailing could hear hoofbeats behind them and knew that one of the smaller centaurs was right on their heels.

"Help!" screamed Tovan, who had been the last to enter the tunnel. "It's grabbing at me. Help me. Please, help me!

Chapter Eighteen
Never Trust A Sphinx

Jamie

Melisande and Jamie tumbled through the opening together and landed one on top of the other on a sunny patch of thick grass. Jeremiah and Mikel came next, barely avoiding landing on top of them and Portia saved herself by leaping over them. Poor Tovan plowed right into the pair, looking as if the devil himself was chasing her. The last to emerge from the tunnel was a small white centaur that collapsed on the ground, pealing with laughter. As she shrieked, she transformed into Crooks the mountain pixie.

"I could strangle her," panted Tovan, glaring at the creature now rolling around on the grass howling with mirth.

"Where did she come from?" asked Mikel, trying not to grin as he helped Melisande and Jamie to their feet. The pixie's laugh was infectious.

Jamie was thrilled to see her. Once again, she was amazed that she had lived with this fascinating creature for so many years, never knowing what she truly was.

Melisande glanced back at the tunnel. "Maybe we could wonder about that later. One of the real centaurs is going to come through at any moment and we need to be gone."

Tovan shivered. "What horrible creatures. I hope we don't run into those monsters again."

"We safe," tinkled Crooks, pulling herself up into a sitting position. "We go through door. Horseman stay inside."

Jamie bent down beside the little creature.

"What do you mean by 'the door'?" she asked. "There wasn't a door in the tunnel."

Crooks looked up at her and gave what sounded to her like a very distinct *purrr* before answering.

"It be the door," chirped the pixie. "The long hole be the door. We at Sphinx. Look."

She leaped to her feet, scampered over to the bushes that edged the small-grassed area, and pointed down between them at something beyond. The others followed and peered through the foliage. They were on the top of a cliff that overlooked a lush, tropical valley beneath. The color was everywhere.

"We're back in Aradell," gasped Tovan. "It's not grey and white anymore."

"But this isn't where the Sphinx was," argued Mikel. "She was in that desert place, not here."

Crooks vigorously shook her head.

"No, no. Land change. Now hot garden. Look. Sphinx."

"She's right," said Tovan. "You can see that Sphinx thing behind those trees. The valley's not quite the right shape and it's not a desert anymore, but that's the Sphinx. The land must have folded over like Azmodeus said it would and we missed it by being in The Hollows."

"Let's get closer to it," said Jamie. "The next door must be there somewhere."

Portia held up her hand. "Wait."

She looked down at the pixie, her expression far from pleasant. "I want to know what Crooks was doing with the centaurs. Doesn't anyone, other than me, find that suspicious?"

The pixie hardly drew a breath before she answered. "I spy and protect for Azmodeus."

"What do you mean?" snapped Portia. "The Willik said that only the six of us could enter this place, so how did you get in without us seeing you? How did you know that we went through the wrong door?"

Jamie moved closer to Crooks as if to protect her from what she was implying.

"You people," said Crooks, drawing herself up to her full height. "I not people. I come here anytime. Only six little people can come in. I not people. I pixie."

"Why didn't we see you?" asked Portia edging closer, her tone menacing.

"Leave her alone," growled Mikel stepping between them. "You, of all people, have no right to question others."

Crooks, however, was not to be intimidated. She stepped out from behind him, spread her legs apart, and placed clawed hands on her hips. Jamie couldn't have been more proud of her.

"I come through mist," she chirped defiantly. "You not see me."

"Portia, that's enough," said Melisande firmly, stepping forward. "I'm sure that everything is fine. After all, we did meet her through Azmodeus."

Portia glared back at her and then turned, pushing between Tovan and Jeremiah.

"Fine," she threw back, over her shoulder. "Then let's get this over with. We're wasting time."

"With friends like that," muttered Jeremiah, turning to follow her, "I'd rather be with my worst enemy."

"Boy are you right," grumbled Mikel, standing beside him. "There are words for girls like her."

"She's not that bad," said Jamie. This war between Portia and the others, Mikel especially, was going to have to stop if they were going to get anywhere. "After all, if Azmodeus sent her with us, there must be a very good reason."

"You haven't lived with her," snapped Tovan. "She's pulled off nasty little tricks all her life. She was the one who turned us over to the trolls and if it hadn't been for Mikel, four of us would have been goblins by now."

"Tovan, we have to support each other on this journey," argued Jamie. "If we fight, we'll never make it."

Tovan glared back at her, eyes flashing. "Don't trust her. She'll let you down in an instant, or betray you, or worse. We three have known her forever and the only person that Portia cares about is Portia. Don't say I didn't warn you."

With that, she strode ahead leaving Jamie shaking her head.

"Don't mind her," said Melisande coming up behind her. "Tovan has reasons to be upset with Portia. We all do, unfortunately."

"Well, I hope we're never in a position where our lives depend on Mikel and Portia cooperating."

Melisande smiled. "We'll worry about that if it happens…a whole bunch."

Jamie returned her smile. Of the four Glockamarians, Melisande was the one to whom she was beginning to feel the closest. Nothing seemed to unnerve her and if it did, she didn't show it. Jamie found herself looking up to Melisande for answers that appeared to be carefully thought through before given. She treated everyone with the same consideration, which made Jamie decide to follow Melisande's lead as opposed to Tovan's in regard to the difficult Portia.

When they reached the valley floor, Crooks gestured to them to be quiet, but it wouldn't have mattered had she not. After seeing what the Sphinx had almost done to Portia earlier, no one was going to take the chance of attracting the monster's attention. With the help of the thick foliage, they were able to actually get within touching distance of her feet, before they were forced to stop.

"Can you see the door?" whispered Melisande.

Jamie took a small step closer. Leaning against the stone leg was an arch covered in vines that didn't seem to lead anywhere except into a wall of stone. Would it open as the other door had or would it be a trap? She could see no other alternative. They would have to take a chance. She realized that the others were all looking at her.

"When I say 'go'," she whispered, "we all run for the vine-covered arch on the Sphinx's right leg."

"You're crazy," hissed back Mikel. "That's just leaning up against a rock."

"She right, she right," chirped Crooks, pointing at Jamie.

"Then let's do it," whispered Tovan, taking several deep breaths.

Suddenly Jamie stopped and looked thoughtfully back at the Sphinx.

"Wait," she whispered.

"What's the matter?" asked Melisande.

"I think we're approaching this the wrong way. The Sphinx asked us the wrong riddle and I didn't see any clue to our next location."

"What are you talking about?" sneered Portia, folding her arms across her chest. "Are you suggesting that we walk up and ask her what she left out?"

"Exactly. The riddle she asked me, Portia, was the standard riddle of the Sphinx. She asks everyone that one. I'm sure that Hera had another one that she wanted her to ask. If we had continued, Hera would have won because we would have missed her first riddle."

"What do you suggest?" asked Melisande.

Jamie squared her shoulders and stepped forward. "I'm going to talk to her," she threw back over her shoulder.

"No!" cried several at once, but she continued her purposeful stride toward the Sphinx.

Tovan suddenly let out a squeal. "The Sphinx is opening her eyes!"

Jamie stopped directly in front of the creature. To the others, she looked brave and confident, but only she knew that her knees felt like jelly and her stomach was doing cartwheels.

"Sphinx!" she called out. "I need to talk to you."

The colossus looked down at the tiny creature before her. "Have you come back to die?" she asked, her great voice booming throughout the valley.

"No! I answered your riddle, but you did not ask me about Hera's riddle. You cannot kill me because I answered yours correctly."

"You have courage," chuckled the Sphinx, "but are stupid. What is to stop me from devouring your soul? What does a correct answer have to do with me sparing your life?"

Jamie shook her fist at her. "Because if I answer your riddle correctly and you harm me, you will be destroyed and I did answer it correctly."

The Sphinx continued to gaze down at her and then chuckled again. "You know your history, little one. Very well, here is Hera's riddle. You will have one minute to respond.

If you break me, I do not stop working.
If you touch me, I may be snared.
If you lose me, nothing will matter.

Name me."

Jamie wracked her brain for the answer. She had heard this riddle before, but the answer kept slipping from her grasp. She realized that the others had mustered the courage to come out of the foliage and were now standing behind her. Their presence touched her heart. That was it!

"Heart!" she called out. "The answer is 'heart'."

The Sphinx looked down at her, immobile for several moments.

"Well done, human," boomed the voice. "You and the others may pass."

"But where is our clue to the next riddle?" she shouted.

A brightly colored flower formed on the ground in front of her. She snatched it up and handed it to Jeremiah, who instantly put it in his pouch.

"Do you think that archway is actually a real door?" Melisande asked Jeremiah.

Without a word to the others, Crooks raced to the vine-covered arch and without hesitation, stepped through the rock and vanished. Jeremiah took a deep breath and followed. The rest raced through, as quickly as they could, with Mikel and Portia bringing up the rear. None of them heard the laughter of the Sphinx as it boomed over and over throughout the valley.

"Beware of Hera, little humans. She does not like being thwarted and will seek to do you harm. Be warned."

153

Chapter Nineteen
Let There Be Monsters

Mikel

Beyond the door on the leg of the Sphinx was a staircase that wound around in an upward spiral that seemed to go on forever. To the relief of all, they came to another door at what appeared to be the top of the stairs, and Jeremiah, who had been at the front of the group, opened it up to reveal blazing sunlight. As soon as Mikel emerged behind Portia, the doorframe disappeared, simply melting away behind them.

"What is that?" squealed a terrified Portia. "What are we supposed to do now?"

When Mikel saw the scene around them, his shock matched that of Portia's. Judging from the looks of horror on the faces of Melisande and Tovan, they were just as terrified. They were on an island; the size of a postage stamp. Several straggly trees and a couple of bushes rose reluctantly from the center, surrounding them on all sides; for as far as the eye could see was water. To the four from Glockamar who had never even seen a small lake, the sight was terrifying.

"It's alright, everyone," said Jamie, her voice shaking slightly. Mikel had the feeling that she was finding the experience just as nerve-shattering but was trying not to show it. "It's either a big lake or some kind of sea or ocean. We have them everywhere back where I come from."

"She's right," joined Jeremiah. "There's nothing to be afraid of."

"As long as there isn't a tsunami," he whispered under his breath and instantly received a quick punch in the ribs from Jamie and a questioning look from Mikel.

"What's a soonamy?"

"Nothing to worry about" countered Jamie who sat down on the ground and sighed. "All I know is that I'm tired…tired and hungry and my nerves are shot. Do you think that before we do anything else, we could rest for a while?"

"I don't think we have any choice," replied Melisande, squatting down on a knoll under one of the trees, her eyes on the scene around them. "I've never seen so much water in my life. It's terrifying."

"I agree," added Tovan, sitting down beside her and looking nervously around. "I don't think I will be able to sleep. Do you think it's safe enough here?"

"I don't really care," sighed Jamie, putting her head down on her pack.

Mumbling in agreement, Melisande did the same and soon they were both sound asleep. Mikel sat down beside them and stared nervously out at the water. Something was not right. His senses told him that all was not as quiet as it seemed to be in those murky depths. Portia went off by herself to the other side of the tiny piece of land and sat down, staring out over the water and that suited him just fine. The light that was there quickly disappeared as the sun dipped below the horizon. It appeared that they were stuck for the night in more ways than one.

Mikel's attention was drawn to Jeremiah who had taken a seat in the sand, right beside his pack. He had pulled the flower out from a pocket on the side of his pack and was turning it over and over in his hands. 'Why had Azmodeus put him in charge of the clues and prophecy?' This had irked him from the beginning. It should have been him. Crooks suddenly appeared in front of Jeremiah so he stood up to have a better look at what was going on.

"Do you know the secret?" Jeremiah asked half-heartedly, extending the flower toward her.

The pixie giggled and then suddenly transformed into an image of the flower. Slowly it unfurled like a curled-up piece of paper, revealing something inside. In an instant, Crooks was back to her pixie shape. Mikel almost whistled. She had actually shown Jeremiah what to do. The boy looked back down at the flower and slowly began to pull the petals apart. Something fell out from the center onto the sand and he bent down to pick it up.

"Thanks, Crooks," he grinned. "Nice work."

The pixie giggled happily and then scampered off. Jeremiah looked down at the object, his smile soon giving away to a look of confusion.

"This is odd," he muttered to himself.

"What looks odd?" asked Mikel, sitting down opposite him.

"This image. It's shaped like a piece of a puzzle. It shows a boat on the water, but it doesn't seem to be going toward anything. Apart from the boat, it doesn't show anything about how to get to any place."

He handed it to him. The feeling of evil and danger came back to Mikel full-force and he shoved it back to Jeremiah pointing to something in the water.

"Look at that shape in the water," he whispered.

"What do you see?" asked Jeremiah. "I don't see anything."

"A monster of some kind. I could sense something when we arrived"

He tore his eyes away from the image and looked at Jeremiah, the other startled by the fierce expression on his face. "We can't go near that water. There's something evil down there somewhere and we'll never make it across."

How do you know?"

"I can feel its presence."

He stood up and walked back to where his own pack sat, propped up against one of the trees, swinging his head back and forth, watching the water. Other thoughts took over. At the moment they were stuck with no way off the island. What if this really was a trap, and they had no chance of escaping? He shivered at that particular thought. How were they going to get there from here? And where was 'there' considering there wasn't even a hint in the image? As he lay down on his pack, he couldn't help but focus his eyes on the other boy. Why had Azmodeus trusted Jeremiah with the prophecy and not himself? He had known the old wizard all his life, so why hand over that responsibility to someone who had just arrived back on Eleusia? The more Mikel thought about it, the more he seethed. Something would have to be done about this in the morning. At first light, he dragged himself up and stumbled over to where Jeremiah lay sleeping.

"Wake up," he demanded.

Jeremiah opened his bleary eyes and starting with Mikel's ankles, looked up at his body to finally rest on his face.

"What do you want?" he grunted.

"Where are the prophecy and the image?"

"What?" muttered Jeremiah, struggling to sit up.

"The prophecy and the image. I want them."

"What's it to you?" asked Jeremiah, suddenly awake and sounding ornery. He got to his feet as quickly as he could, Mikel realizing for the first time that the two of them were the same height. He noted out of the corner of his eye that the girls had suddenly noticed what was happening.

"I want the prophecy and the image," he demanded. "Azmodeus made a mistake in giving it to you. He knows that I'm a better leader."

He put his hand on his sword hilt and in response, Jeremiah reached for his staff.

"Since when have you led anything," snarled Jeremiah. "I'll show you who the leader is. Come on. Give it your best shot." He gestured menacingly with his staff.

"You've got a big mouth, boy," sneered Mikel. "Let's see how you feel after I separate your head from your shoulders."

Two things happened at once. Jeremiah was pulled backward by something with tentacles. He lost his balance and fell flat on his backside in the wet sand. Mikel, in turn, received a sharp piercing message.

Mikel!

The thought blasted into his mind, resulting in him taking a step backward. He turned to Melisande, who was now standing a few feet away, glaring at him with such anger that even the other girls appeared to be taken aback.

"How dare you behave like this? Azmodeus gave Jeremiah the prophecy for a reason. It is not yours to take away."

"It is not up to you to tell me what to do."

"Maybe not. But if this quest fails because of your actions, I hope we both come out of it alive. I want to be there when Azmodeus hears what you have done and I would not want to be you. The wizard will not be pleased."

Mikel stared at her for another moment.

"Fine."

"Apologize to Jeremiah."

He sent her a dark look and then turned to Jeremiah.

"I apologize. I was..."

The girls screamed Jeremiah scrambled toward them as fast as he could move and Mikel suddenly felt sick. The Wickersnit had taken on the shape of a fierce lop-sided land-walking octopus and was fighting fiercely with what appeared to be an oddly shaped ball of mist. Suddenly the mist dissipated, leaving Bandi fighting with nothing. He turned to Mikel and actually appeared to have a sheepish look on his face.

It away went. Hard was the catching.

Mikel was aware of the terrified cries behind him and knew that the time for secrecy was up.

Turn back into your regular shape, Bandi, and try not to look too terrifying.

The Wickersnit did just that and to his credit, tried to look a little more appealing. Unfortunately, he ended up looking a little worse. Mikel turned to face the others who were bunched together as far back as they could safely go.

"This is Bandi, everyone. He is a Wickersnit who is able to change shape, like Crooks. In fact, they are cousins. He won't harm you."

Slowly, the others relaxed, although they stayed where they were.

"But…but what is he doing here?" stammered Jeremiah nervously.

Mikel took a deep breath. "You know how Crooks is an assistant to Azmodeus?"

There were heads, nodding all around.

"Well, Bandi is my assistant."

The Wickersnit's head was nodding so hard, Mikel was afraid it would damage itself.

"But Azmodeus is a wizard," said Melisande, looking closely at him.

Mikel simply stood looking at the ground making no response.

"You are a wizard!" cried Jamie. "That's your magical talent. Right?"

"I'm not a wizard," he replied, stamping a foot in anger. "Azmodeus says I am, but it's rubbish."

"Well, if you already have an assistant," chuckled Melisande, "then you must be well on your way."

"Who was he fighting, anyway," asked Jeremiah.

Mikel turned to Bandi.

The creature be here.

What?

Yes. I with him did fight but no could catch. The creature now be gone. Chase him, did I. He poofled. He you make mad so with Jeremiah you fight.

Mikel shivered. How long had it been with them this second time? When did it reattach itself to the group?

Thank you, Bandi. You're a good friend.

The creature responded with what sounded like a small sigh of satisfaction.

But I warn you to be careful. Hera knows you are here now.

Bandi snorted. *I fast be too.*

He refused to say another word on the subject. Mikel looked over at the others and shrugged his shoulders.

"I apologize. That creature must have reattached itself to me sometime after we left the cave. That wasn't me arguing. Sorry."

"Don't worry, Mikel," said Melisande, with a watery smile, trying to avoid looking at Bandi, and failing miserably at that. "I have a feeling that our problems have just begun. Now come and have something to eat."

He nodded but noted that the others seldom took their eyes off Bandi as they ate and quietly discussed what was meant by the new clue. A short time later, part of the answer was surprisingly revealed.

"Look what we found," shouted Jamie from behind the scraggly trees.

Tovan and Jeremiah stood up and peered through the branches, laughing when they caught sight of Jamie and Melisande, dragging two rowboats along the edge of the water behind them. Saved! They were saved!

"Oh no," moaned Mikel when he saw what they were pulling into view.

"We don't know where they came from," grinned Melisande. "When we decided to walk around this little island, there they were, tied to a tree on the other side."

"Well, they weren't there this morning," said Portia. "I know because I slept over there."

"We have to use them," said Jeremiah to Mikel.

Mikel simply stared back at him and shrugged his shoulders. They didn't have a choice.

"There's land out there," called out Portia, pointing to a blotch in the distance.

Jeremiah looked down at the puzzle piece and then back up at Mikel. A blotch of land had appeared that had not been on the image the night before.

"I don't like this," he murmured.

"Neither do I," Mikel whispered back, "but what else can we do?"

The boy stuffed the image into his pouch and picked up his pack. Jamie picked hers as well and gave a very heroic sniff. Mikel looked at her with concern.

"Are you coming down with a cold?" he asked.

"Nope," she retorted. "Just gathering up my Harriet courage. Come on. Let's go."

He shook his head. Girls. He would never understand them.

The group gathered their belongings together, but when it came to getting into one of the two rowboats, some clear choices were made without anyone speaking a word. Jeremiah got into one and Mikel instantly chose the other. Melisande and Tovan joined Mikel, and Jamie got into the boat with Jeremiah after having a quick search for Crooks. There was no sign of the pixie now that they had a chance to leave. Portia appeared to be unsure of which one to approach. Bandi had changed into a fish and had slipped unnoticed into the water much to the relief of the others who could not yet get used to his ever-changing appearance. He had told Mikel that he needed a bath and having lived with him by his ear most of the time since leaving Donagal, he couldn't help but agree.

"Come on, Portia," called Jamie. "Get in here with us."

Mikel breathed a sigh of relief. The girl was the last one to get into a boat and as soon as her feet left the sand, both boats pulled away from the shore, turned, and headed out onto the lake.

"We don't have any oars," called out Melisande from the other boat. "We have no control over where we're going."

"Neither do we," called back Jeremiah. "Hang on. We obviously have no say in this."

The boats headed straight for the blotch of land, which appeared to be more like a large island the closer they came to it. Panic was etched on everyone's faces. Halfway there, Mikel noticed a movement out of the corner of his eye and glanced down into the water. At first, he thought that the water was fairly shallow and that the lake bottom was moving faster than the boat. It struck him at the same time that he heard Tovan cry out that this was not the bottom but a huge presence of some sort moving beneath them.

"There's a monster down there," shrieked Tovan, pointing into the water.

Everything happened at once. The boats stopped as if they had hit a wall, sending everyone tumbling forward. Jeremiah, who had been lifting his hands to get a firmer grip, shot over the bow and into the water just as a massive reptilian's head rose out of the depths in front of them. It lifted higher and higher until it towered in the air above them, each eye as large as one of the boats and a fanged mouth capable of swallowing both boats together. Its scales glinted gold and green in the sunlight, with water sliding down from them, threatening to drown the occupants of the boats.

"You are trespassing," boomed a rough, gravelly voice from above. **"These waters are my domain, and you were never invited to travel upon them. You never asked permission."**

Taking a deep breath and trying not to shake from head to foot, Mikel stood up.

"Please accept our apologies. We were not aware that we were trespassing and would most certainly have asked you for permission had we known."

"Nicely said," thundered the voice. **"But your apology does not excuse you."**

The serpent ducked his head down toward them. The others hit the bottom of the boats screaming and Mikel squeezed his eyes shut, standing ramrod straight in the center of the boat like a mast. The head swept past the sides of their boats and plucked something delicately from the water. When they finally had the courage to look up, poor Jeremiah was dangling by his cape from one of the monster's teeth.

"I believe that I will have this one as an appetizer," gloated the creature, obviously enjoying their terror. **"However, if you can answer my riddle correctly, I will be generous and let you go as I have just eaten the occupants of the harbor villages. My appetite for the moment is somewhat sated."**

His laugh threatened to deafen them all as Jeremiah fought to keep from falling from such a great height.

"This is not one of Hera's riddles by the way. Oh yes, I know about your quest as does everyone else in this rumor mill. This riddle, however, is only for me. Who will answer?"

Terrified silence greeted this question and then Melisande got slowly to her feet.

"I will," she replied, sounding strangely calm. "But if I answer correctly, you must let us all go."

"No", yelled Mikel, gesturing to her not to do it.

"I can do it," joined in Tovan. "Remember what you said about doing riddles."

Melisande was the one who didn't feel strong enough at solving riddles. What was she doing? Ignoring them both, she stood her ground.

"Ah, a young damsel. I prefer damsels you know. Part of my heritage. Yes, I will let you go if you provide me with the correct answer."

The serpent smirked and chortled, obviously convinced that this would not happen.

"Now. My riddle is this. In what way do you prefer to die? You have one minute to respond."

"That's not a riddle," blustered Jeremiah, hanging on for dear life.

"Quiet boy! Of course, it is. There are numerous ways to die, you know. Swallowed whole by a massive beast, dropped into a volcano, flung from a massive height, swatted like a fly against a mountainside…oh, so many lovely ways to die. Half a minute to go, damsel. If you don't solve it, I eat you all. Not that you're much to swallow, but I haven't yet had dessert."

Again his laughter thundered around them. While the creature had been carrying along with his monologue, Melisande had been mind-linking with Tovan and Mikel. Mikel couldn't come up with a reasonable answer and it appeared neither could Tovan. The serpent suddenly stopped laughing and lowered his head so that one eye was level with the girl.

"No answer?" snorted the monster. **"Dessert time!"**

He flicked Jeremiah up into the air and within a second, the boy vanished into the gigantic mouth.

"No!" screamed everyone together.

"That wasn't a minute," shouted Jamie. "You cheated. You've just ruined your reputation as a sea serpent because you didn't keep your word. Wait until the others hear about it. You won't ever be able to show your face to the other monsters."

"Momsters almays chmeat," he mumbled.

"Never!" the girl shouted back. "They might be mean and nasty, but they always keep their word."

For a moment, the serpent looked confused and then appearing to come to a decision, opened his mouth and dropped Jeremiah into the water.

"Well?" he demanded, looking down at Melisande.

"Old age!" shouted the girl. "We all want to die of old age."

"Now you have cheated. No one has guessed my riddle before. Who told you?"

"How could anyone have told me the answer when there are only the six of us out here?" smiled Melisande looking quite innocent. "The answer came from my own mind."

The five in the boats looked dumbfounded. Mikel grinned. She had done it without any help.

"You must let us go now, sir," Melisande said as politely as she could under the circumstances. "Apart from being incredibly handsome, you don't strike me now as one who would break an agreement."

She bowed and the monster visibly preened, pleased with her compliment.

"Very well, but can I just keep this one?" he asked, eyeing Jeremiah with speculation.

"No, you promised," said Melisande firmly. "All of us must be released."

Jeremiah, in turn, was struggling to reach one of the rowboats. Despite the extended hands trying to help him, his cape kept wrapping around his feet and dragging him beneath the water. Jamie was about to dive in to help him when a roar of frustration rolled over them.

"You have won. But that doesn't mean I have to make it easy for you."

The monster lowered the upper half of his body swiftly and horizontally to the water creating an ear-splitting smack. The water crested out from either side of his body, creating gargantuan waves that caught the boats and Jeremiah and sent them hurtling toward the island. They clung to the sides of the boat, too terrified to shout as the land shot toward them. Just as it appeared that they were going to be dashed to pieces, on the rocky shore, the water calmed and they slid up onto the beach amidst the grating sounds of the boat bottoms being ripped to shreds, coming to rest not far from a dark, flat wall. The battered occupants quickly stumbled out of the boats, having no intentions of being carried out onto the water again by the little vessels.

"Jeremiah!" gasped Tovan. "If he hit the shore like we did, he could be killed!"

All thoughts of their own aches and pains vanished in their concerns for the boy.

"You three go that way down the beach," directed Mikel. "We'll go this way."

They took off as fast as they could to check the lengthy expanse of the beach. The rocks made it difficult to maneuver quickly and Mikel was grateful more than once for the solid boots that had been given to him by the elves. His thoughts were in chaos. If anything happened to Jeremiah, the quest would be at an end and besides, he was growing to like him. He had to be safe.

Tovan spotted the bobbing head first. "There he is," she shouted, heading for the water. "Hurry. It doesn't look as if he's conscious. He could drown."

"Wait, Tovan," cried Jamie. "You don't know how to swim. I'll get him."

Before Tovan had a chance to ask her what she meant by the word 'swim', a huge shadow passed overhead, cutting out the sunshine and sending chills over the three girls.

"Another monster!" shrieked Portia.

A large creature lowered its feet to the water, back winding with enormous wings to steady itself, and lifted Jeremiah out of the water with its talons.

"No!" shouted Jamie. "Leave him alone!"

The creature paid her no attention but continued to lift the boy into the air and disappeared into the clouds above.

"What was that?" asked Portia, her voice shaking with fear and shock.

"A dragon," whispered Jamie, collapsing on a rock. "They have all kinds of dragons in this horrible place. Oh, what do we do now?"

"What about Jeremiah?" sobbed Tovan, covering her face with her hands. "What about Jeremiah?"

Jamie wiped away the tears that were forming in her own eyes.

"I've been so stupid, Mikel. I've been equating these adventures with someone I've read books about and didn't give the feelings of the people in them a second thought. It's a different thing to experience it and feel the pain in your heart when something happens to a friend or in my case, a supposed newly found brother."

"We'll find him," said Mikel, patting Jamie awkwardly on the shoulder. He knew deep down that that wasn't going to happen. Jeremiah was lost to them. What were they going to do now?

Chapter Twenty
Hiding In The Dark

Kara

The spell cast on Kara had not worked properly. Whether it was her hysterical screaming at the time it had been cast or the fact that she was basically good and had little evil inside to work with, Kara hadn't lost her sense of self. When she regained consciousness, she had found herself in the corner of one of the hallways, having been tossed there by the troll on his way out of the chamber. She had been very bruised and sore but other than that, couldn't determine any other injuries. As she stumbled through the corridors, no one had looked at her strangely, which she had found odd. How could any of these horrid little creatures not notice that she didn't look like them? It wasn't until she raised a hand to open one of the doors that she realized that she was not as she had once been.

Kara had screamed and pulled back against the wall, shaking and sobbing uncontrollably. The arm and hand that reached out in front of her was identical to the hands of those goblins around her. She forced herself to breathe deeply and to bring herself under control. Tentatively, she had touched her face and then examined her feet and ankles. No wonder no one had been looking at her strangely. She looked just like them. She forced down the wave of nausea that swept through her.

"Get a hold of yourself," she had whispered.

That had been a second shock. The words she had spoken were incomprehensible guttural noises. They hadn't made any sense to her at all. Only her thoughts were working in a language she could understand. She obviously looked like a goblin, but how was she to communicate with others if she couldn't understand the words?

Goblins had passed her as she remained cringing against the wall, but none had even spared a glance at her. They walked with eyes focused on the floor in front with no one talking to anyone else.

Taking a deep breath, Kara had stepped in behind a group of five that were pushing a cart away from the chamber in which she had met the hideous woman. She had tried to copy their walk and kept her eyes down so that she wouldn't be noticed. The little group had wound its way through hallways and corridors, coming at last, to what sounded like a kitchen. Just before they reached it, Kara had pulled back into a dark passageway and then scurried away into its cobblestone depths. It had led to the lower levels of the Sanctuary, filled with small storage rooms and much deeper down, a row of empty cells. Kara had surmised that this was where the five of them would have been housed to wait, had Mikel not removed the door in time. One appeared to be locked, but she was not in the mood to investigate.

For the next few days, this was where Kara hid. She found an old storage room that possessed a few blankets, and she made this her living quarters and a place to hide if anything came too close. She learned to time it so that she could sneak into the kitchen for food, when others were asleep, and on one of her excursions, discovered an underground grotto that had a natural well for fresh water. For the most part, she cried. She had never been more lonely or frightened in her life.

Kara had been there for about five days before realizing that this type of existence wasn't going to help anyone, including herself. This was the perfect opportunity to find out what was going on in the Sanctuary. Even though the thought of sneaking around that horrible place and taking a chance on being caught terrified her, she was fed up with being a coward. Most of the goblins occupying the building had at one time been other Glockamarians. Who knew? Maybe there were others like her who didn't succumb to the spell.. She began to explore the passageways that led from the grotto where she got her water. There was a warren of tunnels, and as she explored, she discovered that some of them led back into various rooms in the Sanctuary. On one occasion, she came to a wall that blocked her from going further. A latch in the center caught her eye and when she pulled on it, a small door opened. Cautiously she peered into the space beyond it and was startled to find heavy material hanging down in front of her face.

'Curtains,' she thought, carefully groping at the material in an attempt to find out where there might be a split. The voices from beyond the curtain, however, stopped her in her tracks.

"They discovered the Morgae in both the canyon and on the island," hissed a voice that Kara did not recognize. "That boy Mikel can sense danger and evil. He knew about the centaurs as well. I don't understand how he knows. We must get rid of him and that beastly failure of a Wickersnit."

Kara froze. Was this their Mikel? He could sense danger? And they were trying to get rid of him? Kara was filled with a feeling of panic. How was she going to save her friend?

"How far have they gone on their quest?" asked another voice that seemed familiar.

"They are past the Sphinx and have survived both my centaurs and the sea monster," replied the other. "At least five of them have. Perhaps I need not worry. One must be dragon fodder by now, but I must not presume."

She gave a nasty chuckle.

"You need help, Spider. I can only involve myself to a point. The three sisters should be arriving soon. They will know what must be done."

"I don't want them here," hissed Spider.

Kara didn't wait to hear anymore. Without turning around, she had moved slowly back into the tunnel, closed the door as softly as she could, and then started to run as fast as possible on her little bent legs.

The following day, she had come face to face with a similar wall but when she had pulled the latch, it had opened onto a balcony. This was to be Kara's most important discovery but she wouldn't know of it for quite some time. As she crept forward, she realized that it overlooked the chamber in which she had met the creature she now knew to be Spider and that she had been turned into a goblin. She could hear voices below and at one point, maniacal laughter, sweeping through the chamber, almost sent her scurrying back into the tunnel.

'I refuse to be a coward,' she thought, becoming more determined as the horrible sound swept through the chamber once again. Taking a deep breath and squaring her thin shoulders, she continued her quiet journey to one of the pillars that formed a part of the railing and peered down.

Spider was enfolded in her chair, gloved hands clasping her robed arms, her red eyes intent on the figures in front of her. There were three, all hunched over and as skeletal looking as herself. They were clothed in black dresses and long, ragged cloaks of indiscriminate colors. One had a floppy black hat perched atop wispy white hair. The other two had scarves wrapped around their heads, making it impossible to see if they had hair.

"So it is agreed," rasped Spider. "If we are successful, we will share Draukenberg and rule together."

"It will be so," replied the crone in the hat. "But what of the wretches on the quest? My spies have told me that they have survived the serpent."

"Mine as well," spat out Spider. "How am I to do anything when I must keep searching for talented brats here in Glockamar? My problem is not knowing where they are but you, Corilla, say that you have a way of solving that dilemma."

"I do," cackled one of the crones in a scarf.

She reached inside her cape and withdrew a small crystal hanging from a slender chain. The Spider pushed herself out of her chair and hobbled down the stairs to examine it.

"It is a crystal eye," explained Corilla. "There are only a few left but it will tell us what we need to know."

"Explain," demanded Spider.

Corilla reached inside her cape and pulled out a second crystal the size of an orange.

"The necklace will be placed around the neck of one of the girls and through it, we will see and hear what they are doing and know where they are. We must use all of our skills to make sure the little rotters fail. Perhaps each one will die a fabulous death. Although, Hera wouldn't like that. She wants to do the dastardly deeds herself."

"They will notice the necklace," argued Spider.

"Trust us, my dear," said the third crone. "You have been at this business for a very short time whereas we've had hundreds of years to perfect the craft."

"Well then," snapped Spider, "answer my question."

"I will take it," said Corilla. "I will await my chance to catch one of them alone, cast the spell, and place it around her neck. She will think that she has always worn it, and when the others ask, they will believe her when she says that they've just never noticed it."

She held up the crystal ball. "We'll see and hear everything through this little treasure and plan many traps ahead of them. They won't get far after with my help. Now, I must go."

She handed the ball to Spider, tucked the necklace back into her cape, and turned toward the window. Her shape dissolved and then reformed into that of a large crow that lifted itself on powerful wings and soared through the open window, heading for a cleft in the roof that would take her outside the mountain. Kara had never before seen a bird and the sight of the creature spreading strange arms and lifting itself off the ground was more than she could take. She crawled back on shaking arms and legs, and slipped through the door, closing it gently behind her. Once inside the tunnel, she leaned against the cool rock, trying to calm herself. What had they meant by these children…children they wanted to destroy? If one was Mikel, were the rest her friends from the Eagles? Whoever they were, they were walking into a trap if the crone succeeded with the necklace. Kara wanted to do something but what? She was alone and friendless, hiding in a place full of enemies. Slowly she pulled herself to her feet. She would return to her little closet and think. Maybe an idea would come to her there.

Halfway down the tunnel, she stopped. Melisande, Tovan, Mikel and Petre. She could mind link with them all. In all the time she'd been a fugitive in the Sanctuary, she'd never thought of trying to link with their thoughts. Mentally, she called out to each in turn and then to all of them as a group. Nothing.

On his way to Donagal, Petre tried to make sense of the faint message that was trying to enter his thoughts. On the island, Melisande and Tovan stopped for a moment but neither could catch the words. To Mikel, it sounded like a faint sigh.

In the chamber, Spider cocked her head, a frown creasing her forehead.

"What is it?" asked one of the crones.

"We have a spy in the tunnels," came the sinister reply.

Chapter Twenty-One
The Maze

Jamie

Portia, Jamie, and Tovan huddled on the beach together while Mikel and Melisande stood behind, gazing around at their hostile environment. Bandi had changed back to his normal, unappealing shape but was keeping his distance. He knew that the others found his presence disturbing and that included Mikel.

"We have to believe in him," said Melisande from behind Jamie. "If anyone can get themselves out of an awkward position, I believe it would be Jeremiah."

For once, Mikel didn't appear to be affected by the girl praising the other boy's ability, which was a relief as far as Jamie was concerned. Not to negate the seriousness of Jeremiah's position, they weren't in a much better one themselves. When they returned to their boats, the supposedly damaged crafts were floating merrily back in the direction from which they had come with all their food and supply packs that they had forgotten in their rush to escape the boats.

"What are we going to do?" asked Portia, looking around in panic. "We have no way of getting off this island now, we're going to starve and die."

Tovan kept rubbing her eyes with the heels of her hands, but no one told her to stop crying. The loss of Jeremiah was almost too much to bear.

"Our quest seems doomed," said Melisande shaking her head. "We've only answered one riddle because the serpent said his didn't count. At the rate we're going, we'll never get through in time."

"Well you did a great job of answering that riddle for someone who didn't feel confident in herself," said Mikel, with a smile. For once it didn't appear as if he were trying to impress her.

Melisande looked back at him with a puzzled expression on her face.

"It was so odd. The answer came into my mind as if someone had actually placed it there and then told me that it was fair because it really had come to my mind."

For a moment they all stopped and stared at her, amazed by her admission.

"But without Jeremiah, it doesn't matter," she continued sadly. She could barely keep her own tears under control. "We need six to finish the quest."

"We won't think like that," sniffed Tovan. "We must be positive. Can I ask you something, Jamie? How did you know that monsters keep their word?"

Jamie suddenly began to laugh.

"No, I'm serious," protested Tovan. "You told that serpent if he didn't keep his word, he'd never be able to face the other monsters."

Jamie laughed even harder.

"I'm sorry," she finally gasped. "Oh, I needed that, Tovan. A good laugh always clears one's head and puts everything back into perspective. I made it up."

"What?"

"I made it up. He really was a stupid beast despite his size, so I just made that all up, about trust and stuff, and he bought it. He's probably still trying to figure it out."

"You mean it's not true?"

"Of course not, silly."

That brought a much-needed chuckle to the rest except for Portia who looked away rolling her eyes, a foul expression on her face.

"That's it," snapped Mikel. "We are not giving up yet. I for one am not going to sit around waiting for someone to solve my problems. I'm going to check and see what's around that corner of that hedge. Come on, Bandi."

In an instant, the Wickersnit altered its shape to that of a shaggy four-legged creature and started to lope after the boy.

"If we could do that," sighed Tovan, "we could change to a shape that could get us off this island."

"Well, we can't," snapped Portia. "I think that creature is disgusting."

Bandi stopped and turned, emitting an angry growl. Mikel was quick to respond.

"Stay still, Bandi. Don't do anything stupid... No! You cannot eat her!"

That brought a startled look to everyone including Portia who took an instinctive step away from the creature. Mikel laughed, gave her a nasty look and Jamie sighed. She could only hope that things would change between the two. However, she was not planning on holding her breath.

"I'll go in the opposite direction from Mikel and meet up with them on the other side," said Melisande, looking back at the hedge "You three stay here and wait for us."

Before the others could protest, she set off.

"We need to stay together," complained Portia as Melisande took off. "Trust those two to do just the opposite," she continued.

"Quit moaning, Portia," snapped Tovan, impatiently. "It won't hurt to find out what's on the other side of the hedge or the other side of this island."

"Well, if that's the way it is, I'm going to see what's inside."

Amid protests, she stood up and marched determinedly toward the opening in the hedge.

"Portia don't!" cried Jamie leaping to her feet. "You can't go in there by yourself. It might not be safe."

Portia simply tossed her hair back and walked through the opening.

"Oh, I don't like this," said Tovan, glancing nervously around. "We shouldn't be separated. I wish that none of this had happened and I was back on the farm with my family."

"I don't remember anything about my family," sighed Jamie, resting her chin on her drawn-up knees. "I keep feeling as if I should, but something keeps blocking my memories. That might have happened when I came from my dimension to this one."

The two sat quietly for several moments, Jamie watching the entrance through the hedge and Tovan's eyes flickering back and forth from one corner to the other.

"There they are."

Jamie looked in the direction in which Tovan was pointing. Melisande and Mikel had emerged from the boy's side of the hedge and they didn't look happy.

"It was the strangest thing," said Melisande as she reached them. "Each side of the island was the same. It faced the way we had come."

"What?" exclaimed Jamie.

"It's true," chimed in Mikel. "The view was identical to this on the other three sides."

"Where's Bandi?" asked Tovan.

Mikel suddenly looked worried.

"On the other side of the hedge, Bandi suggested to me that he follow the dragon and try to find Jeremiah. I told him that its not a wise thing for him to do because Hera would come looking for him and the Crystal Spires were a long way from here. He assured me that he could do it, suddenly transformed himself into an eagle, spread his enormous wings, and launched himself into the air. You should have seen him. The real thing is much better than the drawings I showed you from Azmodeus's office. I'm worried because it's not safe for him to be alone."

"He should be alright," said Melisande, patting him on the shoulder.

"Not really. If Hera knows where he is, it will be an easy task for her to capture him without the protection of a magician like me. She could actually kill him."

"Then why didn't you stop him?"

"Because he's a stubborn fool who doesn't think things through," sighed the boy. "Some protector, I am."

"I'm sorry, Mikel. But we have our own problems to solve. Come on. I'm sure Bandi will figure something out if he gets into trouble. Where's Portia?"

Tovan shrugged her shoulders and pointed to the mass of foliage behind them.

"She got tired of waiting and went through the entrance in the hedge."

"That idiot has cow poop for brains," muttered Mikel, kicking at a pebble on the ground in front of him. "Why won't she do as I ask, just for once?"

"It's almost as if someone wants us to go in there," sighed Jamie. "We're not going to get anywhere staying out here. Remember the image we found at the Sphinx?"

"Well, it didn't show a hedge," said Mikel, "Only a blob. We also have no food or supplies, so if that's the way we must go, then let's do it."

"I agree," said Melisande. "We're not accomplishing anything out here."

Tovan nodded although somewhat reluctantly. She dragged herself to her feet and joined the others who had already started to pick their way carefully through the rocks and toward the hedge. When they reached it, they stopped and nervously examined the thick tangle of leaves and branches. Mikel peered cautiously around the edge into the interior.

"This is odd," he said softly. "It's like there's a pathway between the outer hedge and the inner one."

"Let me see," said Jamie, squeezing around him and peering in.

"Oh no," she sighed. "I think this is a maze."

"What is that?" asked Melisande.

"It's like a puzzle. It's a bunch of pathways with hedges on either side and you have to follow the correct path to get through it. There are lots of dead ends and traps along the way to trick you because if you don't find the right path and stick to it, you could be lost in the maze forever."

"Sounds wonderful," grimaced Melisande. "Just what I wanted to do on this lovely afternoon."

"Well," shuddered Tovan taking a deep breath. "Since we have no other option, let's get on with it."

Without looking back, they took their first nervous steps into what resembled a quiet, dark green cavern. Jamie was caught between fascination and fear. She had never been inside a maze that she could recall and under different circumstances would have been truly excited. Due to the height of the hedge which was more than twice her height, only a little sunlight was able to reach the interior. Despite the blue sky directly above, she felt as if she was walking in the twilight. The further she walked, the hotter it became. Not only was the sunlight having difficulty penetrating, she felt as if the air was suffering the same fate, and it quickly became stifling.

It did not take them long to come to the first split in the path.

"Which way?" asked Mikel looking back at Jamie.

She stopped and scratched her head. There was a trick to mazes that she had read somewhere, but what was it? The right…there was something about keeping to the right…or was it the left?

"I think…I think we have to stick to either the left or the right wall all the way through it. Sometimes we'll double back on ourselves, but if we stick to one wall, eventually, we'll get through…I hope."

"Well, that's better than nothing," replied Melisande. "Let's keep to the right wall. I think I can already see that path to the left ending in a dead end down there."

There was a mutual agreement and they started off, keeping their hands trailing on the right wall of the hedge. They hadn't gone far when Mikel stopped, his whisper sounding harsh in the eerie silence.

"Listen. Something is up ahead."

Whoever or whatever was there did not try to make any effort in hiding its presence. Branches snapped and heavy feet scraped at an uneven pace on the gravel beneath.

"There's no place to hide," hissed Jamie, backing up against the hedge.

Tovan glanced over her shoulder, looking as if she wanted to run back through the maze. Suddenly, Portia stumbled into view and the group gave a collective sigh of relief.

"Portia!" cried Tovan. "Where have you been?"

"I don't know," said Portia, looking at them through glazed eyes. "The last thing I remember is walking down one of these paths and then there was this…there was a…I don't remember."

"Where did you get that necklace?" asked Melisande, peering at the jewel hanging on a chain around her neck.

The glittering object instantly caught everyone's attention.

"Well, I've…I've always had it, I think," she stammered.

"We probably just didn't notice it before," said Tovan, her eyes suddenly wide and glassy. "You've always had it."

"Yes," said Melisande almost dreamily. "You've always had it."

Jamie looked over at Mikel who appeared to be fighting whatever was happening.

"It's evil," he whispered before succumbing and responding in the same dream-like voice,

"Yes. You have always had it. It has always been yours."

Overhead, a crow squawked as it winged its way back to the borders of Aradell. Jamie looked up at it and then turned to Portia.

"You've never worn that necklace before," she stated almost defiantly. "You've never had it. We would have noticed."

Four pairs of eyes turned to her as one, the same, strange, glassy look in all of them.

"I've always had it," retorted Portia, her expression one of pure malice.

"That's right," agreed Melisande, her stance defying Jamie to argue.

All four nodded together, looking at Jamie like puppets, manipulated by strings. Something warned her not to push the issue. The situation was very wrong, but for the moment, she decided to play along.

"You're right," she replied, smiling. "I just didn't notice it before."

The others visibly relaxed and then continued down the path with their hands brushing the hedge wall to the right as if nothing had happened. Jamie felt drawn to the necklace and had to work hard to avoid looking at it. She felt something evil attached to it. Mikel had said so as well, before being caught up in whatever was happening but none of the others seemed to notice. It was as if they were under some sort of spell. Why wasn't she? Why hadn't she been taken in by it then?

At the next split in the path, Melisande turned and smiled at Jamie.

"We stay to the right wall?" she asked.

Jamie nodded and smiled back, although something clenched in her stomach. Melisande was behaving as if nothing had happened. They continued their cautious journey through the maze, the silence becoming oppressive. It was as if the hedge was listening to every word they uttered and as a result, the odd comment made came out as hushed or whispered.

As they rounded a particularly sharp corner in the path, they came upon a frightening sight. The path forked to the right and left, but barring each path was a door. Standing in front of each were turtle-like creatures, boney shells covered with spikes, encasing their bodies. They were standing upright on green scaly legs and holding needle-shaped swords and round shields. Their long necks and faces were those of serpents and Jamie, who hated snakes, found her stomach heaving at the sight of the serpentine movement of their heads. One of them had a monocle resting in an eye socket, which was strange because they didn't have eyes.

"You cannot move forward," hissed the creature on the right.

"Well, that's kind of obvious," muttered Mikel.

"You must answer the riddle of the maze," lisped the one on the left. "If you answer incorrectly, you will die."

"Why is it that we're always going to die in this place?" moaned Tovan.

"One of these doors leads to the place of the next riddle," hissed the two creatures together. "The other leads to The Hollows. If you answer the riddle incorrectly, you must either go to The Hollows, and find a door that leads back to us, or you may refuse to enter and wander through the maze forever. You have one minute to decide upon your answer."

"One minute," gasped Tovan. "Is one minute all we have for each riddle?"

Jamie frowned and then shrugged her shoulders.

"We have no choice. We must try."

The others agreed without hesitation.

"Tell us the riddle," demanded Portia before anyone else could answer.

The turtle creatures looked at one another and then recited the riddle together.

Pronounced as one letter and written in three,
Two letters there are and two only in me.
I'm double, I'm single, I'm black, blue, and grey,
I'm read from both ends and the same either way.
Name me.

The group was silent for several moments.

"Well, I don't have a clue," said Melisande.

"Neither do I," whispered Tovan. "And Jamie can't answer because she solved one already."

Portia had been examining the two guardians with interest. She suddenly smiled and stepped forward, placing her hands on her hips.

"I will answer this one."

Mikel grabbed her arm and spun her around.

"We have to discuss this, Portia. What makes you think that you can just decide?"

Portia ripped her arm from his grasp and glared at him.

"Each of us has to answer one riddle and I choose this one because I think I know the answer."

"Your time is almost up," hissed one of the creatures.

"Let her try, Mikel," pleaded Melisande.

He reluctantly stepped back, shaking his head. With a smirk, Portia turned away from him and defiantly faced the two creatures.

"The answer is 'eye'," she stated clearly.

A gust of wind swept through the maze and the door on the right began to slide open.

"You have succeeded," cried both creatures, their outlines beginning to blur. In a moment both had turned to mist and vanished. The monocle dropped to the ground beneath, just before they disappeared and Tovan picked it up and held it out to show the others. It was a plain glass circle with nothing pictured on its surface.

"Well," mumbled Mikel, looking over her shoulder. "At least it's not another maze."

Tovan handed it to Jamie, who put it into her pouch. They would examine it in more detail when they had time. Perhaps it was important.

"Well done, Portia," smiled Jamie. "I would never have thought of that answer. How did you do it?"

"It was easy," replied the girl, haughtily tossing her hair over her shoulder. "The answers so far seemed to have something to do with being opposites. The answer to the first riddle was heart, which the Sphinx didn't have. The sea monster had said that his riddle hadn't counted, but his riddle had been about ways of dying, opposite to living till old age. Why was this turtle thing wearing a monocle when it didn't have eyes?"

"Well, it was a complicated riddle, and I'm glad you answered it. You did really well. Now we know the riddles are connected to the one asking."

A slight blush touched Portia's cheeks and she turned away which surprised Jamie. She wondered if Portia had seldom been praised for anything in her life after having heard the stories about her father from the others. They had also said that Portia always seemed to be focused on revenge for supposedly being slighted, and had never stopped to consider the effect it was having on everyone, including herself. Was that how her father had treated her? Jamie couldn't help but feel a bit sorry for her.

"Well, come on everyone," said Melisande, moving toward the open door.

"Wait," cried out Jamie, as they all began to move forward. "The image. We have to find the next image in order to know where we are going next. The monocle wasn't the clue. There was nothing on it."

"Does it really matter?" asked Portia. "Jeremiah has the other ones, and he's probably dead."

Mikel looked at her as if she were some malignant disease and Jamie sighed. Portia was back in form.

"We must continue to believe that we're going to meet up with him," Mikel snapped. "Now help us out or go drown yourself in the lake. Better still, I'll drown you."

"Enough!" cried Jamie. "Stop your bickering and look!"

No one noticed the door on the right slowly closing as the one on the left opened. Once open, it too began to close. Neither did any of them spot the shadowy shape hovering over the doors, manipulating their movements from above. Cloaked in shadows, the goddess appeared to be part of the hedge, as she quietly worked her evil.

Their search proved fruitless.

"It must be the monocle in your pouch," suggested Melisande. "There is nothing else around that could be considered as a clue."

Jamie shrugged her shoulders.

"I think you're right. Perhaps…"

"The door's closing!" shrieked Tovan. "Hurry!"

Without pausing to check, they tore through the opening, the last one getting through as the door banged shut behind with a nasty clang. Hera's laughter filled the maze before she too vanished like mist into the air.

"Well, we seem to be out of the maze," noted Mikel, looking around.

"Or in the middle of something worse," muttered Jamie.

"Or we took the wrong door," whispered Melisande. "Look at the colors in here or should I say lack of color."

They took stock of their surroundings, and what they saw was far from comforting. They were in a stone building at the end of a hallway. Open doorways were scattered down its length and torches in sconces provided them with enough light to see. Everything was in black or varying shades of grey, which meant that they had slipped through to the shadow world again. Tovan groaned and clasped her hands onto her head.

"But we answered the riddle," argued Mikel. "The right door was the correct door. The snake thing said so."

"We came in through the left one," whispered Jamie. "Think about it. Only the left one was open when we rushed through."

"We've been tricked," whispered Portia.

Jamie nodded her head in agreement. "Well, we'll have to go on. We can't really go back."

It took every ounce of courage left in them to begin the walk down the hallway. Jamie wasn't the only one to feel that her legs wouldn't hold her up. Her knees were knocking so hard they hurt. Mikel and Melisande pulled the swords from their scabbards and held them out in front. The others had left swords and staffs in the boats so had nothing with which to defend themselves. The hallway ended at the top of a set of wide stairs leading down into a large room. Although there were torches lining the walls, they didn't throw off enough light to see what was in the center. They crept down the stairs and stopped at the bottom. It was deathly quiet and Jamie sensed immediately that there was something evil and sinister about the place.

"Are those bones on the floor?" squeaked Melisande, gazing down in horror at the littered floor. "I think we should go back."

Before any of them had a chance to respond, a figure moved into the light at the top of the stairs and they all froze. It stood over seven feet tall and had the head and lower body of a bull. Its hands were enormous, and muscles rippled on its torso and into its legs. The sword it was carrying was longer than Mikel and about as wide. None of them missed the animal fangs it possessed for teeth or the flaming red eyes.

"What is that?" croaked Tovan.

"It's a Minotaur," cried Jamie, "and it eats humans for breakfast. Run!"

Chapter Twenty-Two
An Invitation To Dinner

Jeremiah

Jeremiah had been unaware of being plucked from the water by a dragon. When he finally regained consciousness, he thought he had been picked up once again by the serpent. But after rubbing his eyes several times in order to believe what he was seeing, he realized that he was flying hundreds of feet above the ground, or rather, something was flying hundreds of feet above the ground while carrying him. He was struck dumb with terror. For someone as afraid of heights as he was, this was the worst thing that could have happened to him. He couldn't see the creature carrying him, but whatever it was, it smelled awful and it seemed certain that he was going to be sick to his stomach at any moment.

He covered his eyes with his hands but couldn't resist peeking through his fingers. If he was going to die, he might as well see where the terrible deed would happen. They were moving steadily toward what he thought to be mountains but it was hard to determine as the structures appeared to be made out of glass columns clustered together in the shape of mountainous shapes, and pointing towards the sky. As they approached, he could see creatures flying around the tips and landing on the pinnacles. He was stunned when he determined what they were.

"Dragons!" he choked. "I don't believe it."

Believe it.

The voice rang through his thoughts like the voice that had spoken to him when he was entering Aradell. He was so startled that he found himself incapable of replying.

The creature transporting him swerved to the right as they began to fly over the smaller of the strange mountainous structures only to soar up towards the taller ones. The boy was suddenly dropped onto a flat ledge just below the peak of one where he sat for a moment, stunned and feeling sick. Slowly, anger began to replace his feelings of fear. All day, he'd been picked up and dropped, and he was tired of it. He staggered to his feet and shook his fist.

"I've had enough," he cried. "I refuse to be treated…cripes!"

His method of transportation had landed on the peak just above him causing his knees to give way. He landed in the dirt with an unceremonious thud.

It was a magnificent metallic-blue dragon with golden horns that flared out from a broad forehead. A ridge of gold extended down the forehead to between black, slanted cat's eyes and then down the powerful neck, over the back, and down the rest of the body to the tip of its equally powerful-looking tail. At the moment, its long neck was twisted down so that its head with its mouth of sharp fangs was only a few feet from his face. As the beast stared at him, it carefully folded huge diaphanous wings over its back.

Welcome boy. I see that you are an anipath.

"A what?"

An anipath…a mortal who can speak to animals. I understand you and you can understand me.

It was certainly true. Jeremiah was having no difficulty in understanding the giant creature peering down at him, although she hadn't moved her mouth. Once again, he thought back to his departure from the gryphons the morning before. It must have been one of them, speaking into his mind, but at the time he had not even really considered such a possibility and had dismissed it as a case of nerves. Where had this strange ability come from? He'd never been able to do this back in Earth's dimension. Was this one of the gifts that the Willik had said that they all individually possessed? Was this his gift?

"I can understand you," he said, getting back onto his feet. The revelation had been such a shock that he forgot momentarily to be afraid of the creature. "My name is Jeremiah."

I am Brax. That is the short version of my name. You would never be able to pronounce the original.

"May I ask you a question, Brax?"

Of course.

"Why did you bring me here?"

The dragon pulled back its jowls revealing her teeth. Was that its version of a pleasant smile? The boy fervently hoped so.

Why for dinner, Jeremiah. His dinner.

The dragon gestured to a spot on the other side of the ledge. Jeremiah's heart leaped into his mouth and he took several shaking steps backward. So involved had he been with Brax, he hadn't noticed that he wasn't alone. Lying on its stomach was a small white dragon approximately twice the size of him.

Brax sighed almost sadly.

I am sorry that you are an anipath. We have so few of you in this world, but my child is hungry.

Jeremiah couldn't answer. He was staring in horror at the baby dragon that was slowly getting to its feet, its eyes never wavering from its newly arrived dinner. The boy looked around in desperation, but there was nowhere to go. The ledge ended on three sides with a sheer drop to the valley below and there was nothing on the ledge that he could use to protect himself.

A wave of excruciating pain suddenly washed over him, and he shut his eyes and dropped to his knees. His leg was on fire. The pain was so intense, he fell forward, beads of perspiration forming on his forehead and then it was gone.

He lifted his head, pushed himself slowly to a sitting position, and examined his left leg. There was nothing wrong with it. What had just happened? He glanced over at the young dragon. The creature was sitting back on the ground, shaking its head to and fro and moaning softly. Jeremiah suddenly realized that it was the little dragon that was in pain.

"Brax," he called out. "Your baby is hurt."

Do not try to trick me. He is simply hungry.

"No, he isn't. Can't you hear him? Let me look at his leg. Tell him to let me look at it."

For a moment, he didn't think that she would allow it and then she lowered her head and crooned something to the little dragon.

You are correct, Jeremiah. He is in pain. Approach.

Tentatively, Jeremiah took a step forward. The little dragon watched him closely as the boy moved around slowly, step by step.

"Brax, could you please ask him to extend his back leg?"

You ask him, boy. His name is Crill.

Jeremiah walked back to the dragon's head and extended a hand toward the creature's nose. Crill pulled back slightly and then allowed him to rest his hand on a space just above the nostrils. The skin was soft and warm, not cold and scaly as he had expected. For a moment, the boy was overwhelmed by the majestic creature. He was touching a dragon, a real live dragon, and a dragon that in the end would probably eat him. He tried not to think of that part.

"Crill, can you understand me?"

Yes.

Once again, Jeremiah felt the pain.

"I want to help you. Can you extend your sore back leg so I can look?"

Crill moved slightly and pushed his back leg out as far as he could. The leg was gashed from the equivalent of his knee to his ankle and was definitely infected. What was he to do with this? He heard Brax's sharp intake of breath when she saw the wound.

"How did this happen?" asked the boy. "He's cut his leg on something sharp."

The child tried to fly despite my refusal to allow it and landed on the ledge below. He was warned about the sharpness of the crystal rocks but ignored me. Obviously when I retrieved him, the wound went unnoticed.

Crill startled Jeremiah by suddenly sending him a message, which the boy passed on to Brax.

"He didn't want to tell you about the wound. He was afraid to."

If you cannot help Crill then you are useless to me. It is now time for dinner.

Jeremiah had had enough. He stood and faced the dragon, hands on his hips and feet apart.

"You know, Brax, I've had too much happen to me today. First, I get thrown out of a boat, picked up by a monster serpent, thrown back into the water, sent careening toward a rocky island on the crest of a gigantic wave, picked out of the water by you, discover I'm dinner for Crill and now you. Now back…right…off!"

I like you, little man. Just for that, I will eat you a little bit at a time.

"You are not funny!" he shouted as he turned back to Crill.

I was not trying to be.

Giving an indignant snort, Jeremiah went back to examining Crill's leg. The infection had to come out, but how? He had no access to medicines and he was certainly not a doctor.

If you cannot help him then Crill must die.

"What?" he cried, spinning around to face her.

We cannot afford to keep sick dragons in our midst. He will die anyway.

"You would kill your child just because he has an infected leg?"

Of course. I can make another child that will hopefully be healthier.

"You can't kill him," he exclaimed, backing up against Crill who trilled softly in his ear. "He's your child. You love him."

Love? I do not understand this word. Now move away.

"I will not!" shouted Jeremiah spreading his arms out in a futile attempt to protect the little dragon. "You cannot purposely kill your child. It's wrong. You must care for him at least long enough to try and fix his leg. After all, you are his mother."

I do not understand your words, boy. What is this mother? I am the bearer only, and Crill is sick. He must die. Move aside now.

"No!"

Then you shall die with him.

"No!" he cried out, turning as he did so to wrap his arms around Crill.

Chapter Twenty-Three
Disappearing Acts

Mikel

"Why didn't you know he was here, Mikel?" cried Melisande. "What happened to your ability to sense danger?"

"I don't know," he shouted, watching with horror as the monster approached. "I didn't feel a thing."

"Everyone run!" screamed Jamie. "Scatter!"

"Circle him!" cried Mikel. "Don't let him touch you!"

Jamie, Portia, and Tovan did not have swords. In desperation, they picked up bones from the floor and waved them menacingly in front of themselves. Suddenly, Tovan vanished. One moment she was there and in the next, she was simply gone but no one noticed except Mikel. Tovan had been in front of him and then she wasn't. He didn't have time for it to even register in his mind, so busy was he trying to survive.

Despite their best efforts, the Minotaur's sword was far larger and heavier than anything they possessed. They tried to attack together, but the creature was too fast for them and they quickly found themselves huddled in a group with their backs against one of the walls. One by one, the bones they'd picked up slipped from their hands with the monster towering over them, ready to deliver a killing blow.

"Run around him!" shouted Mikel. "Don't just stand there!"

Everyone did exactly that except for Melisande, who seemed to be frozen with fear.

"Melisande, move!" screamed Jamie.

She didn't. The Minotaur raised the sword above his head as Melisande screamed and covered her face. In desperation, Mikel raced toward the monster, his sword flailing about in front of him. He didn't expect to hurt the monster but hoped that the blow might divert him long enough for Melisande to get away. The Minotaur suddenly turned to face him and knocked the sword out of his hand.

"All of you stop running," it bellowed. "I just wanted to scare you. I won't hurt you."

"Yeah sure," cried out Mikel, picking up a large bone. "As if we'd believe something that looks like you."

The Minotaur raised his sword in an almost threatening manner and pointed it at Melisande who gave a sharp scream.

"I would never hurt her. She's too pretty."

Balls of colored light suddenly began to swirl around the creature's head. A strange look came over his face and then…he wasn't there. His sword clattered noisily to the ground as the bone Mikel was going to hit him with whooshed through thin air.

For several moments, no one moved or spoke. All that could be heard was heavy breathing coming from different parts of the room.

"Where did he go?" cried Jamie, looking around, terrified.

"Down here," yelled someone as if from a great distance.

"What was that?" asked Portia.

"Me. I'm down here. Watch where you step."

Mikel looked down and around his feet. Sitting on his backside and rubbing his head was the Minotaur…all twelve inches of him. He bent down and peered at him.

"What happened to you?" he asked, part of him relieved but the other part slightly amused by this turn of events.

"I don't know," groaned the now shrunken little monster. "One minute I was trying to explain my predicament to all of you, and in the next, I was here."

"Well, that's great," chuckled Mikel standing up. "Now I can get rid of you by simply squashing you."

The Minotaur leaped to his feet. "No!" he yelled. "I wouldn't have hurt her. Look, it's not my fault I'm a monster. Cerce did this to me. She turned me into this creature because my mother boasted that she was prettier than Cerce."

"Who is Cerce?" asked Tovan coming closer.

"The daughter of Apollo…you know, the sun. She's always turning people into animals. Why, she turned half of Ulysses' crew into pigs."

"I don't know who all these people are that you're talking about," snapped Portia, "but you eat people. Look at all these bones. Step on him, Mikel."

"I don't eat people," spat out the Minotaur. "If you look at those bones, you'll discover they're cow bones and they've been here forever. I've got a garden at the back where I grow everything I need. After all, I'm a half bull, and also vegetarian."

"What about your fangy teeth?" queried Mikel, bending down again.

"They came with the spell Cerce used, but I would never use them to eat people."

"Okay," said Jamie. "But where are the people who have obviously come through here before? Surely we're not the only ones you've seen."

The creature shrugged. "I've never seen anyone else. You're the first ones."

Jamie looked over at Mikel.

"That's probably why you weren't warned against him. He really isn't evil."

"I'm not!" came a shout from the floor.

Mikel nodded. It made sense and if that was the case, he should be able to tell whether someone was good or evil as soon as they met them. That would help.

"How did that happen to him?" asked Tovan, looking at the others. "One minute he was a monster and now…look at him."

"She did it," came a delighted voice from behind.

Melisande was sitting on the ground with her back against the wall, her hands open, in front of her. Floating above them was a small ball of light. The girl looked up at them with a silly grin on her face.

"It was Gamma and her friends who actually did it together."

The three others peered closer at the ball of light. When they realized what it was, all three of them grinned including Portia. Inside the glowing sphere was a tiny creature, slightly raspberry in color, wearing a green tunic and sporting a pair of transparent raspberry-colored wings.

"She's a fairy," continued Melisande. "She and her friends were sent here to help us."

"By who?" asked Portia.

"Someone named Rosamund, but she won't tell me anything more. I think Rosamund was the one who gave me the answer to the riddle."

"You can understand her?" asked a startled Mikel.

"Of course. Can't you?"

He looked at the others. Between shrugs and shakes of their heads, it was obvious that they couldn't understand her either.

"All I can hear are little bells," said Portia.

Mikel and the others nodded in agreement.

"That's it, Melisande," grinned Jamie. "Remember what the Willik said? Each of us would discover some of our magical strengths and talents on this quest. Obviously, one of yours is to be able to talk to fairies."

"Hey," shouted a voice from the floor. "What about me? Tell her to make me bigger."

"Why?" glowered Mikel. "You'll just chase us around again and act like a bully."

"No, I won't. At least ask her if she can make me bigger."

No one spoke as Melisande listened to the sound of tiny tinkling bells.

"Gamma said that she and her friends will only double your current size because they don't trust you."

"Well, that's better than this, at least." replied the Minotaur sullenly. "Say, can they change me back to my human form at the same time?"

Again, Melisande listened to the bells.

"No," she replied. "I'm sorry, Minotaur, but they say that only Cerce can do that."

"Drats," snorted the creature. "She'll never do that. Can you at least call me Adonis? That was my name before she changed me."

"Alright," said Melisande after getting a nod from the others. "But the minute you don't behave, we're going back to calling you Minotaur."

"Agreed. Now tell the fancy fly to get on with it."

Melisande crossed her arms and frowned down at him.

"Please?" he added.

Gamma joined the other colored spheres that were beginning to circle Adonis' head. The four of them watched in amazement as his body slowly grew and expanded until he reached a height of approximately two and a half feet.

"Well," he grumbled. "I guess this will have to do."

"What do you say to them," snapped Melisande.

"Uh…thanks…thank you."

"That's better, Adonis," she grinned.

"Now, how do we get out of here?" asked Jamie.

"Wait a minute," said Portia, looking around. "Where's Tovan?"

The rest stopped and gazed around the room.

"I haven't seen her since we came down the stairs," added Mikel, shoving his hair out of his eyes and then he stopped. "I remember something during the fight with the M…Adonis but I was too busy running around to really pay attention. I think she disappeared."

"That's impossible," blurted out Portia. "No one can disappear."

"Oh, shut up Portia," he snapped back.

"Enough!" demanded Jamie. "Both of you be quiet. She must be around here somewhere. Where are you, Tovan?"

"Maybe we should search around," suggested Melisande. "She might have been hurt with all the running around and we didn't notice."

For the next few minutes, they searched the area including the walled garden where Adonis grew his vegetables. Mikel and Melisande even braved the dark to check the rooms at the top of the stairs. There was no sign of the girl.

"Maybe she ran away," sneered Portia. "She probably took off the minute Adonis appeared."

"Stop it, Portia," replied Jamie, finally appearing to lose patience with the girl. "You always have to consider the worst about people. Stop being so nasty."

She turned away from her, Mikel was surprised that Jamie had spoken to her in that manner. It was obvious that Portia was getting on everyone's nerves which filled him with deep satisfaction.

"Maybe she found a door," suggested Melisande. "Adonis do you have one?"

"This way," he replied. He bounded over the floor to the far wall and yanking on a latch, pulled open a door. They could see that it was twilight and hoped that they would be outside the maze on the other side of the island. However, when they finally filed up the steps to have a look, the hedge still surrounded them and there was no sign of Tovan.

"I don't believe it," laughed Adonis, spinning around in merry circles.

"What don't you believe?" asked Mikel.

"I haven't been outside since Cerce put me into the temple."

"Why not?"

"Look at the door, idiot…no, I take that last word back. Sorry. I was too big to get through the door. All I could do was open the door and look outside and smell the air. You have to admit that the air in there is pretty rank. The only place I could go was into the garden area. It was lonely…"

He sniffed and looked away. Mikel actually found himself feeling sorry for the little guy.

"I can't imagine what it must have been like, Adonis. It must have been terrible."

Adonis looked up at him and opened his mouth to say something. Changing his mind, he walked away from him as fast as his awkward legs would take him.

"What are we going to do?" asked Jamie, coming up to him. "We're still inside the labyrinth and Tovan is nowhere around. What could have happened to her? Where has she gone?"

"We have to keep going," he replied. "We can't stay here, that's for sure."

Melisande listened to a series of bells.

"Gamma said that she and her friends will fly over the maze and try to find a way out," said Melisande.

Mikel nodded and then stopped, tilting his head as if listening. Thunderous grindings and explosions appeared to be coming toward them from across the lake. Beneath them, the ground began to shake to the point where they started to lose their footing.

"What is that?" he shouted, his voice almost lost in the noise.

"It feels like an earthquake," cried Jamie. "Where can we go?"

"Everyone, back into the building," shouted Adonis. "We'll be safe in there. It's happened before. Come on."

The group rushed back down the steps and through the door, into the temple. Adonis shut the door behind them, the ground continuing to shift beneath their feet. Mikel couldn't see the others as he grabbed for the wall and slid down its length. Huddled in a ball with his hands over his head, he waited for the worst to happen and fervently hoped that both Tovan and Jeremiah were safe.

Chapter Twenty-Four
To Save A Dragon

Tovan

One minute Tovan was waving the bone at the Minotaur, terrified to her toes that they were going to become his breakfast, lunch and supper, and in the next, a soft golden mist surrounded her. Her terror turned to curiosity and then to a wonderful feeling of peace and calm. Tovan couldn't remember when she had last felt so relaxed and almost happy. As the mist gently wrapped itself around her, she had the sensation of being carried. Someone she couldn't see was there with her. But to her surprise, she was unafraid.

"Who is there?" she asked, quite calmly.

"You do not know me, but eventually, I will reveal myself to you. I am here to help."

Tovan sighed. It was a woman's voice and one that would be difficult to forget. Tovan likened it to rich honey on a piece of thick bread. Now where had that come from? Tovan wasn't one for flowery, descriptive language, and yet her thoughts didn't feel silly.

"Your friend is in trouble, and you must not only save him but the one that he protects."

"How am I to do that?" asked Tovan, not feeling the slightest bit concerned about such a task. She was so relaxed that nothing could have bothered her. "I don't have any weapons."

"You don't need weapons," replied the woman. "You have your hands and your mind. In order to win this battle, you must discover your most special gift."

"But what is it?"

"You must discover it for yourself, for if you do not, three of you will perish."

Hadn't Jamie said something about every time you turned around in this place, your life was being threatened? Tovan didn't have time to contemplate the thought. The floating sensation ended abruptly, and her feet came to rest on solid rock. The mist dissipated as quickly as it had appeared, and she found herself facing Jeremiah, who seemed to be protecting a fairly large creature that was cowering behind him.

"Jeremiah!" she cried. "You're alive!"

He stared back at her as if she'd suddenly grown two heads. Brax pulled back and looked curiously down at the human who had materialized out of thin air.

"Wh…where did you come from?" stammered Jeremiah.

"A chamber in the middle of the labyrinth. You know…the shadowed wall on the island. It turned out to be a maze. We were being attacked by a Minotaur, and then suddenly, I was drifting in a mist, a wonderfully warm and comfortable mist. This voice told me that she was here to help and that we would meet her sometime in the future, and then suddenly, I was here."

"Why?"

Tovan shrugged. "Something to do with saving you and whatever it is you're protecting. What is it, by the way?"

Jeremiah moved aside but kept his arms around it as if protecting it still. Tovan looked at the creature and gasped.

"A dragon? You're saving a dragon? But from what?"

Jeremiah pointed a shaking finger at a spot above her head and behind her. Slowly she turned.

Tovan had never screamed before in her life, but the sight of the huge monster wrapped around the pinnacle above her was too much. She fell to her knees and gave a scream that would have knocked the socks off of professional screamers everywhere.

"Easily frightened, isn't she?" stated Brax aloud, lowering herself to speak the common tongue as opposed to mind-speak. She knew within seconds of meeting her that the girl did not possess the boy's skill. "Has she come to help Crill?"

"I think so," he quaked.

Tovan continued to stare at the monster frozen to the spot. Could dragons speak? Brax lowered her head to have a better look, but all Tovan could do was stare back at the creature, speechless and horror-stricken.

"How can she help, boy? She doesn't look as if she's going to be much good for anything."

"Tovan," called out Jeremiah, his voice cracking under the strain. "Turn around and look at me."

She remained rigid, the eyes staring out from a chalk-white face riveted on the dragon. She was absolutely terrified.

"Tovan, if you don't turn and look at me, all three of us are going to die. Turn around."

Something in his words or tone of voice got through to her. She slowly rose to her feet and turned to face him.

"How can you help Crill, Tovan?" he asked.

The girl blinked and shook her head as if to clear it. "I don't know," she whispered. "The voice told me to use my h…hands and brain."

"To do what?"

"I don't know."

"Come over here, then."

Tovan forced herself to walk across the space, separating her from Jeremiah. She could hear the little dragon moaning behind him.

"What's wrong with it?" she whispered again, conscious of the huge monster hovering behind her.

"He's got an infected leg," said Jeremiah, turning to Crill. "Because he's hurt, his mother was going to kill him. That's why I was protecting him."

"She was going to kill her own child?"

"Brax doesn't see it that way. She just laid the egg, and if anything goes wrong with the hatchling, she gets rid of it and lays another egg."

"That's terrible," fumed Tovan, her terror suddenly replaced by anger. "You need a good talking to, whatever your name is. You don't just kill off your babies because they're hurt, you know."

Brax gave her the semblance of a smile, and Jeremiah shivered.

"Don't be taken in, Tovan," he cautioned quietly. "I'm discovering that a dragon smile is not something that is proving to be a positive thing for those in her direct vicinity."

"Very astute, boy, but I like this one. Maybe I'll start with her before sampling you."

"Disgraceful," snorted Tovan, straightening her shoulders to have another go at the beast.

"Don't threaten her," Jeremiah hissed. "Not unless you want to end up as her main course. Now take a look at this."

Tovan turned with a defiant flourish and moved closer to Crill, but not before she'd called Brax several inappropriate names that, luckily, the beast did not understand. At Jeremiah's encouragement, the little dragon extended his leg for the girl to examine. She gasped when she saw the extent of the infection.

"Jeremiah, I can't heal this. He needs medicines and someone who knows what they're doing."

"You have to do something," he hissed. "Brax will kill us all if you don't try. Someone sent you here because you could help, so think."

Jamie bent down, looked closer at the wound and then placed her hands on either side of the gaping sore. As soon as she touched the leg, a strange thing happened. A surge of power flooded through her, and Jamie forgot everything except the infected leg. Focusing on the wound, she found that she could actually see into the leg – the veins, tendons, muscles, and pockets of infection were clear. Slowly, Jamie drew those pockets of infection toward her, feeling the pain within herself as it flowed through her. She mentally pulled at the broken tissues, carefully locking them into place and then knit the ends together. Through it all, Jamie could feel the intensity of Crill's pain, and at moments she felt so weak and sick that she didn't think that she would be able to continue. As the edges of the gash drew together, healing as if the wound had never existed, a wave of weakness washed over her, and she pitched forward into the darkness. Throughout the process, not once had Jamie's hands moved from either side of the wound.

Chapter Twenty-Five
A Devious Spell

Spider

"Foiled!" screamed Spider. "I thought that Minotaur had them for sure. Why, he turned out to be no more frightening than a cockroach. What a pathetic little coward, and who is this Rosamund?"

"Regretfully, she's our cousin," said Zorna, sitting back in her chair.

"And she's sickening," chimed in Corilla. "She's a good witch, and I'm ashamed to say. She is always rescuing mortals from the bad things that we throw at them. Don't suppose you've heard of the sleeping girl who pricked her finger on a spindle. That was one of my best bits of wickedness, but Rosamund interfered and almost destroyed me. She has nothing to do with us. Can't stand the sight of us."

"We can't stand her either," chortled Druet, the third sister. "Always prancing around telling us what we were doing was all wrong and nasty. Pompous little tweedle."

"So, what's she doing now?" sneered Spider. "Running a home for unwanted fairies?"

"They've actually made her queen of the little suckers," replied Zorna quite matter-of-factly. "Wears a crown and can move around in the air like a ghost. Scares the pudding out of you when she suddenly shows up."

"What do we do now?" hissed Spider through gritted teeth, making a not-so-successful attempt to keep her temper in check.

"Hold on to your knickers there, Spider," said Corilla. *"My, my, these young ones are impatient. First, we need some eats, dear. Can't plan wicked comings and goings on an empty stomach."*

They were sitting in the courtyard beside the dead Laurel Tree with the crystal ball on the table between them. The magic in Glockamar had been gradually dissipating, leaving the valley in growing darkness. The magic shell covering the valley was slowly weakening, and soon the once fertile valley would begin to resemble the interior of a cave. This suited Spider just fine. She was beginning to hate the light.

Spider gestured to the troll guarding the entrance.

"Food," she demanded.

"No, no, dear," chuckled Druet. "Not that way."

The witch spread her hands over the table, and a wide assortment of dishes was suddenly in front of them, steaming or chilled depending on what they contained. From her vantage point, Spider spotted a few mouse and frog specialties that the three sisters seemed to thrive upon. She grimaced. They were not on her list of favorites.

"There," cackled Druet. "Much better. Now while they're asleep, we can plan."

She pointed to the ball that clearly showed Mikel and Jamie asleep in front of Portia and Melisande. They had decided to stay within the safety of the temple after the ground finished folding and get some well-deserved rest, which suited the plans of Spider and the witches perfectly. Time was what they needed now.

"It's that Jamie girl that has me worried," muttered Spider, reluctantly helping herself to some toasted mice. "She knew that Portia didn't have the crystal before she entered the labyrinth."

"Too true," agreed Zorna. "Only someone who is immune to magic can do that."

"Immune to magic?" sputtered a startled Spider. "Is that possible?"

The three crones nodded in unison.

"It's rare," said Druet. "But there are a few around who are capable. Jamie does appear to be one of those. I'm also curious about that boy, Mikel. He originally fought the spell and realized that it had an evil purpose. There's something strange attached to him as well...like some sort of shadow. Drat. This puts a ruddy kink into our plans. I'm tellin' you."

"It's a Wickersnit," snapped a voice behind them.

Druet and Corilla were so shocked that they fell out of their chairs. After getting over their fright, Zorna and Spider stood their ground and waited. Druet and Corilla struggled to their feet as a figure glided toward them.

"Gosh, Hera, my love," sputtered Corilla. "You could have given us some notice."

Hera ignored her and carried on. "He's the little traitor that failed at poisoning the Willik and attached himself to the next budding wizard. That boy, Mikel, is a newly hatched wizard but doesn't yet believe it, so he is vulnerable. The Wickersnit was the reason your Morgae failed. However, at the moment, that creature is also vulnerable. He has traveled too far from his master, and he will be sorry for making that decision."

"We have to stop them...get rid of them," growled Spider. "So, what do we do?"

"Several things, young one," said Corilla, who had gone back to munching on her frogs. "We may already be in luck in that the one boy has been devoured. Our mission is done...their quest is finished. However, we need some safeguards if that hasn't happened, like sending a spell through the crystal that will make the others despise Jamie. We need dissension in the ranks, don't you know. With some luck, we won't have to do a thing. The others will get rid of her for us."

"Yes," mused the Spider. "An excellent plan. I would like to see her destroyed. What else do you have in mind?"

"Oh, something quite devious," snickered Hera. "I have a plan that may get rid of several of them. Watch through your crystal ball. I believe you are going to enjoy this."

With that, she was gone.

The three sisters were silent for a moment. Suddenly, they broke into shrieks of cackling laughter and screams of merriment, the sounds of which curdled the blood of all who heard. Spider grimaced and attempted to cover her ears with her gloved hands.

"Keep your eye on the crystal, sisters," gasped Corilla at last. "I don't think we want to miss this."

"I want to see the last image they received when they answered the riddle," replied Zorna, wiping her eyes, which hadn't shed tears in a hundred years and weren't doing so now. It was simply a habit. "If any survive Hera's plan, I want to know where they will be headed next so that we can make sure that someone or something is waiting for them...something unpleasant...something capable of finishing them off."

Spider gave what could possibly have passed as a small smile. "What diabolical schemers you are."

"Thank you," beamed the three.

"We do try," added Druet almost humbly.

At that moment, a troll entered the courtyard.

"Mistress." His voice was as deep as the tunnels from which he came. He bowed low and remained in that position until she told him to straighten up.

"What is it?" she muttered, all signs of the smile gone.

"I regret to inform you that we searched the tunnels but found nothing."

Spider rose to her feet so quickly that she knocked her chair over.

"There is someone or something there. I felt its thoughts," she shouted at the now cowering creature.

"I'm sorry, mistress, but I took a core of soldiers into them, and we scoured the tunnels from top to bottom. We found nothing."

"Aagh!" screamed the Spider, pointing a gloved hand at him and shouting the incomprehensible words to a spell. The troll froze in position and turned to stone in an instant.

"You know," said Zorna calmly, not taking her eyes from her meal. "You really must learn to control your temper, dear. At the rate you're going, there won't be a troll left to defend us when the battle comes."

"There is a spy in the tunnels," muttered the Spider, embarrassed because Zorna was right. She was starting to possess too many statues of trolls and goblins. Perhaps she should ease off.

She whistled, startling the crones almost out of their chairs.

"There must be a better way of doing that noise thing, dear," grunted Zorna, straightening her hat. "It is most disturbing to the senses."

Spider glowered at her but made no comment as two tiny owls flew to her outstretched hand. Individually, each was the size of an apple. Together, they fit into the palm of her gloved hand.

"Beak and Claw will find whoever it is."

"Not too imaginative with names, is she?" whispered Corilla to her sisters.

"Go into the tunnels," she instructed the birds. "Observe what comes and goes and return to me when you have spotted an intruder. You know what will happen to you if you are not successful."

Both hooted in response and lifted off her hand.

"Now, we'll find out what's going on there," she smiled slyly.

"Come dear," said Zorna. "It's time to see what Hera has conjured up for these human creatures."

Spider returned to the group full of suppressed excitement and took her place awkwardly at the table. Four sets of eyes of different shades of red and yellow —filled with the same horrifying green of evil – stared intently into the ball.

The four remaining children were sound asleep on the floor of the cave with the Minotaur curled up by the wall. Spider and the witches had sent a spell through the crystal to ensure they would sleep. If truth be told, none of them had needed a spell to put them to sleep. They had all been beyond exhaustion.

"Where is that other girl?" asked Spider, suddenly aware of Tovan's absence.

The three sisters looked at each other in amazement.

"She hasn't been with them since they came down the stairs," said Druet.

"Ah," snorted Corilla. "She probably went and hid when Minotaur appeared. We'll find her."

"Maybe she'll run away," suggested Zorna.

They looked at each other and once more broke into peals of laughter. After all, where could she go? Spider closed her eyes and tried to cut out the horrible sound. Nothing disturbed her as much as the laughter of the three sisters. However, she would be patient. She had promised that the four of them would rule Draukenberg together but had no intentions of doing it. She would get rid of them as soon as this nonsense with the silly quest was over.

"Something is happening," whispered Druet.

She was right. The walls of the grotto were shimmering and glittering in the dark as if water was running down the sides. It wasn't water. As they peered closer, they could see exactly what was causing the strange movements. The three sisters sighed with satisfaction and envy. Why hadn't they thought of this most evil of plots?

"All of them will be destroyed," hissed Spider, her face contorting into what could only be described as a hideous leer. "They have no chance to escape from this for any of them."

Chapter Twenty-Six
Bad Times For Jamie

Mikel

The shaking and rolling did not last long, but no one moved when it ended. As the minutes stretched out in the darkness, each member of the little group found themselves nodding off and slipping into a deep sleep. Such a deep sleep might have been considered normal under the circumstances, but four scheming creatures hovering over a crystal ball a fair distance away were helping to induce this one. It had been an easy enough task for the young people who were completely exhausted, and the lack of food had also taken its toll.

As a result, none of them noticed when the long, narrow shapes began to slither and undulate down the walls of the chamber with the intent of destroying the five sleeping forms below. Eerily silent, the snakes slithered lower and lower, carefully winding around arms, legs, torsos and necks and tightening so as not to awaken anyone until it was too late. The sound of their scaly bodies slithering over the rocks was almost as terrifying as the hissing that began to fill the silence.

Mikel had been dreaming of being trapped in a spider's web when he suddenly awoke to find his dream horrifyingly real. Instead of a web, it was the bodies of snakes wrapping around each of his friends and beginning to squeeze the life out of them. The creatures were everywhere – long slippery bodies that were covered in slime, which kept him from being able to grab them.

"Help!" screamed Melisande. "I'm being squeezed to death!"

Cries of pain and terror were coming from everywhere. He had to do something. They had little time left, and the pressure around his chest was beginning to hurt beyond any pain he had ever felt before.

"Watch what you wish for." The words of Azmodeus suddenly came back to him. He had fought against the thought that he was a wizard ever since that moment. It couldn't be real. Another squeeze made him gasp, and he could hear someone sobbing. If he didn't find out now, there would never be another opportunity to try.

"I wish for the snakes to be gone," he gasped, trying to keep from yelling out in terror.

No one was going to hear that, he thought, a cold chill creeping up his spine. What if he really wasn't a wizard? What if his wish did not work? It was then that he noticed that the snakes squeezing him had loosened their grips slightly.

He took as deep a breath as he could and cried out, "I wish the snakes to be gone."

The snakes around him pulled back far enough to allow him to stagger up into a standing position. He noticed that the creatures had pulled back from the others as well. Shouting with all his might, he cried, "I wish the snakes to be gone."

The creatures began to struggle against some unknown force that seemed to suck them back into the rocks from where they had come. Shaking from the fear and effort, Mikel looked cautiously around. It had taken only a minute for every reptile to disappear, which he found astonishing. At this point, Mikel had to admit that something about him was not normal. The thought gave him little comfort until he heard the moans and frightened sobs of the others. It suddenly hit him what would have happened if it hadn't been for him and his weird ability. He decided to rethink this wishing thing.

"Snakes," sniffed Jamie, holding her sore arms and trying to stop crying. "I hate snakes. Yick!"

"Those are called snakes?" gulped Melisande, looking around to ensure the creatures were gone. "I've never seen one before, and I never want to see one again."

"What did you do, Mikel?" gasped Portia, rubbing her sore neck.

He looked over at the group and was startled by the looks of utter astonishment on their faces. He probably would have looked the same if it had been someone else. He shrugged his shoulders nonchalantly and tried to control the red flush that was creeping up over his face.

"Just something Azmodeus taught me," he replied, pretending to take an interest in adjusting his boot.

"If you say so," replied Jamie, shaking her head in amazement.

"All I know," said Melisande, stumbling to her feet, "is that I am staying away from anything that moves like those horrid things do and thank you, Mikel. I don't know what you did, but you saved our lives."

Their attention was drawn to sniffling in the far corner. Adonis was sitting on the ground, his shoulders shaking uncontrollably. Melisande got up and hurried over to him.

"Adonis, it's alright. They've gone."

"I…I…almost got eaten," he sobbed. "I was halfway d…down a s...snake when M…Mikel saved us."

The girl patted his back, comforting him until the sobbing stopped. "You have to be brave now, Adonis, and show us the way out."

Adonis nodded, got up slowly and stumbled shakily over to the door. He pressed his head up against it and listened. Hearing nothing, Adonis yanked on the latch, pulled it toward him and peeked out. Sunlight poured through the opening, and he almost danced for joy, his frightening adventure forgotten.

"Hey, everyone," he called out to the rest. "There are colors out here – every color that you could possibly imagine."

"What?" mumbled Portia, rubbing her bruised arms as she joined him.

"Look," pointed the Minotaur.

Mikel gestured to the others. "Come here. We're back in the right place. Somehow we've moved from The Hollows to Aradell."

He followed Adonis up the steps and slowly one by one, the girls joined them. He had been right. They were back in Aradell, the land of colour and wonderful fresh morning air. The hedge was gone and glinting back at them was the water lapping up against the shore. The scene on the other side of the water was thankfully changed from the identical scenes that had greeted them from all sides of the island the day before. Now green fields, forests and a magnificent range of mountains swept up from the lake on the other side.

"Great," glowered Portia, pointing at the water. "How are we going to get across that?"

"We need something to eat before we do anything," said Melisande.

"That's easy," grinned Adonis. "Come with me."

"I'm not going back in there," snapped Portia. "Who knows what will happen this time."

"Then you stay here," replied Melisande. "I'll help."

"I can too," said Jamie, stepping forward.

Melisande turned and gave her an angry, disgusted look. "We can manage," she replied in a cold voice.

Jamie quickly stepped back as if she had been slapped.

"What did I to deserve that?" she asked but Melisande had already disappeared down the stairs.

"I'll come," said Mikel, glaring at Jamie as he passed her. The girl took another step back, tears beginning to well up in her eyes. Mikel noticed but didn't care. After getting over the scare of the snakes, all he could think of was his hatred of Jamie and how they had to get rid of her from the group. He never stopped to question from where this feeling had suddenly come.

Unaware of what had just occurred, Adonis was already scampering across the floor of his now former home, leading them through a set of doors into an enormous garden filled with every kind of fruit and vegetable they could think of and then some. Melisande found several bags to carry ropes she found and with Mikel's help, filled up the empty spaces in each of their own packs with fruits and vegetables. Portia reluctantly joined them for breakfast with a white-faced Jamie following behind. Feeling much better after a satisfactory meal, they all felt more positive as they traipsed back up the stairs to the outside and down to the lake. The horrors of their terrifying awakening were receding into their memories. They had to focus on what was coming next.

"We might be able to make a raft," suggested Mikel, eyeing the pieces of driftwood. "That rope might come in handy, Melisande."

At that moment, a shadow passed over them, the size of it blocking out the sun and becoming larger as it descended.

"The dragon's back!" someone screamed.

Everyone scattered. Mikel took refuge behind one of the larger trees and watched as a magnificent, massive dragon descended gracefully onto the beach with Jeremiah sitting quite comfortably on its back and Tovan appearing to hold onto his waist for dear life. What had happened to the boy who had been terrified to ride gryphons? Jeremiah grinned and waved at them as the huge creature landed on the sand and extended a leg so that the two could scramble down. Jeremiah gave her a bow and appeared to be talking to the beast before he turned and ran inland. Although Tovan had no idea what the two had been saying to one another, she followed his lead and bowed politely before following.

"Morning, Jamie," Jeremiah called out as he approached her hiding spot on the ground behind a bush.

The girl looked up and stared at him in shock. "Jeremiah!" she gasped. "Where have you been?"

"It's an amazing story," he grinned. "I'll tell you all about it later. Tovan's here too."

He looked around and waved at the others who were beginning to cautiously approach while keeping watchful eyes on the dragon standing calmly on the beach.

"Brax will take us to the other shore," he called out.

"You can't be thinking that we'll ride on that awful creature, can you?" gasped Portia.

"Why not?" smiled Jamie "It can't be much different than riding a gryphon."

Jeremiah and Tovan both appeared startled as the three girls and Mikel turned to Jamie, looks of undisguised dislike on their faces. When Jamie saw their expressions, the grin vanished from her face. Mikel had no intentions of explaining the situation because he had no idea what was causing it and quite frankly, once again, he didn't care.

"Do you have another idea?" Jeremiah asked, obviously oblivious to the tensions swirling around him. "Brax has to get back to her baby and said that this would only be a small detour."

"Ride on a dragon?" gulped Portia.

"Can she carry all of us?" asked Melisande.

"Of course," he replied. "It's either that or stay here. Come on. She's promised she won't eat any of us."

"That's big of her," mumbled Mikel, turning toward the beach. "But what is our other choice?"

It took a bit of work to get them all aboard, but eventually everyone plus the bags and packs were squeezed onto the dragon's back. Brax lifted easily from the sand and skimmed across the water to the opposite beach. She landed with a bit of a bump causing Portia to hit her nose on Mikel's shoulder, but other than that, they each arrived in one piece. They dismounted a great deal faster than they had mounted and on Jeremiah's orders, bowed respectfully to the huge beast before backing away from her as quickly as they could. When Tovan bowed, the dragon lowered her muzzle to within inches of the girl's face. Tovan closed her eyes. The dragon's nostril was bigger than her head.

"She told me to take care of you, Tovan. You have as rare a gift as I do."

With that, the dragon sprang from the beach and was airborne in seconds.

"You could talk to that creature?" exclaimed Melisande.

Jeremiah nodded. "I've become an animay – someone who can talk with animals. Brax and I had a lovely visit."

Tovan punched him in the arm.

"You would have been dinner if I hadn't saved your skin."

Before Mikel could ask her what she meant, Melisande suddenly realized that they were missing someone.

"Oh no," she groaned, glancing around. "We forgot the Min…I mean, Adonis."

"Ah, the poor little wretch," chuckled Jeremiah. "Well, he has the run of the island now."

Mikel looked back at the island and started to laugh. "Well, they certainly didn't forget him," he pointed. "Look."

The little Minotaur was streaking across the water toward them. As he got closer, they could hear him shouting the most inappropriate comments at the little specks of light surrounding him, and these continued even after they had plunked him down on the sand in front of the group. His eyes were squeezed shut as he continued to yell, but the fairies simply tinkled merrily as they flew in circles above him. Jeremiah and Tovan stared at the tiny creatures in amazement.

"Are those fairies?" she asked.

Mikel nodded. "And Melisande can talk with them."

Jeremiah grinned. "It looks like a lot of talents have emerged."

Adonis kept up his bellowing and finally, Melisande decided to take the situation in hand. "Minotaur!" she shouted. "Control yourself right now!"

The little creature stopped his cursing and warily opened one eye. "The name is Adonis, woman."

"Only if you act like an Adonis," was her quick retort.

He opened both eyes and got to his feet. "Alright, alright, most gracious lady," he muttered. He gave her a courteous bow and almost landed face first in the sand.

"That's a Minotaur?" laughed Jeremiah.

Adonis gave him a miserable look. "Stop your laughing, boy. When I was my normal size, you would have run from me in terror."

"It's true," confirmed Melisande, trying to look serious. "If it hadn't been for the fairies shrinking him down to this size, he would have chopped me to little pieces."

"I apologize," replied Jeremiah, trying to control his snickers.

"Well," said Mikel looking around. "We'd better get on our way. Could you give me the monocle, Jamie? Maybe we can make sense of it now."

Jamie pulled it out of her pack and handed it to Jeremiah. Mikel's relief at seeing the other boy return safely dissipated into the morning air. He had asked for the object. Why had Jamie automatically given it to Jeremiah? He shot her a dark look, which made her cringe. For one terrified moment, he thought he was actually going to hit her, which, even through the spell, made him pause long enough to wonder why he would do such a thing. And then the thought was gone.

"There's nothing on the outside," said Jeremiah, examining both sides carefully. "But there seems to be something on the inside."

For several minutes, he struggled to find a way of opening the monocle, but nothing worked. He shrugged his shoulders in defeat. Mikel finally lost patience, grabbed it and slammed it against a rock beside him. It shattered into pieces that scattered everywhere, but the object that Jeremiah had noticed on the inside was left alone on the rock.

"Now, that's how to make a decision," laughed Melisande.

Jeremiah bent down and picked up the piece.

"This is strange," he remarked, looking slightly confused. "It looks just like the other one. They both look like puzzle pieces."

"Pull out the other one," suggested Jamie. "See if they fit together."

The others turned to her and glared. Jeremiah did not notice their reaction and did as she had suggested, unaware of the negative feelings swirling around him.

"They don't fit together, but one side of both is the same. They look like walls of rock."

"What's on the other side of this one?" asked Tovan.

Jeremiah turned it over.

"It's a castle or fortress with a huge bridge attached to it."

"And I suppose you've seen a castle before?" sneered Mikel.

Jeremiah looked up, slightly taken aback by the tone in the other boy's voice.

"As a matter of fact, I have," he replied and then looked back at the image. "Other dimensions have castles as well as this one."

The others crowded around.

"Strange," said Jamie. "There was nothing in the monocle when we first found it."

"Go away, Jamie," hissed Portia.

Jamie took a quick step back as the others stared at her, their glares threatening and hostile.

"Let's get on with it," snapped Portia, turning away, but not before she threatened Jamie with a fist. "It looks like we're going to be walking all day."

As she turned, the sun glinted off her necklace.

"That's pretty," remarked Jeremiah. "You didn't have that when we started, did you?"

Jamie held her breath as the others turned to face him.

"She's always had it," they said together, their expressions daring him to challenge them.

Jeremiah stared at the jewel for a few more seconds, a strange look coming over his face. It appeared as if he were struggling with something.

"Yes," he replied, overcome by the spell. "You've always had it."

"Yes," chorused Tovan. "You've always had it."

Mikel felt quite satisfied to see the look on Jamie's face when the two turned to scowl at her. The girl shivered and took several steps backward, away from the group. The group moved away from the lakeshore, the Minotaur hopping and skipping to keep up.

Partway up the slope, Mikel stopped and scanned the sky. Bandi was overdue. Jeremiah and Tovan had returned, but what had happened to the Wickersnit? His concern for Bandi deepened.

Chapter Twenty-Seven
Staggering News

Azmodeus

"It's good of you to see me again," said Azmodeus, bowing respectfully to the Willik.

For this interview, the two were in a small room close to the elf's private chamber.

"I knew you would return, my friend. Please tell me what Rudana reported to you."

She gestured to the chair opposite from her, and he sat down.

"Rudana's instructions were that we would be able to find the seed of the Laurel Tree but that it would be necessary to go to her sisters for that answer."

"Hmm," mused the Willik. "That is a dangerous quest to make. Few have survived a meeting with the Furies."

"I agree. However, she made a mind link with Petre just as we were prepared to mount the gryphons, which she also hooked into my mind. It warned the boy to be brave, and at that moment, I felt a strong suspicion that the boy was critical to this quest, but I did not know how. It is for this reason that I have come to you. What part does Petre play in all of this?"

The Willik placed her elbows on the arms of her chair and templed her fingers in front of her face. She sighed deeply.

"Placing the seed inside the tree is not all there is to restore it to life, Azmodeus. The gods and goddesses have never been so simplistic in their demands. The person who places it there must also place themself inside the tree. They must become part of the tree. Hera has been very thorough in her plans for revenge. I believe that she has promised Spider the right to rule Draukenberg when this is all over, and then she will then retreat to safety in New Olympus while this world and all who are in it are destroyed."

Azmodeus rose from his chair, clasped his hands behind his back and began to pace back and forth in front of her, deep in thought. The Willik did not speak. Finally, the older man returned to his chair and sat down with a heavy sigh.

"If I were to say that I would do it, you would tell me that I was too old. Am I correct?"

The Willik nodded. "It must be a child, Azmodeus, a willing child. As cruel and barbaric as the whole thing might sound, it must be a child."

Azmodeus gave her a stricken look. "Petre is the one," he stated, his voice shaking.

"Yes," said the Willik. "Rudana knew when she saw him that he had been marked for the task. Her mind link to him erases any doubt."

"Sapphire," sighed Azmodeus. He hadn't used her given name in many years. "How can I tell a young boy that in order to save our world, he must sacrifice his life?"

"In exactly that way, my friend. If he chooses not to do it, our world is doomed, and many will die. The trolls will also not return to their roles as tree keepers."

"It is a vicious circle," replied Azmodeus, shaking his head. "If the six children are successful, and we are able to stop Spider, Petre must lose his life. If we cannot stop her, we all die."

"You are quite correct," agreed the Willik. "If she wins, the trolls, goblins and all the dark creatures will be hers. War will erupt in our world for the first time, and many will die. Oh, Draukenberg will survive as a country, but it will be a hideous one, and once we are all subdued or dead, Spider will look beyond to the other countries on Eleusia and possibly to other dimensions. We must stop Spider, Hera, and Azmodeus for the sake of our world and those beyond. The fate of many may rest on the life of a young boy, for without his sacrifice, the trident will not come between the good and the evil."

"What do you mean?" asked Azmodeus.

"It must all happen at once. If all the players are not in place at the same time, we cannot win. The six must complete their journey according to the prophecy and be standing in the chamber of the Sanctuary at the time of the constellation alignment. When the trident is placed between good and evil, the seed of life must be placed in the Laurel Tree."

"Ah," sighed the old wizard.

The two sat in silence for a long time. When Azmodeus stood and left the chamber without her permission or a formal bow, the Willik did not reprimand him, but he didn't miss seeing the single tear that rolled down her cheek.

Chapter Twenty-Eight
The Furies

Petre

"What I don't understand is why someone doesn't destroy Spider before the date that the constellations are aligned. Shouldn't we be looking for Sharra? Wouldn't it be better than all this?"

Petre gestured to the confusion around them. Everywhere they looked, swords were being sharpened and bows restrung for new arrows being made by the women. Although they were also warriors, their smaller hands were better suited for the delicate feather work.

"Only Hera can destroy Spider as far as we know," replied Azmodeus. "As for Sharra, if those on the quest are successful, they will find her when they answer the sixth riddle."

"Will it come to war, Azmodeus?"

"Not if all fall properly into place."

The older man cleared his throat and looked away. Petre gave him a curious look. Ever since he had joined the wizard that morning, the older man had seemed preoccupied with something and had had difficulty looking directly at him. He tried to think of something that he had done wrong but, for a change, could think of nothing. This was a first for him because he had always been used to knowing exactly what it was. Trouble was his middle name, according to everyone who knew him.

"Petre," Azmodeus began, turning back to him. "I…"

"Everything is ready, Azmodeus."

The wizard looked up at the big man standing beside him.

"Thank you, Yonnus. Where is Crutchin?"

"He's with the beasts."

"Good."

He got to his feet and gestured to Petre to follow him.

"Come, boy. It's time we were on our way."

"But what were you going to say to me?"

Azmodeus gave him a thoughtful look. "It will keep for a while, my boy. Now come."

Peter shrugged. He would have to accept this for now. The three walked down the main street of the tree city to where the griffins were stabled. They found Collpepper and Arynn putting their packs on the griffins when they arrived.

"Is it far?" asked Petre.

"Not by gryphon," replied Yonnus. "However, they will only take us to the edge of The Hollows, and we will be on our own from there."

"I guess I should be nervous about that part," said Petre.

"Yes, you should," grunted the big man, his expression troubled and his voice grim.

The boy gulped but continued at a relentless pace. If the three of them could do it, so could he. In no time at all, they were perched on the griffins and winging their way toward the southwest. It was a beautiful morning, and for many miles, Petre could see nothing that would cause an alarm. Shortly before noon, however, he spotted a grey haze on the horizon. The closer they came to it, the more pronounced it became, looking more and more like a wall of cotton than one of mist. It was not advancing toward them but continued to hover in one spot.

"The Hollows," shouted Yonnus, who was riding behind him.

Petre shivered. He thought of the safety provided by the treetop city of Donagal and wondered for a moment if he should have stayed there.

The elves landed their griffins smoothly on a flat section of the meadow a short distance from the mist, and the four travelers clambered down. Packs of supplies were dropped down to them, and then the two elves were once again airborne with waves and shouts of encouragement. They would not return until Azmodeus called for them, and as they gradually became specks in the sky, Petre sighed.

"Wishing you were going back with them?" grinned Yonnus.

Petre nodded and then took a deep breath.

"If you're not afraid, I won't be," he replied with heroic determination.

Yonnus grunted. "Who says I'm not afraid, boy?"

At the look on Petre's face, the big man laughed. "Don't worry. We have Azmodeus with us, and as long as we stick together, we should be fine."

He ruffled Petre's hair and picked up his pack. The boy reached for his, slung it over his back and followed the others toward the mist. At the edge of the grey wall, Azmodeus stopped and removed a rope that was hanging from his own pack.

"From this point on, we stay roped together," he explained, tying one end around his waist. "No matter what happens, stay attached to this rope. The creatures that live inside the mist are all up to no good. Unfortunately, some of them also remember me from former trips, and if they find out I'm back, they will do everything to make sure that I don't escape from them again."

Petre tried to control his shaking as he tied himself in behind Azmodeus.

"Buck up, lad," whispered Crutchin as he tied himself in behind Petre and passed the rest of the rope to Yonnus. "He's only trying to scare you."

Petre was not so sure.

"What about the Furies?" the Wildenchin asked Azmodeus.

The wizard stroked his beard.

"That's going to be a bit of a problem," he replied slowly. "We will not know how they intend to show themselves until we get in there. I'm sure they know we're coming. Rudana would never miss an opportunity to provide us with a welcoming committee, if one can call it such. Ready?"

He led the group forward and stepped into the mist without hesitation. The rest had no choice but to follow. It was dense and cold. Petre realized instantly why Azmodeus had tied them together. He could see nothing, absolutely nothing, and it was the eeriest feeling he had ever experienced. All that kept him moving forward was the tugging pressure on the rope, and Petre could only trust that the older man wouldn't lead them into holes or other dangerous traps. The other thing Petre noticed was the lack of sound, which was strange. It wasn't that it was simply quiet; it was much deeper than that. He couldn't even hear his own breathing. Panic began to set in. It started as a tight curling sensation in his stomach and then began to expand outward.

"Breathe slowly," he whispered to himself. At least, he thought he had whispered. The problem was that he hadn't heard it. Suddenly, they were through. For a moment, however, he wasn't certain. He could see trees and hills ahead of them, but there was no color to them. Everything was in shades of grey, white and black.

"Isn't this a wonderful place," muttered Crutchin sarcastically. "I can honestly say I would not be happy here."

"Me neither," replied Petre.

Azmodeus sighed as he looked around. "No, it's a bad place to be at any time.

"Where to now, Azmodeus?" asked Yonnus.

"The Furies will be in a place called the Crags, which is somewhere in those peaks," he replied, pointing to the mountains in the distance. "They are not as far away as they appear. Everything is distorted in this place, so be careful and stay roped together. The Furies may even choose to confront us before we get there."

They followed him in silence. Petre was grateful that he could once again see and hear, but as he followed Azmodeus down the incline, he again noticed the quiet. Nothing moved or made a sound in this place. It was like walking into someone's painting.

At the foot of the incline, Azmodeus brought them to a halt. What had originally appeared to be an open stretch of land from the top of the hill was nothing more than an evil-smelling bog.

"How do we get across this?" asked Petre. "There doesn't appear to be any path."

"I hate to think what's causing this stink," muttered Yonnus.

"Maybe I can get us over it," suggested Crutchin.

Azmodeus shook his head.

"The problem is that you don't have much control, my boy. We could land in this muck part way across."

"True," agreed Crutchin. "I guess it's up to you, oh fearless leader."

The wizard raised his eyebrows, and the Wildenchin grinned.

"Someone has to lighten the mood," he offered as an explanation.

Azmodeus walked to the edge of the swamp and thoughtfully examined its width.

"Any good swamp has a safe pathway through it. It is simply a case of finding it."

He held out a hand and closed his eyes for several seconds. Petre watched in fascination as the older man's beard began to shorten, and when it finally stopped, what was left was a good three inches shorter than it had been before he had begun the spell.

"I see it," he said at last. "Follow in my exact footsteps."

They lined up carefully behind him, holding on to the pieces of rope that attached them to the person in front. Azmodeus placed one foot cautiously in front of the other, and the three followed behind, imitating his movements and placing their feet in the same spots when they reached them.

Petre figured that they were almost halfway across when it happened. Shapes began to rise from the mud around them, and the stench became unbearable. It was impossible to tell if the creatures had any body shape, for they were simply blobs of dripping mud and slime. Circles emerged on what would have been the forehead of a human, but Petre didn't know if they were mouths or single eyes.

"I was afraid of this," sighed Azmodeus.

"Wh…what are they?" stammered Petre.

"Mud men," grumbled Crutchin from behind. "Their actual name is Yelti, and they are nasty creatures. Let Azmodeus do the talking, or we're going to end up like them."

Petre swallowed hard. Was he ending up like them? Mud men? Yelti? A shiver of horror snaked up his back, and he suddenly realized that he couldn't move his feet. Looking down, he almost leaped out of his skin. His feet were mud, and as he watched, a horrible mushy sensation moved over his ankles. He was turning into the mud!

The Yelti edged closer, and Petre grabbed at the rope in front of him, hanging on for dear life. The squishy sensation had moved from his ankles to his knees, but he was too terrified to look down. Was this how he was going to end? A mud man?

Crutchin raised his hands, and the mud men stopped their advance. "I am a Wildenchin, a creature of the earth like you. You cannot harm me or those who are under my protection."

"We are not bound by your rules," boomed a voice from one of the creatures closest to them. "We may take who we want."

"You may not," shouted Crutchin. "You must allow us safe passage across this bog, or you will be sucked back into the earth, never to return to the surface. That is how you will spend the rest of your days."

"He lies," thundered another voice. "Power such as that does not exist."

"It does," countered the Wildenchin. "Listen to the sounds that are coming to you from deep inside the ground."

The Yelti stopped and cocked the upper parts of their bodies as though listening, although Petre saw nothing that resembled ears on what might have been their heads. All at once, Petre could hear a dull pounding coming from beneath them that vibrated up his legs and along his backbone.

"You are being warned," cried Crutchin. "Do you dare challenge the power of the earth itself?"

The Yelti looked around in nervous confusion.

"I say let them go," shouted one.

"No," argued another. "It's a trick."

They all began to yell at once, and Petre realized that his feet and legs had returned to normal.

"Move!" hissed Crutchin to Azmodeus.

The wizard jerked on the rope, and the three others did their best to keep up with him without falling flat on their faces. They had almost reached the other side of the bog when the arguing stopped.

"They escape!" shouted one.

"It was a trick!" cried another.

Sounds of pursuit filled the air.

"Hurry! Run!" bellowed Azmodeus. "We'll just have to trust our luck."

They plowed after him, following the narrow path as best they could. Petre slipped off into the slime several times, and each time, he was picked up under the arms and carried forward by Crutchin. Just as they were about to reach more solid ground, a dark, ugly cloud appeared above them from out of nowhere and began circling above their heads. Flashes of light streaked throughout its interior and crashed in jagged forks around them. The mud creatures shrieked with fright and vanished into the murk, leaving the four to their fate. Before they had a chance even to try to run, they were sucked up into the cloud, held together by the rope that connected them. The turbulence bounced them back and forth like rag dolls. Because of the rope, they smacked into each other, ricocheted away and then had the breath wrenched out of them every time they were pulled back. By the time they were deposited on a rocky shoal in the mountains, far above the valley of the Yelti, they were a bruised and damaged lot. The cloud simply moved away from them and vanished.

"By all that's mighty, Azmodeus," choked Yonnus. "Couldn't you have created something a little less dangerous?"

"It wasn't me," groaned the wizard, sitting up and rubbing his elbows.

"Well, it wasn't me," muttered Crutchin, trying to stand up and not succeeding. "That was well beyond my capabilities."

Petre didn't even try to speak. His head hurt and his mouth felt full of dirt.

"Greetings, little frogs," rasped a voice slightly above them. "It's so nice of you to drop in."

Laughter greeted this comment and the four turned to see who had spoken. Hovering above them were three of the most horrific creatures Petre had ever seen.

"I had a feeling that this was your doing, ladies," sighed Azmodeus getting to his feet.

The monsters hovering in the air looked like shadows in tattered clothing. Their heads and faces were hidden in hoods, and the arms that could be seen through the shredded sleeves were simply bones ending in clawed appendages. They didn't appear to have legs. What was left of their tunics wafted back and forth as if being blown by a breeze except for the fact that there wasn't one. The air was completely still.

"Let us get rid of that thing first," cackled one of them.

In an instant, the wizard's beard was gone. Azmodeus fingered his bare chin.

"What is it about my beard that gets all the ladies upset?" he asked.

If Petre hadn't been so terrified, he would have laughed at the melancholy look on the old man's face.

"It will take him much longer to grow it back here," screeched another.

"I take it these are the Furies, Azmodeus?" asked Yonnus. His voice didn't sound as strong and confident as it normally did.

Azmodeus nodded as the three lowered themselves closer to the ground in front of them. They were taller than Yonnus and terrifying to look upon. As they turned their attention on each of their captives, Petre had the distinct impression that the creatures were wondering what each of them would taste like.

"We know what you want," the three chimed in together and Petre had to resist covering his ears. It was a horrible sound, blending sawing on metal with the screaming of animals. "You want to know the whereabouts of the seed."

"If you would be so good as to tell us," replied Azmodeus courteously.

The three screeched with laughter. The sound was so horrifying that the four were forced to their knees, covering their ears with their hands.

"We tell nothing unless we receive something in return," said one. "You know that, Azmodeus."

"If we tell you, then one of you will have to remain behind with us," said the second.

"But which one will it be?" asked the third.

The shadowed faces turned to each of the four. Petre's teeth began to chatter, and his knees were knocking together so hard he could barely stand.

"Let them decide, sisters," cried one. "Let them decide whose fate will be forever locked with ours."

This response drew another onslaught of maniacal laughter. Suddenly the ground was moving around the four and at first, it appeared to be alive with snakes. Vines of all thicknesses sprang from the ground and wrapped themselves around arms and legs, imprisoning each where they knelt or stood.

"Don't struggle," warned one of the Furies. "The more you do, the tighter the vines will become."

"You will have one night to decide," said another. "When morning comes, you will tell us who will stay, and we will tell you the location of the seed."

"This is unfair," shouted Crutchin. "You can't do this to us."

"Oh yes, we can," replied one. "After all, we're doing it, aren't we?"

With that, the creatures rose into the air, screeching into the night. They circled their prisoners several times, deafening them with the noise before flying into the sky and disappearing from sight.

"Azmodeus?" croaked Petre, his eyes round with terror.

"Hmm," replied the old man, looking down at his bonds. "I'd say we were in a bit of a bind."

"That," snorted Yonnus, "is an understatement."

Throughout the cold, chilly night, the four argued about who would remain with the three Furies. It wasn't that any of them wanted to stay; they simply couldn't bear the thought of one of their friends suffering such an end.

"I'm the irrelevant one," said Petre for the hundredth time. "Seriously, what good am I? I have no gifts or skills to speak of."

"No," snapped Azmodeus. "I will not have it. It's me they want. They know that without my magic and safely trapped in the Hollows, I would no longer be a threat to the despicable creatures who live in here."

"I disagree," growled Yonnus. "All I have are my muscles. We need you out there, Azmodeus, where you can do some good. I will stay."

"It has to be me," argued Crutchin. "Of all of us, I would be the least affected. As a Wildenchin, creatures like this do not affect me. The rest of you would be driven insane."

And so the arguments went on with no decision having been made by the time the grey around them lightened slightly so they could see. Dawn heralded the arrival of the three horrific creatures, who could be heard approaching long before they were seen. As they swept into sight, Petre tried to make himself smaller within the vines, but all that happened was that the green ropes tightened their grip.

"Well, trapped chickens," snarled one of the Furies. "Have you decided?"

"We will tell you," replied a suddenly calm and almost indifferent Azmodeus, "when you tell us the location of the seed."

"Stubborn to the end," chuckled a second. "You will never change, Azmodeus. Very well. The seed is inside a crystal that hangs on a gold chain."

"And where is this chain?" asked the wizard.

"In limbo," replied the third. "Only the chosen one has the ability to recover it, and in order to do so, he or she must die. Only then can he or she make the final choice in his or her heart and give the ultimate sacrifice."

"But that doesn't make sense," protested Petre. "If they have to die first, haven't they made the ultimate sacrifice?"

For some reason, this question seemed to strike the creatures as hilariously funny. Like the night before, the sound was deafening and the boy felt that his skull was going to break in two. Crutchin was right. How could anyone live in their presence for long without losing their sanity?

The three stopped laughing suddenly and leered down at their victims.

"And who has chosen to stay with us?" asked one.

"I will," replied the four in unison.

"Ah, such devotion," smirked the second. "Aren't we protective of one another?"

"So, which one shall it be, sisters?" asked the third.

They were silent for a few moments, as if contemplating their decision.

"I will stay," said Azmodeus. "I am the one that is any sort of challenge to you."

"No Azmodeus," said Yonnus. "I am the one…"

"Quiet!" snapped the tallest of the Furies. "We have decided. The three that have not been selected will be sent away. The fourth will remain with us."

The vines disappeared from their arms and legs and slithered back into the ground.

"Go and do not return," demanded another.

They were enveloped in a thick mist and lifted off their feet. It was not as violent a trip as their arrival on the mountain had been, but it was just as uncomfortable. Three of them found themselves in a place quite unexpected. The fourth ended up at a cave entrance higher up the mountain. All four were shocked by the choice the Furies had made. Azmodeus was devastated.

"Why would they have chosen him unless they had known? They must have known how critical he was to our quest. Ah, poor boy, and we are now quite undone."

On the ledge outside the cave, Petre looked up at the three Furies in horror. "Wh…why me?" he whispered.

"I think our shapes alarm him," chuckled one. "Shall we go with the old ones?"

"It would be more motherly," agreed the second.

Their shapes blurred, and suddenly before him were three kindly-looking old grannies. The change was more comforting to Petre, but it didn't make him feel any better. He was still stuck in The Hollows with the three Furies and supposedly forever.

"But why did you choose me?" he asked again.

"Because you are important to their quest," was the response. "We get so bored, and you are our new amusement. Come along."

They waddled into the cave, and Petre reluctantly followed. The tunnel wound for a short distance into the mountain and opened up into a grotto that made Petre forget his predicament for a few brief moments. He was stunned. Pillars of marble swept up to a ceiling that was painted with characters and constellations of the sky. Grand dwellings of white and pink brick surrounded a tiled courtyard dotted with fountains, benches, trees and ponds. The scents from the many gardens were overpowering, but Petre loved it. He was in paradise!

"Did you think we lived in squalor, young man?"

Petre turned to face the speaker and gasped. The Furies had changed shape again. Three beautiful women now stood in front of him, garbed in long gowns that seemed to wrap around their bodies, trimmed with strange shapes at the hem and on a seam running up the side of the gown to the shoulder. Each had a hairstyle of intricate curls and braids, and each had hair of a different color from the other two.

"This is what we really look like, boy," chuckled the dark-haired one closest to him. "We only take the other shapes to frighten. I am Razna. My blonde sister is Rethnie, and the redhead is Rindelle. Welcome to our home."

They moved gracefully down the steps and into the courtyard.

"But why did you choose me," he asked once again. "If I'm supposed to be your new amusement, I'm afraid you'll find me lacking."

Rindelle turned back to him. "You are being used by that old man, silly boy. Do you think that Azmodeus really cares about you, Petre? You are just another pawn in his game."

"What do you mean?" spluttered Petre. "Of course, he cares about me."

"So, you don't mind being used as a sacrifice?" asked Rethnie.

"A sacrifice?" Petre blanched. "I don't know what you mean."

"Come, Petre," said Razna, smiling kindly. Unfortunately, the smile didn't reach her eyes. "Let us have something to eat, and we will tell you the story of your fate had we left you with the wizard."

Petre stumbled down the steps missing the sly smile exchanged by the sisters. Oh, this was going to be too much fun. The boy was gullible as well as trusting. Obviously, Azmodeus had not told the boy of his role in this little adventure, so they would take care of that oversight with a little help from the world of lies and exaggerations. He was putty in their hands. Besides, they needed his youthful essence in order to keep their enchanting appearances. The others had been too old, so there had been no doubt from the beginning as to whom they would keep. Poor boy. It was a shame that he was the chosen one. Ah, well. There was nothing wrong with all of Draukenberg looking like The Hollows.

Chapter Twenty-Nine
Caught Like A Rabbit In A Poacher's Bag

Bandi

Bandi had tried his best to follow the trail of the dragon but had not counted on the Crystal Spires being so far away. He had to stop several times and was worried he would be too late to do anything to help Jeremiah if he couldn't make better time. Part of him had also wanted to impress Mikel. He knew the boy was not happy about being considered a wizard. Nor was he happy with having Bandi as an assistant. But Bandi had felt the bonding as soon as the boy had entered the Willik's chamber, pointing him out in the shadows. It was meant to be just so long as Mikel never found out that his assistant was a coward.

Bandi's home village was deep in the jungles of Hvedrung, the country to the east of Draukenberg. Anyone not knowing the village was there would have walked right by it, so carefully was it camouflaged. Bandi was the youngest in a family of eight and was considered to be the runt of the family. In fact, he was really the runt of the village. He was the smallest and the weakest of the Wickersnits his age, and the fact that he was the fastest and most adept at changing did not hold much weight with the others. He couldn't help but think that his parents were slightly ashamed of him, but that didn't matter now. The Sorgochs had seen to that.

The large ape-like creatures had easily found their village, and most of his friends and family were now likely slaves of the creatures. Those that were not were probably dead. The Sorgochs constantly raided the Wickersnit villages because the smaller creatures had no way to fight, only to camouflage. Unfortunately, the Sorgochs had the ability to see through their attempts and caught them easily. They wanted the smaller creatures to go into their mines to dig out a rock spice that could only be found in those particular hills and was much in demand in the big cities. The Sorgochs were too big and clumsy to do the work, so they raided villages throughout their territory to find replacements. They had to do it often, as life in the mines was usually short.

Sitting on a sheltered branch, Bandi thought back on that terrible day. He had been out in the jungle pretending to be a great hero, swinging back and forth from tree to tree in the shape of a small monkey, when he heard crashing coming through the foliage on the ground. Hiding behind the trunk of the tree, he smothered a gasp when he saw the Sorgochs. He needed to warn his village. Some of them might be able to escape. But no, he just sat there, frozen like a stick, too terrified to move. He heard the cries a short time later and was so ashamed of himself that he turned and raced through the trees jumping from one to the next, away from the village, as fast as he could go. He didn't pay any attention to where he was going, and then suddenly, she was there. Grabbing him by the scruff of the neck, she held him out from herself and peered at his terrified face. He tried to squirm and change, but she just laughed.

"It's no use, little Wickersnit," she had laughed. "You cannot change while you are around me. I need you to do a job for me, and if you do, I will have your family released from the mines."

And so he had agreed to take the poison to Donagal.

The eagle, Bandi, shook himself out of his reverie and tried to untie the knot in his stomach. He wouldn't be able to fly with his mind and emotions in such turmoil. He slowly calmed himself down and then lifted off from the branch, his huge wings lifting him easily into the air.

For the next hour, he drifted on the air currents, which carried him toward his goal without much effort on his part. He could finally see the Crystal Spires as the sun peaked in the sky before starting its downward journey. Now to find Jeremiah.

Suddenly he was snatched from the sky and tossed into some sort of enclosure that felt like a bag. His eagle shape transformed instantly into that of his own natural shape. As he grasped frantically at the sides of the bag to avoid being tossed around, he heard a familiar laugh.

"Did you think that you could get away with failing to do the task I asked of you, Wickersnit? You strayed too far away from your master, and now you must suffer the consequences."

Bandi closed his eyes and let out a small, pitiful moan. Whatever Hera had planned for him, he would probably have been better off as a slave in the Sorgoch mines.

Chapter Thirty
Forest of Death

Jamie

Melisande peeked out from behind a tree. "Do you think it's safe?" she whispered. "Do you think that there might be someone there who will help?"

The little cottage looked innocent enough. It sat nestled between several large evergreens, the sloping roof of the round structure touching the ground except for the entrance, where it arched up over the small wooden door. It was neat and clean, with a path leading to the door edged with whitewashed stones, and smoke drifted enticingly out of the chimney. All in all, it looked cozy and welcoming.

'A little too cozy and welcoming,' thought Jamie coming up behind the group.

"I don't care," muttered Portia. "I'm hungry, and I want more than vegetables and fruit. Sorry Adonis, but it just isn't enough."

More than one looked at Portia in amazement, although she didn't seem to notice. This was the first time they had heard her apologize to anyone. She stepped forward out of the safety of the trees and marched purposely toward the cottage. The others followed. Only Jamie held back.

"I don't have a good feeling about this," she called out. "I think we should be more cautious."

No one turned to even look back at her except Adonis, who, for the entire journey, had kept watching her with a questioning expression on his face. Had the spell not worked on him, she wondered? For most of the trip up the mountain, the others had verbally threatened her with physical punishments if she came too close and at one point, Portia had thrown rocks at her. Tears had rolled down Jamie's cheeks on several occasions. She had never felt so wretched in her life. At least they were pretending she didn't exist as they marched up the hill to the cottage, and she didn't have to endure any more abuse. She watched them for a moment and then, shrugging her shoulders, started to take a step forward. Suddenly, something yanked on her hair from behind.

"Ouch!" she yelped, jerking backward.

"Not safe, Jamie girl," squeaked a voice in her ear. "Mustn't follow others."

Jamie stopped her struggling and looked around. Hovering in front of her face was a pink and white bird the size of a sparrow, which, as she watched in amazement, turned into the shape of a small Crook with wings.

"Oh, I'm so glad to see you," croaked Jamie, her eyes filling up with tears at the sight of her friend. "I've had such an awful time, Crooks, and…."

"Get down," hissed the pixie. "Get down low and watch."

"But…" protested the girl.

"Do as I say," snapped Crooks.

Jamie could not ignore the urgency in the creature's voice. She did as she was told and crouched behind a tree, her eyes on the group who had now reached the path leading to the cottage. The door opened slowly, but she couldn't see anyone inside. The others hesitated for a moment and then walked up the path, one by one disappearing through the doorway. As the last one stepped inside, the door closed behind them.

"What is in there?" whispered Jamie.

Crooks shook her head vigorously, her fingers to her lips in a warning to keep silent.

Crouched behind the tree, Jamie waited for what seemed to be an eternity. Her legs were cramping, and her neck and back were aching from being curled into a ball shape. She was just about to ask what they were waiting for when the door of the cottage opened, and a small squatty shape emerged. It stood in front of the door and looked around, finally peering intensely at the wood in which Jamie was hiding. The girl held her breath and then let it out as slowly as she could when the creature looked away. Either her eyes were deceiving her, or the creature strongly resembled a witch from a fairy tale, right down to the pointed hat. It suddenly spread its arms, and the witch shape changed into that of a large black crow. It lifted from the ground and flapped its way around the cottage in a circle. It continued to circle the cottage; each pass further out from the last one. The creature was searching for something, and Jamie was pretty certain that she knew what that something was. She tried to make herself even smaller and remained curled up into a ball long after the bird had disappeared over the hill behind. In fact, she didn't change her position until Crooks told her it was safe.

"What was that?" she asked, pulling her aching limbs up into a standing position.

"A witch," replied Crooks. "She help Spider. Not a nice one. Come. Friends need help."

"Why should I care?" snapped Jamie, the hurt and anger finally surfacing. "Even if I'm able to help them out of whatever, they'll only continue to hate me."

Crooks flew directly into the girl's face and stopped a scant inch from the tip of her nose. Her expression was one of puzzlement, but Jamie would never have known because she had to cross her eyes in order to see her, and that hurt.

"You angry," said the pixie. "Why?"

Trying not to look at Crooks because every time she did, she saw three of her, Jamie told her about the necklace and what it had done to the others. When she was finished, Crooks backed off and sat down on a branch just above Jamie's head. At least the girl could now focus on the pixie.

"Well?" asked Jamie.

"Shh," warned the little creature. It appeared to be listening to something that the girl could neither see nor hear.

Jamie waited a little bit longer, but finally, impatience got the better of her. "Crooks, answer me."

The pixie didn't move for several more minutes while Jamie fumed beneath her. Finally, she shook herself and looked at the girl. "Seeing eye."

"What?" asked Jamie.

"Azmodeus. He tell me. The necklace is seeing eye."

"You were talking to Azmodeus?"

Crooks just carried on without acknowledging her question. "It very bad. Must smash it. Witches see us. Witches can trap us."

Jamie tried to make sense of the strange explanation. "So, the necklace really is bad. I knew it. If the witches can really see what we're doing through it, no wonder it was so easy to put traps in our way."

The pixie nodded.

"Is that cottage a trap then?"

Again, the creature nodded.

"But why are they being mean and cruel to me? They want to hurt me, Crooks."

"Spell," was the reply. "The witches put spell through eye. You no feel magic like others. The witches want you hurting even die. Then no six for quest."

"I don't feel magic?" gasped Jamie. "Do you mean that it doesn't work on me?"

Crooks only looked at her.

"Of course," Jamie mused almost to herself. "I was the only one who knew that Portia hadn't had the necklace all along. Then all of a sudden, the rest turned on me. If I get hurt or worse, the quest ends because there would only be five. If that cottage is a trap and that creature harmed the others, then it doesn't matter, does it? The quest would still be over because there is only me."

"You think right," was the pixie's reply. "Now we go. Must save others."

She flew out of the woods toward the cottage, and Jamie followed after giving the tops of her cramped legs a bit of a rub. At the path to the cottage, Crooks paused long enough for Jamie to reach her and then darted quickly up the walkway. When the door opened before the pixie reached it, Jamie stopped and did not continue forward until Crooks gestured to her to come. She followed the creature over the threshold and into the interior. The door slammed shut behind, and suddenly, they were in pitch-black darkness.

"Where are we?" whispered Jamie, suddenly feeling very afraid.

"This not good," she heard the pixie reply. "This not good place."

"I can't see, Crooks."

"You will, soon. Move forward."

Jamie took several tentative steps forward, and gradually, the dark outlines of trees took shape. "Where are we?" she asked again.

"We in The Hollows…in Black Hags Forest. It be a horrible forest. We never find friends. We never leave Black Hags."

"What are you talking about?" quaked a trembling Jamie.

"No one ever come out of Black Hags," whispered a voice near to her ear. Crooks was sitting on her shoulder as close to her neck as was possible. "Magic not work in woods. Everyone die in here. Everyone die. It be forest of death."

Jamie moved slowly forward, with Crooks clinging to her neck. If magic didn't work in Black Hag Forest then the little pixie was incapable of changing shape or taking off in flight. She was stranded…they were both stranded. At least the lack of magical ability would not affect her, but that would not make any difference if they met up with the wrong inhabitants.

The trees were packed closely together and, from what she could detect, were leafless. Their thick, scarred trunks were enormous ancient relics whose roots started at a point well above her head and entered the ground to disappear deep within the earth. Out of the corner of her eye, she spotted movement from the roots and the ground, almost as if they were rolling and undulating, but when she turned to look, all was still. She crept around one behemoth and into a bit of a clearing, pausing to look carefully into the surrounding shadows before stepping out from behind her protector. It was deathly quiet. A sudden movement caught her eye to the right, but when she turned to look, there was nothing. She caught another to her left, but once again, there was nothing. She moved into the center of the clearing and stopped. Crooks suddenly grabbed her ear and pointed.

"Imps!" she squeaked.

At first, Jamie saw nothing but shadows between the trees and darkness behind the roots. Then, like a series of tiny red lights going on almost one at a time, eyes began to peer back at her from the depths.

"What are imps?" she whispered in a squeak that was almost as high as the one Crooks had emitted.

"Horrible nasties. They eat creatures. Like you best. Like all peoples best."

Jamie thought she was going to be violently sick. Was that what had happened to the others? Had they been caught and ea…ea…she couldn't say the word even to herself.

She waited in the center of the clearing, watching the imps advance, terrified to the bone. What would Harriet have done at a moment like this? She thought of the haunted house mystery, remembering when her heroine had been trapped in the basement of the old relic, and shadowy creatures had begun to stalk her. What had Harriet done? And then she remembered. If Crooks hadn't been hanging on for dear life when Jamie began to scream and thrash around with her fists, she would have fallen off.

The noise and threats startled the creatures into pausing momentarily before beginning to creep toward her once more. Each was carrying a bat-shaped piece of wood with spikes poking out at the ends. They were short, stocky creatures with skinny arms and short legs. Their eyes were round and red, and tusks emerged on each side of the mouths extending from the lower jaws. Long, pointed ears like those of a mule seemed to be growing out of the cheek area. Each wore fur leggings and strange headpieces. She hoped that the things sticking up from bands wrapped around their foreheads weren't bones.

Now you would think that someone who was standing in the middle of a clearing, screaming her head off as these creatures crept toward her, would be too terrified to notice all these details, but Jamie had plenty of time. The imps formed a circle and then began to chant as they hopped around her. She couldn't help but take in details about them as they did this, and as a result, the images became permanently etched in her mind. She had nightmares about them for years.

The imps stopped their chanting and circling, and Jamie stopped her screaming. They glanced back and forth at one another, and then suddenly, she knew they were going to attack. She didn't want to die like this. She couldn't die like this. She began to scream again.

The creatures raised their bats in readiness, but before any of them could move, the ground opened up around them and swallowed them whole. Within minutes, there wasn't an imp left in the glade. Jamie stood in shocked silence for several moments, and for the first time in a long time, Crooks was speechless.

Suddenly, from out of the shadows, three figures emerged, laughing and congratulating each other. Two of them looked familiar, but where was the wizard's beard?

"Azmodeus?" she cried with relief. "Yonnus?"

She didn't recognize the third man, but the sight of the wizard and Mikel's father was too much. Her knees gave out, and she landed with a thump on the ground.

"Ah, my girl," said the big man, lumbering over. He placed a hand under each arm and hoisted her back to her feet. "I always seem to be hauling you up from the ground."

"Where did you come from?" Jamie asked, grateful for the fact that Yonnus kept his hands on her to keep her steady.

"The Furies sent us here of all places," replied Azmodeus. "It's a long story which I will relate to at another time. But if it hadn't been for your screams, we would never have found you. Where are the others?"

Jamie shook her head. The tears started up, and her bottom lip trembled so hard she couldn't reply.

"Others trapped by witch," stated Crooks for her.

Azmodeus peered down at the creature clinging to Jamie's ear.

"Why Crooks," he chuckled. "You got caught in an awkward shape for this place."

The pixie pointed at the flame glowing in the wizard's hand. "Magic not work here. Your magic work."

Azmodeus laughed and held out an object that Jamie recognized immediately.

"There are some interesting toys in Earth's dimension, and every time I'm there, I have to collect a few. The sudden disappearance of the imps we owe to Crutchin."

He flicked off the barbeque lighter and stuffed it into a pocket hidden deep within his massive cloak. "Now, what does Crooks mean that the others were trapped by a witch?"

Slowly Jamie told them what had happened, stopping often to sniff or hiccup. "And that's when you rescued us," she ended, finally feeling calmer and more in control.

"She knew where you were because of the crystal," muttered the wizard. "How long has Portia been wearing it?"

"Since the maze on the island," replied Jamie. "She went off by herself and came back with it. But where would the others be? Do you have any idea?" She gestured to the forest surrounding them.

"You know where they'll be if they're still alive, Azmodeus," said the strange man standing beside her.

"This is Crutchin," said the wizard when he saw the question in the girl's eyes. "And this, Crutchin, is Jamie."

The two gave each other a brief smile.

"What does Crutchin mean?" asked Yonnus.

"Hag's Breath," replied Azmodeus, stroking his hairless chin out of habit. "It's the headquarters for the imps and other horrible nits. That's where we'll find the others. Without magic, we are at an extreme disadvantage, but we must try. It's time for our own brilliant minds to provide the answers, my friends. Come."

He strode off into the trees, and the rest followed. With or without magic, Jamie felt much better being with her companions. Even Crooks didn't cling quite so tightly to her ear as they waded through the shadows.

Chapter Thirty-One
Into Hag's Breath

Jamie

Jamie peered through the bushes at the horrifying sight that greeted her in the valley below. Hag's Breath was even more terrifying than its name, and those that dwelled there were something out of a nightmare. Hundreds of hairless creatures resembling monkeys with their long arms and short legs were leaping and shrieking around the edge of a deep steamy pit. Every so often, some of them would stop and point to the trees on the hill and scream with laughter. As she watched, Jamie realized that there were other strange beings interspersed throughout the mob. Some were tall and gangly and covered in dark robes with hoods that hid their faces. Others flitted above like tattered black ghosts with no features whatsoever. What she had thought was a large pile of rocks suddenly began to move, and the only thing that she could relate it to in her mind was some form of a fairy-tale giant. Large ape-like creatures were everywhere.

She couldn't see where her friends were until Crutchin pointed at one of the larger trees with enormous roots wrapped around its trunk, forming a strange-looking room. She realized that it looked like a prison cell and that there were others similar to it in the trees along the side of the hill. Peering at the one closest to her, she spotted Jeremiah sitting on the ground inside with his arms wrapped tightly around his legs. He looked terrified. She assumed that the others were trapped inside the other trees.

"What are those monsters going to do with them?" she whispered, her voice shaking. "Throw them into the pit?"

No one responded, but she was pretty sure they thought the same thing. Yonnus pointed at what appeared to be a waterfall on the opposite side of the valley from where they were crouched.

"Can we get down to the valley floor from behind that?" he asked. "There seems to be a path leading from the pit to behind the falls."

Azmodeus nodded. "That's where their leader, King Kartoudik, dwells. There have been many strange stories about that tyrant, and I have wondered about those I have heard more than twice. There is usually a germ of truth to rumors. Come. I have an idea."

He took them back as they had come and then branched off to the right. They circled the valley and headed toward the waterfall, cautiously watching their steps and keeping as quiet as possible. What happened next made them hurry much faster. The roots suddenly parted in each of the tree cells, and imps carrying sharp, pointed spears and the swords they had confiscated from other victims hustled out the prisoners. Adonis and the young people were pushed together into a group, the little Minotaur trying to remain in the center to avoid the prodding spear points.

"Stop that!" they heard Mikel shout when one of the points nicked his arm. "Keep those things away from us."

The imps simply hooted with laughter and pushed them forward. It didn't take long before Jamie and the other three realized that the destination for the group was definitely the edge of the pit.

"They're going to push us in!" came a cry from Tovan. "We're all going to die."

Melisande and Portia both screamed, and Jamie had to stop herself from doing the same.

"Whatever you're planning," whispered Crutchin to Azmodeus, "you'd better be quick about it. We only have a few minutes to save them from the look of it."

Jamie gasped. If Crooks hadn't stopped her earlier, she would have been down there with the others. She shook her head. She wasn't in a much better situation up here. They didn't have an ounce of magic between them, and there were only five of them, if you counted Crooks, against hundreds of those creatures. Her stomach in knots and her body shaking, Jamie followed the rest behind the falls.

It was quite spectacular, really. The water had been halted in flight and rippled back to her in hundreds of shades of grey, looking almost silver in spots. She found it ironic that there could be such beauty in a horrible place like The Hollows. For a moment, Jamie almost forgot their predicament, so enraptured was she by sight, and then a tug from Yonnus had her moving forward once again. The path that Azmodeus found moved in a zigzag fashion down the face of the rocks behind the falls.

"Why are there no guards?" asked Yonnus in a harsh whisper.

"There are," replied Azmodeus. "In fact, we're actually wandering into a trap."

"What?" protested Yonnus and Crutchin in unison. Jamie opened her mouth, but nothing came out.

The wizard held up his hand. "If the stories about Kartoudik are correct, then all will be well."

"And if they're not?" choked out Crutchin.

All he got in response was a shrug.

They crept down the path behind the ice, one following after the other. At the bottom, the path turned left into a huge cavern dotted with stalagmites and stalactites, the colors of the frozen waterfall. Torches had been placed in sconces that rose from the cavern floor, and slender, dark creatures protected by chest armor, shields and helmets stood in groups facing them, their swords drawn in preparation. In the center on an elevated platform was a huge creature twice the size of Yonnus, its enormous bald head bobbing back and forth like a balloon attached to a mountain of lumpy material.

"The soldiers look like elves," whispered Crutchin.

"They are," replied Azmodeus. "They're the Black Shadows of Gorlin and a nasty bunch at that."

"Who's the bloke up there?" asked Yonnus, gesturing to the creature on the platform.

"Kartoudik."

"Azmodeus," smiled Kartoudik, beaming down on him as a father would on a badly behaved child. "You've been keepin' us waitin'. My spies have bin followin' ya since ya entered the woods."

"I'm aware of that," smiled the wizard, granting the king equal amiability. "We didn't hurry, as a result. We knew that you would not begin the festivities until we got here, so there was no need to rush."

"Ah yes," sighed the king, looking smug. "Our sacrifices to Hag's Breath. It has been a long time since it received such young and pleasing gifts. And now we have all of ya here ta add ta that. What a night."

"Ah, but you might change your mind, Calliotrope," said Azmodeus, looking keenly and intently at the king. "Situations do not always have to remain the same."

The king looked back at him through narrow, beady eyes.

"What ya suggest is nigh impossible," he snapped. "The damage be done."

"You only think it has," replied the wizard calmly. "Chances are strong that the condition can be reversed."

The two verbally sparred back and forth, neither seeming to win the argument. Jamie had no idea what the two were talking about, but Crooks was enthusiastically nodding her head. Before Jamie could ask her what was going on, the tyrant bellowed, and the Gorlin elves raised their swords.

"I grow tired of this," shouted Kartoudik in a sudden rage. "No one tells me what to do here. I am my own master, and I intend to stay the master. Take them."

The elves moved forward, surrounded them and then prodded them forward toward an opening in the waterfall that revealed a path down toward the pit. Kartoudik, or Calliotrope as Azmodeus had called him, rose from his throne and waddled awkwardly down the steps. Crutchin watched him with interest.

"There is something familiar about that movement," he muttered, "but I can't for the moment figure it out."

Before Jamie could ask him what he meant, they were all prodded forward. They had just reached the top of the path, where they had a clear view of their group at the edge of the pit when one of the girls screamed. Mikel's body was lifted above the crowd and tossed toward the pit, where it hung suspended in the air for a moment before it dropped like a stone into the abyss.

"They threw him in," screamed Jamie with such force that Crooks grabbed her hair for support. "They've thrown Mikel into that hole!"

The screaming and laughter grew louder, and several imps grabbed Tovan and began to drag her toward the edge of the pit. Suddenly, the noise died away, fizzling like a fire when water is poured on the burning embers. The imps clutching Tovan let her go and stepped away from her, expressions of shock and horror on their faces. Rising out of the abyss, looking quite composed, was Mikel. When his feet became level with the edge, he moved toward it like someone walking neck-deep in water, eventually landing safely on the ground beside his friends. Horrified, the creatures of Hag's Breath backed away from the group, leaving a large space around them. Azmodeus did not waste the opportunity.

"This is what I came to tell you," he bellowed, his voice carrying easily over the silent mass. "The spirits of the pit are not pleased with you. By rejecting your gift, they have rejected both you and your leader."

Mumblings began, and sly looks were sent in Kartoudik's direction. Azmodeus gestured, and the group by the pit moved as quickly as they could without being obvious up the path toward him.

"Send your guards out to protect you from the mob and then move back into the cavern," Azmodeus instructed the king. "You are going to have to help us whether you like it or not."

Seething with rage, Kartoudik swept back into the cavern with his strange, waddling stride.

"Ya have condemned me ta death," he shouted over his shoulder. "Druet told me I would die if I left The Hollows."

"I can assure you that you will not die," replied Azmodeus. "If you stay here, Calliotrope, they will kill you anyway. Your sacrifice has been rejected."

"Only because ya raised that point," yelled the king. "If ya hadn't brought that to their attention, they would never have thought of it. They are too stupid."

The noise outside the cavern grew in intensity, and Kartoudik looked nervously at the cavern entrance. "Guards," he demanded, appearing to have come to a decision. "Move outside and protect the entrance to this cavern while I prepare myself to talk to me people."

The Gorlin leader stepped forward and eyed both the king and his captives suspiciously. "You are planning to leave and take them with you," he stated flatly.

"How dare ya question me," shouted Kartoudik, taking a threatening step toward the creature. "I intend to show our people why our sacrifice was rejected. I need to consult with the spirits, and then we will send all of these worms to their deaths. Now go! Leave three behind. I canna do everythin' myself."

Still, the guard hesitated.

Kartoudik sucked in his breath. "Go!" he bellowed.

The shout reverberated over and over again throughout the cavern, forcing everyone in the chamber to wince. Several stalactites actually fell off the ceiling, and the elf leader took off at a run taking all his guards with him.

"Come on!" shouted Kartoudik.

He loped off toward the back of the cavern, his top half swinging in opposition to his lower half. The cavern was immense, but eventually, they arrived at the back wall and an entrance to a tunnel. It was obvious that Kartoudik was far too big to get through.

"That will do, Sluggitt," he stated imperiously.

Huge hands lifted to the front of the brown, mud-spattered robes and undid the fastenings. When the masses of material fell to the ground, Jamie didn't know how to respond when she saw what was underneath. A little man with an enormous head was perched on the shoulders of a gigantic, powerfully built creature with a small head. Sluggitt reached up and carefully lifted Kartoudik to the ground. The little man's body came to the wizard's knee, but his head was large enough to bring his total height to the top of Mikel's head.

"So that was it," chuckled Crutchin. "I knew something was not quite right. Had forgotten what it looks like when one person sits on the shoulders of another in order to create one character."

He was the only one who found the situation amusing.

"I can hear a lot of noise at the far end of the cavern," said Jeremiah, looking nervously over his shoulder.

"We must hurry along," warned Azmodeus.

Jamie felt that Kartoudik hadn't heard him or was purposefully ignoring him. "Ya have been a superior help, mate," he said, peering up at the giant. "I couldna have done it without ya. Now go back to yer people. Get out of here before they find ya."

Sluggitt grunted, reached down and patted the top of Kartoudik's head with a huge hand. Grunting again, he set off at a good pace toward a darker section of the cavern.

"You'd better know what yer doin', Azmodeus," Kartoudik muttered. "I know where the door is, but if you can't promise me that I won't die and that ya can change me back, I ain't goin'."

"The fairies can't change him back," said Adonis and for the first time, Kartoudik noticed him. "Melisande's fairies were able to make me smaller, but they weren't able to change me back to my original form."

"They can change Kartoudik," replied the wizard. "Rosamund is a sister to Druet, the witch who changed him into this in the first place. Kartoudik is actually the dwarf, Calliotrope."

"I am that," said the little man, puffing out his chest.

"You're a dwarf?" gasped Jamie.

"Now that's rude," blustered Calliotrope. "Ya don't see me questioning what ya are even though I know you're a human girl. Anyone with a brain can see that I'm a dwarf."

"I apologize," replied Jamie. "It's just that you don't look like the other dwarves I've met."

"More like Mr. Balloon Head," chuckled Jeremiah, who received an instant frown from the wizard but a stifled laugh from Crutchin. Calliotrope ignored them and focused his attention on Jamie.

"And exactly how many have ya met?"

"Well…actually," she stammered. "I haven't really met any. I briefly saw three the other day."

"Jumpin' to conclusions," huffed Calliotrope. "Ain't that just the way."

"Oh, she's always doing that," sneered Portia.

The others quickly agreed with her and turned their backs as if shunning Jamie. None, including Jamie, saw the eyes of Azmodeus dart to the crystal or the furrows that settled between his bushy brows.

"Don't worry," he said to Calliotrope. "Rosamund is equal to her sister, so she will be able to reverse the spell. On the other hand, Adonis, you must be turned back by the goddess Cerce or another god or goddess equal in stature to her."

"Azmodeus," interrupted Yonnus. "I believe it's time to continue. There is a great deal of noise coming this way."

At that, Calliotrope turned and jogged into the tunnel with the others following. They had to keep pace with the little man, which was not all that fast and at several points, Jamie was terrified that his head would bounce off either the walls or the tunnel's ceiling. As it was, it was barely escaping bumps and scrapes as he maneuvered down the dark path. Azmodeus had flipped on his trusty barbeque lighter once again, so at least there was some light.

The tunnel branched off several times in other directions, but Calliotrope seemed to know exactly where he was going. Without warning, it ended, sending the group bursting out through the opening onto a ledge. Ahead of them was a gorge. They were trapped by the noise of their pursuers getting closer.

"How do we get across?" shouted Mikel.

"We don't go across," replied Calliotrope pointing to a spot in the air above the gorge. "That's the door to Aradell."

"We have to jump?" gasped Melisande.

The dwarf nodded.

"We'll fall into that gorge," protested Tovan.

"Are you certain about this?" asked Azmodeus. "And are you willing to go first?"

"Well, it has been a long time," muttered the dwarf. "And I was comin' from the other direction."

"I'll go first," said Crutchin. "Even in The Hollows, I can draw some power from the earth."

Azmodeus nodded, and Crutchin got ready to leap.

"Hurry," whispered Jamie. "They're getting closer."

The angry shouts were indeed getting louder by the second. They were obviously in the tunnels and knew exactly where they were headed.

Crutchin leaped and vanished in a flash of light that crackled and spat like bacon in a pan.

"All of you!" shouted Azmodeus.

Calliotrope jumped, followed by the girls, Jeremiah and Adonis. Yonnus flew through next, and Mikel and the wizard brought up the rear just as the imps shot through the tunnel. The invisible door had brought them all back to Aradell onto a stretch of grass halfway up the mountain from where Brax had dropped them off beside the lake. A short distance away was the cottage that had led them into The Hollows. Before any of them had a chance to breathe a sigh of relief, several things happened at once.

The wizard's missing beard appeared, and before the last hairs had grown into place, he snatched the necklace from Portia and smashed it as hard as he could on the nearest rock. Those affected by its evil magic shook themselves as if coming out of a stupor and looked around. At the same moment, Crutchin gave a startled yelp.

"The dwarf is floating away. Help him, Azmodeus!"

And right on the tail end of the Wildenchin's cry came Tovan's scream. "Mikel! Mikel's been killed!" She pointed and screamed again at the boy who was lying face down in the grass, the shaft of an imp spear embedded in his back.

Melisande called to the fairies and asked them to not only retrieve the floating Calliotrope to ground level but to also ask Rosamund if she could return him to his original form. At the same time, Jeremiah yelled to Tovan to join him beside Mikel. The spear was not in as deep as he had originally feared and after he had pulled it gently out of Mikel's shoulder, he gave her a questioning look.

"But I've only done it once, and I don't know what I did," she whispered. "To top it all off, it was on a dragon, not a human. Remember?"

"Try," he encouraged.

Jamie moved up behind the two of them, frightened for Mikel but at the same time confused by the comments exchanged between Jeremiah and Tovan. What had she been doing with a dragon? Tovan put her hands on either side of the wound, sighed deeply and closed her eyes. Jamie, along with the others, watched in shocked amazement as the sides of the wound drew together, in minutes disappearing altogether, and then Tovan fainted.

"She did that last time too," grinned Jeremiah. "The fainting part, I mean."

"The last time?" gasped Jamie, kneeling down beside Tovan and lifting the girl's head onto her lap. "She's healed other things?"

"Yah," continued the boy. "Except last time, it was a wounded dragon."

Mikel opened his eyes, shook his head and pushed himself up into a sitting position.

"Why are you all looking at me?" he asked.

"I believe it was because you were at death's door," smiled Azmodeus. "Young Tovan was able to save you."

Mikel's hand brushed the spear and he recoiled from it when he looked down and saw the bloody tip.

"It hit me as I jumped," he replied with a shiver. "I remember feeling this horrible pain in my back and then nothing."

Azmodeus sat down on the nearest rock and leaned on his staff.

"So tell me, young ones. How has everyone faired so far?"

He was deluged with six versions of everything they had experienced so far and Jamie had to smile when she saw the amused expressions on the faces of Yonnus and Crutchin. It was so wonderful to have a moment in what appeared to be a safe environment with friends. Too soon, would the dangers begin again.

"Well, well, well," beamed the wizard. "Melisande can call the fairies and Tovan has displayed a talent that hasn't been seen in several hundred years. Anyone else who's made discoveries?"

"Mikel is a magician," replied Jamie. "He saved us from the snakes that wanted to strangle us."

"I've also lost Bandi," shrugged the boy. "He took off to help Jeremiah and never came back."

Azmodeus frowned but did not respond.

"Magic doesn't work on me," continued Jamie. "But that's all."

Portia shook her head angrily. "Well I don't know why I've been dragged along. I can't do anything."

"Don't worry, my dear," smiled Azmodeus. "Your quest is not complete and who knows what might happen before it concludes. Anyone else?"

"Well, I seem to be able to talk to animals," volunteered Jeremiah. "So far I can understand dragons and I think the gryphons."

"Excellent, my boy," smiled the wizard, nodding his head in approval.

"Azmodeus," asked Jamie. "If magic doesn't work in Hag's Breath, how was Mikel able to levitate?"

"But I didn't," replied the boy.

"Well then, what happened?"

Mikel shrugged. "A wall of air rose from the bottom of the pit and pushed me back up. It stayed there until I walked off."

Crutchin grinned from ear to ear. "I considered that to be one of my finest moments."

They all had a laugh over that.

"Well done, my man," chuckled Azmodeus.

Tovan sighed and opened her eyes.

"Welcome back, little healer," grinned Crutchin. "That was certainly something to see."

"Indeed," said Yonnus. "Your group is in good hands…hands…did you get it? I think I made a joke."

"You did, father," chuckled Mikel, winking at the wizard. "I think you're getting better at picking them up. Wouldn't you say so, Azmodeus?"

Yonnus beamed and the old man rolled his eyes. Yonnus had never been good at seeing the humour in anything.

"Well now," continued the wizard. "This is indeed remarkable. The Willik knew that you all had the potential to develop unique and powerful talents and look what's happening."

"We need some help though, Azmodeus," began Melisande, but the wizard put up his hand to stop her.

"I'm sorry, young ones," he said, getting to his feet. "We three dare not stay in case we inadvertently assist you. Please, for all our sakes, do not say another word. We must be off."

"Please Azmodeus," protested Mikel, rushing over to the wizard. "I need to ask you about…you know…Bandi."

He lowered his voice. "Where could he have gone? Do you think Hera has him?"

"Not now, my boy," warned the wizard. "Do not ask another question or make another comment. I was so intrigued by your newly discovered gifts that I allowed us to stay longer than I should have. Come, my friends. This time we travel my way."

Crutchin gave them a quick wave and a grin.

"Be safe," boomed out Yonnus.

Azmodeus grabbed the two men by their elbows and the three vanished.

"Here's your hat. What's your hurry?" muttered Jeremiah, shaking his head.

"I wanted to ask him about the lake monster," sighed Melisande. "I wanted to know if his riddle counted."

Mikel looked over at Tovan who was now standing and brushing herself off.

"Thank you, Tovan," he said sincerely. "Thank you for saving me."

"You're welcome," smiled the girl. "However, you need to know that I haven't a clue as to what I'm doing."

Jeremiah turned to Jamie looking slightly abashed. "I'm sorry about the way I've been treating you. I don't know what came over me."

"I think we all are," said Melisande. "Whatever caused us to behave like that in the first place?"

"Jamie didn't like Portia's necklace," said Tovan. "I remember that part. You didn't have it when you started out, did you?"

"No," replied Portia slowly. "No, I didn't."

"Where did you get it?" asked Jamie. "Who gave it to you?"

"It was …a flying creature," said Portia, a look of wonder crossing her face. "I remember now. It was when I went off by myself into the labyrinth. This creature was there and it gave it to me. I honestly felt that I'd had it all along."

"Beware of gifts," muttered Mikel. "The Willik warned us about that. It must have something to do with either that Spider person or the goddess, Hera. What a horrible pair they are."

"But why didn't it affect Jamie or me?" asked Adonis. "I never changed my feelings toward her."

"Magic doesn't affect me," replied Jamie. "You must be the same."

"Can we take a moment to rest?" sighed Calliotrope, mopping his head with a huge handkerchief.

The rest turned to him in surprise. In all the chaos, they had forgotten all about him.

"You look much better," laughed Jeremiah. "He's right. I don't know about the rest of you, but I'm exhausted. Surely we can take a few minutes. I'm curious, though. Why is your name Calliotrope, but you were called Kartoudik in The Hollows?"

"Ah," replied Calliotrope, looking slightly abashed. "The critters named me. It means Fat Head."

When the others broke out in laughter, he joined in.

"They thought I was an important demon so made me king."

Calliotrope's comments had relieved some of the tension and also made them realize how tired they were. The decision was made to rest where they were and most of them gratefully collapsed on the grass. Mikel lay on his back, sighed and closed his eyes while the rest sat in a group with their faces turned up toward the sun. At one point, Jamie noticed Jeremiah sitting on a tree stump apart from them. He seemed to be studying the piece of parchment that contained the original prophecy. He looked up briefly and moved over to make room for her on the stump.

"What are you doing?" she asked.

"I'm just making sure that we are covering all the bases," he replied. "We just seem to be going from one problem to the next, and we've only solved two riddles. We're running out of time."

Jamie could only nod. Her brother was absolutely right. Nothing seemed to be working out for them. The two sat together quietly, each lost in their own thoughts.

"Come on, you two," called out Tovan, sometime later.

Jeremiah returned the prophecy to his pouch and followed Jamie back to the others. The sun was beginning to sink behind the mountains and it was time to move on. Melisande looked around at the little gully in which they had been resting.

"Maybe we should stay here for the night," she suggested.

Calliotrope shook his head.

"We can't take a chance on running inta Druet or any of her sisters. I think we might have stayed here too long as it is. It will be safer ta camp in the woods up there than ta stay here."

The others agreed. Mikel and Jeremiah took the lead followed by Melisande, Adonis, Tovan and Portia. Jamie and Calliotrope brought up the rear. Of Rosamund's fairies and Crooks, there was no sign. Jamie didn't worry. The little pixie disappeared and showed up when she wanted to, so the girl didn't give her absence another thought.

They trundled up the path, concentrating on the ground in front of them. The light was fading quickly and all of them knew that they would have to set up some form of camp before it got too dark to see.

Suddenly, Mikel stopped. "Danger," he hissed. "I think we are walking into a trap."

Everyone looked around in desperation. Where could they go? What could they do? They moved forward stealthily, straining to hear any sound beyond them in the trees and bushes. They had not gone far when what they were dreading, happened.

The strange soldiers did not rush out to capture them. They were just simply there and knew they could take their time.

Chapter Thirty-Two
Lunchtime In Toria

Spider

It had not been a good day for all concerned and that included Spider and her co-conspirators. She gasped in horror when Azmodeus arrived on the scene and watched with growing anger as he helped them all escape from the trap that Druet had so carefully laid. When he ripped the crystal from around the neck of their ignorant victim and all images became lost to them, she screamed her fury to the skies, causing at least one crack to form in the mountain wall behind the Sanctuary.

Throughout this performance, the three crones had watched her with growing disgust, and Corilla decided to finally put a stop to it. "Really, Spider," she sniffed. "If you ever hope to become a member of our order, you are going to have to learn to behave with more self-control."

Spider stopped to catch her breath. "But did you see?" she panted. "The wizard smashed the jewel. He helped them to escape, and then he smashed the crystal to smithereens. How are we to know what they're going to do now?"

"Oh, the eye has not been destroyed," scoffed Zorna. "It has already repaired itself and is now lying somewhere, waiting for one of us to pick it up."

Druet was pacing back and forth, throwing vile curses at the crystal ball each time she passed it.

"When I see that dwarf again, he'll wish he'd never been born. How dare he go with them! How dare he show them the way out!"

"No matter," said Corilla, calmly clearing off the table and carefully setting the crystal ball on a shelf against the wall. "We

are far from defeated. Azmodeus and his friends are not going to stay in Aradell. They can't. If any of them help the riddle solvers in even the smallest way, the quest will be over."

"But he helped them in that imp place," sputtered the Spider. "Shouldn't that be the end of it then?"

"Oh no," replied Corilla. "The Hollows is not Aradell. If they get caught in that place, then anyone there can help. Unfortunately for them and fortunately for us, very few are willing. However, the other reason is that the cottage and Hag's Forest were not part of the clues. They were traps. Anyone could have helped for that reason alone."

"True," chimed in Zorna. "However, judging from where they have re-entered Aradell, they are still halfway up the mountain, not far from Druet's cottage. At the top of that mountain is the trap that I had arranged if Druet's plan failed. All is well, my dears."

She gave a hearty cackle. "Oh, I wish I could see them trying to answer the next riddle. Once they set foot in this place, they won't be leaving."

"That's what you said about the cottage," whined Spider, "and we won't be able to see what is happening."

She carefully lowered herself into her chair. No matter how hard she tried, she always looked awkward and clumsy when seating herself. So far, the other three had been too wrapped up in their thoughts and plans to have noticed. She hoped it continued.

"Oh, we'll figure that part out later," said Corilla, flicking away that concern with a wave of her hand.

"I have a concern," mumbled Druet, tapping her chin with the tip of an exceptionally long fingernail. "Her highness might start to get agitated with our lack of success. She's been quiet up until now, but something tells me that she won't stay that way for long."

Hera?" queried the Spider. "But she can't. If the other gods and goddesses find out, she'll be punished."

"She has her ways," chuckled Zorna. "Look what she has done already. Remember the snakes? And the doors closing on the

island? None of it was accomplished with the permission of the godly council or whatever that nutty place is called."

"If she's that good," sneered the Spider, "why doesn't she just get rid of the blighters and be done with it? Too difficult for her Highness?"

"Sarcasm is not going to resolve this," harrumphed Corilla. "Hera is waiting for her moment of triumph. So far, it has been just a game to her, with us doing all the plotting and her enjoying the results. Somewhere down the road, she will have her revenge, and the six will meet their ends. Now, there are plans to be made, but first, we eat."

"Food," muttered the Spider. "All you ever do is eat."

"Better to plan our evil mischiefs when tummies are full."

"I have better things to do," she muttered, ambling toward the hallway.

It didn't take her long to get to the entrance to the tunnels. She was angry. Actually, it would have surprised everyone if she hadn't been. It was her normal mood and any other would have shocked the inhabitants of the Sanctuary. It had been two days since she had sent Beak and Claw into the tunnels to find the intruder, and neither had been seen since.

Hauling up the long robe, she tromped down the steps leading to the lower levels and then stopped. Even the smallest bugs inhabiting the horrible place would hear her coming at this rate. Closing her eyes, she mouthed the words to one of her simpler spells and levitated into the air. Opening her eyes once again, she propelled herself forward, drifting down the remaining steps and out over the floor like some ghostly apparition from a nightmare.

Chapter Thirty-Three
A Visit With King Hagmar Sylxidor

Jeremiah

They found themselves surrounded by fierce looking soldiers covered from head to toe in strange leather armour, carrying spears, swords and arrows notched in large bows. One of the soldiers shouted something at them in an unfamiliar language and then cried out something else to his men. They gestured with their weapons and the little group was forced to move with them up a rocky, desolate-looking mountain side covered with scrub brush and few trees. A cold, bitter wind howled around them and Jeremiah did his best to try to shelter Adonis who was only wrapped in a sheet. The trek to their destination took the entire night. Their captors said nothing to them despite Mikel and Melisande's attempts to draw them into a conversation. All they did was urge everyone to move forward with gestures from their spears and swords. They didn't appear to want to harm them, but no one was willing to test that theory by challenging them.

"How did they know we were here?" whispered Tovan to Portia.

"I don't know, but I can guess."

"They look like Mongolian warriors," said Jeremiah to Calliotrope. "You know, the ones that fought for Genghis Khan."

"They kinda are," the dwarf whispered back.

"But Genghis Khan was a real person," said Jamie. "How could he be in Aradell?"

"The person who lives here ain't the real Khan. He thinks he's like the real tyrant and calls himself King Hagmar Sylxidor. Did ya two ever hear the story of Rumplestiltskin?"

"I think so," replied Jamie thoughtfully. "Didn't he give some girl the skill to spin gold out of straw?"

"I didn't," whispered Jeremiah. "That would be a story for girls."

He received looks from both of them that implied he was an idiot.

"You're right, Jamie," said Calliotrope. "He gave her the magic, but she had ta give him her first-born child unless she guessed his name, which she did. Anyway, that lout sitting on his throne in yonder castle be Rumplestiltskin."

"We have to get our next riddle from him," she sighed. "Every challenge seems to be harder than the last."

As they moved further up the mountain, the path began to wind through scraggly-looking trees, and what began as a dirt forest floor changed to gravel at some point during the night and then toward morning, became a cobblestone road. As the sun's weak rays began to peak over the mountains to the east, the exhausted prisoners were allowed to pause on the crest of a hill overlooking a valley beneath. It was an impressive sight despite their dire situation.

A huge walled palace sat on an outcrop of rocks that overlooked a wide gorge. The walls of the gorge were so sheer and straight that they looked as if they'd been sliced down and shaped by a very sharp knife. To attempt to climb down either side would be suicide, and Jeremiah wondered how they would escape. The only place to cross the gorge appeared to be a bridge that went from one side to the other but didn't look entirely safe. It didn't seem to have anything propping it up, and even from this distance, he could see it swinging back and forth in a fairly gusty breeze. He sighed and shook his head. They were in a terrible predicament.

Their captors urged them forward. The road dipped slightly before winding up toward the gates of the wall surrounding the palace, eventually becoming a very narrow pathway with a steep rock wall on one side and the gorge on the other. They had to walk in a single file, and Adonis was the only one who didn't seem to be bothered by the danger of the situation. His size gave him the advantage. The path led them through a set of enormous gates and into the courtyard of the castle grounds, which appeared to house a small village. Jeremiah was so exhausted he barely noticed the silent groups of people coming out of homes and shops to stare at them. Looming up ahead was a large and ominous-looking castle, the sight of which gave him the shivers. Everything about it, from the peaked windows to the pointed turrets, shouted out warnings of danger to him. He was pretty certain Mikel was having the same thoughts. The group was pushed and prodded around to the side of the building, shoved through a small door and down the stairs into a dungeon. The door to one cell clanged open, and they were all unceremoniously shoved inside. They were soundly trapped.

"What have we gotten ourselves into now," mumbled Melisande.

"But we were supposed to come here," groaned Jeremiah, looking around. "The castle was our last image."

"Does that mean that one of you will have to answer the next riddle here?" asked Adonis.

"Probably," mused Jeremiah. "The Sphinx gave us the first riddle and clue. That led to the labyrinth. The lake monster said that his riddle didn't count, and we didn't get a clue from him, so he must have been telling the truth. You guys got one in the labyrinth, and you had to answer a riddle, and the clue you got is this one showing this palace."

"I think we have to answer our next one here then," was Jamie's conclusion.

"But what good will it be if we're prisoners?" asked Adonis.

The question was left hanging in the air.

"I have to sleep," sighed Calliotrope putting his pack on the ground to use as a pillow.

"I can't," mumbled Jeremiah, sitting down on the ground. "I want to be awake when that door opens and see what's coming in."

There were mutters of agreement around him, and the others joined him. After several hours of quiet discussions and listening to Calliotrope's snores, the door to their cell banged open, and they were herded out into the damp hallway by guards dressed in similar uniforms to those who had brought them in. The girls were sent into one washing chamber and the boys into another, and although no one said a word to them, the gestures of the guards were clear. They were to clean themselves up and get themselves presentable, which they all did with a sense of relief. The two groups were shoved together, and the guards prodded them forward to a different set of stairs from the ones they had used to enter the dungeon.

No one spoke as they traveled through many hallways and up even more stairs. The further up they went, the more elaborate and grand the furnishings and the more expensively dressed the people who stopped and silently stared at them as they passed. Jewels glittered, and silks and satins glimmered in shades of every color of the rainbow. The men and women were dressed alike in long robes, with elaborate headpieces sitting on carefully styled hair that hung to the shoulders in a myriad of braids. Men and women alike carried scrolls and fans, the latter being used sparingly as they warily watched the strangers. Not on any level did they see children, which struck Jeremiah as odd. What he did see were many animals similar to the cats found in Earth's dimension, all sitting like statues and staring intensely at them, tails slowly twitching back and forth. It was an eerie sensation that left him feeling uneasy and nervous.

The group arrived at a pair of elaborately carved gold doors that reached from floor to ceiling. The head guard nodded to the two standing stationary at the door, and one abruptly turned and tapped out a coded message to someone on the other side. The two massive panels were pulled open from the inside and entered a monstrous chamber. The walls were covered with horrid pictures of battles that were so graphic in the horrors of war that Jeremiah looked away and kept his eyes focused on the man seated on a throne at the end of the room. Apart from half a dozen guards standing behind him, the massive room was empty. Jeremiah sucked in his breath. Something told him that this encounter would not end well.

The man on the throne was dressed in a similar fashion to those in the outer hall, but his robe and headpiece were much more elaborate. Heavy chains hung around his neck, and considering his short, round shape, Jeremiah was amazed that he could hold them up when he stood.

"Ah, how nice to meet my trespassers," he smiled benignly. "We have been waiting a long time to meet you." He came slowly toward them down the steps from the throne.

"He's dangerous," whispered Mikel. "I can feel it."

The little man stopped in front of them.

"I am Hagmar Sylxidor, king of this land," he stated pompously. "What has brought you to my kingdom?"

Jeremiah furrowed his brow. This man looked more like Santa Claus than the paintings he had seen of Mongol warriors.

"We were just passing through, your majesty," he replied. "If we were trespassing, we apologize as we were unaware of it."

"Why?" demanded the king.

"I beg your pardon?"

"Why were you passing through?"

"We entered the land of Aradell by mistake," he replied smoothly. "We have been trying to find our way out for a few days now."

The others kept their faces as expressionless as possible. Unfortunately, the king was not to be taken in so easily. He stared at each of them in turn and then returned to his throne. When he seated himself comfortably, he glared down at them for a moment more and then spoke.

"Word has reached me that a group made up mainly of children has been traveling through the land of Aradell seeking riddles and pictures. You appear to be that group."

"I'm certain…" began Jeremiah, but he was not allowed to finish.

"Quiet!" bellowed the little man. "The group is also traveling with a small Minotaur and a dwarf. I see both with you. You are on a quest. Your task is to solve six riddles, and you have only solved half of them."

"Now, how had he known that?" muttered Melisande.

"And why did he say half?" hissed Mikel. "We've only answered two riddles."

"Yes," stated Jamie, rather defiantly. She placed her hands on her hips for emphasis. "We are those people, as you well know, and you are obliged to give us a riddle and an image."

"Really," drawled the little man. "What if I don't?"

"You must, or Hera won't like it."

The king gave a bit of a start. He knew exactly what Hera would do.

"Fine," he snarled and then a sly smile crossed his features. "What is my real name?"

"That is not a riddle," scoffed Jamie, "and your real name is Rumplestiltskin."

King Hagmar Sylxidor turned every shade of red known to the skin, leaped out of his chair and stomped up and down in fierce, uncontrolled rage.

"How did you know?" he shouted. "How did you know?"

"Everybody knows," replied Jamie boldly. "Now, ask your riddle."

The King clambered back up onto his throne. His little, beady eyes moved back and forth, his gaze resting briefly on each of his victim's faces. An expression of pure malicious evil took over his face. Jeremiah instantly rejected the Santa Clause comparison.

"Who is going to answer?" he asked in an oily voice.

He looked intently at each one and then pointed at Jeremiah. "I think that this one should be yours."

Jeremiah opened his mouth to speak, but nothing came out.

"Oh, don't try to thank me," he sneered. "I knew that you were the one most anxious to respond. Now what is it? I remembered it just a moment ago. Close your mouth, boy. You look like a drowning fish."

Jeremiah closed his mouth so hard that he rattled his teeth.

"Did you know that fish can drown?" the king carried on as if they were all having a casual afternoon chat. "They drown in air. Isn't it amazing that we drown in their environment, and they drown in ours? I hope you never experience drowning. It's a nasty business. Now for the riddle."

Jeremiah's knees weren't the only ones shaking.

My thunder comes before lightning. My lightning comes before clouds.
My rain dries all the land it touches. What am I?

The silence that existed between them seemed to go on and on. Jeremiah kept shaking his head, a look of complete puzzlement his only expression. He tried to remember Portia's explanation of how she had figured out the riddle in the maze, but it didn't seem to make sense in this situation. She had connected the "heart" with the heartless Sphinx, the "old age" response with the sea serpent's talk of ways to die and the "eye" answer with no eyes in the turtles. He looked frantically around for a clue for this one, aware of the king's evil smirk, which was growing with the satisfaction of knowing that he had probably won. There had to be something that would help somewhere in this room…something that was the opposite.

"You know, dear boy," drawled Hagmar. "This is a game of skill, not endurance. Answer the riddle."

"Think, Jeremiah, think," pleaded a desperate Jamie.

"Can we help him?" asked Portia.

Suddenly Jeremiah's frantic gaze rested on one of the horrific war paintings on the wall. It showed soldiers being chased and slain by invaders, but the image behind them caught his attention. He thought of the descriptions provided in the riddle. It was opposite the mountain they were on. It fit, but was he right?

"The answer is a 'volcano,'" he offered tentatively, his fingers crossed behind his back.

Without saying a word in response, the King took a coin from his pocket and flipped it toward the boy. Jeremiah caught it and stuffed it safely into his pouch without looking at it, his body beginning to shake with the relief of being right.

"Now, my friends," smiled the King. "You can't possibly think that I would now release you to continue your quest, do you? I have grown quite attached to all of you. You will remain here as my guests, and each day, one of you will be sent to amuse me."

He laughed heartily and then suddenly lurched forward in his chair, pointing at Adonis.

"Beginning with you," he roared. "Grab him."

Before any of them had a chance to respond, the little Minotaur was lifted off his feet by two of the guards that had brought them into the chamber.

"Take him away," instructed the King. "Put him in my special waiting room. We will find out tomorrow just how good a Minotaur is at defending itself from one of my pets. Unfortunately, you are so small. The battle will only be a brief one, I'm afraid."

Adonis was carried kicking and yelling from the room while his friends loudly protested and struggled to reach him despite the grip of their captors.

"Return the peasants to their cells," commanded the King, ignoring their cries. "I am bored with them for the moment."

The guards hustled them out of the chamber and back down the route they had taken a short time before. By the time they were pushed back into their cell, most of the fight had left them.

"What are we going to do?" sniffed Melisande, her cheeks wet with tears. "They're going to kill Adonis tomorrow and then one of us each day after that. Oh, the poor little thing. He must be terrified."

Jeremiah began to examine the door and the hinges that held it to the rock wall.

Tovan shook her head.

"I don't think we're going to find these as easy to remove as those on the wagon."

"I don't care," he grumbled. "There has to be some way out of here."

He wandered restlessly around the cell, poking his fingers into nooks and crannies in search of a weak spot. At the back of the cell, he stopped and bent down to peer at something.

"What have you found?" asked Jamie.

"I don't know, but there appears to be a rectangular shape back here that resembles a small door. Come and look."

The others scrambled to their feet and rushed over.

"I see it," said Portia. "Maybe if we dig away at the crack, we'll be able to push this section out."

They searched the chamber for bits of rock that could be used to try and dig around the edge, but after a lengthy amount of time, they had made little to no progress.

"It's no use," sighed Tovan, sitting back on her heels. "It doesn't want to give at all. Maybe it isn't a door. Maybe it's just the frantic scrapings of others who have occupied this space."

"You might be right," muttered Melisande. "I don't think that we've made even the tiniest indent."

Without warning, their cell door opened, and a grinning Mikel gestured to them to come out. One by one, they crept cautiously through the door into the outer hallway. The guards were completely unaware of what was happening. All three were lying on the floor with their legs stretched out in front of them and their backs propped up against the wall. Contented snores filled the air. A young girl dressed in the elaborate clothing they had seen in the upper levels of the castle was standing quietly in front of them, her hands clasped neatly in front of her.

"What happened to them?" whispered Melisande, gesturing to the guards.

"Just a little trick I've learned to do recently," chuckled Mikel.

"How did you get out of the cell without us seeing you?" demanded Portia.

Mikel turned his back on her refusing to answer, causing Jeremiah to shake his head. Who needed enemies when you had Mikel and Portia around?

"Don't talk," whispered the girl. "Follow me quickly."

She led them in the opposite direction from the door they had used to enter the dungeon and stopped in front of a curtain at the end of the hall. Pulling it aside, a hallway was revealed behind, and they crept through. The girl waited until the last one had entered, then drew the curtain back into position, hiding the hallway entrance.

"Now we can talk," smiled the girl. "My name is Ping, and I have been sent to help you."

"By whom?" asked Mikel.

"It is not important," replied Ping. "My job is to get you as close to the bridge as possible."

Portia emitted a sharp gasp. "Are you expecting us to cross that thing?" she asked.

Jeremiah pulled out the coin he had received from the King. On the one side of the coin was a path leading from the bridge to what appeared to be a cluster of village houses.

"According to this, we have to do just that. Our next spot for a riddle is on the other side. We have to head for a cluster of houses."

"Great," muttered Portia. "I wouldn't mind it so much if I thought something was holding that bridge up."

For some reason, Jamie found the remark funny and grinned back at Portia.

"Maybe we should ask Gamma for some fairy wings," she chuckled.

"Are you kidding?" replied Portia. "We'd all need a hundred pairs."

The picture of them covered in fairy wings struck Portia and Jamie funny at the same time. Both began to giggle, and it took the threats of the others to make them stop finally.

"If we get caught because of you two," scowled Jeremiah, "I will never let you forget it. Be quiet, both of you."

Jamie grinned back at Portia, who responded with a roll of her eyes and a merry smirk. Jeremiah was surprised by Portia's reaction. This was definitely a first.

"How are we going to find Adonis?" asked Melisande. "I, for one, am not leaving without him."

Ping looked at her, the expression on her face one of sorrow.

"I am sorry, but rescuing him is impossible. He's in the waiting room, in a cage on an island in the middle of a moat. There are great beasts that guard the cage and creatures of terrible horror that swim in the water. The bridge across the moat can only be lowered by knowing the secret word, and my father changes that word every day. Only he knows the charm to subdue the beasts."

"Your father?" choked Tovan.

"Unfortunately, yes," replied the girl in a small voice. "I am one of many children."

"But where are the rest of the children?" asked Jamie. "I didn't see any in the castle."

Ping looked slightly sheepish as she responded. "The children are kept as cats until they reach their sixteenth year. In that way, they are not a burden. They can look after themselves, and the adults need not have to bother with them until they are trainable."

Jeremiah was speechless. All those cat creatures he had seen had been children?

"What a horrible practice," muttered Melisande. "Children should be cared for and loved."

"It depends on your perspective," replied Ping casually. "Our young people are most independent when they change and do not need to rely on others to make responsible decisions."

"Is it possible to get Adonis out of there?" asked Jeremiah, trying to get over the image of himself as a cat.

"Nothing is impossible," said Mikel, his eyes flashing, the intensity of his comment instantly bringing Jeremiah back from his musings. "Adonis will not be left behind. Can you show us where this waiting room is?"

Ping nodded but looked far from happy.

"Come along then but do not expect to rescue him. He is doomed, and nothing can save him."

She led them down the hall and into a new tunnel.

"We just seem to go from one mess to another," muttered Portia.

Tovan nodded. "Even if we figure out a way to rescue Adonis, we're still stuck on this side of the gorge."

Despite Ping's description of the waiting room, which frightened them to their toes, it was nothing like the reality of the situation that greeted them a short time later.

"Oh, mercy," whispered Jeremiah. No one could have summed it up better.

"Lions and tigers," whispered Mikkel. "What are we going to do against those?"

"And crocodiles in the moat," replied Jamie. "We don't have hope."

"Is that what they're called?" asked Melisande. "I've never seen creatures like that. They appear to be quite horrible."

"And dangerous," added Mikel.

They were peering through an opening in the tunnel wall into an enormous cavern. An island sat in the center with a crocodile-infested moat surrounding it. The island was high enough that the creatures couldn't climb up the sheer cliff-shaped sides, and their only purpose appeared to be to guard the moat. The lions and tigers roamed the island's surface with the cage holding Adonis attached to the roof, just high enough above them to be safe for the moment. The cats, however, were very aware of him, pacing restlessly beneath and constantly glancing up at what they soon hoped would be a meal.

"This ain't going to be easy," mumbled Calliotrope. "But we can't leave him where he is."

"What about following the tunnel behind us?" asked Tovan.

"What tunnel?" asked Jeremiah, looking around.

"That one," she said, pointing to a small opening in the wall that could easily have been excused as a shadow.

"I didn't even see that," said Jeremiah. "It's worth a try. Maybe it will take us closer to Adonis."

The rest agreed. Following one after the other, they climbed up the slanting slope of the second tunnel. Ping remained standing by the window opening, slowly shaking her head.

Within a short distance, the path veered to the right into a little grotto lit by lights from the chamber below. In the floor was a hole right above the Minotaur's cage.

"Well done, Tovan," said Melisande. "Look where it led us."

It made sense that no one would be foolish enough to cross a bridge and put a captive into a cage surrounded by ferocious beasts. They had put him into the metal structure and lowered him into the cavern.

The cats below paced back and forth, hungrily eyeing the cage.

"Hold my belt," said Jeremiah, lowering himself onto his stomach and crawling toward the hole. "I hope he doesn't weigh more than he looks."

Mikel lay down on his stomach and grasped Jeremiah's belt.

"Come on, everyone, grab on," he said. "Form a chain."

One at a time, they got down on their knees, one behind the other and grasped the belt of the person in front of them.

"Okay," hissed Jeremiah from the front, "Everyone slowly moves back and pulls."

Grunting, puffing and tugging with all their might, hoping that all their belts would hold, they pulled the cage slowly up through the hole in the ceiling. Tugging the heavy structure onto the solid ground, Adonis was finally out of the grotto. As quickly as they could, they set to work releasing him. The little Minotaur was sitting in the center of the cage, his arms covering his head, his shoulders shaking.

"Adonis," whispered Melisande. "It's us. Look at me. Come on. We have to get you out of this cage."

At the sound of the familiar voice, the little creature looked up, his face contorted in grief and covered with tears. Not many people have ever met a Minotaur, but to see the little face with such an expression of despair would have softened even the hardest of hearts. He had the same effect on each group member, and willing hands reached forward to either hold the cage to balance it or wrench the doors open.

"Come on, buddy," said Jeremiah reaching in. "You're safe now."

"Well, as safe as we all are," muttered Mikel.

Adonis clambered awkwardly out of the cage, wiping his face with the backs of his clawed hands.

"I wasn't really worried," he sniffed heroically. "I knew that Melisande would find me."

He gazed up at the girl with a look of adoration. Melisande's eyes widened in surprise, and several of the others chuckled.

"Why, Melisande," grinned Jamie. "I believe that you have an admirer."

The girl scowled at her, but that didn't erase any amused expressions.

They moved back into the tunnel, shocking Ping with their success.

"Ping," said Jeremiah turning to their rescuer. "Where do we go now?"

She stared at him in amazement for a moment and then, raising a delicate hand, gestured all of them to follow her. She continued down the tunnel, and the rest followed, Adonis keeping close to Melisande. Ping led them down winding slopes that, at times, seemed to crisscross one another. Had they been alone, they probably would have become hopelessly lost in a very short time, but the girl seemed to know exactly where she was going. They emerged into a room that was no longer part of the tunnel. In fact, it appeared to be an old shack.

"We're in the village close to the wall," said Mikel, peering out the window. "In fact, I can see the bridge spanning the gorge. Didn't you say we had to cross that, Jeremiah?"

The other boy gave a start. That was the first time Mikel had addressed him directly without yelling or being sarcastic.

"Right," he replied. "Although I'm not sure how."

"This is as far as I can bring you," said Ping. "If my father finds out what I have done, he will deal harshly with me."

"Why did you help us?" asked Tovan.

"It was my destiny," replied Ping, her cheeks coloring slightly. "I have been waiting for you since my dream several years ago."

"A dream?" questioned Portia. "You helped us because of a dream. Why that's the s...."

Melisande elbowed her in the ribs, and whatever she was going to say ended in a "whoof."

"Well, whatever the reason," said Tovan, "we are very much in your debt. We will never be able to thank you enough. Neither will the rest of the people of Draukenberg if our quest is successful."

The girl nodded and bowed slightly. "Before I go," Ping replied, "you must consider how to cross the bridge carefully. A wicked goddess lives on the other side of the chasm. She has a habit of changing anyone who disagrees with her into different kinds of animals, so none of our people are allowed to cross to that side. Not that they would want to go. Our gates are never open, and every time people or animals are seen crossing from the opposite side, our guards chase them back with arrows. My father thinks that they are enchanted beings, and if he lets them in, they'll enchant all of us as well. Be very careful."

"What is the name of the goddess?" asked Adonis, his voice shaking.

"Cerce," she replied.

"No!" he bellowed.

"Be quiet," warned Ping. "Someone will hear us."

Jeremiah put a hand over the Minotaur's mouth.

"Isn't that the goddess that turned Adonis into a Minotaur?" asked Tovan.

Adonis nodded vigorously despite Jeremiah's attempts to hold him.

"I must go," said Ping. "I wish you much luck." She turned and was gone.

"You didn't have to do that," snapped Portia, glaring at Melisande while still holding her side.

"What?" asked the girl, who had already forgotten what she had done.

"That elbow to my stomach. I was only going to say that that was special…having that dream."

"No, you weren't," replied Melisande quite matter-of-factly. "Now, how are we going to cross that bridge?"

Calliotrope walked over to the window and looked up. From there, they had an excellent view of the guard lookout above the bridge. Jeremiah followed his gaze. As they watched, the guard turned from the bridge and marched to the back of the round turret to look out over the city. He paused for several moments and then marched back to the front. A short time later, he marched back to overlook the town and, after several minutes, returned to view the bridge. This back-and-forth motion was non-stop.

"I have it," grinned Jeremiah.

"What?" asked several at once.

Except for Adonis, who sat moodily in the corner, the rest moved closer in order to hear.

"I'll see if I can get this right. There once were two countries separated by a bridge that spanned a chasm half a mile across – something like this one. A woman wanted to escape from one country and get to the other, but if she were caught escaping from the country she was in, she would be shot. People coming across the bridge toward her country were not shot at but simply told to go back."

"What were they shot with?" asked Melisande.

"Guns," replied Jeremiah. "You don't have them here, thank goodness. By watching, she discovered that it took the guard three minutes to get around his tour. She would be able to make it halfway across the bridge by that time, and then when the guard reappeared, she would wave at him as if she were coming from the other side. The guard would tell her to go back, and she could walk off the bridge to the other country."

"Brilliant," grinned Mikel.

"But how are we going to get from here to the gate on this side?" asked Portia. "People are going to notice that we look different."

"Not if we put these on," said Tovan, pointing to an assortment of old clothes piled in the corner. "We don't have to go far to get to the bridge."

There were enough dirty tunic-like garments for the girls that none of them were too excited to handle, let alone put on, and battered headpieces that shielded their different features from view. Jeremiah and Mikel found some old work jackets and hats, and Calliotrope, much to his disgust, ended up pulling on a small jerkin and headpiece that resembled a bonnet. With his beard tucked into the jacket, he looked like an exceptionally short, ugly person who most people would not want to look at twice. At least, they all hoped that no one would. Adonis was a problem until Melisande got the idea to swaddle him in an old blanket with his head covered, and Mikel, who Jeremiah had to agree was the strongest, would carry him like a bundle of rags.

"We'd better go," warned Jeremiah, who'd been watching by the window. "I think they've discovered that we've escaped. Guards are beginning to appear from everywhere. It won't be long before they check here."

"Here comes the tricky part," sighed Calliotrope as he opened the door and stepped out. The rest followed him out into the compound.

"Walk slowly," whispered Jamie. "We don't want to draw attention to ourselves."

"Too late," hissed Portia.

Pounding down the square toward them was a regiment of at least a dozen soldiers. They stood their ground waiting for the inevitable.

Chapter Thirty-Four
Never Eat Strange Food

Petre

It had been so long since Petre had eaten that he'd almost forgotten how food tasted. The table that he had been asked to sit at was covered with all kinds of delicious-looking food, and after getting a reassuring nod from Razna, he began to eat. He knew he was making a pig of himself, but he couldn't help it. He was ravenous.

The Furies watched him with interest, and after a few minutes of stuffing everything that he could into his mouth, he realized that they were not eating.

"Oh, dear boy," laughed Rethnie. "We stopped eating eons ago, although I must admit, you seem to be enjoying it so much, I'm tempted to try it once again."

Petre put the fruit back on the plate and wiped his face with his sleeve. His father would be ashamed of him if he could see him now. Picking it up, he continued at a slower, more polite pace.

"You said that Azmodeus was just using me," he said between bites. "What did you mean by that?"

"Do you honestly not know why he allows you to hang about?" asked Rindelle.

"I thought he liked me," was the cautious reply.

The Furies went into shrieks of laughter. Petre shuddered. Their appearances had changed but not the horrible, shrill sounds of their laughter.

"Oh my, that was a good one," said Razna, wiping fake tears from her eyes. "No, my dear. You are the sacrifice."

"For what?" he asked.

"You have seen what is happening to the trees, have you not?"

"Yes."

"And you know it's because the trolls, the tree guardians, have left their tasks in order to be the servants of Spider."

The boy nodded.

"Do you know why that happened?"

Petre gave her a thoughtful look.

"It's because she destroyed the Laurel Tree inside the mountain."

"Good," said Rethnie. "At least we don't need to explain that. But do you know how to bring the tree back to life, boy?"

"We need the seed that we are searching for."

"Yes," said Rindelle. "But do you know what must happen to that seed in order for it to come back to life?"

The food in Petre's stomach was beginning to feel like lead, and he was getting angry. The Furies were thoroughly enjoying his lack of understanding of this whole issue, and the constant questioning was beginning to get on his nerves.

"No," he snapped. "Give me some answers. Now. I'm tired of these silly games. If you have something to say, then say it."

"Very well," said Razna, sitting back in her chair, a smug expression on her face. "An innocent, a child, must willingly place the seed inside the tree along with himself or herself. They must give up their own life and become one with the tree."

Peter's face lost its color as he stared back at her.

"And that child is supposed to be me?" he asked shakily.

"Oh yes," replied Rethnie. "You have been marked as the chosen one. It is you who has to do this, and Azmodeus knew that. That's why he made sure you were with him at all times. It certainly wasn't because he liked you."

Petre pushed himself back from the table and stood up. "That's not true," he shouted. "You are making this up...all of it!"

The three shook their heads.

"We have no reason to do such a thing," smirked Razna. "Often, the truth is far more interesting than fiction. Humans are such ridiculous creatures that just watching their antics is amusement enough."

Petre couldn't listen to it anymore. He ran to the door of the temple and didn't stop until he was at the pool on the other side of the grotto. He sat down heavily on the bench in front of it. How could Azmodeus have done this to him? Why had he never told him about his horrible role in all of this? The old wizard had expected him to simply throw his life away without any explanation?

The longer he sat, the angrier Petre became. If anyone thought he was going to do this, they were idiots. He was not going to throw his life away just to save some stupid old trees, and no one was going to convince him to do otherwise. The next time he saw Azmodeus, he was going to tell him exactly what he thought of him. Another more satisfying thought struck him. If he were a prisoner of the Furies, then he wasn't going to be available to do this silly thing. He wouldn't have to confront Azmodeus about anything. Part of him was angry that the wizard would never know how he felt, but the other was relieved that he had an excuse. Good. He'd stay right where he was and not worry about leaping into a tree to save the world.

Slowly, the anger began to seep out of him and he slumped forward, staring into the water. He wished he were back in the Glockamar and that none of this had ever happened. A small feeling of guilt niggled at him. He knew that his friends were in Aradell, trying desperately to find and solve Hera's riddles. Some of them might be hurt or dead. Maybe he was being selfish. No. They at least had a chance to get through and live, whereas he, on the other hand, was a walking dead man. He sat up straighter and shook his head. Any of them would have felt the same in his place.

For the next few hours or days, he was never too certain how much time went by during his stay with the Furies. All he seemed to do was eat and sleep. He fell asleep on the bench and woke up in a bed sometime later with the three sisters hovering over him. It could have been his imagination, but they seemed to be chanting. He woke up starving, wolfed down the food they gave him and then promptly fell asleep. Each time he ate, he fell asleep, and each time he woke up, the sisters were hovering and chanting. The strange thing was that instead of feeling full and rested, he felt as though he were growing weaker. It was becoming more of an effort for him to get off the bed, and he couldn't get enough food when he was awake. He was starving.

If it hadn't been for the Furies disappearing at one point, convinced that their prisoner was too weak to move, Petre might have literally wasted away to nothing. As it was, he woke to discover that he was alone. Pulling himself off the bed, he stumbled into the garden and moved on, shaking legs toward the table covered with food.

Don't eat the food.

He looked groggily around for the speaker, but seeing no one, continued on toward the table, convinced that his befuddled mind was hearing things.

Don't eat the food. It will make you sleep.

Again he looked around, but the grotto was empty.

Drink the water from the pool.

Changing direction, he shuffled over to the pool closest to the table and, using his hands as a cup, gulped down as much water as he could. He instantly felt more alert than he had in quite a while, and to his amazement, the ravenous hunger that had engulfed him for so long disappeared.

Follow the singing.

At first, he couldn't hear it. But gradually, a strange, high-pitched melody that seemed to be a combination of several voices began to seep into his overtaxed brain. He stood up and followed the unusual sound to the entrance of a tunnel at the back of the grotto. The closer he got to it, the more he could make out the melody, but the words were foreign to him. For a moment, he stopped and peered down the tunnel that seemed to be lit from within the rock walls. Taking a deep breath and worried that he was stepping from the frying pan into the fire, he entered the tunnel.

It led in a straight line to another smaller cavern deeper into the mountain. In the center of the space sat three women, who he knew immediately were not the Furies. One sat spinning at a loom, another appeared to be cutting off different lengths of thread from a larger skein, and a third was sitting beside the spinner, snipping threads with a golden pair of scissors. They also ranged in age. One was quite young, one middle-aged, and the third was ancient.

"Hello, Petre," said the youngest one, although neither she nor the other two looked up at him. Their eyes never left their work.

"Hello," he replied. "May I ask who I am addressing?"

"Of course, you may, but first, how did you come into the clutch of the Furies?" asked the middle-aged woman.

"They brought me here," he said. "Razna wanted to tell me about my fate."

"Razna?" smirked the ancient crone. "What are they calling themselves now?"

"Why Razna, Rethnie and Rindelle."

The three chuckled softly but still did not look up from their work.

"What a silly threesome," smiled the youngest. "Their real names are Alecto, Tisiphone and Magaera, but they like to change their names as often as their appearances."

They continued to work in silence.

"But who are you?" asked Petre as the silence lengthened.

"We are the Fates," replied one. "I am Clotho, the one beside me is Lachesis, and the third is Atropos. We are the ones who record the journeys of all creatures through their long or short lives. We are also the ones who rescued you. Your destiny is not to die in the chamber of the Furies."

"If you spin the threads," said Petre, "then everything we do is decided upon by you."

The three chuckled again.

"Oh no," replied Clotho. "We can weave a general pattern, but it isn't finished until individuals choose their own paths. We can predict, however, what those paths will be."

"Can you predict mine?" asked Petre, not knowing if he really wanted to hear the answer.

"Most of it," replied Lachesis.

"Can you tell me?"

"Of course not," snorted Atropos. "It is, however, quite a special one. Some are born with unique tasks to perform, and you are one of those. Had we not rescued you from those essence-sucking creatures back there, you wouldn't have survived long enough to make the choice that's written into your destiny."

"Essence sucking?" he quaked.

"They suck the essence of youth out of young ones they catch," explained Lachesis. "In that way, they can change their shapes to that of young beauties instead of what they really are…old crones."

Petre shivered.

"Why is my destiny special?" he asked, praying they wouldn't say that he had to leap into a tree.

For the first time, the three stopped their work and looked at him. Petre took a sudden step backward. All three had eyes as white as the shiny stones he collected from rivers. He had difficulty focusing on any one face, so horrifying did their appearances become.

"Look into your heart," they said in unison.

"Wh…what am I to see?" he stammered. "I'm not magical like my friends. I have nothing to offer."

"Petre," said Atropos. "True magic resides in the soul and in the heart. That is where you make choices, and it is the choices you make that determine the path of your thread, not magical skills that are obvious to others. Not spells cast by those who can. The magic of choices is making them for the sake of others and not for the sake of the self."

The three went back to work.

"But how can I make choices if I am a prisoner of the Furies?"

Clotho laughed.

"When you made the choice to enter our tunnel, the Furies lost control over you. You are free to decide your own fate once again."

"But where should I go?" he asked.

"Follow the ants. Beware of the nymphs at Ornoaka, and watch for the red bugs of the sky. They will help. Now make your choice. You can go back to the Furies or follow the ants. Life is one constant series of choices."

"Thank you," replied the boy. "May I ask another question?"

"You may ask," said Lachesis, "but we may not answer."

"I have friends on a quest in Aradell. Are they alright?"

"I still weave their threads," replied Clotho. "But there is tension on them. They are in danger."

"Thank you again," replied Petre.

He felt numb. They were not safe, but at least they were still alive. Were they being faced with choices as horrific as the one facing him? He would have to give all of this some deep thought.

The three women nodded in response but did not look up from their work. Petre swallowed. Choices. The magic was in making choices for the other, not for the self. He spotted the ants leading further along the tunnel in the opposite direction from the grotto of the Furies, and Petre made his choice. He had no intentions of having anything further to do with the Furies and so turned and followed the ants. They led him to the end of the tunnel, and to his amazement, he found himself beyond The Hollows and into the sunshine with brilliant color everywhere. He had no intentions of trying to find Azmodeus or the others. He still burned with an intense anger and a feeling of betrayal. What he wanted more than anything was to return to his home and try to find his father.

Petre knew that they had flown in a southwest direction when they had left Donagal. Originally, he had been flown from north to south to reach the elfin city, so he deduced that if he headed in a northwest direction, he'd eventually come to his home. Full of determination and purpose, he started off. The sun was high in the sky, so he figured that he had several hours of travel time before he would have to find someplace to spend the night. A path wound down from the mountain into the valley beneath, and he followed it despite thoughts that often, the obvious things seemed to lead into traps outside his mountain home.

It didn't take him long to reach the valley floor. He followed the path into a grove of trees and tried to ignore the fact that half of them were beginning to show signs of dying.

"I can't be the only one who can save them," he muttered under his breath. "I just can't be…and not that way. Not by throwing myself into a tree."

He straightened his shoulders and determinedly followed the path, refusing to look left or right. The path met up with a river and then ran parallel with it for some distance. Petre found the rushing water restful and soothing to his agitated nerves. The streams inside the valley were much narrower and more tranquil. They didn't rush along like this one, which seemed to have a life of its own. As he walked along, he thought about the message that Clotho had given him. He had to be aware of the nymphs, whatever they were, at Ornoaka, wherever that was, and to watch for red bugs in the sky that would help. He also had to look into his heart. Each time he tried to do that, he thought of the trees, and guilt nagged at his conscience.

"No one can expect me to kill myself in order to save trees," he muttered again. "That is just not fair."

He gradually became aware of a soft thundering sound which seemed to grow louder the further on that he walked. Sometime later, Petre came to the top of a magnificent waterfall that roared over the edge of a cliff and disappeared in a cloud of mist and spray into another valley far below. He had never seen water cascading down a mountainside before, and the magnificent sight left him speechless. The sound was overwhelming, and he could barely hear himself think. Engulfed with sheer joy, he yelled at the top of his lungs but could hear nothing but the thunder of water roaring over the cliff. It was as if his voice had been swallowed up and had become part of the wild sound of the water.

The path also ended at this point, and when Petre looked around, he realized that he was going to have to cross the river. He had seen a shallower part further upstream and reluctantly decided to backtrack to the spot. With luck, he would find a way to climb down into this second valley and see the water from below. He couldn't imagine what the falls would look like from that angle, but the thought excited him.

He turned and walked swiftly back up the path to the place he had noticed earlier. There was a gravel shoal that crossed the river about halfway and only looked ankle-deep. From there, he could see rocks poking out, and if he were careful, he would be able to jump from one to the other to reach the opposite bank.

Peter pulled off his boots and tucked them into his belt. Stepping gingerly into the water, he gasped at the cold and then cautiously placed one foot ahead of the other. As he moved out toward the center, he could feel the tug of the flow and, several times, almost lost his balance. Forcing himself to slow down, he made sure that each foot was firmly planted before lifting the other off the gravel bottom. He was almost at the end of the shoal and about to jump onto one of the rocks when he felt his hair pulled.

He stopped and tried to look around.

"Only fools try to cross this river," hissed a harsh little voice in his ear.

He tried to twist the other way to see who was speaking. His hair was yanked again, and something pushed him from behind.

"Don't do that!" he snapped.

"Silly little boy," came a voice in his other ear. "Didn't anyone warn you about crossing the Ornoaka?"

Peter groaned. Well, now he knew what the Ornoaka was, and from where he stood, he was at a definite disadvantage.

Suddenly the air around him was full of chirping little creatures with wings. They pulled at his hair and clothes, pushed him from behind and tugged at his legs. His arms began to windmill as he tried to keep his balance, but the little creatures were too much for him. He plummeted into the water. As he fell, he reached out blindly for the closest rock and clung onto it while the creatures chattered above him. Several dove down, pinching his hands and pulling at his fingers.

"Leave me alone," he tried to shout, but it came out as a watery sputter.

These had to be the nymphs that Clotho had warned him about. She could at least have told him what they looked like, but then again, he hadn't spotted anything when he had started across. They had just appeared. More of the creatures attacked, and his hands were losing their grip on the rock. The drag of the water was pulling at the rest of his body. Petre panicked. How was he to get out of this mess in one piece?

From out of nowhere, strange red bugs appeared. They went after the nymphs, flying at their faces and getting tangled in their wings. More than one nymph ended up in the water and, squealing angrily, drifted away. Their arrival sent the rest of the nymphs flying quickly toward the shores on either side of the river, and Petre sighed with relief. The little bugs were the strangest things he had ever seen, with their bright red bodies covered with black circles. They hovered above him as if to say that all was well. He raised a hand to thank them, realizing instantly that he had made a mistake. The water caught him, yanked him from the rock and sent him tumbling head over heels down the stream, caught in the current.

He righted himself at one point and tried to swim to the closest shore, but his clothes weighed him down. Keeping his head above water was proving to be more and more difficult, and then he heard it…the roar of the falls!

"Help!" he shouted, ending up with a mouthful of water.

His head was pulled under, and he tried to struggle back to the surface. It was too much. He didn't have the strength, and his lungs began to burn from lack of air. His last thought as he was swept over the falls was whether dying inside a tree would have been worse than this.

Chapter Thirty-Five
From Goblin To Mouse

Kara

Kara never spotted her. She was sitting in a corner feeding her tiny, new friends crumbs from a piece of dried bread she'd stolen from the kitchen. They had arrived the day before yesterday, and at first, she had thought they were strange little bees of some kind. She had been eating pieces of gara fruit, and after trying to coax them to her for some time, one had landed close enough to feed. The other was quick to follow, and soon the three were sharing the rest of her small, pilfered meal. Kara couldn't believe her luck. They were two of the most beautiful little beings she had ever seen, and even though they flew just like the horrible creature the old woman had turned into, they were so much nicer.

At night, they had perched on the shelves above her head, and for the first time since her arrival in the Sanctuary, Kara had slept deeply and dreamless, somehow feeling safe in their presence. Yesterday, they had followed her everywhere. She had shared her food with them, and they had even allowed her to stroke the spiky things on their strangely shaped arms.

"There you are!" rasped a horrifying voice.

Beak and Claw fluttered into the air, squawking in shock, followed by a terrified Kara leaping to her feet. When she saw who it was, she backed up against the wall, praying that the rocks and dirt would swallow her whole.

"I send you on a mission, and what happens?" shrieked the crone. "I find you making friends with a slave."

With that, she pointed a gloved hand at the two birds and yelled out her spell. A flash of light filled the air, and the creatures fell to the floor as mice.

"From predators to prey!" she shrilled.

The two mice scampered around in a circle for a moment and then vanished into the dark shadows. Spider turned her attention to Kara.

"And what are you doing here, slave? Why are you not with the others?"

She flicked a hand, and light filled the corner. Kara had nowhere to run.

"Your eyes…they're blue!" she rasped.

Kara was too terrified to look away. Spider floated closer, red eyes staring deep into blue depths. Suddenly, the witch backed away.

"You can understand me, can't you?"

Kara continued to stare.

"Answer me!" screamed the woman.

Kara slowly nodded.

Spider glared down at her, her expression suddenly thoughtful.

"The spell didn't completely work," she murmured to herself. "Imagine that."

She leaned forward, coming almost nose-to-nose with the girl.

"What is different about you, I wonder," she smiled, the effect so horrible that Kara shut her eyes. "If I wasn't pressed for time, I'd take you apart and find out."

Kara thought she was going to be sick.

"Well," said Spider straightening up and backing away. "I can't have you running around as free as a bird. No. Let's have you follow your friends."

She pointed her gloved hand; there was another flash of light, and Kara felt as if she were spinning away to nothing. When the mist cleared away, she was lying on the ground, and everything around her was huge. The hands stretched out in front were clawed, and her arms were covered with fur. She tried to scream, but all that came out was a squeak.

"You liked my feathered pets so much," boomed a voice from far above, "you can suffer their fate. Run! It won't be long before you're caught and end up in the cook pot for my three guests."

Kara ran. She was on four feet, and her nose twitched. She also seemed to be dragging something behind, but she was too frightened to worry about it. A hole showed itself in the wall before her, and she tore toward it, dodging rocks that were now the size of boulders and small hills. Into the hole she shot, the sound of Spider's laughter followed her in. It was dark and damp, but still, she ran…right into something that screeched and scraped ragged claws across her face. She squeaked loudly but kept on running, aware that the other two mice were right behind her.

The next afternoon, Kara sat beside Beak and Claw, nibbling away at the grain they had found in the storage room. The three had become inseparable since Spider had turned them all into mice, although Kara still bore the scratch across her face that Beak had given her when she'd careened into him in the little tunnel. Since their transformation, they had explored many of the mouse tunnels that crisscrossed behind the walls and had even found ways of getting in and out of the upper chambers. Kara couldn't communicate with the other two, but they followed along wherever she went. They sensed her cautiousness when they entered open rooms, and when she hid, they did the same. The good thing about the Sanctuary was that there were no cats, although she wouldn't have known one if she had met up with such a creature. None existed in Glockamar. Nor had they run into any other mice, which was strange had Kara stopped long enough to think about it. Mice were quite common in the mountain community, and the many tunnels in the Sanctuary indicated that mice had lived there at some point in the past. Kara, however, did not give the mystery more than a thought.

They finished their little meal, and then the three methodically washed their faces before carrying on. The lack of light didn't bother her in her mouse form. With her new ability to smell, she was able to sniff her way through the tunnels. She led them back up into the chamber, where the Spider met with the three crones. In this way, she could keep an ear on what the three were doing even if she couldn't figure out what it was that they were actually trying to accomplish. Somehow, she felt that it was important that she at least knew.

She found them on the porch by the dead tree, perched around a table and peering intently into a crystal ball. Kara skittered across to the rock wall that circled the now-dead tree and squeezed under the ledge of one of the bricks, followed by Beak and Claw.

"I can see nothing!" roared Spider, pushing herself away from the table. "What good is that? We need to find that necklace and put it back on one of the girls."

"Patience, dear one, patience," soothed Corilla. "The necklace is gone for the moment, and we only have the ball. We do know the brats are somewhere in Rumplestiltskin's city. Remember. The ball only shows us what it chooses, not what we necessarily want to see."

"That's why we need the necklace," snapped Spider. "At least we would know what was happening. All we know through that lump of crystal is that they have escaped their cells. Where are they? What are they doing?"

"At least we know they have no way of getting across the bridge," said Druet. She reached for another wriggling beetle and popped it into her mouth, chewing and talking at the same time. "As long as we know they are still there, all is well."

"I think we should all be a little more concerned about the seed for the Laurel Tree at the moment," said Zorna. "I think that Azmodeus is trying to track it down."

"Why be concerned?" replied Spider flippantly. "They can't do anything without a child who's willing to sacrifice his or her life for them, and there's been no sign of that. Besides, I've transformed all the children."

Kara shivered. All her friends gone? All of them goblins?

"Not all of them, Spider," said Druet. "There's that boy that escaped with the Wildenchin."

"Yes, he's been on my mind," mused Zorna. "That Wildenchin is a close friend of Azmodeus, so what was he doing with the boy unless he's the one? The wizard is not with the six in Aradell, of course, so where is he? All those rotten kids have with them is that stupid dwarf and the Minotaur."

"Let's see if we can get anything from the ball," suggested Druet.

The four hovered once again over the ball.

"Show us, Azmodeus," commanded Druet.

Smoke filled the space, and a blurred image appeared.

"Why you can't tell if it's him," sputtered Spider. "That could be anyone. Besides, he's just sitting there."

"Whoever it is, he doesn't look happy," muttered Corilla. "That could be a good thing if it's the wizard. Show us the child chosen for the tree."

Again, the ball misted over and then cleared.

"Silly gadget," snorted Spider. "All it's showing is a waterfall."

"Not just any waterfall," said Corilla, peering closer. "That's the Ornoaka. I wonder why it's showing us this?"

"I think it's time to change our focus, sisters," said Druet. "We can't leave anything to chance at this late date. I think that I will take a trip to Aradell. If, for some reason, those children get across the bridge, we have to stop them from getting any further."

"Cerce is on the other side," chuckled Zorna, tapping her chin thoughtfully. "If we can herd them in her direction, she will take care of them for sure. Perhaps a few polerats will do nicely."

"Ooh," shivered Druet, grinning gleefully. "What a nice touch, sister."

"Corilla and I will investigate the Ornoaka and try to find the wizard," continued Zorna.

"Another shape than birds," said Corilla. "One more to our liking."

Her outline blurred and reformed into the shape of a bat.

"Excellent," chuckled Zorna, and the other two followed suit.

In minutes, the three were flapping up through the night sky of Glockamar. The magical ceiling constructed by the original Glockamarians had finally failed, thanks to the extra help given by Spider and her cronies to destroy it. The valley was now open to the elements, and at the moment, Spider was enjoying the rain pounding down on the steps outside and the sudden powerful gusts of wind that battered at anything in their path.

She turned and left the porch, returning to the chamber inside. Kara scampered back across the floor to the hole in the wall, followed by Beak and Claw. Once inside, she stopped to think. What was this business about a seed being placed inside a tree by a child? Who was Azmodeus? Kara didn't know what good a mouse could be in this situation, but she was going to do everything she could to stop Spider. She would have to keep her eyes and ears open.

Chapter Thirty-Six
The Village

Jeremiah

The soldiers sporting unsheathed swords and other ugly-looking weapons shoved aside the little rag-tag group standing beside the shack and disappeared inside. Without a word, the seven ragged inhabitants moved unhurriedly toward the gates that opened onto the forbidden bridge. No one even glanced their way. Despite the soldiers rushing about, the rest of the population was going about their business, ignoring everyone else. As they reached the shadows under the archway, Mikel gratefully deposited Adonis on the ground and sighed.

"It won't be long before they decide to look here," he whispered.

"Then we'd better get to work," replied Jeremiah. "We have to count how long it takes the guard above us to move from the front of the turret to the back and then again to the front."

"The boy's right," agreed Calliotrope. "And we all have ta have the countdown perfectly."

"And then hope that Cerce doesn't find us," muttered Adonis.

For the next ten minutes or so, they watched the guard above them and counted. By the time they were ready, each of them had an identical count to the others except for Adonis. Melisande told the Minotaur to forget the count and follow the lead of the others. She suddenly thought of something else.

"If we have to run, Adonis will never keep up. How do we get him to the middle?"

"I'll carry him," said Calliotrope.

"He's too heavy," replied Melisande.

Adonis snorted. "I can run. Even though I'm little, I'm fast."

"Maybe we can put him in the middle of one of our capes and carry him," suggested Tovan.

Adonis pulled himself up to his full height and puffed out his chest.

"No one is going to carry me again," he snapped, glancing over at Mikel. "I said I could run, and I can."

"Are you sure?" asked Melisande, genuine concern showing in her eyes.

Adonis looked up at her and smiled. His adoration for her was obvious, and the rest tried to cover up their chuckles. Melisande ignored them.

"Alright," said Calliotrope. "When one is a man, one should be treated like a man."

Adonis puffed out his chest even further.

"Mikel can take off the bar that keeps the gates closed," he continued. "We'll start the count just as the guard turns ta go to the back of the turret. Count in your heads as we run, and then turn and face the city. The wind doesn't look too strong, so the bridge should be quite stable. Ready?"

"This better work," muttered Portia.

Mikel crept over to the gate and lifted the bar out of its cradle. Jeremiah kept his eye on the street while the others watched the guard. As soon as he turned, the group spilled through the gate and onto the bridge, running for all they were worth and counting at the same time. True to his word, Adonis kept up with them and even passed a couple.

"Now!" shouted Jeremiah.

They stopped and turned, appearing to be walking toward the castle from the other side. They had timed it perfectly. The guard was just coming into view around the turret to look at the bridge. What he saw was a rag-tag group of people crossing the bridge toward him, and he quickly held up his notched bow, shooting the arrow out over the chasm toward them. The arrow landed harmlessly a few feet ahead of them. They could hear him shouting to others, and that was all the prompting they needed. Turning, they continued across the bridge, running as fast as their legs could carry them, collapsing on the ground when they reached the other side.

"We did it," laughed Jamie, pulling off the old clothes she'd put on for a disguise. "You are brilliant, Jeremiah. Positively brilliant."

"Well done," grinned Mikel, helping Jeremiah to his feet. "That was excellent."

Jeremiah grinned back. He knew without saying a word that Mikel had finally accepted him as someone worthy and capable. Who knew? Maybe they would actually become friends.

"I think we have a problem!" cried Tovan suddenly, pointing back at the bridge. "Look!"

Those on the ground scrambled to their feet and looked back at the palace.

"Oh no," moaned Melisande. "It didn't work. What gave us away?"

The gates to the King's palace were open, and ranks upon ranks of soldiers were trotting at a quick pace over the bridge toward them. Ahead of them raced two of the lions that had been in the waiting room.

"I can't run anymore," gasped Portia. "My legs feel like lead."

Calliotrope tapped his chin with the tip of a finger. "I think I can handle this problem," he replied.

Stretching a hand toward the bridge, he began to mumble under his breath. To Jeremiah, who was standing closest to him, it sounded like he was talking to someone. Suddenly, Calliotrope's hand formed a fist, and the half of the bridge closest to them, vanished. He then sharply moved his fist, pointing it toward a patch of ground a short distance away and to the amazement of everyone, a hill covered with flowers and bushes took shape where there had been nothing before.

The troops came to an abrupt halt, soldiers behind colliding into the backs of those in front. For a few seconds, there was absolute silence and then pandemonium broke out. Those in front turned and yelled at the others to retreat. Everyone seemed to be shouting at once. The cats seemed to be enjoying the run back, nipping at feet as the soldiers ran. Only the group on the opposite side, staring back in total shock, was silent. It took time, but eventually, the soldiers were back in the palace with the doors shut tightly behind them.

"Awesome," whispered Jamie.

"What did you do, Calliotrope?" asked Jeremiah, looking at the dwarf with awe.

"All dwarves have that capability," he beamed. "You know that Eleusia is alive. She can move her land around at will."

"Like when the land folds over in Aradell?" asked Melisande.

The dwarf nodded.

"The thing is that what is tak'n away must be put somewhere. Nothing can jist vanish inta oblivion. It has ta change inta something else. I just asked that she remove half the bridge and remake it over there. Luckily, she obliged this time."

"This time?" asked Portia.

"Oh ya," replied Calliotrope. "Sometimes she can be quite stubborn and refuses ta do anything. Mind you; I think the old girl has a good reason whenever that happens."

The ground rumbled slightly beneath them.

"Sorry, my dear," he responded quickly. "I shouldn't have referred ta ya in that way but tank ya."

There was a second rumble but much milder than the first. He beamed around at the rest who were staring at him with their mouths open.

"She is alive," whispered Portia looking down at the ground around them.

"How wonderful," whispered Melisande, her eyes like saucers.

"And only dwarves can do this?" asked Mikel.

"We are the people of the earth," he responded. "The gift was given ta our ancestors when we arrived in Eleusia in order to build our tunnels and homes underground. But we must never abuse the privilege. If I had hurt any of dem soldiers, I would have been punished."

"Right," said Jeremiah, pulling off the rest of his disguise. "Well, thank you, Calliotrope."

The rest expressed their gratitude as they, too, removed the old tunics and headpieces.

"Well, one thing's for sure," muttered Portia. "There's no retreat for us. We're stuck on this side whether we want to be or not."

Jeremiah rummaged through his pouch where he kept all the image pieces and pulled out the coin the Rumplestiltskin had given him.

"Here it is. Look. It has two sides. One shows some kind of village, but there's nothing on the other one."

"May I see that?" asked Jamie coming up behind him.

Jeremiah handed it to her, and she studied it carefully. Was this where they were supposed to go? But how were they to get there?

"Well, let's find it," demanded Portia. "I'm starving, and hopefully, we can get something to eat there."

The rest agreed, except for Jamie.

"But what direction should we take?" she argued. "It may be where we are supposed to go but what if it's just a red herring or possibly a trap?"

"Red herring?" questioned Melisande.

"It means something put there to confuse us."

Tovan sighed. "The village does look very inviting."

The other four agreed with her, and Jamie had no choice but to follow the others in a direction that might take them there. They had been walking for some time when Mikel paused.

"What's that noise?" he asked, looking toward the south.

The others stopped and listened. A strange yipping could be heard a fair distance away, but as they listened, it seemed to be coming closer.

"Polerats!" snarled Calliotrope. "Someone's put them on our trail."

"What are polerats?" asked Tovan.

"Ya done want ta know," cried the dwarf. "Come on. We have ta git out of here. Hurry, or there won't be enough left of ya ta run!"

The little group ran as fast as their legs could carry them, but no matter how much ground they covered, the polerats seemed to be gaining. It was only a matter of minutes before they were going to have the first view of their pursuers. They were being chased toward the top of a high, treeless hill that did not look very inviting. The grass was yellow, and if there ever had been trees or bushes, they were now collections of leafless spindly sticks. Every time they tried to go in a different direction, they were herded back to the hilltop. On the other side was a valley that looked much more inviting, and ahead of them was a village.

"There it is," cried Jeremiah. "The village…ahead of us."

"Stop!" howled Portia. "I can't run anymore."

"They've stopped!" shouted Mikel.

Panting with the effort and almost sobbing, they turned to face their pursuers. What greeted them, shocked them to their toes. The creatures were large, bluish-grey rats with teeth that most wild cats would have envied. At the moment, those teeth were very visible beneath little black eyes that appeared to glint with glee. What was astounding about them, apart from a horrible howling bark, were their corkscrew tails which were used for travel. The creatures could hop over and through obstacles bouncing on their tails and moving at an incredible pace.

"They're making certain that we go toward that village," choked a startled Melisande. "They weren't after us to hurt us. They just wanted to herd us in this direction."

"I hope this isn't a trap," muttered Jamie.

Jeremiah shook his head. If anyone was going to see the problems in something, it was going to be Jamie.

Tovan pointed to the village.

"It looks like we're being welcomed."

Villagers dressed in old-fashioned clothing enthusiastically waved to them to come ahead, and as they approached, they noticed a table covered with delicious food. Fruit, steaming vegetables, meat pies and newly baked bread covered the surface along with water and fruit juices. It never crossed the minds of any of them to be wary of this situation. They were starving, and when Portia used the Willik's comment that there were those along the way who would help them, they felt justified in eating the food.

"Azmodeus told us you were coming," sang out one villager.

"We've been waiting for days," encouraged another. "Come. Sit down and eat."

They did not have to be asked twice. The food was delicious, and they began to relax and chat amiably with each other. Jeremiah was the first to notice that they all appeared to have become friends, totally supportive of one another and happy to be in each other's company. Even Portia was smiling, which was a miracle as far as he was concerned. So intent was he on focusing on the group and their conversation, he didn't notice the villagers gradually slipping away or the cottages beginning to shimmer and slowly fade.

"You know," stated Jamie. "That coin had a picture of this village on one side and nothing on the other. Is this where we have to answer a riddle?"

"Neither side tells us where to go next," added Melisande. "Let's see that coin again, Jeremiah."

He took it out of his pouch and handed it to her.

"The other two pieces are puzzle pieces," he remarked. "This one isn't."

"The first puzzle piece was inside a flower," said Melisande, examining the coin more closely. "The second was inside the monocle."

She looked up at the others. What she was implying suddenly sank in.

"Find a way to open it," suggested Mikel, the others nodding in agreement.

They moved in closer to Melisande and leaned forward expectantly to get a better look. It took several minutes of twisting and turning the top and bottom halves before the two separated, revealing the contents. Melisande pulled out the puzzle piece and held it out for all to see.

The one side was identical to the other two they had collected, showing what appeared to be the wall of a room. This third one, however, was slightly different in that it revealed a corner of the room as opposed to just a wall. The colors were so dark none of them could figure out what it actually was. The girl turned the piece over, revealing the image of a strange house that appeared to be built within an enormous tree. The house was tall and thin, and judging from the number of windows that could be seen, consisted of many levels or floors.

"What a strange house," exclaimed Tovan, her expression one of perplexity. "Is that where we have to go next?"

"But where is it?" asked Portia, looking around at the others. "How do we get to it?"

Jeremiah suddenly noticed that they were alone in a small, grassy meadow with a whimpering Adonis sitting under their table, his arms tightly wrapped around his drawn-up legs. He was shaking from head to toe.

"What's wrong, Adonis," he asked.

"I think that is where Cerce lives," he whispered, pointing at the puzzle piece. "She'll find us. I just know she will."

"I think so," replied Calliotrope, shaking his head. "Them polecats were chasin' us straight to her, and this village jist vanished. Those were her tricks fer certain."

The others looked around in astonishment. There was nothing left of the village or the villagers, only an open field. Jeremiah felt his insides turn to ice. Calliotrope was right, and they had just walked into another trap.

"Oh, quit snivelling, Minotaur," snapped Portia. "If that's where the next riddle is, then that's where we have to go. Now, where does this Cerce live?"

"Portia!" exclaimed Melisande. "Don't speak to Adonis like that. For a moment, I thought you were becoming a half-decent person, but I guess I was wrong."

Portia glared back at her and then stomped off in a direction that she hoped would bring them to their destination. The others shook their heads and followed. No one said a word about the vanishing village, although it was on everyone's mind.

There was something else about their surroundings that was disturbing. It was simply too quiet. The four from Glockamar didn't seem to notice, and Jeremiah assumed that they were used to the silence of the woods back in their valley. He, however, found the lack of sound unsettling.

"Are there no animals in this wood?" he whispered to Adonis.

"Who would want to live here," he muttered back. "All this land belongs to Cerce."

The Minotaur continued to creep along, his eyes darting to and fro.

The sun was beginning to set when they came to the crest of a hill. Beyond them in the distance was the house they had seen in the image on the coin. For once, Portia had made a good choice. Either that or they had been led there, which wouldn't have surprised anyone. Jeremiah realized, in thinking back over their journey, that in many ways, there had never been a choice in the routes they had taken. They had simply been led through Aradell.

"It is hers," gasped Adonis, falling onto his knees. "That place does belong to Cerce."

The small group stared gloomily down at the strange building.

"Do you think she knows that we're here?" muttered Jamie. "Stupid question."

"Are you sure that's the only house that looks like this in this area?" asked Melisande hopefully.

"I think we should stay here tonight," suggested Calliotrope, pointing to a copse of trees a short distance away. "It's going ta get dark soon, and we don't want ta go stumbling around this close ta the castle of a nasty goddess. Maybe tomorrow, we can scout around and see if Melisande is right. Maybe that house ain't our destination."

The suggestion was a good one, and they were too tired to argue. They hiked over to the trees and pushed through the foliage until they found a small clearing. As they settled in for the night, Portia approached Jeremiah.

"Let me take first watch," she suggested.

"Sounds good," he replied. "I think we'll need to take turns tonight. Wake me up for the second one."

Portia nodded.

It did not take long for all of them to drop off to sleep, so Portia thought. She waited until everyone was either snoring gently or breathing evenly before making her move. She crept over to the edge of the clearing and stopped, her ears straining to catch every sound. Reassured that all was well, she picked up her pack and disappeared into the woods. She'd had enough of the quest and had no intentions of dealing with this Cerce creature.

Portia was wrong. Jamie had noticed. Suspicious over the girl's offer to keep watch, she had only pretended to sleep. Portia never volunteered for anything unless there was something in it for her, and lately, there had been too many mutterings on her part about going home. As Portia vanished into the trees, Jamie got quietly to her feet and followed.

Unknown to all of them, the food had been tampered with. Despite his best intentions, Jeremiah never woke up in order to take over the watch and not far into the woods, Portia and Jamie slid to the ground in drugged stupors. When a triumphant Cerce arrived later on, she was initially perturbed that the Minotaur was absent, as were two of the girls. She had so desperately wanted to deal with the Minotaur once again. However, five of the birds in her hands meant that the quest was destroyed. She had her minions cart them away, pleased with the fate she had in store for them. It didn't matter that the others were missing.

The little Minotaur had been the only one not to eat the food and, unable to sleep, had crawled deep into the center of a thickly foliaged bush. When Cerce arrived, he could only watch in horror as his friends were taken away. He had stayed hidden long after they were gone, shaking with terror. When the rays of the sun peeped over the hill the next morning, he desperately tried to figure out what to do.

"I must find Jamie," he whispered to himself. "I must find Jamie."

With that burning thought in his mind, he raced into the woods, following the routes the girls had taken.

Chapter Thirty-Seven
The Pirate

Petre

Petre found himself standing on the riverbed, watching in fascination as varieties of different fish swam by and wondering how it was possible that he was breathing underwater. One minute he'd been hurtling over the waterfall, an unconscious wreck and in the next, he was standing on the bottom of the river contemplating a casual stroll.

'I'm dead,' he thought to himself. 'That's it. I'm definitely dead.'

"In a manner of speaking, you are," came a voice through the water. *"Come ahead, boy, and don't dawdle."*

Petre was so startled that it never crossed his mind to resist. He took a few tentative steps forward, finding the water only slightly heavier than walking through air on land and looked around. It was a marvelous sight. Fish, every shape, size and color, swam past, paying no attention to him whatsoever. He was relieved about that. Some of them were larger than he was. Great ropes of underwater plants rooted in the sandy riverbed rose upward like willowy dancers, the leaves drifting back and forth in the current like filmy skirts. He could see the sunshine playing on the surface of the water above him, and the rays moved through the water in constantly shifting beams. Shells in a multitude of shapes and colors littered the riverbed, but when he bent down to retrieve a particularly attractive one, it suddenly grew legs and scuttled away. He didn't bother reaching for anymore.

"Are you coming, boy?" repeated the strange voice.

"Yes," he replied without thinking. He stopped short. He wasn't coughing. His mouth hadn't filled up with water. What was going on?

Moving forward once again, he became aware of a small hill jutting up in front of him. It was a very strange mound. There was a wooden door on the side facing him with a large brass handle in its center and brass hinges holding it to the rock. To one side of the door was a flag drifting lazily back and forth in the ebb and flow of the water. On its face was a grinning skull, a scarf wrapped around its forehead. On the top of the mound was a similar flag and a sign that had one word blazed into its surface.

"Pierats," sounded out Petre. "What kinds of rats are pierats?"

"Open the door," said the voice. *"Come in."*

Petre hesitated, trying to think.

"Come in," demanded the voice. *"It's not as if you have any other place to go."*

Petre sighed and pulled the door open.

He was sitting on top of a clothing chest. A scarf was wrapped around his head like the skull on the flag, and perched on top of this was a black hat with three corners. He had a thick, black beard, gold circles hung from his ears, and one eye was covered with a black patch. His jacket, which reached almost to his knees, was trimmed with gold braid down the front and around the cuffs, and heavy black boots with rolled-down tops covered his legs from foot to knee. One hand was not a hand. His arm ended in a nasty-looking hook, and the other hand, which was a hand, was resting on the hilt of a sword tucked into a wide belt. Petre had never seen anyone like him in his life.

"Welcome to 'Davey Jones Locker," boomed the big man.

"To what?" asked Petre, trying not to sound rude. He knew instinctively that this was not the place for rudeness. "I'm sorry, sir, but what are you?"

"A pirate," said the stranger, grinning broadly.

"A what?"

"A pirate. They were nasty men who roamed the seas many years ago in Earth's dimension, and they would rob from anyone who had money and then…you don't know what I'm talking about, do you?"

Petre shook his head.

"I've wanted to play the part of a pirate for years, and I finally get the perfect opportunity, and who do I end up with? I'll bet you grew up in Glockamar, didn't you?"

Petre nodded.

"Drat! I thought you were one of those new arrivals from Earth's dimension. They would have been impressed. Well then, who are you?"

"I'm Petre."

"Well, Petre," sighed the stranger. "You will have to do. Now, tell me what's been happening in Draukenberg?"

Petre began to tell him the story as he knew it, starting with the prophecy, the six who were now attempting to solve the riddles and Spider and Hera's devilish plots. This last bit of information brought a frown to the man's face. Petre's story came out quite stilted at first, but as he began to warm to his subject, it came out in a rush. Every so often, the pirate stopped him to clarify a point and then urged him to continue.

"And what part do you play in this story, young Petre?"

Petre looked away.

"You are the one who has to put the seed in the tree, aren't you?"

"Yes," whispered the boy.

"Tell me your story."

Slowly Petre told him about the Furies, the message from the Fates and his anger at not being told by Azmodeus.

"Ah, I understand," said the pirate with sympathy. "It is a great deal to ask of an untried boy. The Fates are right, you know. The only real magic is to consider others before one's self. But to expect you to give up your life for the sake of the trees is really asking too much."

The expression on the boy's face brightened. "That's exactly the way I feel."

"After all, what could happen? The evil side of this world would win. Darkness and bitter cold would cover the land, and many of its inhabitants would die."

Petre looked away, a stubborn expression replacing the former relieved one.

"The fairies, elves, sprites, Wildenchin..."

"Wildenchin?"

Petre's sudden interest was not lost on the man.

"Oh, they'll be the first to go, I would imagine. They are so close to the land that as the trees die, so will they."

"Crutchin," whispered Petre. "Crutchin would die?"

"If he is a Wildenchin, then yes."

Petre thought for a moment and then took a deep breath.

"Am I dead, pirate?"

"If you choose to be, then you will not have to throw your life away on a tree. No one will know. They will simply find your drowned body on the shore of the river and grieve for your loss. If you choose to live, then it will take more courage than you have ever been required to give."

"Well," said Petre thoughtfully. "I think I know what it was like to die once. It can't be any worse a second time."

He suddenly thought of what the Furies had said…only the chosen one could find the seed, and in order to do so, he had to die first. Hadn't he done just that? Hadn't he drowned in the river?

"You have made your choice then," stated the pirate.

Petre nodded and was suddenly engulfed with bubbles and swirling water. He was traveling toward the surface of the river at an incredible speed, and the higher he went, the more he coughed and sputtered. He was drowning again! He shot through the surface and was catapulted onto the bank, landing with a thud that knocked out whatever little air he had in his lungs. With a moan, he collapsed and blacked out.

Down in the underwater room, the outline of the pirate dissolved to be replaced by the form of a youthful-looking young man dressed in shorts of intertwined leaves and winged boots. The hat perched on his curly hair was also winged. The youth looked thoughtful. As mischievous as he was, even this trickster knew when a situation had to be taken seriously. Things were worse than they had been told. He left the hill in the same manner that Petre had only moments ago, but without all the fuss of nearly drowning. Mercury, also known as Hermes, kept moving up into the clear blue sky and was soon lost from sight.

Chapter Thirty-Eight
The King Under The Mountain

Azmodeus

Azmodeus, being as sensitive to the pull of magic as he was, had felt the eye of the glass crystal on him as he sat deep in thought. The tingle had encircled him, an uncomfortable feeling that could be recognized by all wizards and sorceresses, and he waited patiently until the feeling had passed. So, the Spider and her crones were searching for them, were they? He had been wondering when they would attempt to catch up with their side of the quest.

As soon as the sensation passed, he stood up and stretched out his old bones. Minutes later, he sensed the searching come again, but it passed over their little group and headed more toward the south and The Hollows. It paused there for a time, which made him wonder. Had they found out about Petre? They knew there had to be another child and had probably asked the crystal where he or she could be found. Had they been shown the answer? This was not good.

"Yonnus, Crutchin," he called to the others. "It's time to be off, and I'm judging from signs I'm receiving that we must go south."

"We can't go back into The Hollows," said Crutchin. "The Furies would never let us enter again."

"True," replied the old man. "But there are other forces at work that are even more powerful than the Furies. Perhaps the boy has encountered them."

"Will they help him?" asked Yonnus.

"Some will," said Azmodeus. "Others will try to hinder him. We must find him."

"Lead on," gestured Yonnus.

Quickly, they broke camp. Picking up their scant belongings and dwindling food supply, they took off in a southerly direction. They had been traveling for several hours when Azmodeus suddenly stopped and gestured to the others to move into a stand of trees just off their path.

"Keep quiet and still," he whispered, scanning the sky with eyes squinting against the sun.

Within minutes, a black shape flapped across their line of vision heading south.

"What was that?" asked Yonnus.

"It is supposed to be a creature called a bat," replied Azmodeus. "However, bats are not active during the day as they are nocturnal. I would tend to think that this one is a friend of Spider, and the shape you see is not her natural one."

"Where is she heading?" asked the Wildenchin.

"If I am correct," replied Yonnus, "the Ornoaka lies in that direction. I used to travel a great deal in this area, and that was one river that everyone warned me to stay away from. There are some nasty creatures living in that area."

"I believe you're right," said Azmodeus. "If Petre has escaped the Furies, then he could still be in trouble."

They continued on, traveling at a faster pace than they had before the bat sighting. At times, the thickness of the foliage slowed them down, but even here in the wilderness, there was obvious evidence that the trees and bushes were dying. The one most affected by the sight was Crutchin.

"Does that witch not realize that without these trees our world will die?"

"But she doesn't want this world, boy," said Yonnus. "She wants it dark and dead so that her friends from The Hollows can join her. I can't even imagine what this place would be like, and I sure wouldn't want to live in it."

"I won't be around to find out," sighed Crutchin. "The trees are not the only things that are weakening."

"What do you mean?" asked Yonnus.

"All the creatures that rely on the trees and everything associated with them will die," replied the wizard. "The rivers will turn dirty, the temperature will drop, and this will become a land of ice and snow. Eleusia as a world will die. The Wildenchin will also age and die."

"What?"

Azmodeus did not look back or break his stride.

"Look at Crutchin, Yonnus. Really look at him."

Yonnus turned and stopped dead in his tracks. Crutchin's hair was showing white strands throughout the blue mass. His face was beginning to wrinkle around the eyes and mouth, and his shoulders were ever so slightly bent.

"Azmodeus!" cried the man. "We cannot let this happen!"

"Of course not," snapped the wizard, stopping so suddenly that the other two bumped into him. He turned and looked back at the Wildenchin.

"Now, why didn't I think of this before, Crutchin? Can you use the ground to try to discover the whereabouts of our young friend?"

"I will give it a try," nodded Crutchin. "It may take some time."

"We can wait," replied Azmodeus."

Crutchin bent down and put his mouth to the ground. For a lengthy period of time, he appeared to be alternately speaking into the dirt and then listening to any reply that might come his way.

"Now I know why he's got such big ears," whispered Yonnus. "He needs all the help he can get to hear what's being said."

"Sh!" chuckled the wizard. "Be careful, Yonnus. You're beginning to develop a sense of humor. I don't know if that's a good thing or not."

"Harrumph!" snorted the blacksmith, crossing his arms over his massive chest.

The strange conversation between Crutchin and the ground carried on for some time. Suddenly, the Wildenchin stopped and pulled himself up to face his two friends.

"There was a boy," he said, his forehead wrinkled with concern. "He came out of The Hollows this morning and made his way down to the river. He was halfway across when the river nymphs attacked, and he fell into the water. His body was swept over the falls."

"Petre is dead?" gasped Yonnus.

"He never resurfaced at the bottom of the falls," replied Crutchin. "No one knows what has become of him."

It was dusk the following day when Azmodeus, Crutchin and Yonnus finally reached the bank of the Ornoaka River. They had been unable to call the elves and their gryphons to help them because their route had taken them too close to The Hollows' border. Crutchin had tried to help them on several occasions, but the landings after the leaps had left Azmodeus and Yonnus too bruised and battered to use this mode of transportation more than a couple of times. It had not taken Azmodeus long to find the spot where Petre had left the river.

"He was carried from here."

"By whom?" asked Yonnus.

"Dwarves," replied Azmodeus after several minutes of consideration. "They picked him up from here and headed off in that direction."

He pointed away from the river toward the hills forming the edge of the valley on the west.

"Was Petre alive?" asked Crutchin, his aging face wrinkling in concern.

The old man shook his head.

"I don't know. There are too many auras in this place, and I cannot separate his from the others."

"We must follow then," said the Wildenchin.

Azmodeus nodded and then looked up into the darkening sky.

"I sense another being. Strange. His aura is quite different. I should know it, but…"

Yonnus turned back to the grey, misty wall of The Hollows and cocked his head. "Listen," he murmured. "Can you hear that? It sounds like mutterings, hissings and whispers. I have been on its edge many times, but never before have I heard sounds coming from inside."

Azmodeus listened for a moment and then sighed and shook his head. "It is the sound of war plans, my friends. The natives grow restless to escape their boundary and trample over the rest of Draukenberg. Come. We must make haste. Petre has been away from us for too long."

The three took off at a brisk walk toward the hills. None saw the bat detach itself from the tree above and veer north toward Grumbletops.

It was dark and very late when the three travelers finally reached the foot of the rugged hills that they hoped housed a very alive Petre. Crutchin bent down again and had another strange conversation with the earth. His message when he finally stood was much different from his first.

"He's there, and he's alive," grinned the Wildenchin. "Shall we continue on?"

Azmodeus looked at Yonnus. The old wizard seldom slept, and Crutchin was capable of going days without sleep. The big man, however, was a different matter.

"We go on," said Yonnus. "I wouldn't be able to rest, not knowing what has happened to the boy."

"Then we go," said Azmodeus. "Would you be so kind, Crutchin?"

The Wildenchin stretched out his hands, and a soft glow rose from the ground in front of them, illuminating a safe path up the hillside. In the dark, it would have been a hazardous trek at best. With the light, they were able to step forward with confidence and move at a much faster pace.

At the crest of the first hill, they could see the land dip down into a small dell. The trees in this section were in very bad shape, and Crutchin sucked in his breath.

"Some are close to death," he whispered. "Soon, it will be too late."

Azmodeus put a hand on the small man's shoulder. The Wildenchin had aged even more since the morning, but neither he nor Yonnus had commented on the fact.

"There is a cavern behind those trees," said Azmodeus. "The boy was taken there. Come."

He led the way down the hill to the dell and through to the hillside beyond. A cave entrance emerged from the shadows of the rock, and without pausing, he walked inside, the other two following behind. Crutchin's strange earth-light guided them through the dark. When their tunnel met a second, the wizard stopped.

"Our welcoming committee is approaching," he explained. "Out of politeness, we will wait here."

The trudge of metal-soled boots could be heard emerging from the depths of the second tunnel, and Yonnus shifted uneasily from one foot to the other. He had never been comfortable in tunnels, and not knowing who was coming to meet them was disturbing.

"They're certainly not hiding their presence," he muttered.

"Nor is there any need," chuckled Azmodeus. "Under the ground, they are the lords and masters."

A group of six dwarves appeared around the bend and approached the three, stopping directly in front of them. Yonnus recognized Maxim in the group and immediately relaxed. Both groups bowed respectfully. The conversation was held in dwarfin, but as all spoke the language, communication was not a problem.

"We expected you," said Maxim. "As soon as I saw the boy, I knew that you would not be far behind."

"Is Petre well?" asked Crutchin.

"He is," replied the dwarf. "Come. We will take you to him."

The dwarves turned back and led the three down the tunnel from which they had so recently emerged. Within minutes, it opened up into a large grotto. Yonnus, who had never before been invited into a dwarfin grotto, found the scene one of strange magnificence. Pillars, intricately carved with strange symbols, flowed from floor to ceiling and multitudes of metal sconces holding blazing torches lined the walls. The furniture was made of metal in different tones and shades of silver and bronze, and the couches and chairs were adorned with furs and bright blankets. Platters of food covered the surfaces of the many tables, and Yonnus' mouth watered at the sight.

"This way," said Maxim, leading the way down the steps to the grotto floor.

The many dwarves, both male and female, eyed the newcomers with unconcealed curiosity but courteously made way for the group as Maxim led them forward.

As they approached the group at the far end, they noticed one dwarf more formally attired than the others. His jacket and pants were made of a rich, black material, and a circlet of gold sat on his brow.

"The King Under the Mountain," explained Azmodeus. "His name is Reygould."

Azmodeus stopped several feet from the king and bowed. Yonnus and Crutchin did the same.

"Welcome," said Reygould, holding both hands out to the wizard. "It has been a long time since your presence graced our chambers, Azmodeus."

His hair and beard were dark brown, and black eyes twinkled merrily above flushed red cheeks. He was indeed a cheery sight after everything they'd been through.

"It is an honor to be here, Reygould," replied the wizard. "These are my friends, Yonnus and Crutchin."

The twinkle left the King's eyes as they alighted on the Wildenchin. He approached Crutchin, clasping his hands in his own.

"My boy," he said. "Your presence reminds us all of how dire the situation is and how quickly we must move to help."

Crutchin bowed his head in acknowledgment.

"The young man is here," said Reygould, turning and gesturing behind him.

The group parted to reveal Petre sitting on a couch behind them, glaring back at Azmodeus with undisguised anger.

"I didn't want to see you," he muttered sullenly. "Why did you not tell me what I had to learn from the Furies?"

The wizard sorrowfully shook his head. He knew immediately to what the boy was referring. "I apologize, young Petre. I had only been told the night before we left Donagal for The Hollows, and somehow I could not get out the words. How do you tell someone you care for that they have to give up their life to save the rest of us? No, Petre. The words would not come, and then after what happened in The Hollows, there was no time. I ask for your forgiveness."

Petre glared at him for a moment more before spotting Crutchin standing slightly behind the wizard. He leaped from the crouch, utter concern replacing the anger on his face.

"Crutchin!" he gasped. "What the pirate said is true. You are dying."

"Pirate?" questioned Azmodeus.

Petre looked up at him, his feelings of resentment toward the old man gone.

"I found him at the bottom of the river inside a hill. It was the strangest thing. I could breathe in the water, and the fish were swimming around me. The man was dressed in strange clothes and called himself a pirate, although he was disappointed when he found out that I'd never heard of one. He told me that as the trees die, so will many others, including the Wildenchin, and then he asked me to choose between drowning, which had already happened to me, and saving the trees."

"And you chose the trees, Petre?" asked Yonnus.

Petre nodded. "I figured that if I'd died once, it couldn't be as bad the second time around."

Azmodeus cleared his throat, and Crutchin grasped the boy by the shoulders. "You are a good and selfless friend," he whispered in a choked voice.

"Not really," sighed Petre. "But I did end up with this. It was around my neck when I came out of the river."

He loosened the ties at the neck of his shirt and pulled out a chain. Attached was a narrow crystal, and inside was a small gold bead.

"The Seed of Life," gasped Crutchin.

Azmodeus sat down on the nearest chair and gazed at it in wonder. "You magnificent boy," he said, shaking his head. "You made the choice. For what it's worth, Petre, I am so proud of you."

The boy's only thought was that if Azmodeus knew how terrified he was, he might not be so gracious with his compliments.

"What must we do, Azmodeus?" asked Reygould.

"The three of us must get to the far side of Aradell by tomorrow night. I have learned that the children following the quest of the riddles must be in the Sanctuary chamber at the same time that Petre puts the seed in the tree. If it doesn't happen together, we will not be able to stop what is happening to Draukenberg and, eventually, to all of Eleusia."

"We can take you on our railway through the mining tunnels," said Reygould. "However, it is becoming dangerous. As the trees die, their roots are no longer holding back the dirt, and some of the tunnels are beginning to collapse."

"What of the gryphons?" asked Yonnus.

"We are still too close to The Hollows," said Azmodeus. "However, if your people can get us far enough away, Reygould, we will be able to call them. Once we are on the east side of Aradell, we will be able to find the six young ones who will be coming out on that side, and the gryphons will have little trouble landing."

The King shook his head. "If you want to get to the far side of Aradell by tomorrow night, then the only tunnel to take is the one that goes east. It doesn't take you further from The Hollows; it takes you beneath it. There are not only creatures that mean to harm you above ground; there are those that live below."

There was silence for a moment.

"We must take the chance, Azmodeus," said Yonnus. "We're running out of time."

The wizard agreed.

"Then come and eat," said Reygould. "While you are refueling yourselves, my men will ready the carts. Who will go with them?"

"I will," said Maxim. "I helped build that tunnel and know it well."

"Thank you," said Azmodeus, bowing to the dwarf.

Petre sighed. Once again, they were going from the frying pan into the fire. However, when he glanced back at Crutchin, he felt his fear disappearing and a steely resolve taking its place. For the sake of his friend, he would not fail.

Chapter Thirty-Nine
Into The Fire

Jamie

"Please, please wake up, Jamie."

The urgency in the voice finally reached her, and she struggled to sit up. Cautiously opening her eyes, she concentrated on getting the unfocused images to blend from multiple to singular.

"Oh, Adonis," she moaned. "What is it that is so important?"

"It's Cerce," he cried. "She came last night and took the others away."

Jamie shook her head and looked blearily around.

"Where's Portia?" she asked. "I remember following her out of the clearing, and then everything got dizzy."

"She woke up a little while ago and went off in that direction. She mumbled something about going home and that she'd had enough of the quest."

In an instant, Jamie was wide-awake, her heart pounding in her chest. Without Portia, the quest would not be successful. Suddenly, she was angry. All Portia had thought about through this entire trip had been about herself and what was best for her. She had never considered the importance of what they were doing and what would happen if they failed.

"Where did she go, Adonis?"

He pointed deeper into the grove of trees.

Jamie struggled to her feet. "I have to get her back. If we lose her, our quest is finished."

"What about the others?" he exclaimed. "We can't leave them alone with that mad woman."

"One thing at a time, Adonis," was the frantic reply. "Portia is the problem that will most certainly destroy us."

She took off through the trees in the direction that Adonis had earlier indicated, with the little Minotaur running to keep up. Despite the fact that the early morning sun was starting to shed more light on the ground beneath, the area of the forest that the two now entered was dark and dank. Branches reached out with grasping fingers, yanking Jamie's hair and tearing at her clothes. Ugly smells surrounded them, reminding her of rotting fruits and vegetables. It was deathly quiet, not a sound to be heard from any direction, and it was not long before the anger at Portia's stupidity seeped out of Jamie to be replaced by fear and a growing sense of hopelessness.

They were scattered all over the place. She, Portia and Adonis were somewhere in the middle of this horrible forest, and they weren't even all together. They had only solved three riddles, she had no idea where this Cerce had taken the others, and surely they were beginning to run out of time. How many days did they have left, if any?

She continued to creep through and around the closely packed bushes and trees, getting scratched and bruised in the process. Adonis stuck to her heels, trying to stay out of the way of the branches that sprang back after she passed. It was rough going for both of them and at no time did they catch sight of Portia or any sign of her having passed this way.

"Do you think we've made a mistake?" panted Jamie, finally leaning against one of the trees to catch her breath. "For all we know, we've been traveling around in circles."

Adonis shook his head and leaned against the trunk beside her. The tree suddenly shuddered as if a switch had been flicked on, the bark melted away behind them, and they catapulted backward into a black space that appeared to fall toward the center of the earth. The drop was short but terrifying, with them landing on the leaf-covered floor of an underground tunnel.

"Oh, that hurt," moaned Jamie, dragging herself to her feet, rubbing her bottom. She reached down and helped the Minotaur to his. "If nothing else, I'm going to be a mass of bruises at the end of this quest…if I live to see the end."

"Listen," whispered Adonis. "Do you hear that? Down there?"

Jamie turned and peered into the gloom. They were definitely inside a fairly narrow tunnel…they seemed to spend the better part of their days in tunnels, thought Jamie glumly…and a flickering light of some kind was brightening up the far end. Suddenly, she heard someone scream for help.

"That sounds like Portia, Adonis. Come on."

The two raced down the tunnel toward the voice.

"Slow down," cautioned Adonis, stopping and holding up a hand as they neared the end. "I've been around long enough to know when a trap is about to spring, and I sure smell a trap here."

Jamie heeded his advice, and the two crept forward toward an entrance that appeared to lead into a huge grotto. Waves of heat rolled out to meet them, and she loosened her cape. Beads of perspiration quickly formed on both foreheads, and Jamie began to find it difficult to breathe. The smell of rotten eggs was everywhere. As they peered around the rock into the cavern, they discovered their problem.

"We're inside a volcano!" she gasped.

Rivers of lava covered the floor of the grotto, roiling and spewing liquid rock into the air as they moved at tremendous speeds from one end to the other. In the center was an island that could only be reached by flimsy rope bridges that zigzagged from one pylon of solidified lava to another. One wrong step would send whoever was trying to cross into the molten streams beneath. Hanging from one of the rope bridges was a basket, and crouched inside was a terrified Portia.

"Help me, Jamie!" she screamed. "The rope holding the basket up is fraying."

Jamie went to move forward, but Adonis grabbed her arm.

"What if it isn't Portia, Jamie? What if she's an illusion? I just know that all the rest of this can't be real. Volcanoes don't exist on Eleusia."

"And what if she's real?" she countered. "That could actually be Portia down there, and I'm not going to take a chance that it isn't."

She took off down a path that led to the first bridge, with Adonis reluctantly following behind. As they reached the structure swaying in the heat, Jamie suddenly found her courage evaporating. There was hardly anything to the bridge. The ropes were old and frayed, and most of the boards were loose.

"Harriet Clarkson, don't leave me now," she whispered.

Cautiously placing a foot on the first board, she grasped the rope handrails and pulled herself onto the bridge. It swayed alarmingly, and she shut her eyes, clutching the cords of rope with such intensity that her knuckles turned white. Slowly it settled, and she opened her eyes.

"Hurry!" screamed Portia. "Please hurry, Jamie!"

Jamie took another step forward and then another. She was conscious of Adonis following but didn't dare turn around to look. She didn't speak for fear of disrupting her concentration. The two made their way across the bridge without mishap and reached the first pylon of rock protruding out of the lava.

"Okay," she sighed as her feet landed on solid footing. "That's one down."

"I...I don't th...think I c...can cross another...another one," squeaked Adonis.

She looked back at the Minotaur and, in an instant, lost her own fear. His features were drawn up in an expression of terror, and he proved beyond a shadow of a doubt that the faces of Minotaurs could lose their color. His little body was shaking from head to hoof.

"You must," she insisted, bending down and putting her arms around him. "There's no way that you can stay here."

"It's alright," his lower lip quivered. "I'll just stay until I get the courage to go on."

"You will not," she insisted. "You will take my hand as we cross this next one, and you will not look down. Now come on."

Standing up, she took his hand and led him to the next bridge. It looked to be in worse shape than the last, and she swallowed hard before stepping onto the shaky structure. Slowly they made their way across the second bridge. Adonis was still shaking like a leaf in a stiff wind, but he didn't utter one word of complaint. When they looked over at the third bridge, they could see Portia clearly. She was clutching the ropes of her net prison, her face so white that the freckles stood out like beacons.

Suddenly, the grotto was filled with wild laughter.

"So mortals can be brave."

The hairs on the back of Jamie's neck stood on end at the sound of the voice. She knew in an instant that she was in the presence of the feared goddess. "Hera," she cried out. "Where are you?"

She found her floating above the island in the center of the volcano.

"Come to rescue your friend, have you?" continued Hera. "Well, it's not going to be that easy, girl."

She gestured to the island beneath. In the center, were the rest of the group's members trying to escape their bonds. Melisande, Mikel, Jeremiah, Tovan and Calliotrope were trussed up like pigs, ready for market. They didn't seem to be able to see her, but their yells were audible over the noise of the lava flow.

"Shouldn't you be choosing your friends?" sneered Hera. "What is saving one life in comparison to saving five? They will die horrible deaths, you know. Lava is not kind."

Suddenly a new bridge shimmered in the air, attaching itself at one end to the rock on which she and Adonis stood and the other to the island. Jamie was now faced with a choice. She could either take the bridge to rescue Portia or the other to try and rescue her friends.

"It's a trick, Jamie," shouted Adonis from behind. "There are no volcanoes on Eleusia. This is all an illusion."

Jamie barely heard him.

"Choose girl," sneered the goddess. "The one or the group?"

"Think, Jamie," cried Adonis. "None of this is real! Those aren't your friends on that island!"

Jamie looked at Portia and slowly shook her head.

"Jamie!" screamed Portia. "Please!"

"Choose!" bellowed the goddess. "Choose!"

Chapter Forty
A Strange Experience At A Farm

Tovan

Unaware of the plight of Jamie, Portia and Adonis, the *real* remaining members of the group found themselves in their own frightening position. When Tovan awoke the following morning, she found herself in a wooden cage positioned in the center of a large barn. There was no sign of the others, just some chickens scratching in the dirt, a couple of ducks and a little donkey.

"Where am I?" she asked of no one in particular. "This is certainly not where we fell asleep."

"I think Cerce found us," said a voice that sounded very much like Jeremiah's. "It appears we're inside a barn attached to the house we saw last night."

"Where are all of you?" asked Tovan, looking around.

"We're right in front of you," huffed one of the chickens, rushing up to the cage. "Look at me. This is terrible."

"Who are you?" asked Tovan, her eyes wide with amazement.

"Mikel," sputtered the chicken. "Melisande is the other chicken, and Jeremiah and Calliotrope are ducks. Portia, Jamie and Adonis are missing, and we don't know who the donkey is."

"And I can't say that I'm enjoying this particular transformation," muttered Jeremiah.

"Well, how da ya think I feel," sputtered Calliotrope. "This is degradin'."

"Well, I'm enjoying it," chuckled the donkey.

The outline of the creature blurred and changed into that of a woman dressed in a gown of shimmering red and gold that fell from her shoulders to her ankles. Her red hair was piled high on her head, and she would have been fairly attractive had it not been for the nasty expression that seemed to be permanently etched on her face. Tovan found herself squeezing into the far side of her cage, as far away from the goddess as possible. The others scurried behind bales of hay, shaking with terror, their hearts in their throats.

"This is indeed a pleasure," smirked the woman.

"Who are you?" asked Mikel, peeking bravely out from his hiding spot.

"I'm Cerce, but then you knew that, didn't you? The Minotaur told you when he saw my house. He and your other two friends have walked into one of Hera's traps, and they won't be escaping from that one. No one escapes from one of her traps."

Tovan gasped. Was she telling the truth? Were the other three captives of Hera?

"I know what your quest is, and I hold the next riddle. It's useless to you now because your quest is at an end, but let's have some fun, shall we? Who will answer it?"

She looked over at Tovan and then at the animals that had slowly crept out of hiding.

"Tell us the riddle, and we will decide who must answer it," said Jeremiah, trying to keep his voice from shaking.

"Very well," replied Cerce, smiling wickedly. "There is a wine barrel over in that corner. How would you know if it was just over half full or just under?"

"I can answer that," said Tovan, her voice quaking slightly, "and I believe it's my turn."

"Are you certain?" asked Cerce. "If you answer incorrectly, your friends will stay in their present shapes until the day they die, which will not be in the too distant future. My dinner pot awaits."

"Mercy," whispered Jeremiah.

"I can answer it," she replied determinedly. "I have spent my life on a dairy farm and have had to figure this out with milk."

"Then answer."

"You tilt the barrel toward you until the liquid reaches the top of the barrel. If you can see the bottom, the barrel is less than half full. If you can't, then it is more than half full."

The others held their breath.

"Correct," laughed Cerce. "And here is the next useless image."

A small box appeared magically between her two fingers, and then she let it go to drift gently into the back of the barn. Their precious clue disappeared from sight into the darkness of the rafters.

"But you must let us go and change us back to our normal shapes," shouted Mikel, angrily.

"I must?" questioned the woman. "I don't have to do anything. I have decided to keep all of you until you have earned your freedom. When I feel that you have, then I will let you go."

"You must let us go," cried Tovan. "We have only a few days left to finish our quest."

"Yes, I know," smiled Cerce sweetly. "Now, out you come."

The door of Tovan's cage suddenly sprung open, and she slowly and reluctantly stepped out, uncertain of what Cerce had in store for her.

"Your job will be to start cleaning this barn," smirked the woman.

She waved her hand, and the neatly stacked bales of hay were suddenly torn apart, and the contents tossed over every bit of the huge floor.

"I expect this to be finished by this evening. If it isn't done properly, I will enjoy one of your friends for dinner."

She turned with a flourish and headed toward the doors. Just as she reached the sunny exterior, however, she did a very odd thing. She reached up and out of the empty air pulled a huge parasol; a thick netting hung to the ground around its circumference. As she walked into the sunshine, she resembled a walking tent. Not even her feet were visible. It was a strange sight.

"Oh no," sighed Tovan. "We're never going to get out of this mess."

"Yes, we will," muttered Calliotrope. "But first, let's get ta work on this barn. I don't intend to be her dinner."

All of them started to pick up the hay as best they could, but it became obvious very quickly that the animals were quite useless at such a task. They simply were not suited physically for the job. Tovan was left to do the majority of the work, and just as the last load was piled carefully in the corner, Cerce returned.

"Not bad," she concluded. "However, the bales are not as tidy as I would like, so, therefore, I think I will have chicken tonight."

Mikel suddenly lifted off the ground and went hurtling out the door of the barn.

"No," cried Melisande, trying to run after him. A quick wave of Cerce's hand sent her spinning back into the barn and into Calliotrope, sending him flying into the dirt with a most appropriate duck squawk.

"By morning, I expect to see excellence," continued Cerce, ignoring the tears running down Tovan's face. "If I do not, then another of your friends will become a meal."

Once again, she raised her hand, and the hay flew everywhere. Turning on her heel, she left.

"Oh no," sobbed Tovan, "What are we going to do? Oh, poor Mikel."

"Drat this body," snapped Jeremiah. "I can't do anything to help."

"Well, Tovan can't clean this barn by herself, "fumed Melisande. "None of us can. We have to find our puzzle piece, and I think we should try and rescue Mikel."

"What?" cried Jeremiah. "In case you haven't noticed, I'm a duck, and you're a chicken. What good are we to a rescue mission?"

"So we let Mikel get eaten for supper?" snapped Melisande.

"She's right," sighed Tovan. "I can't possibly do this barn again, and even if I do, it won't be good enough, and one of you two will be taken to the kitchen tonight. I think we have to try."

"You're both right," stated Calliotrope. "Well, let's see if we can find the kitchen without being seen. That's going ta be our first hurdle."

Tovan led the assault on the kitchen. Creeping stealthily forward, she stopped at the entrance to the barn and peeked out. The sun was beginning its slow walk toward the horizon, and nothing seemed to be stirring in the outer courtyard.

"Where would the kitchen be?" she asked the other three.

"Look for wet cobblestones," suggested Melisande. "The kitchen is usually the door from which they throw out the dishwater."

"Well, there are no entrances like that on this side," replied Tovan.

"What's down that alley?" asked Jeremiah.

"Stay here. Let me check it out first."

Tovan crept out of the barn and headed toward the dark, shadowed alley to their right. She kept her eyes glued to the windows that overlooked the courtyard, and every time she detected movement in their shadowy depths, she pulled back against the barn wall. It was a slow, ponderous journey, but eventually, she reached the alley and poked her head around the corner. Sure enough, there in all its glory was the kitchen entrance. Not only could she tell by the wet cobblestones in front, it was festooned on either side with cans filled to overflowing with old food stuffs, much to the delight of an overabundance of flies enjoying the feast. She gestured to the others to join her.

Without hesitation, they left the safety of the barn and raced across the space that separated them from Tovan. Despite their attempts to keep quiet, they found it impossible to stifle the natural clucks, squawks and scrabbling claws. When they reached her, Tovan could only look at them with disgust.

"What was all that about?" she fumed. "If the inhabitants didn't know we were leaving the barn before, they sure know now."

"Sorry," mumbled Jeremiah. "I just don't seem to have any control over this body."

"This is not going to work," muttered Melisande. "If I keep having to move like this and Jeremiah and Calliotrope keep up what they're doing, which is worse…."

"It is not!" snapped the boy.

"…we'll all be caught," she finished without acknowledging his comment.

"There has ta be a way," grumbled Calliotrope. "I have fought many a mean battle and survived tem all. I don't intend to end up in a cook pot, and nither shall any a you."

"I agree," replied Tovan. "Listen, what about this? If Melisande and I could mind link with Mikel, then maybe we could convince him to try to levitate and lift himself out of that window."

"As long as Cerce hasn't taken away his magic," agreed Melisande. "Let's do it together."

Jeremiah was left to stew in his own juices while the girls closed their eyes and concentrated. Their message hit Mikel as he was crouched on the chopping board, waiting in terror for the chef's axe to fall on his now scrawny neck. He gave a piercing squawk, leaped off the table and plummeted to the ground.

I can't do it! he shrieked to the girls. *"I keep trying, but nothing is happening."*

Yes, you can! shouted Tovan into his mind.

Focus, you idiot, screamed Melisande. *Do you want to die? Wish for it! Wish! Wish!*

The axe thumped down, barely missing Mikel's tail feathers, burying itself deep into the wooden floor. Mikel made a wish with such intensity that he felt as if his head had just exploded. The cook let out an undignified curse as Mikel suddenly lifted himself off the floor and, using his feet like a duck in water, ran as fast as he could through the air and out the window. Before he could lose his concentration, Tovan raced forward and snatched him out of midair.

"Come on," she hissed to the other three.

Clutching a stunned Mikel to her chest, she raced back to the barn door, passed it by and was around the far corner with a chicken and two ducks hot on her heels before the frustrated cook had made it to the kitchen door.

"How do we get out of here?" she panted to the others, pulling into the shadows when she spotted the guarded gate. "And how do we get our clue?"

"Let me down," hissed Mikel. "I can do this on my own."

"Stop being such an ungrateful wretch," snapped Tovan as she plopped him down beside her. "Now help us try to figure out a solution to our predicament."

Cerce's soldiers were guarding the only gate in the brick wall that encircled the house and the barn. It was obvious that Cerce was not willing to be surprised by unwanted guests. She kept her home very secure. On top of everything, a moat surrounded the entire enclosure with a narrow bridge leading from the gate to the other side. There didn't appear to be any way to get through to the outside safely, and Tovan's heart sank.

Keep going, said a gentle voice that four could hear. *The guards won't see you. Trust me. Don't worry about the clue.*

"Did you hear that?" whispered Tovan, looking down at the others. "I recognize that voice."

Jeremiah nodded his head vigorously. "I could hear it too," he replied in an amazed voice.

"Well, I didn't," muttered the dwarf.

"We can't just simply walk out of here," argued Mikel. "Maybe it's a trap being set by Cerce."

"I don't think so," replied Melisande. "I agree with Tovan. There's something familiar about that voice. I do trust it."

"Well, we can't stay here," said Jeremiah, looking nervously around. "We're sitting ducks."

When the others just looked at him, he glared back and snapped, "That wasn't a joke."

"Come on," said Tovan. "Do as I do. Don't stop, don't question – just keep up."

She moved quickly toward the gate with the other three in tow. The guards didn't notice them. They passed through the gate unobserved and walked as quickly as possible over the bridge.

Run! cried the same voice when they reached the path on the other side of the moat. *Run for the forest! Run!*

They didn't have to be told twice. Tovan took off at a fierce gallop with the two chickens and the ducks close to her heels. What the birds lacked in wings, they made up for in their legs and never lagged behind as they raced for their lives across the meadow.

They were halfway across when shouts could be heard coming from behind them. Jeremiah glanced over his shoulder and then wished that he hadn't. Cerce, complete with her netted umbrella, was leading the chase perched on the back of a creature that looked like a huge cat with red, slathering jaws. Behind her were a dozen soldiers carrying enormous swords and mounted on similar creatures.

"Run!" he cried.

They were a dozen yards from the wood when disaster struck. Tovan tripped and went sprawling on her face, and the others plowed right into her, feathers flying and bird shrieks filling the air. Their pursuers were on them in an instant. When Tovan finally had the courage to look up, she discovered they were completely surrounded with no hope of escape.

"What made you think that you could escape me?" laughed Cerce. "Once I have you in my grasp, you are in it forever…or until you die."

Tovan dragged herself to a sitting position and put her arms around the others who were crowding up against her for protection.

Cerce turned to her soldiers and gestured nonchalantly to the prisoners. "I grow tired of this. With war coming, I must be ready, and these five are becoming irritating fleas. Kill them."

Tovan pulled the other four closer to her as the warriors on their terrifying mounts approached. One of the soldiers raised his sword to strike, and she covered her eyes with a raised arm and screamed. Sobbing uncontrollably, she waited for the blow to fall. She could feel the shaking bodies of Mikel and Melisande jammed up against her body, and her last thought was of her family, who would never know how she died.

Chapter Forty-One
Rosamund

Tovan

Nothing happened. Tears streamed down her cheeks, and she tried to control the shuddering sobs that wracked her body, but…nothing happened. It was utterly silent.

"What are you doing, Rosamund?" shrieked Cerce. "You have no power over my land."

"No, but I do over my own," replied a voice that both Melisande and Tovan recognized instantly.

Tovan dropped her arm and stared at the amazing sight that greeted her. The soldiers and hideous mounts were frozen in their last poses. The soldier who had raised his sword looked as if he were about to slash down on her unprotected head, and she could see frozen saliva in the process of dripping from his mount's fangs. To her astonishment, the other four had reverted to their original shapes and were struggling to their feet. Calliotrope had landed on his back and was now manfully trying to struggle up into a standing position.

Getting shakily to her own, she looked up into the eyes of Cerce. The netting on her umbrella had been pulled aside, revealing her face, and she was glaring down at Tovan with evil malice. The woman's body was motionless, but her eyes, filled with rage, began to dart back and forth between Rosamund and the four young people. Calliotrope, she ignored.

"Thank goodness you got as far as you did," said a voice next to Tovan's shoulder.

Tovan turned and took a startled step backward. Standing behind her was an elderly woman with snow-white hair piled high on her head and twinkling blue eyes. She was as round as she was tall and dressed in an old-fashioned floral dress with puffed sleeves to the wrists and pointy-toed boots. A large white apron was stretched across her middle, and all Jamie could think of when she saw her was that the woman resembled her idea of someone's sweet little old grandmother. The little balls of light floating above her head told her immediately who this funny person was.

"Rosamund?" she asked.

"Yes, of course, my dear," replied the woman. "Now, I want all of you to move back into the trees. I have some unfinished business here."

They did as they were told, watching over their shoulders as they went. Tovan felt that Rosamund didn't appear to be strong enough to take on Cerce, so she wasn't going to take any chances. If they had to run for it, she would make certain that they had a head start. Although she couldn't hear what Rosamund was saying to Cerce, she could easily tell that the goddess was not happy. Suddenly, the netting vanished from Cerce and with a shriek, she turned and raced back to her castle, her troops thundering behind.

"You will pay for this, witch," shrieked Cerce over her shoulder. "I will not forget or forgive."

Rosamund ambled over to them, chuckling merrily to herself, a satisfied smile on her face.

"She can't tolerate sunlight. Now, follow me, young ones. It's time you had some relaxation."

Melisande followed immediately, a look of absolute adoration on her face. The others grinned at each other and stepped in behind them. They hadn't experienced much being saved on this trip, so that they would take advantage of the moment. Calliotrope reluctantly followed. He'd always been a bit suspicious of the witchy types.

The Dell was a beautiful place. It was an outdoor room that had been carefully formed out of the actual foliage. The branches of the huge trees that formed the walls met overhead in a protective canopy, which at the moment was full of birds of every shape and color. Flowers filled the spaces, their various aromas drifting through the air and combining to form a heady perfume. It would have been easy to forget the trials and tribulations of the outside world, but unfortunately, Tovan could not. They had lost Jamie, Portia and Adonis, and not only was she concerned terribly about her friends, she knew their quest had ended with them gone.

When they were comfortably seated on roomy chairs made of branches and vines, Rosamund looked at the long faces with sympathy.

"Have faith," she said. "I have confidence that your friends will be found. First of all, tell me what has befallen you so far."

Each contributed sections of the quest as Rosamund listened quietly, nodding her head at times. It was a bit of a disjointed telling, but by the end, she had a fair idea of all they had encountered.

"You have done well to come so far," she commented finally, smiling kindly at each one in turn. "But unfortunately, you are not yet done. Let us have a look at the clues you have discovered so far. They should point the way to your last riddle."

"The last riddle?" exclaimed Tovan, furrowing her brow. "But we have only answered four."

"Four?" questioned Rosamund. "But that cannot be possible if you have traveled this far and have stayed with the path. Tell me about finding the clues."

"Well, first, there was Jamie's riddle," volunteered Jeremiah. "She answered the one for the Sphinx. Here is the image we got at the Sphinx."

He handed her the piece, which she carefully put on the table before her.

"And then Portia answered the one for the guardians on the island, and I got this one from Rumplestiltskin. All of them have what looks like the picture of a wall on the opposite side from the image."

Rosamund examined the two briefly before putting it with the first one.

"And I answered Cerce's," said Tovan. "But she floated it into the back of the barn, and we didn't have time to look for it."

There was a rustle above their heads, and a small box drifted down from between an array of colored balls of light into Rosamund's hands.

"No, my dears," laughed Rosamund. "My little helpers were way ahead of Cerce. They went after it as soon as she released it. Now let me have a look at this."

Rosamund carefully examined the outside of the box and handed it to Jeremiah, who then passed it on to the others.

"What do you see outside the box?" she asked.

Several minutes passed as I each examined the box.

"There are two figures that seem to be hovering in the air," responded Tovan finally. "One looks like a woman, and the other looks like…."

"Bandi," gasped Mikel. "She has Bandi."

"Who?" asked Rosamund.

Reluctantly, he told her the story of meeting the Wickersnit and his own unpleasant discovery of being a wizard. He also explained his two yelling incidents and how Bandi had discovered the source of the problem.

"Not only that," responded Melisande, her eyes glowing, "Mikel made the snakes disappear on the island, and Crutchin was able to levitate him out of the pit in that horrible Hag's Breath place. The monsters were too scared when they saw him rise up to do anything more to us."

An embarrassed flush spread over Mikel's face, and he turned abruptly away from her.

"It's not going to help if we can't find the others or answer the rest of the riddles," he grumbled.

"Time will tell," replied Rosamund softly, opening the box and removing the puzzle piece.

On the one side was the image of the strange walls on the back of the others, except that this image gave the impression of being part of the main chamber of a house.

"Oh dear, young ones. This one will be far from easy," she sighed.

She attached the piece to the others, and together the resulting image revealed what appeared to be a large, grand room – one that would be found in a castle or fortress. The images of rocks had been the walls of the room.

"Where is this place?" asked Tovan, examining the picture. "I've never seen anything like it."

"It's the main hall of Mohandas Keep," replied Rosamund with obvious distaste. "The name means 'not to be seen' and lives up to its name. It is almost impossible to find because it is built into the side of a mountain. One must fly into it. This is where you must go to answer your last riddle, but it is the home of the tyrant King Friere, and he is one of the most dangerous creatures in Aradell."

Tovan shook her head and tried to control the knot in her stomach that had formed due to Rosamund's description.

"But we have a problem. Mikel hasn't answered a riddle yet, and Melisande never received a clue when she answered hers because it wasn't one of Hera's riddles. There's still two to answer."

"That is odd," mused Rosamund. "Are you saying that you crossed the lake without encountering Brutus?"

"Brutus?" they asked in unison.

"Do you mean the monster that lives in that lake?" asked Tovan.

Rosamund nodded.

"Well," said Melisande thoughtfully. "He did ask me a riddle about how we wanted to die but said that it didn't count as one of Hera's riddles."

Rosamund laughed, her voice pealing out like a thousand tiny bells.

"That old trickster. Of course, that was one of Hera's riddles. You answered it correctly, Melisande, because Gamma whispered the answer into your mind, so it legitimately came from your own mind. You have answered five riddles."

Jeremiah shook his head. "But we didn't get an image from him."

Rosamund looked at the clues in front of her, her expression one of puzzlement.

"Who came the closest to Brutus after you solved the riddle, Melisande?"

"Why, Jeremiah, I think," she replied, looking over at the boy. "He was still in the monster's mouth when I solved the riddle."

"Check your clothing, Jeremiah," instructed Rosamund. "Check for anything that might not have been with you when you started this quest."

The boy diligently went through his clothing, but the only thing he found in his cape was a shell the size of the palm of his hand.

"You probably got that when you were sent shooting toward the island," sighed Mikel.

Jeremiah looked at the shell more closely. "Maybe not," he replied. "Remember? All of the clues have been inside objects."

Before anyone could stop him, he slammed the shell down on a boulder, smashing it into pieces. Tucked inside was a stone with a small piece of paper wrapped around a puzzle piece.

"Well done, Jeremiah," laughed Rosamund. "He might have tried to be tricky, but Brutus knew that he had to leave that clue with one of you. What does it show?"

The boy laughed. "The two turtle things in the maze and the others found them without his clue."

"What is the image on the other side?"

Jeremiah turned it over and placed it carefully into the puzzle's center. It fit perfectly and showed a large wall-sized mirror to the right of a door that appeared to lead into a dark hallway.

Tovan turned to Rosamund. "What I want to know is how we get to this place and who is the person with this Bandi creature on the outside of the box."

"It be Sharra," said a yawning Calliotrope, who had just awakened from a short, well-deserved nap in time to hear the last part of the conversation. "I would know that young lady anywhere."

Something suddenly seemed to catch Mikel's attention. He stood up and walked over to the edge of the glade, facing the direction from which they had come.

"What is it?" asked Jeremiah, coming to stand beside him.

"I don't know," he replied. "Someone's in terrible trouble, and I have a feeling that it's Jamie and Portia."

"How do you know?"

"I don't really, and it's just that…something is telling me I'm needed. Maybe it's just a suspicion, but something is wrong."

Jeremiah stared at him for a moment. "What is the message?"

Mikel didn't answer him. Instead, he began to move into the forest, slowly at first and then faster. "Come on," he shouted back over his shoulder.

Jeremiah didn't hesitate but plowed through the underbrush after him. Tovan and Melisande stood up to follow, but Rosamund stopped them.

"It's alright. The two of them will manage. Sometimes, resolving the prophecy does not solve all the problems. Sometimes things have to change in order for a prophecy actually to be resolved."

Chapter Forty-Two
A Theft Is Planned

Spider

"Your plots haven't worked," snapped Spider. "The ball shows very clearly that the wretched brats are back together again. No one has died, and they've escaped Cerce. What good are your powers if you can't stop brats?"

"I told you that luck was with them," replied a sullen Corilla. "Rosamund has been helping them all along. She was probably the one that got that Tovan girl to the dragon. It's embarrassing to call her our sister."

"They are not all there," uttered Druet. "Jamie and Portia are not with them, which is indeed strange. I wouldn't be a bit surprised if Hera has involved herself, which is entertaining."

"What of the other child, the chosen one?" demanded Spider, ignoring Druet's comments.

The four leaned toward the crystal ball resting on its stand in the middle of the table. Corilla cast the spell.

"Ah, now this is better," muttered Zorna, almost to herself. "The ball is showing us the main hall of the dwarf kingdom. There is Reygould...Azmodeus and behind...there...the boy. Do you recognize him?"

"No!" spat out Spider. "All the creatures look alike to me."

"Look, he's showing Azmodeus something," continued Zorna. "It can't be! The boy has the seed! The boy has the Seed of Life around his neck!"

"Foiled!" shrieked Spider. "I am undone!"

Corilla pulled away from the table. "Oh, do stop that horrible noise, Spider. All the yelling in the world is not going to solve this problem. I must think."

"So far, your thinking hasn't solved a thing," muttered Spider, trying to regain her composure.

Druet stood back from the table and crossed her arms. "I can't tell where the children will be coming out of Aradell, that is if they come out, but if Azmodeus and the boy are to join them by tomorrow, Reygould will have to send them through the mines under The Hollows, and I know where the mining tracks exit on the other side."

"I think you are developing a cunning plan, sister," grinned the toothless Corilla.

"We must get the seed away from the boy," continued Druet. "Without that seed, nothing will happen even if the children arrive here. Everything must be done together: the seed in the tree at the same time, the triad stands between good and evil, whatever or whoever they are. We go after the boy."

Silence reigned. Hidden in her spot with Beak and Claw, Kara held her breath. Who was this boy they were so interested in?

"How do we do this?" asked Spider, breaking the silence. "And what of Azmodeus? He will be able to stop an attack with his magic."

Druet smiled an evil, sly smile.

"Listen carefully," she said, gesturing to all of them to come closer.

Chapter Forty-Three
Tragedy Strikes

Petre

Petre rather enjoyed the ride at first. The cart they had all piled into hovered above one wide rail. There was nothing between the bottom of the cart and the rail except for air, which Maxim explained was what made it move. The dwarf worked the controls from the front, and as it sped over the rails, Petre felt terrified and excited all at once.

The cart traveled swiftly through tunnels lit with a strange glow that seemed to originate from the rocks. The passageways twisted and curved at an alarming rate, but Maxim didn't exhibit any outward concerns, so the boy relaxed slightly. Yonnus was hanging on for dear life, his large bulk squeezed into a space meant for someone much smaller. Azmodeus looked quite calm, his beard and hair streaming out behind him, and Crutchin crouched in a corner, looking old and ill. At the sight of his friend, Petre mentally urged the cart to move faster. Time was obviously running out for the Wildenchin.

They had been traveling for quite some time when Maxim slowed the cart to a standstill at the top of what appeared to be a steep incline. Beyond them was darkness.

"The Hollows," he muttered. "From this point on, keep as low in the cart as you can."

"Easy for you to say," grumbled Yonnus, finding it impossible to scrunch down any lower than he was.

"You must do your best," growled Maxim. "These are the caves of the swidgits. They are bat-like creatures the size of large birds. They secrete a poisonous substance through their skin; if they touch you, it will seep into your body and eventually kill you. It is a slow and agonizing death."

"Thank you for the warning," said Azmodeus. "I will be prepared to repel them as much as possible."

Maxim nodded, and the cart moved forward slowly at first, then picked up speed. The front of the vehicle began to glow with the strange light that Petre had seen in the rocks further back, and he realized that the same type of stones had been embedded in the cart frame. Maxim could see, but that also meant that the swidgits would be able to see them. The boy shivered. Maybe if the creatures lived in constant darkness, they would be blind. One could only hope.

The cart moved forward quickly but not as fast as before. The darkness obviously made it too dangerous to travel at a quicker pace. They came to their first obstacle, a short distance into the darkness. Dirt from a recent cave-in was partially covering the tracks.

"Azmodeus," shouted Maxim over his shoulder. "Can you clear it?"

The wizard stood up and raised both arms, his boney fingers gesturing to the pile of dirt in front of him. Slowly the debris receded to the side. As soon as the track was clear, Maxim pushed forward once again. There were three more cave-ins, each more severe than the previous ones, and Petre could tell that the old man was beginning to tire. His beard was now only several inches long.

"It's almost as if these have been purposefully made in order to slow us down," shouted Yonnus.

"Or to wear me out," muttered Azmodeus.

They had just risen to the top of another incline when the light from the cart revealed a terrifying sight. The track had been scattered with dirt from top to bottom, and clinging from the walls and ceiling were huge winged creatures glowing a pale white. They didn't make a sound but just clung to their perches, staring at them through round orbs that Petre assumed were their eyes.

"Swidgits," spat out Maxim.

"What do we do?" asked Crutchin, peering over the edge of the cart.

"If we stay here, we're dead," replied the dwarf. "We have to make a run through them and hope we make it to the other side. We're at the edge of their territory. They won't follow us into the next cavern because that one is outside The Hollows."

"Do you mean that we are almost through?" asked a hopeful Petre.

The dwarf nodded. "I wondered why they hadn't attacked before," he said. "They were waiting for us here because they knew Azmodeus would be at his weakest."

"I still have some surprises up my sleeves," muttered the wizard.

"I can look after the dirt," said Crutchin.

"No," replied Azmodeus gruffly. "Every time you use your powers, it ages you faster."

The Wildenchin sighed. "What good is it if we all end up dead anyway?"

Azmodeus looked at him with a deep concern for a moment, nodded slowly and then looked away. "Alright then. Let's go."

Yonnus struggled to release his sword from its scabbard and finally succeeded. "I'm ready," he growled.

Maxim nodded, and the cart shot forward.

Everything happened at once: Dirt spewed up from the tracks ahead of them; the swidgits detached themselves from their perches and, with horrific shrieks, began their attack; balls of light seemed to come out of nowhere and exploded into the white bodies that appeared to be everywhere; and Yonnus swung his sword with wild abandon and bloodcurdling cries. Petre crouched in the bottom of the cart, eyes tightly shut, convinced the end was near.

The battle seemed to go on forever, and it was suddenly over. The cart emerged into a brightly lit cavern, and Maxim kept it moving to the end of the track before bringing it to a halt. Fresh air assaulted Petre's nostrils, and when he opened his eyes, he found himself looking up at the blue sky and fluffy white clouds. They had made it!

He sat up and looked around, the smile on his face turning into a grim line of worry and concern. Maxim was hunched over the controls, gasping for breath. Azmodeus, who looked worse for wear, was bent over a sleeping or unconscious Yonnus, and Crutchin was crumpled up in the corner as white as death.

"Help me," cried Azmodeus, his voice weak and strained.

Petre scrambled up and helped the wizard stretch Yonnus out into a more comfortable position.

"What's wrong with him?" asked the boy.

"He's been touched by a swidgit. We'll have to get help if we're going to save him."

Azmodeus then turned and lifted Crutchin gently from the corner where he had fallen. Maxim had recovered enough to take the limp body from him and carry the Wildenchin to a spot under the nearest tree. He removed a blanket from one of the packs and wrapped it around the small body. Removing a second one, he trotted back to the cart and gave it to Azmodeus, who tucked it around the now shivering but still unconscious Yonnus.

Petre walked unsteadily over to Crutchin and knelt down. The Wildenchin had aged years since he had made his determined statement in the cavern to remove the dirt. Beneath the blanket lay a very old man. Petre took hold of a wrinkled hand and gently squeezed.

"Don't leave me, Crutchin," he whispered. "I need you. Please don't die."

The Wildenchin gasped for breath and opened his eyes. "You don't need me," he replied softly. "You are brave, Petre, but you must still be braver. I..."

Crutchin coughed, the raspy sound tearing at Petre's heart.

"I need you as a friend," choked the boy, tears running down his face. "You are my only true friend. Please hang on. Once I put the seed in the tree, you will be alright."

"I will always be your friend, Petre. Always."

A strange glow began to emanate from the Wildenchin's body. It became so bright that the outlines of his features blurred, and Petre had to look away. When he looked back, Crutchin had vanished. All that was left were his blanket and clothes.

"Always," floated a voice on the breeze. "Always."

Petre put his head in his hands and began to sob. He felt a hand on his back and became aware of Azmodeus and Maxim standing behind him.

"Did he die, Azmodeus?"

"In a manner of speaking," replied the old man softly. "The earth claimed him back."

"Will I ever see him again?"

"I don't know. There are more mysteries in this universe than anyone can count."

A groan came from the cart.

"Come. We have not yet lost Yonnus, but if I cannot figure out a way to save him, we will."

Azmodeus turned his back on the boy and rushed over to help his friend.

Petre looked over at the cart. What could he possibly do to help? There had to be something. They couldn't have two friends die in one day.

He raised his face to the sky and closed his eyes. "Don't let Yonnus die," he whispered.

At that moment, a dark figure rose up from behind one of the rocks and raised cloaked arms toward the boy. It was positioned so that neither he nor Azmodeus was aware of its presence until Petre felt a tingling around his neck. He reached up to grasp the chain, but it melted through his fingers like mist.

"Azmodeus!" he gasped.

As the old man turned, the dark figure tucked away its prize and vanished from sight.

"The Seed of Life!" choked Petre. "It's gone!"

Chapter Forty-Four
No Choice

Bandi stared up at the statue in awe. The creature was beautiful, and for a second, he forgot about the monster standing behind him. It was of a woman who seemed startled by something and was caught turning around. It was so life-like that he felt if he touched it, she would actually move.

"Do you like her?" snorted the voice behind. "She angered me some years ago, and as a result, this became her fate. Do not mind the link, Wickersnit. You are capable of speech."

"Sharra, this is?" he squeaked, nodding in agreement to her request.

"Of course," snapped Hera. "Who else do you think it would be? Now, for your punishment. Turn and face me, chameleon."

Reluctantly the Wickersnit turned to her.

"Originally, I was going to destroy you. After all, you failed at what I sent you to do and got caught by an inexperienced wizard. No one fails me without paying the price."

Bandi began to shake. He was terrified because he knew what the goddess was capable of doing.

"However," continued Hera, "a new idea has come into my mind. With the last riddle and image, the urchins will be forced to come here…hopefully including that rotten little man, Azmodeus. So far, I have been toying with them and thoroughly enjoyed the experience. This place, however, will be their grave."

She threw back her head and laughed. "Now for you, my little shape-shifter. You failed me the last time I gave you a task to do, but this time you will not fail. Let me show you why."

She pointed a long, elegant finger at a cage hanging from the ceiling in the corner of the cell. Bandi had glanced at it when he had entered the enclosure, but out of sheer terror, he had not thought about it. Several occupants resembled oddly shaped mice. He gasped. They weren't mice. They were tiny Wickersnits holding out their arms, appearing to plead with him.

"These my people are," he whispered.

Hera laughed.

"Oh. They are more than that. They are members of your own family. I was able to rescue your mother and brother from the mines but could not find your father. Thanks to your cowardice, no one warned the village that day, and most of your people were taken as prisoners."

Bandi moaned and bent over, clutching his sides. How had she found out about that? Shame flooded through him as he rocked from side to side, wishing with all his might that his actions that day of the attack had been different.

"Oh, do stop that awful caterwauling," snapped Hera. "You should be thanking me for my kindness and generosity. Now stand up."

"But prisoners, you have them here," groaned Bandi as he pulled himself up and took a deep breath.

"Of course," replied Hera, giving a flip of her hand as if it were of no consequence. "I had to make them smaller to fit into their new home, but they have food and water and will remain quite safe as long as you do what I tell you to do."

Bandi shivered. He couldn't imagine what Hera had in mind but, for the second time, felt he would probably have been better off in the spice mines.

"If what you ask, I do, let them go home, you will?"

"It depends on you," chuckled Hera. "Now, this is your new task."

Bandi listened, shocked and terrified, as Hera described what he was to do.

"Cannot I do this," he protested. "Trying so hard they are."

There was a sudden grinding of metal in the corner. The cage holding his family was being lowered and stopped when it reached several inches down.

"Can you see what is under the cage, chameleon?" asked the goddess.

Bandi glanced over and cried out. A large barrel full of water was sitting directly below the cage.

"There are only a few days left before the time allowed for the quest will expire," she continued. "Each day, I will lower that cage, one cage length toward the water, until you have completed your task. Will you finally develop the courage to rescue your family this time, or will you remain a coward?"

Bandi suddenly felt angry. His hatred for the goddess was clearly etched on his face. There was no way to get out of this, and in the end, he would probably be hunted down and destroyed by everyone in Eleusia.

"Do it, I will," he snapped. "Choice, I have none."

Hera gave a nasty laugh.

"Of course, you don't," came her droll reply.

Chapter Forty-Five
The Sixth Riddle

Mikel

Mikel stopped and listened.

"There," he pointed, taking off again toward what appeared to be a small hill within a thick grove of trees. "They're in there. Hurry!"

"Who is in what?" shouted Jeremiah, but when Mikel didn't reply, he simply shrugged his shoulders and followed him. Mikel stopped when he reached the hill. Clouds of dust were emerging from a tunnel entrance that could only be attributed to a recent cave-in.

"Oh no!" he cried. "Dig, Jeremiah! We have to dig them out!"

He attacked the cave entrance with his hands, and responding to the desperate urgency in his voice, Jeremiah did the same without asking why.

After several minutes of frantic digging, both of them stopped, and Mikel dropped his head into his hands.

"It's no use. We're too late. They're buried under all that dirt, and we can't reach them."

"Are you talking about Jamie, Portia and Adonis?" asked Jeremiah.

Mikel simply nodded.

"But, Mikel," he cried, leaping to his feet. "You have magic. Dig them out with your magic?"

Mikel hesitated for only a moment before turning to face the cave entrance. "I wish Jamie, Portia and Adonis to be set free."

Nothing happened.

He repeated the wish in a louder voice, but it was no good. Nothing moved. Jeremiah looked over at him and slowly shook his head, dirty cheeks stained with watery tears. It was too late to save them now.

Mikel's attention was suddenly drawn to the trees. It might have been his imagination, but it was almost as if the ones in their vicinity were beginning to move.

"Get back!" he shouted.

They moved quickly away from the hill, which was now rippling and rolling like someone under a blanket trying to get out. It didn't take much urging to get Jeremiah to move when part of the hill came loose and was tossed in his direction.

"Wow," he gasped. "Those trees are actually digging through the dirt!"

He turned and gaped at Mikel. "How is this happening? Did you do that?"

Mikel didn't respond. His eyes never strayed from the tunnel entrance, and when he spotted the first body, he tore forward with Jeremiah on his heels.

The trees had literally torn the top off the tunnel, which now resembled a small gorge. Digging carefully down into the dirt with their roots, they lifted the three bodies up and out, depositing them gently on the grass. Adonis began to cough and moan, but the girls remained motionless. Mikel watched Jeremiah hurry over to Jamie and squat down in the grass. He cleared the dirt out of her mouth and, taking a deep breath, put his mouth down on hers and seemed to blow air into it. Mikel had never seen anything like it. What was the boy trying to do? He was conscious of Portia groaning behind him, which eased his mind a bit, but why wasn't Jamie breathing? Jeremiah continued to count and breathe, turning his ear to her mouth to listen in between. Suddenly, she sobbed and began to choke. He quickly turned her on her side as she brought up the dirt and phlegm that had been lodged inside.

"You healed her!" Mikel exclaimed, kneeling beside him. "Is this a new magic skill of yours?"

"That wasn't magic. I learned to do that in my good old life-saving course."

"Well, good job," grinned Mikel, slapping the other boy unexpectedly on the back. A startled Jeremiah looked back at him and grinned.

Jamie wiped the dirt off her face with the inside of her cape, which did little good except to allow her to see better. When she looked up at Jeremiah and saw Mikel, tears began to roll down her cheeks.

"You're alive," she sobbed. "Oh, I thought I had killed you…I was certain it was a trick but…but…I just didn't know. I…I could have been wrong. Adonis kept telling me it was all an illusion, but…I just didn't know."

With that, she pulled her knees up to her chin and covered her face with her hands. She began to cry as if her heart were broken.

"It's all been too much for her," said Adonis from behind.

"She had to make a choice," said Portia, her own eyes filling with tears.

Mikel turned to look at her.

"What choice?"

Taking a deep breath, Portia told them what had happened. "When Hera told her to choose, I expected her to go down to the island to rescue all of you. She stood there for the longest time and then came over to me and pulled me out of the basket and onto the bridge."

The girl stopped and swallowed hard as a tear rolled down her cheek. "Hera told us that she would give us a head start out of the cavern because she was a sporting soul. Ha! We barely got into the tunnel when she started to bring it down on top of us. Don't you see? Jamie didn't know if she had given all of you up for me, and I was the one who got us into the mess in the first place."

At this point, Portia began to cry in earnest. "No one else would have done that for me. I've always said that my family would want me back and that I'm important to them, and…well, it's not true.

They don't like me or care for me. They wouldn't have chosen me over something important to them. Oh, Jamie, I'm sorry."

Jamie pulled her head up and wiped her face again, resulting in a worse mess than before. "It's alright, Portia," she sniffed. "I took a chance that Adonis was right and the others were illusions. However, I somehow knew that you were real and would not leave you behind under any circumstances. We're family now. You're my sister."

She gave the girl a shaky grin, who, in turn, responded with a similar one.

"We are, aren't we," whispered Portia.

Jeremiah suddenly pointed at Portia's wrist. "Look! Look at her bracelet! It's glowing!"

True enough, the ball attached to the chain was glowing almost as brightly as it had before the Willik had put it on her wrist.

"But I haven't saved anyone's life yet," protested the girl.

"Maybe you've started to save your own," said Rosamund coming up from behind.

She smiled down at the little group. "Come, children. We have much to do before tomorrow morning."

She chuckled, the tinkling sound bouncing through the glade. "I think we have some cleaning up to do as well."

They helped each other stand up and followed Rosamund as she waddled back in the direction of her glade. Jeremiah put an arm around Portia's shoulders and hugged her before letting her go. She was very grateful that the dirt on her face hid the blush that must have covered it from neck to hairline. Mikel, however, stood and watched them, a frown on his face. He couldn't forgive Portia for what she had done. Jamie and Adonis had almost died because of her selfishness. What if he hadn't been close enough to be there to know, or what if the trees hadn't helped? He shivered at the thought and followed the rest, determined at some time to deal with Portia.

"Why did the trees help us?" asked Tovan when they got back to the dell.

Rosamund smiled.

"Someone who cares," she replied. "One day, you might be lucky enough to meet the Spirit of Eleusia, who will explain it all to you. I would say that Mikel had a hand in it as well."

Calliotrope left early the next morning to make his trek home to his people. "They must be warned," he grumbled. "Until this curse is lifted, we must prepare for war. I have much ta share with my people."

With hugs all around and promises that they would meet again, the dwarf started with a new walking stick and a pack full of supplies. As he disappeared from sight, a feeling of loss settled over everyone. He had been with them and helped through several tough adventures. He had been like a member of the quest in many ways, and they felt they were losing a valued friend. After his departure, the rest sat around Rosamund's table, examining the clues.

"As I explained before," said Rosamund, "Mohandas Keep is in a gorge, and the only way to get to it is by flying there. I cannot understand why your last clue ends there, as it is very difficult to get to. One needs some manner of flight. Jeremiah, do you think that Brax might oblige?"

"She might," was his response.

He closed his eyes and opened them with a laugh after a few minutes of concentration. "Brax is willing and will be here as soon as possible. She told me that she can't bring her son, Crill, because he is just learning to fly and is being, and I quote, 'somewhat idiotic about it.'"

The others laughed as well and then turned back to the discussion of the tasks ahead of them.

Mikel straightened his shoulders. "The sixth riddle must be mine. I'm the only one who hasn't answered one."

He suddenly looked puzzled.

"What's wrong?" asked Rosamund.

"Well, the strange thing is that whenever we were faced with solving a riddle, something kept me back from volunteering. It felt like something was telling me that it wasn't my turn."

For a moment, the little woman looked thoughtful, as if she knew more than she was telling, and then she got back down to business.

"For this last one, I can give you a clue. It is the most difficult riddle, and in order to answer it, you must look deep within yourself. You must look beyond what you are shown in order to decipher the message."

"I don't understand," said Mikel looking confused. "Do you know what the riddle asks?"

"No, but I have my suspicions," replied Rosamund. "You must try hard to understand this last riddle. Our fate rests upon that understanding."

Mikel gulped. Jamie patted his shoulder in sympathy as the girls looked at each other with concern. It just didn't seem to get any better for them.

"You have all done well so far," said Rosamund cheerfully. "More than many adults could have done. You will also conquer this challenge, and you, Adonis, will stay with me until this is all over."

"I can do this," huffed the little creature.

"But we have a job to do," smiled the fairy queen. "We must get the spell broken that keeps you a Minotaur, and until we do, you must remain in Aradell."

The expression on the little guy's face was so woebegone that even Jeremiah felt sorry for him.

Melisande bent down and put a hand on his shoulder. "You have been very brave, Adonis. No one could have asked more of you. But I would constantly worry about you if you came with us, which could put me in danger. Please stay with Rosamund for my sake."

Adonis grabbed her hand, his lower lip trembling. "But I won't be there if you get into trouble."

She put her hand over her heart. "Yes, you will," she smiled. "You will be right here the whole time."

For once, no one snickered at the look of adoration that shone from the eyes of the little Minotaur.

"Alright, Melisande," he said, his voice a little stronger. "I will stay here, be brave for you and find a way to return to normal." He grimaced. "Even if I have to face Cerce again."

She kissed him on the forehead, and he blushed crimson. "Ah, don't go doing that," he groaned.

This time, there were laughs all around.

"Be brave," said Rosamund. "Now you must go. I see Brax beginning to land."

"Come on, everyone," said a determined Mikel. "The sooner we start, the sooner it will be over."

"I hope you mean that positively," sighed Portia.

Rosamund watched the group gather their packs and approach Brax with appropriate bows and comments. She had not been truthful with Mikel, for she knew that this last riddle was not similar to the other ones they had previously answered. It had been changed intentionally from the one that Hera had originally wanted to be asked by Friere, and if the goddess found out about the change, it would destroy the only chance they had of breaking this curse. The Willik and the elves had been hard at work throughout the quest in order to keep Mikel as the last responder to the riddles. Rosamund was at a loss as to how the ancient elf had done it. Friere had been reluctant to change the riddle at first, but the Willik had convinced him through ways to which only she had been privy. Rosamund was also worried about what the goddess might have in store for the group on their arrival at the Keep. They had escaped all her previous traps, but if Hera had been serious about destroying them, they would all be dead by now.

"No," she whispered. "So far, she's just been playing with them."

A cold sensation crept up her spine. It was time to change the rules of the game. "Gamma," she called.

The little fairy was there in an instant.

"Take a small troupe and go and find Azmodeus. Tell him to get here as fast as he can."

She watched as the group climbed safely onto the back of the dragon. Jeremiah sat in the front, grasping the dragon's shoulder ridge. The others sat in a row behind, each with their arms wrapped around the waist of the person in front and each hoping they wouldn't fall off and die. Brax did her best to keep at a smooth, steady level as they flew up to the top of the mountain range. As she flew over the crest of the tallest peak and began her dive down the other side, the air was filled with terrified shrieks and cries. Mikel was scared witless by the speed and down slope of her descent. The dragon's amused laugh drifted over them as she began to circle down to the ground.

As she back-winged in order to land, Mikel spotted the gorge below them. The dragon was landing on a snowy meadow above what he hoped was Mohandas Keep and their final destination.

"But if we're up here," asked Portia, "how are we going to get down into the castle?"

As they slid down onto the ground, Jeremiah was busy asking Brax the same question.

"We are to follow the path over there," he finally explained, pointing to a narrow opening between two rocks. "Brax said that it would take us to a set of stairs that descends into the back of the castle. She is too big to take us to the main door in the gorge, so we have to take it from here."

He turned back to the dragon and bowed. "Thank you, Brax. We couldn't have made it this far without you."

The rest also bowed, and Brax took off in a flurry of snow.

"Well, come on, everybody," moaned Mikel, hoisting up his pack. "Let's get this over with."

With a few mutterings of agreement, the group started in the direction Brax had indicated. It began to snow lightly, shortly after they left the two rocks behind, but they trudged on, thankful once again for the solid boots the elves had originally given to them. The path wound steadily downwards, and the snow became deeper. The path they were following had surprisingly little snow on its surface, but the drifts on either side continued to rise. Eventually, it was impossible to see over the top.

"This isn't so bad," stated Jeremiah giving a hopeful smile.

Whether it was the actual words or poor timing on his part, the sky above began to fill with dark, ominous clouds, and a chill wind blew toward them down the tunneled pathway.

"Oh no," he cried. "I never should have said that."

"Murphy's Law," sighed Jamie.

"What?" asked Mikel.

"Just an expression from our former world. You say something like, 'This isn't so bad,' and it gets bad."

Mikel gave her a puzzled look, shook his head and carried on.

The wind picked up, and snow blew in circles around them, getting denser with each powerful gust. If it hadn't been for the walls of snow on either side, they probably would have become separated from each other and wandered off in different directions. The howling noise of the gale made it almost impossible to hear one another.

"Did we miss the stairs leading down?" shouted Jamie. "I haven't seen any turn-offs."

"Keep going," Mikel shouted back. "We mustn't stop."

They tried to move faster, but fighting the wind was like pushing against a door that someone was trying to close from the other side. Suddenly, the blizzard stopped, and the clouds rumbled away.

"This is better," he grinned. "Now, maybe we'll be able to find those stairs."

With no warning whatsoever, the ground suddenly disappeared beneath their feet. They fell, screaming and yelling, tumbling down what appeared to be a circular ice slide. It twisted and turned in a downward spiral taking its captives with it. They were completely out of control and collided heavily with one another as they slid down the icy surface, finally spewing out onto the floor of what appeared to be a dark grotto. It was the massive hall that they had seen in the completed puzzle. The floor and walls were covered in dark, reddish-colored brick, and the arched ceiling was so high that it disappeared into the shadows above. Portraits of men and women dressed in expensive clothing and covered with jewels peered down at them from lofty heights. The distorted, terrified looks on their faces and in their eyes were not at all reassuring. Pennants of different families that none of them would have recognized hung limply from the beams above; their colors faded, their cords covered in spider webs. The only light in the massive hallway was coming from torches in sconces placed at intervals along the walls. It was a dark, somber and very frightening place.

They struggled to their feet, rubbing sore arms and knees, and cautiously looked around.

"What are those?" asked Tovan, her voice shaking slightly.

She was pointing at the wall beside them. At first, Mikel couldn't see what had caused her to be so frightened. And then he saw them…the shadows of men, women and children hanging in baskets on what appeared to be leafless trees…their mouths open as if silently screaming…their eyes wide with terror.

"What kind of place have we landed in?" squeaked Melisande, her eyes the size of saucers.

"Come on," replied Mikel, his voice cracking slightly. "Let's keep going."

At the end of the room, they were faced with a doorway in front of them and a massive mirror covering the wall on the right. They could see themselves clearly in the reflection, and what they saw was deflating. Their clothes were dirty and worn, and the faces that stared back at them seemed to have aged. They were not the carefree band that had set off from Donagal so many days before.

"I don't understand it," whispered a shaking Tovan, looking around. "I don't see or hear anyone. Who or what are we actually waiting for?

"You are waiting for me," hissed a voice that seemed to come from all around them.

A shadow glided through and across the walls, one moment in front of them, the next behind.

"You are tressspassssing on my mountain. Why?"

Mikel sucked in his breath. If this was the dreaded King Friere, he sounded like a snake.

"We are searching for the sixth of Hera's riddles," he replied, his voice quaking. "We were told that we would find it in this castle."

"That issss possssible," hissed the voice, the words seeming to slither around the six shaking figures. "But you are tressspassssing in my home, and how impolite to not usssse my name."

"I apologize, King Friere," he croaked, trying to bow respectfully even though he didn't know where Friere was. "I should have used your name. Can you help us?"

The shadow stopped in the mirror in front of them and then began to move forward. The closer he came, the more distinct his shape became and the more sinuous his movements. Slowly he emerged into the hall, moving out of the mirror as if it were a wall of mist.

King Friere was terrifying. His head was that of a cobra, the hood flaring out and up from behind. The scales were shades of green and yellow, each one reflecting back the faint light coming from the torches in the chamber. The result was a sinuous, rippling effect that made Mikel shiver. Cold and emotionless yellow eyes drifted from one terrified member of the group to the next, and no one could hold his gaze for more than several seconds before turning desperately away. A robe of intense black covered Friere from neck to ankles but failed to cover the scaled clawed hands or feet.

He stood without moving for several long minutes, appearing to enjoy the sight of the shaking, terrified humans in front of him. Finally, he spoke. "I have waited for you for many dayssss. You have come for the sssssixth riddle. However, it will not assssist you. Thosssse who enter my kingdom, remain assss you can sssssee."

He pointed to the walls around them, to their horror, the shapes of captured people silently screaming began to form behind the bricks on all the walls. Friere filled the hall with harsh laughter, which ended as quickly as it had begun.

"You may anssssswer the riddle, but it will do you no good."

"What is the riddle?" asked Mikel, bravely stepping forward despite the fact he was shaking like a leaf.

"Are you the one who is to anssswer?"

"I am."

"Yesssss…it should be you. Look into the mirror. What do you ssssee?"

Mikel was taken aback by the statement that it should be him but turned and looked at the mirror. It was so clear that everyone in the grotto was reflected back to him. Slowly, however, everyone began to fade except for himself, Jamie and Jeremiah. He turned and looked quickly back at the group. They were all there, but when he looked back at the reflection in the mirror, there were only three.

"I don't understand this riddle," he said, looking up at Friere.

"If you don't undersssstand," replied the serpent, "then your quesssst is losssst. I am sssso very pleassssed that you will be sssstaying with me assss my permanent guessssstssss, but unfortunately, before that can happen, ssssomeone elsssse would like to meet with you. Sharra is down thossse stairssss. She has missssed her children."

Friere's cold, bitter laugh followed them through the doorway into the semi-darkness of a hall. The only place to go was to descend the set of stairs they could see ahead of them. They cautiously moved toward them and began to descend rickety, metal steps that seemed to go down and down forever. The area at the bottom of the stairs was dark and damp and smelled of rotting garbage. Ahead of them was an open door to a room that looked very much like a…

"A cell!" gasped Jamie. "This is the castle dungeon."

Mikel!

He stopped and peered into the dark shadows that filled the hallway in the other direction.

Bandi? Is that you?

I, it is. I need you. You can come?

I'm coming.

He took off down the hallway toward Bandi without saying a word to anyone. He raced down the hallway, traveling as fast as he could over the rough, cobblestone floor. The message from Bandi had sounded a bit frantic, as if he were in trouble and needed help. The hallway was dark and dank, with only a faint glow of light helping him to find his way. There were no rooms along its length, and the only sound was his panting as he ran. The hallway ended suddenly and opened up into a large room with enough light for him to discover that it was round with a dome-shaped ceiling and empty of any furniture. In the center was a circle outlined on the floor, and Bandi was crouched in the center of the circle.

Mikel hurried over to him, noting as he got closer that the expression on the face of the creature was one of pain. Tears were running down his cheeks, and he moaned softly as he rocked back and forth.

What is it, Bandi? What's wrong?

Sorry am I, Mikel. Sorry, am I.

Mikel heard a soft click and was suddenly aware of a closed-in sensation as if something had been dropped over him. He couldn't see anything, but when he moved away from Bandi with his hands in front of him, he came up against a hard wall.

What is this? he asked as he moved around the wall feeling his way.

Sorry, am I?

Bandi continued to rock back and forth.

Mikel discovered that he was encased in something round and clear. He could see through it, but he couldn't move through it. It was as if someone had put a glass bowl over them.

Why are we in this strange prison?

Magic work not here. You magician be. Hera not want your magic working.

Michael looked back at him.

Then why are you here, Bandi?

Slowly, the Wickersnit's shape began to change. It seemed to grow thinner and longer. His face began to lengthen and flatten. Mikel backed away from him in horror. Forming in front of him was a snake twice his height and just as wide. The boy shrieked at him.

What are you doing?

She me told, kill you must I.

Why?!

If kill you I do not, mother and brother drowned will be.

Bandi slithered toward Mikel and then slipped behind him, wrapping himself around the boy's legs and then moving upward and encasing his body. Mikel shouted at him as he moved.

We are friends, Bandi! We are bonded to each other!

Sorry am I, Mikel.

She's not going to let you leave this cage alive, Bandi. Your mother and brother are probably already dead. She's evil, Bandi!

Bandi continued to wrap himself around Mikel, squeezing harder and harder as he went. Mikel's struggles and shouts began to weaken, and finally, they stopped altogether. He lay limp and quiet within the coils.

Chapter Forty-Six
The Final Trap

Jamie

No one had noticed Mikel leave. They had entered the cell, too entranced by its occupant to be aware of his departure.

"That statue," exclaimed Melisande. "She was one of the images in our last puzzle piece. Didn't Calliotrope say it was Sharra?"

"She's beautiful," whispered Portia, gazing up at the alabaster statue in wonder. "She looks so real, doesn't she?"

Jamie gazed up at the figure with a puzzled expression. Couldn't it be…could it? Had Hera turned her mother into a statue?

"She was quite beautiful if you like that type," came a voice from behind.

They all turned at once.

"Hera," whispered a horrified Jamie.

The woman standing in the doorway could only have been one person. She was stunningly beautiful, her blonde hair a mass of intricate curls arranged charmingly around her head. Her toga was a glistening white, trimmed along the edges with gold thread stitched into elaborate ancient Greek symbols and patterns. Ropes of gold coins hung around her neck and wrists, and ribbons of gold material were laced carefully and intricately through her hair. She was the picture of a New Olympus goddess.

The five tried to run, but there was no place to go. Hera stood at the cell door, pealing with laughter at their pathetic efforts to escape her. After several minutes of this mayhem, she grew bored, waved her hand, and they all froze in place. No matter how hard they struggled, it was impossible to move. Hera had them firmly caught in her trap. Jamie panicked. Why had the spell worked on her when she was supposedly immune to them? Was the goddess that much more powerful than the witches?

"Why are you doing this?" she gasped. She had been frozen in place, looking directly at the goddess. "We have done nothing to you."

Hera laughed again. "Oh, you are all quite irrelevant in the large picture of my plans. I have wanted to get rid of all you pathetic creatures for a while, and to be honest, I really was very angry with Sharra. I'm sure she went out of her way to attract Zeus and so, therefore, had to pay."

"How evil and petty," fumed Jeremiah, who could just barely see her out of the corner of his eye. "Why go to all the trouble of turning my mother into a statue, making up a prophecy and having all of us go on a stupid quest if we were irrelevant."

"Boredom, my dear fellow," she replied, moving slowly into the room, eyeing each of them as she passed. "There is nothing at all to do in New Olympus. At least in Earth's dimension, I was able to harass the creatures like you on a regular basis – but not here. Oh no. The Council decided when we arrived that the occupants of this world would be left alone. I tried to change their minds but to no avail. The only way I could force the rest of the Council to recognize the fact that none of you were worth saving was by creating havoc and war between all your peoples, which I am in the process of doing. The gods and goddesses will never stand for that, as your people promised never to fight with each other, so they will probably destroy all of you in the end. I will never be accused of instigating it. No one will suspect me. I must admit that it has been vastly entertaining."

"The Olympus Council won't let you get away with it," argued Jamie. "The Willik has sent messengers to tell them what you have been doing."

Hera laughed again, the tone of it raspy and evil.

"Those pathetic creatures never even made it halfway before I destroyed them. The Council knows nothing of my doings and whereabouts."

"Please let us go," cried Tovan. "We've done all you asked."

"No, my dear, I can't let any of you go," replied Hera, her response full of fake regret. "I can't afford for any of you to repeat what I just told you. Besides, my plot is reaching its climax, and I refuse to miss it."

She made a gesture, and suddenly, metal boards slapped against the window just above their heads, sealing off air and light. Water could be heard trickling along the floor at their feet, and Jamie was filled with a growing terror. The cell door shut with a bang and was swiftly covered with the metallic-looking boards that had covered the window. They were securely locked in.

"What are you doing?" she cried, struggling to move. Everyone began to yell and scream at once, and she couldn't help the sobs or the tears that ran down her face.

"Stop that horrible noise!" shouted Hera, placing her hand on the statue of Sharra. "I would advise you all to practice holding your breath. It will bode well for you when the water covers your faces."

They cried out to her to let them go, to please not do this to them, but Hera simply replied with a nasty laugh and disappeared, taking the statue of Sharra with her.

The five continued to cry out and beg for her to come back but to no avail. One by one, they stopped, too exhausted emotionally to carry on.

"The water has covered my foot," sobbed Portia. "What are we going to do?"

"Mikel," called out Jamie. "Can you do something with your magic?"

No one answered.

"Mikel?" she repeated. "Mikel, where are you?"

Still, no one answered.

"Didn't he come into this cell with us?" she cried.

"I thought he was right behind me," sighed an exhausted Jeremiah.

"Try to mind link with him," suggested Portia, trying to hold back her sobs.

Melisande and Tovan tried, but nothing came back to them.

"What about your fairies, Melisande?" begged Tovan. "Surely you can get through to them or Rosamund?"

The girl tried her best, but there was just emptiness in her mind and nothing more.

"I can't hear anything. It's like there is a wall around my mind."

"Mine too," wailed Tovan. "Everything just feels black and empty."

"We have to do something," cried Portia. "The water is up to my knees."

"Mikel, where are you," whispered Jamie to herself. "We need you…we need you…now!"

Chapter Forty-Seven
Time Is Running Out

Azmodeus

"I came as soon as I received your message," said Azmodeus, getting to his feet.

He had arrived with one hand on Petre and another on a now unconscious Yonnus. He pointed to the sick man, a look of desperation on his face. "Can you heal him, Rosamund? A swidget touched him when we were escaping The Hollows. It is critical that you help him."

Rosamund knelt down beside the unconscious man and touched his face, now covered with sweat. His breathing was labored, and a purple sheen was beginning to form around his mouth. She placed a hand on either side of the big man's face, closed her eyes and concentrated.

"I've done all I can for the moment," she sighed, getting to her feet a few minutes later. "Azmodeus, you must hurry to Mohandas Keep. That is where the six have gone for the last riddle, and I have a horrible feeling that that is where Hera will take her revenge. We are past the point of others not being able to help them. That woman is going to follow through with the curse with or without six riddles."

The wizard nodded and got quickly to his feet. "You will stay here, Petre," he said, holding up his hand when the boy began to protest. "I will be bringing the others back here. I have already contacted the Willik, who will have gryphons and riders waiting for us when we return."

He looked over at Yonnus, who had been moved to a vine bed within Rosamund's grotto. She patted his arm when she saw his expression of worry and concern.

"I can't continue helping him while you are still here. Go now and hurry."

Azmodeus nodded. "Yes," he sighed. "There is even more at stake now."

As Petre watched in amazement, the wizard walked away from the grotto and suddenly disappeared from sight. He emerged into the room that the six young people had occupied a short time before. Azmodeus was very familiar with this particular castle and its monstrous owner. One of these days, he would have to do something about Friere. He was also completely without his beard. The trip from the cave to Rosamund's grotto had taken most of its magic, and this one to Mohandas Keep had taken the rest. He crept quietly toward the door at the end of the hall, hearing for the first time the faint cries coming up from the dungeon beneath.

Before he had a chance to enter the hallway beyond, Friere glided out from the wall. "What made you think you could ssssneak your way into my home?" the monster hissed. "You are a fool, wizard. I warned you the lasssst time what would happen if you showed up again."

The wizard felt a moment of panic. Without his beard, Friere had the power to destroy him, and he knew that the snake had picked up on that point. Slowly and sinuously, the creature began to move toward Azmodeus, who in turn moved backward and away from him.

"I have alwayssss wanted a wizard in my grand display of the living dead," Friere smirked, the reptilian eyes glinting.

In his right claw, he clutched a golden rod the length of a grown man, entwined with snakes and vines that appeared to be starting to move and slither around its length. The wizard knew the power that the rod held and also that it was the main source of Friere's strength. With his beard, he could have defended himself, but without it, he was at Friere's mercy.

A plan quickly formed in his mind. If he could play to the creature's huge ego and narcissistic cravings for a few moments, it might be enough time to let his beard grow out.

"I have come to warn you, Friere," he shouted, standing confidently with legs astride and arms folded across his chest.

"Warn me? What kind of warning could a little thing like you provide a mighty king like mysssself. All fear me, including you!"

"Those of New Olympus do not fear you, and if they find out that you have been helping Hera with her monstrous plan, you will be punished."

"You sssspeak ridiculoussss nonssssssensssse. Why should they punish me? The Willik promised me no harm if I sssswitched the riddlesss."

"But I didn't promise you anything. The gods and goddesses formed a pact with the Draukenbergians that they would never bother us or interfere with our plans as long as we cooperated and lived in peace with each other. Hera has broken that pact and promise. When the Olympian Council hears what she has done, she and all who assisted her will be punished."

Friere was quiet for a moment.

"What have you to say for your horrific actions?" asked Azmodeus.

"What horrific actionssss? All I did wassss assssk the boy a riddle and ssssend them off to meet Hera. She wanted to congratulate them for anssssswering all the riddlessss."

The snake gave a semblance of a smile, pleased with how he had handled this.

"That's a lie, Friere. You knew that she had no intentions of keeping them safe. You allowed them to go to their deaths."

A terrible thought crossed Friere's mind. He had been proud of the fact that Hera had involved him in her diabolical scheme and had been looking forward to having six more bodies in his forest of living dead. He had even stayed out of the way when that Spider monster had come to check on the statue. But what if the wizard was right? What would happen to him if the Olympus Council discovered his involvement? Azmodeus watched as all these thoughts were communicated through the variety of expressions on his reptilian features.

"They are…are sssstill alive…I think…down there," he almost whispered. He pointed through the door to the top of the stairs.

"If they are all still alive, Friere, I will not mention your participation in Hera's diabolical scheme. But you must promise to release all your prisoners that you keep in that horrific forest of death of yours and never kidnap another. However, if any of the young ones are harmed, that will be a different matter. I will inform the Council."

Friere straightened up, his contrite expression turning to one of fierce anger. "That issss too much to assssk of me," he hissed.

The wizard was beginning to lose his temper. Time was running out for the young people, and their voices were becoming fainter.

"Would you rather spend eternity in the seventh realm?"

Friere's face actually appeared to turn bright purple with anger. "Alright. I will do assss you ssssay, but you must promisssse not to passss my name on to the Council."

Azmodeus could have cheered. He knew that the monster would never keep his word, but at the moment, it would do. His beard had returned, and he was ready. "Only if all the children are well."

He rushed through the door and down the stairs as fast as he could. At the bottom, he could hear more clearly the cries that were coming from behind the sealed door of the cell in front of him. With a fierce shout, he threw a spell at the door, which exploded outwards, releasing wave after wave of wretched-smelling water. Azmodeus had to leap back up the stairs in order to escape from being swept away. As soon as the water subsided, he rushed into the cell.

He was horrified at the sight that greeted him. The young people stood as if frozen in place and soaked to the skin. All were sobbing or gasping except for Tovan, who did not appear to be conscious. The water had reached their ears, but as Tovan was the smallest, it had reached even further. He went to Tovan first. She was still alive but barely.

"You have to release us," croaked Jeremiah. "I can give her help, but we need to be able to move."

Azmodeus looked around in a panic. Hera had put this spell on them. He didn't have the power to undo it himself. There was only one who could do it. He closed his eyes and concentrated, ignoring the cries for him to unfreeze them.

Sapphire. Can you hear me?

There was silence for a moment, and then the Willik responded.

Faintly. I sense that something is wrong.

Hera has placed a motion spell on the young ones. They are in a terrible state. Would it be possible for you to help me break it?

There was a second moment of silence before she responded.

I will join minds with you. Follow my lead.

Azmodeus felt the warmth of her presence and joined with her as she chanted an ancient spell so old that even the wizard did not recognize it.

Heads were the first to show signs of movement, and as the spell continued, they could finally feel life return to all parts of their bodies. Not one remained standing when the spell was completed. All collapsed to the ground, emotionally and physically exhausted from the horrific experience. Jeremiah tried to calm the shaking that had taken over his body and dragged himself over to an unmoving Tovan.

With a quick word of thanks to Willik, Azmodeus moved quickly from one to the other, checking for injuries. The experience horribly shook all, but they were more concerned for Tovan than themselves. They hobbled or dragged themselves over to where Jeremiah was trying desperately to help her and silently watched as he tried as hard as he could to get her to breathe.

All at once, Tovan choked, and Jeremiah turned her over on her side as the water spewed out of her mouth. Gasping for breath, she tightly held onto the boy's hand as she tried to calm herself.

Melisande sat down beside her and gently pulled the girl up into a sitting position, holding her tightly. Tovan could only hiccup and sob, and she was so weak.

"Well done, son," said Azmodeus, gently patting the boy on the back. "You appear to be getting a lot of practice out of that skill of yours. Now, let us get out of this stinking, smelly hole as quickly as we can. Several of you try to support Tovan."

Struggling to help each other, they stumbled into the hall beyond and stopped at the foot of the stairs.

"I am going to take you all back to Rosamund's grotto, where we can get you some food, rest and clean clothes," said Azmodeus, guiding them into a circle around him. "I could use some help from you, Mikel. Just wish for the grotto."

Silence greeted his request. He looked around and suddenly realized the boy was not there. "Where is Mikel?" he asked.

"We don't know," replied Melisande. "We realized he was missing when we were frozen inside the cell. We never saw him leave."

The others nodded in agreement.

"In fact," continued Jamie, "none of us saw him come into the cell."

The wizard frowned and stood in thoughtful silence for a moment. He suddenly came to a decision. "I want you five to return to the grotto as quickly as possible, and then I will search for Mikel. Form a circle around me and take each other's hands. Quickly."

The five did as they were told, and before they could blink, they were back in the grotto. None of them had ever experienced such a thing before, and all they could do was gape at one another as Rosamond hurried over. They had felt nothing but a sudden whisper of wind briefly touching their faces.

"I didn't even have time to take a breath!" exclaimed Portia.

"I must go back," explained Azmodeus to Rosamund, anxious for his beard to return. "Something has happened to Mikel, and I must find him."

She nodded and quickly herded the others over to her living area. They were soaking wet, and all looked physically and emotionally exhausted. She called for blankets and towels. Other instructions were lost to the wizard. His beard returned in a rush, and he was back in the dungeon in seconds.

The place was as silent as a tomb. He stood outside the cell and strained to hear anything that might give him a clue as to the whereabouts of the boy. He had been straining to hear for several minutes when the sound of faint cries caught his attention. He looked around and was surprised to discover that the sounds were coming from the cell itself. Cautiously, he stepped into the interior. The sounds were stronger here but struck him as cries that might be coming from something or someone small in stature. Creeping toward a large barrel shoved into the corner, he spotted a cage that might have housed a small bird hanging above the water, and the cries were coming from the cage. He was completely surprised by what he saw.

Two tiny Wickersnits were crying out to him. Their arms raised pleadingly toward him. One appeared to be female, and the other was smaller and male. He unhooked the cage, carried it gently out into the hall and placed it on one of the lower steps. Because of their size, he couldn't make out anything they were trying to say. He had a sudden thought that Mikel's disappearance might have something to do with Bandi and that the two in the cage might be relevant to the situation and have information that might help him in his search. Murmuring softly to himself, he formed the words that would shrink him down to their size, and as soon as he reached the height he required, he rushed over to the cage and released the catch.

"You we thank," cried the sobbing female falling into his arms as she emerged. "You we thank."

The young male simply stood beside him, trying to shake the wizard's hand between sobs.

It took several long moments of comforting them and trying to ask questions before he finally got some of the information he needed.

"The witch woman," explained the female between hiccups, "she us find in mines, and us bring here. Bandiloimaa she had. Drown us she would if kill he not do."

Azmodeus finally understood. He had a horrifying thought.

"Who was he supposed to kill?" he asked with trepidation.

"Boy. He wants not to do it. Boy, his friend was. Bandiloimaa, his assistant, was."

The wizard felt cold from the shock that shot through his body. What a dastardly plan. Hera would pay for all she had done, and he hoped with his soul that Bandi had not carried through with his task.

"Did you see the boy?" he demanded.

"He into cell did not come."

"Did he go somewhere?"

She pointed a shaking finger down the hallway from the cell. "He that way ran."

Azmodeus had to think quickly. He couldn't leave these two alone, and the only one who could help them get back to their right size was, hopefully, Rosamond. They would have to get back into the cage so that he could carry them with him.

That took some doing. The thought of going back into the cage was terrifying to both of them. He was finally able to convince them that this was the only way they would be able to save Bandi and Mikel. Reluctantly, they climbed back in, held tightly to the bars as Azmodeus resumed his normal height and then kept their eyes closed as he carried the cage as carefully as possible while trying not to run. He followed the hallway down its length keeping as quiet as possible. Who knew what was lurking around the corners of Friere's castle? When he reached the circular room, the sight that greeted him left him horrified.

"No, Bandi, no!" he shouted, rushing down the steps, depositing the cage on the floor as he went. "You must stop!"

Mikel was wrapped in the coils of an enormous snake that the wizard instantly knew was Bandi. The boy didn't seem to be moving, which filled Azmodeus with a terrible, gut-wrenching fear. When he reached the dome that surrounded the two, he did not stop to think but shattered it with his own spell and then stopped dead in his tracks. The snake that was very slowly turning back into a Wickersnit had tears rolling down its face, and the boy wrapped in the coils was smiling.

"He couldn't do it, Azmodeus," grinned the boy. "He stopped because he's my friend and assistant. He's an honorable friend."

A huge sigh of relief came out of the wizard in a blast.

"Wicked woman makes me," cried Bandi. "Dead be my mother and brother. Drowned. Kill Mikel, not I could do. Not right thing."

Azmodeus shook his head and pointed to the cage. "No, they are not, Bandi. I have them with me, and we will take them to Rosamond in the grotto. She can hopefully help them."

The Wickersnit's sodden face turned to one of joy. He instantly altered back to his original shape and leaped toward the cage, leaving Mikel to drop unceremoniously onto his backside. Picking up the cage, he warbled messages in his own language to the two occupants.

"I'm glad he had a change of heart," muttered Azmodeus, relieved that his beard had returned once again. If he had more days like this one, he'd wear out his face.

"So am I," replied Mikel, rubbing his arms. "He is much stronger than he looks. It was not a pleasant experience, believe me."

"Bandi, bring your mother and brother over here," instructed Azmodeus. "We must get back to the grotto and make our way back to the Sanctuary in Toria. The final conflict is about to begin."

Bandi waddled over, the cage held carefully in what appeared to be a blanket. He had shaped his body around the structure, creating a safe pocket for his family and was beaming from ear to ear…or from the location of where ears were usually on a person. It was hard to know where any of the body parts were on a Wickersnit.

Moving close to the wizard, it was only seconds before they found themselves safe in the grotto. The elves and gryphons had arrived from Donagal, and the riders were sitting with the others enjoying a meal. The five had been outfitted in clean, dry clothing with new boots that had been brought from the elfin city. Mikel sighed with relief when he saw Yonnus and Petre. It appeared that, for a short time, they were all safe and together.

Several hours later and feeling much better with a nap and a good meal under their belts, Azmodeus and the rest of the group had learned almost everything they had missed from each other's adventures. Petre's part in what had to be accomplished had not been shared with good reason. It would have been too much to bear on the part of the rag-tag group that sat around the circle. The boy had remained quiet throughout the discussion, but only Yonnus and Azmodeus noticed and, with heavy hearts, said nothing.

Actually, Petre was quite overwhelmed by the stories of how Jamie and Jeremiah had entered Eleusia. Having lived inside the mountain, he had never heard the story of the Draukenbergian king and queen or the triplets until Azmodeus had told him the story in Donagal. To find out that horrid Portia was one of the group was more than a bit disturbing. He had to admit that she had improved slightly, but at the moment, he didn't have time to bother with her. He winced. He didn't have much time at all. The Wickersnit and its tiny mother and brother had been almost too much for him to take in. Mikel was a new wizard, and this strange creature was his assistant. And what about Melisande talking to fairies and this Jeremiah speaking with animals? Where had all of this come from? He could only sit back and be amazed.

"Now, what of the riddles?" asked the wizard.

"Well, that's the strange part," replied Mikel. "Everyone was given a riddle that could be answered, and we solved them. But the last riddle was mine, and I couldn't figure it out. I'm afraid that we are short. I'm sorry, Azmodeus."

"Tell me what it was," he said.

Mikel described what he had seen in the mirror, but instead of looking grim and shaking his head, the old man simply smiled.

"That is a riddle that only you can solve, Mikel. It must be solved before the alignment occurs tonight so that all our efforts have not been in vain. When the time comes, it will be up to you."

Mikel looked down at his hands, and his heart sank. He had convinced himself that Azmodeus would tell him the answer, and instead, he was leaving it up to him. Mikel had always felt confident about his decisions in the past. For the first time in his life, he was at a complete loss.

"Master," asked Melisande, "what I want to know is what was the point of the riddles and the quest? In the end, they didn't seem to make much difference to the outcome. Hera took off with the statue, and we were left to die. It wasn't as if the riddles were that difficult to solve either."

"Hera had three goals in mind," replied Azmodeus. "The first was to destroy Sharra, and the second was to murder the triplets and the three strongest, most talented Glockamarian children who could possibly become threats in the future. All parts of a prophecy must be fulfilled in order for a curse to be lifted, so all of you had to go on that quest to answer the riddles in order for the rest to be fulfilled. Her third goal was to create a situation in Eleusia where evil would battle good through war, which she is currently trying to instigate. She despises the fact that she cannot play evil tricks and schemes on us as she did with the humans on Earth. The Olympus Council would never allow it and would punish her severely if she were caught. Not knowing Hera is responsible for all that has been happening, the gods of New Olympus would destroy us if they found out because we would have broken the agreement not to war amongst each other in order to stay in this world."

"But we don't want to have a war," argued Mikel. "Hera is doing it, and someone has to tell the Olympus Council."

Azmodeus frowned for a moment and slowly stroked his beard in thought. "I don't believe that Hera had planned for that last riddle," he mused, "for it reveals something she does not know. That is a mystery I must follow up on. Friere mentioned he had agreed to change the riddles, but who had asked him to do so?"

Rosamund smiled. "I can explain that story to you later, Azmodeus."

"What about the Tree of Life?" asked Petre, trying to look innocent so that he would let nothing slip to the others about his own part that he must play. "And what about the stolen seed?"

"That was the idea of the Spider," Azmodeus replied his expression one of disgust. "She felt that by killing the tree… Hera provided the information on how to do it…the trolls would leave their roles as tree-keepers and become her own private army. The trees would die, bringing devastation and destruction to Eleusia much faster than Hera had originally planned. I'm certain she most appreciated Spider's brilliant thinking."

The last was said with a great deal of bitterness.

"To answer your second question, I am hoping that when we enter the grotto, the seed will guide you…I mean, us to it."

No one except Yonnus and Petre caught the relative error in the statement.

"What did you mean that the last riddle may not have been 'hers'?" asked Mikel, a look of puzzlement on his features.

Azmodeus smiled at him and then abruptly stood, not responding to his question. "It is time. We must get into that mountain unobserved and make our way to the central chamber of the Sanctuary. It is critical that we reach that room before the alignment forms over Eleusia. So much depends on the triad standing between good and evil."

"What is the triad?" Jeremiah asked, but this question also went unanswered as all moved to gather belongings in order to get ready for the flight.

"I have a question, Azmodeus," said Jamie, coming up beside him. "We are supposed to be in the Sanctuary tonight, but when we entered Aradell, we had thirteen days left. By my calculations, we were only in there six days."

The wizard chuckled. "You've discovered one of the problems of that place. Time in Aradell does not work the way it does here."

"Then we were lucky to get out when we did."

The old man nodded. "In more ways than one, my girl."

Yonnus, looking much healthier than Azmodeus had seen him that morning, walked up behind them and pointed to the Grumbletop Mountains in the distance.

"Are those clouds wrapped around the top of the Mountain above the Sanctuary?" he asked. "I'm certain I can see lightning."

"The clouds are not moving either," commented Mikel. "They look like they're just sitting there in one spot."

"She is called Spider for a reason," sighed Azmodeus, shaking his head. "We're in for a bumpy ride."

Chapter Forty-Eight
A Magnificent Theft

Kara

Kara ran down one of the tunnels with Beak and Claw at her heels. She was so proud of herself that she felt her little body would burst. Between the three of them, they had out-witted the Spider. It had taken several hours, but they had accomplished the impossible. Working together, they had retrieved the Seed of Life from the floor where Spider had thrown it in anger, and now it lay hidden in one of the many tunnels the three had explored. Kara actually had been amazed at how quickly Beak and Claw had caught on to the task. For mice, they had proven to be amazingly intelligent. Now as they raced toward the main chamber to see what was going on, she felt confident that even though they had played a small part, at least they'd helped squelch some of the creature's plans.

The task had been relatively easy. Druet was the one who had been waiting for the boy and his friends when they had come out of the mining tunnel. Using a simple retrieving spell, she removed the necklace from the boy's neck and returned to the Sanctuary. Spider had been having another one of her fits and had thrown it at the statue Hera had brought with her. The sight of it had incensed Spider. She wanted it gone and out of her sight, but Hera had only laughed.

"After all you stupid creature, she was my rival, not yours. It doesn't matter. The statue will be destroyed when the three constellations align. For now, I will remove her. I would hate to think what you would do to her in my absence."

That hadn't been good enough for Spider. After Hera had left, she had ranted and raved throughout the Sanctuary, turning to stone anyone or anything that got in her way. The three crones simply watched in disgust. With Spider out of the way, the three mice got to work and carefully and quietly pulled the necklace across the floor and into one of their tunnels. From there, it had been an easy task to hide it away. Now that it was safe, it was time to see once again what the evil creatures were up to.

They squeezed through a little hole, one after the other and took their places behind the rocks that circled the dead tree in the courtyard. From there, they discovered that they could see and hear everything being planned without being discovered. Spider was standing with her back to the tree, glaring at the three witches in front of her.

"Couldn't you have done more?" she shouted.

"Now, ducky, we've done all we could," replied Corilla calmly. "We've shared our crystal ball and Seeing Eye with you; we have flown into dangerous situations to spy and play nasty tricks on the brats; we've retrieved the Seed of Life…we have done all we can."

"It hasn't been enough," screamed Spider. "My spies tell me that those brats are out of Aradell, and the blasted wizard has joined them again."

She gestured to the tree behind her. Kara looked up and almost fainted. Perched on the bare branches were two of the largest flying creatures she had ever seen, and one of them seemed to be eyeing the rocks they were hiding behind with keen interest. She crouched down further and gestured to Beak and Claw to do the same.

"Yes, dear," simpered Zorna. "We know. However, all is not yet lost. They will have to fly here in order to get inside the mountain on time. It will be very difficult to do this through the storm we will create."

The three crones shrieked with laughter.

"What do you mean?" snarled Spider.

"Why don't you come and watch," hissed Druet, her smile looked more like a leer. "You might want to add some touches of your own. You are powerful enough."

The three hobbled forward, and Spider turned to join them. Kara shrank back. The four monsters were coming straight toward their hiding spot. She moved slowly back into the hole behind, and Beak and Claw quietly followed. Once safely in the tunnel, she led them down another one that opened on the other side of the tree. Kara had no idea what the four had in mind, but it didn't take long to find out.

The sky suddenly blurred, and she was looking up past walls of rock to what looked like a sky but a much different one from the one she had known. Not realizing that the sky she had grown up beneath was fake and placed there by a massive spell, she was unaware that the three witches had destroyed the spell, and she was now viewing the actual Eleusian sky. Fluffy white things seemed to move in this one. The bits of fluff joined together as she watched and melded into huge grey pillows. Loud noises came from the centers, and suddenly, streaks of fire zigzagged out from their depths. Enormous drops of water, some looking like round white balls, began to fall in sheets buffeted around by something she could not see. Having never been outside the mountain, Kara had no idea she was watching a terrible storm with gale-force winds, heavy rain and hail. It was terrifying.

The three crones cackled with amusement and satisfaction.

"They'll never be able to get through that storm," said one.

"I hope for your sakes you're right," snapped Spider. "Just to be safe, I'm going to retrieve that necklace. The safest place for it is around my neck."

'Uh, oh,' thought Kara.

Leading the other two back into the tunnel, they scampered as fast as they could down its length and into another that led them deep into the Sanctuary. They were not quite at their little refuge when a horrific scream that seemed to rock the very castle foundations burst down their tunnel.

'I think she's discovered it's missing,' thought Kara nervously.

The tunnel shook again, and Kara ran faster. The voices of the witches followed them down.

"I have searched everywhere," bellowed Spider. "The necklace is nowhere to be found. Was it one of you who took it?"

"Now really, dear," replied Druet, sounding disgusted. "We're on your side, remember? Why would we take it, and for what reason?"

"Then who?" demanded Spider.

"That, we cannot answer," crooned Corilla. "But we can certainly bring it to us. Come, sisters. The retrieving spell. It should be a simple task with all of us involved."

The three formed a circle and held hands. The words they repeated together were unintelligible, but Spider could feel the magic building in the room.

Back in her little retreat, Kara crouched over the necklace. The terrible shaking had stopped, and her heartbeat began to slow to a more normal pace. Beak and Claw were cowering in one of the corners of the small hole, their noses twitching and their eyes wide. Perhaps the worst was over. If what she had overheard in the many conversations held between Spider and the witches was accurate, someone was coming who knew what to do with the seed in order to save them all. She would keep it with her and go back and listen. Hopefully, she would discover who the person was and be able to get the necklace to him. At least she knew the person was a boy.

Suddenly, her world shifted. The little hole and the other two mice vanished in a swirl of color and light. Kara desperately clung to the necklace, but at one point, it slipped from her claws. As quickly as it had begun, the trip was over. She found herself encased in dark, heavy material that was almost suffocating. She shook her head to clear it and swallowed hard to keep herself from being sick. Whatever had happened, it had left her feeling nauseous and wretched. As she rested where she was, she could hear muffled voices, and there was something familiar about them. Her stomach gradually settled down, and she did not want to waste any more time. She carefully climbed upwards, her little claws clutching the fabric until she eventually reached an opening at the top.

Poking her head out, Kara found herself looking at more material that seemed to be bobbing around as a voice began speaking quite close to her. Where was she? She tried to concentrate on the words being said, but they remained muffled and indecipherable. Pulling herself up so that half her body was out of the opening, she could peer over the material and what she saw almost made her lose her grip. She looked at the three crones, who appeared to be quite pleased with themselves. Kara could clearly hear what they were saying.

"Calm down, dear," said one. "You've got your lovely necklace back."

"What I would like to know is who took it," snapped a voice that seemed to come close to Kara's ear. "We have a thief and a spy somewhere, and I intend to find it or them."

Kara darted back down into the material folds. Her little body shook with terror. She was in the folds of Spider's cape…on the monster's back!

Chapter Forty-Nine
The Songmaster

Jeremiah

The turbulence began to affect them when they were still several miles from the mountain. Clouds churned in front of them, and the noise of the thunder was deafening. When the first blast of wind hit, it almost flipped two of the griffins, and if it hadn't been for the flight straps holding them on, several of the riders and their passengers would have tumbled off into the void. Such a storm had never been seen on Eleusia, and Jeremiah was fairly certain that it was not an exaggeration to say that even Azmodeus was probably slightly panicked about the situation.

"We'll never make it through this," shouted Jamie to Jeremiah, sitting in front of her.

All he could do was shake his head. The wind whipped away his attempts to reply. He could see Azmodeus on the griffin ahead. He was perched behind the rider, Petre clasping his waist and Yonnus struggling to keep upright behind the boy. He, Jamie and Melisande were on the one behind, and somewhere off to the right, Portia, Tovan and Mikel were squeezed onto a third. Bandi had turned himself into a small mushroom and was safely tucked into Mikel's pouch...well... as safely as he could be under the circumstances. The wind grew in intensity, and suddenly, they were drenched in sheets of cold rain. Lightning flashed around them, and the thunder made talking impossible.

I'm terrified, cried Tovan into the minds of her friends.

There was a mental rumble of frightened agreement.

Do not lose hope, came the wizard's message to all.

The blasts of wind grew fierce. It was as if the wind itself was a creature of the sky trying to tear them from their own struggling mounts. At one point, it felt like the griffins were making no headway. Trying to keep steady and on a direct course was beginning to prove too much for them. They were going to have to turn back. Tears of frustration appeared in Jeremiah's eyes. They had come so far, through so much, only to be defeated in the end. When the hail began, he knew they were doomed.

All at once, the wind stopped, and the thunder ceased to crash around them. They could still see it, but it was as if they were flying through a tunnel of calm, and the storm was a moving mural on the walls, ceiling and floor. Music drifted around them – the most beautiful and haunting melodies. Jeremiah turned to look behind and was amazed by what he saw. Flying behind, keeping pace but not trying to overtake them, was a magnificent white dragon of gigantic size.

Who are you? He asked.

I am the oldest one, rumbled a deep baritone into his mind. *I am the protector of my people, the Guardian of the Crystal Spires. I am Athouloo, father of Crill.*

You are helping us, sir?

You saved my son. I will see you safely on the mountain. I, too, know of the monster that rules there.

Thank you…oh, thank you, sir.

The dragon bowed his head in acknowledgment. By now, the others had noticed their unique escort. Only the elves, griffins and Azmodeus seemed unperturbed by the creature's presence. The rest gawked at him and grasped their safety straps more tightly.

"It's alright," shouted Jeremiah. "His name is Athouloo, and he is helping us."

Without the roar of the wind, his words carried easily to the others.

"Well, well, well," smiled Azmodeus. "It appears that Jeremiah has come into his own in more ways than one."

The flight to the mountain was smooth and uneventful. Athouloo kept pace with them, and the melodies continued to float through the air keeping the terrible storm at bay.

As they approached the south end, Collpepper gestured to a ledge about halfway down the side of the mountain, and Azmodeus nodded. The three griffins dropped toward it, but the dragon stayed behind, his magic remaining with them until they reached the ledge.

Jeremiah quickly hopped down and looked back at Athouloo.

Thank you, sir. You have saved us.

Yes, but now it is your turn to save us all. Be safe, little one.

The great beast turned to begin his flight home.

"In all my years," declared an amazed Azmodeus, "I have never seen the Songmaster. In fact, I have never before heard of him leaving Aradell."

"The Songmaster?" asked Jeremiah.

"That's what we call him. He is the most famous of all dragons. One day, I will tell you the stories. Was it his son you saved?"

The boy nodded, feeling slightly embarrassed.

"There were reasons for all of you to go on that quest, and they had nothing to do with Hera's schemes. Someone else wanted you to complete it for entirely different reasons, it seems."

Suddenly, the storm returned in full force, and they scurried toward the cave entrance where the others had taken refuge.

"What do we do now, Azmodeus?" asked Mikel, approaching with the others.

The wizards' expression became serious.

"We will move together into the mountain," he explained. "When we reach the Sanctuary, we will split into two groups. Yonnus and Petre will search for the necklace that holds the seed of the Laurel Tree. It will draw you to it, Petre. The rest of us will make our way to the main chamber. This is the most dangerous part of the journey. Keep your eyes and ears open."

The elves insisted on joining them, assuring that others would be traveling from Donagal, arriving at any moment. Azmodeus agreed, aware that the dwarves would probably be joining them at some point. Silently, the group moved into the tunnel that would take them to the Sanctuary and a very uncertain future.

"Too bad dragons can't fly into mountains," mumbled Jeremiah.

As they approached the Sanctuary, the steps of the group slowed and became more cautious. The tunnel widened slightly as it joined another, which judging from the polished appearance of the ground, was used on a regular basis. Azmodeus called a halt and pointed down the new pathway.

"This is where we part," he said. "Petre and Yonnus must go that way and enter the main chamber from the back. You know the route, Yonnus."

Both nodded.

Azmodeus turned his attention to Petre. "Can you feel the presence of the seed?" he asked.

The boy nodded, and the wizard placed a hand on his shoulder. "Words escape me, boy," he said softly, his eyes reflecting the pain he was feeling inside.

Petre looked up at him and gave him a resigned smile. "It's okay, Azmodeus. I've grown accustomed to the thought, so to speak."

The old man squeezed Petre's shoulder gently and then dropped his hand. "Keep in contact with Melisande as you go so we know where you are at all times."

Petre and Yonnus turned left into the second tunnel.

"What is it that Petre has to do?" asked Jeremiah, who had watched this exchange with growing curiosity. "Ever since we met with him again, he's barely said a word. I tried to talk to him about whatever was bothering him, but he didn't want to talk about it. He didn't want to talk about anything. He seems to be deeply worried about something."

"You are absolutely right," sighed the wizard and then shook his head. "He carries a great burden, but I cannot as yet share it with you. Now everyone…"

Before he could say another word, they suddenly found themselves surrounded by a group of hostile-looking humans carrying a variety of strange weapons. One had an actual spear, but the rest carried pieces of fence posts, planking or tools. One of them even threatened them with a cooking pot.

"Greetings," smiled Azmodeus at the motley group. "Am I correct in assuming I'm addressing what is left of the Glockamarians?"

One of the figures closest to the group removed his headgear.

"Is that you, Master?"

"Father!" shouted Tovan, pushing everyone frantically to get to him. "You did get away."

Talman wrapped his arms around his daughter. "Tovan, Tovan," he cried, hoisting her into the air. "I can't believe it. You're safe."

"Are you all here?" she gasped. "Momma and Anmarie?"

"We are, and now you can join us," he laughed.

They were interrupted by a flurry of questions from the rest of her group, asking about family members.

"Is my mother safe?" cried Melisande. "Has anyone seen her?"

"What about my father?" joined in Portia. "Has he been looking for me?"

The group fell silent when Portia finished her question. Individuals looked back and forth at each other, their expressions almost hateful. Portia stepped back out of fear.

Talman answered her question as gently as he could. "Your father joined up with the Spider and became one of her most important interrogators."

"He hunted us down one after another," replied another hotly. "He took the children first and then came back for the adults."

"If we find him," snapped another, "he'll live less time than it takes to wring his scruffy neck."

Portia gasped and then cried out in horror. Jamie and Melisande quickly drew her into the protection of their arms and let her cry. They were horribly shocked as well by the revelation. Having only heard stories about Portia's father, the anger and hatred in the voices and gestures still took Jeremiah aback.

"It doesn't surprise me," muttered Mikel. "He was the reason we ended up prisoners of the trolls."

"Well, come on, girl," said Talman, putting a hand on Tovan's shoulder. "Let's get you home to Mom."

Tovan shook her head and released herself from his grasp. "No, Father. I can't join you until after we finish our task," she said, gesturing to her group.

"What do you mean?"

"Your daughter is part of a prophecy," replied Azmodeus. "For the past several weeks, she has been on a quest with these other young people. She must be in the main chamber of the Sanctuary…."

"With that monster?" exploded Talman. "I won't allow it."

He grabbed Tovan's arm and pulled her away from the others. "Have you seen what that creature has done to our people?" he shouted. "My daughter will not be allowed anywhere near her."

Jeremiah looked up at her father's face. He looked like a crazed person who was incapable of thinking rationally.

"I must go, Father," Tovan argued. "If we six do not follow through with the prophecy, Spider will win. She will destroy all of Draukenberg. The trees are already dying and…."

"What is Draukenberg?" her father demanded. "What are you talking about, Tovan?"

Jeremiah suddenly realized that Tovan's father knew nothing about the world outside the mountain. The rest of the Glockamarians were beginning to get agitated and restless. Tovan looked at the wizard, her eyes pleading with him for help.

"She must come with us, Talman," he stated calmly. "Without her, we will not have a chance of defeating Spider and her dark forces."

"I am her father," stated Talman firmly. "She will do as I ask." He raised the club he was carrying in a threatening gesture.

"Ah, dear," sighed Azmodeus. "I was hoping to avoid this."

He raised his hand, muttered a rhyme that no one else understood, and the Glockamarians froze as they were. His beard shrank to one-quarter of its length.

"What have you done?" gasped Tovan.

"Oh, they're alright," replied the old man. "This spell is not like the one Hera used on you. As soon as we are out of sight, the spell will leave them, and they'll be as good as new."

He turned suddenly and faced back down the tunnel they had just recently traveled. "Maxim," he smiled. "You have arrived in good time."

The dwarf and a regiment of soldiers emerged out of the darkness.

"We used our west route of tunnels and rails," he explained. "The rest are following, and Calliotrope is bringing his troops from the Lanfreth Fortress. They are right behind us. The elves from Donegal were arriving on their griffins ahead of us."

"Excellent," replied Azmodeus.

"However," continued Maxim, "the creatures from The Hollows are also on the move. Mudmen, Black Mountain trolls, ghosts, the creatures from Hag's Breath – all manner of horrors traveling by air and land. They outnumber us five to one. That doesn't include the trolls and goblins already under her power. You must not fail, Azmodeus."

"No, we must not," he sighed.

"What was he saying?" asked Jeremiah.

The conversation had been held in dwarfin, so it had not been understood by the rest of them.

"Oh, he wishes us luck," replied Azmodeus blandly. "Now, let us be off."

They followed him into the second tunnel.

"That was a lot of words for 'good luck'," muttered Jamie.

"Maybe dwarfin is a wordy language," was his droll reply. Jamie punched him in the shoulder.

Chapter Fifty
The Truth About Spider

Kara

"Wait," cried Corilla, her eyes darting around the room, her mouth set in a taut line. "They have come through. They are in the mountain. How could that have happened? No one could have flown through that gale we created."

The other two crones were also looking alert and worried.

"What are you talking about?" demanded Spider.

"Azmodeus and the brats," said Druet, looking nervously back at the entrance to the chamber. "They're here and on their way to this chamber."

"I thought you said the storm would stop them," hissed Spider in low, menacing tones.

Kara curled herself up into an even smaller ball.

"Luck is with that group. Something protects them, but what, we don't know."

She glanced over at her sisters, a meaningful expression on her face. "I believe that we have overstayed our welcome. It is time to go, Spider. Thank you for your hospitality, but perhaps we'll come another time."

"You will not leave now," cried Spider. "You will stay to the end."

"I think not," replied Druet, an attempt at a pleasant smile crossing her haggard features. "Our work is done."

"What work?" bellowed Spider. "You have failed at everything you have tried, and now they are here. You have been useless to me, and you will stay."

She threw back the sides of her cape, revealing the body of a black, hairy spider complete with eight legs, four of which were now raised menacingly toward the witches who were screaming and holding on to each other in terror. Spider was actually a spider! Only her face resembled a human's, although the red eyes made the features look more horrifying perched on such a grotesque body. Kara hung onto the fabric for dear life as she caught sight of the legs weaving around on the edges of her vision. Suddenly, the spinnerets in Spider's body got to work, and the air was full of long strands of sticky webbing shooting out toward the three crones, whose cries became horrified, ear-splitting shrieks.

Kara clung to Spider's cape, swallowing hard in order to stop herself from being sick. She barely had time to realize what had happened before it was over. One minute the three crones had been standing in front of her, and the next, they were three sticky, coated bundles of struggling masses now attached to the wall. No one was going to have a chance with this monster.

The chamber and hallway outside were beginning to fill with armed trolls and goblins.

"The enemies have entered the Sanctuary," she screamed. "Stop them because if they don't kill you, I will."

Groups of them scurried out of the chamber, each taking a different entrance.

All at once, Kara caught a message being sent between Petre and Melisande, and her spirit soared. Her friends! They were here! They were here in the mountain! Her joy was so great that tears began to roll down her little furry face. Kara hadn't realized how lonely and frightened she had been until she heard those familiar voices within her mind. She was about to mentally shout out to them when she remembered that Spider could hear them. Kara would have to get off the creature and be far away in order to communicate with her friends without Spider catching her. She knew that the creature was listening. Her head was furiously twisting back and forth in an effort to discover where the messages were coming from.

Kara looked cautiously around. They were close to the throne, but she was too high off the ground to take a leap. Besides, Spider would probably notice. As she was looking over the creature's shoulder, she spotted the necklace which had been hastily placed around Spider's neck after it had been retrieved from Kara's refuge. She felt a little thrill when she realized the clasp had not been properly closed. With a little manipulation, she might be able to pull it around and get it off the bristly neck.

She crept up the material and braced herself on the top fold of the hood. Placing tiny claws on the clasp, she pulled it apart and held her breath. Spider was so busy screaming instructions she didn't notice what was happening. Carefully, Kara pulled the chain toward her, gathering the links into a fold in the material in front of her. The tiny crystal with the seed inside proved to be a challenge; for a moment, she thought her quest would fail. It caught on the cape material in front of Spider's throat, and she couldn't get it to budge. The creature gestured toward the trolls, and the seed miraculously became dislodged. Kara heaved a sigh of relief and gathered in the rest of the chain.

Her next thought was what to do with it, and once again, Spider unknowingly obliged her. Curling her grotesque shape into a position allowing her to sit on her throne, she lowered herself into its depths. Kara wasted no time. Pulling the chain behind her, she scampered down Spider's back and onto the back of the chair. Following the circular, curved pattern in the wood, she could get to the floor unobserved and just in time. The monster heaved herself back out of the chair in order to bark out instructions to a new group of supporters who had entered. Hidden within the shadows beneath, Kara breathlessly pondered her next move.

The throne was on a long oval dais with two steps leading down to the floor. In her normal shape, it would have been easy to climb down, but as a mouse, it would be next to impossible, especially carrying an awkward chain. And yet, she couldn't stay where she was. As soon as Spider realized that the necklace was gone once again, the first thing she would do would be to check under the chair.

Kara looked across at the tree in the courtyard. If she could reach it, she could hide the necklace underneath. Two trolls stood between the throne and the tree. They would spot her in a moment and simply stomp on her. She shivered at the thought, and her mouth went dry. What was she to do? She couldn't move forward, and yet she couldn't go back.

As Kara pondered her predicament, a strange thing happened. One of the trolls approached and placed his sword vertically on the steps forming what could be used as a slide. He returned to his spot, and then both trolls turned to face the tree, their backs to the throne. As they were behind the throne, Spider never noticed. Kara did not wait to question their actions. She raced over to the sword and semi-scampered, semi-slid down its length, dragging the necklace with her. She did not stop until she was across the floor, behind the rocks and under the tree. Only then did she stop, panting for breath and look back. The trolls had turned back to the throne, the one having retrieved his sword.

Why had they done that? They had helped her, and yet, supposedly, they were under the control of Spider. Were there goblins and trolls like her where the spell had not worked? Confused but not wanting to waste any more time, she tucked the necklace into an alcove beneath the tree and raced into a tunnel under the rocks that would take her to where Beak and Claw waited. The three of them then continued down the tunnel as fast as their legs would carry them. Kara had to find the others and warn them that Hera could hear their mental communications.

We're passing an underground well, Melisande. Ask Azmodeus if we are close.

Both Spider and Kara heard the message at the same time.

Stop sending messages! She can hear you!

Petre had stopped dead in his tracks. Who had that been? It sounded like…

Kara?

Yes. I'm on my way. When I get there, I look for something small, but I don't mind linking anymore. The spider can hear you. She'll track you through your mind links.

Chapter Fifty-One
A Horrifying Discovery

Spider

The spider stopped when she heard the messages from the tunnels. Who was Kara? Who had recognized her, and how long had she been in the Sanctuary? The spy in the tunnels had never been found, but...look for something small? Had the spy been that strange little goblin? The one she had turned into a mouse? Spider hissed angrily. She had been duped. She should have destroyed the creature when she had had the chance.

"More problems, Spider?"

The creature spun around, knowing who belonged to the silky, condescending tones. "What do you want, Hera? We are close to the final battle, and I don't have time for...."

She stopped with a gasp. Hera stepped over to the edge of the dais, exposing the marble statue of Sharra behind her.

"Aagh!!" shrieked Spider, taking several stumbling steps backward. "You took her away. Why did you bring her back? You know how much I hate and detest her. Aagh! No!"

"Really, Spider," drawled the goddess with a smirk. "What a performance. After all, she is your better half...Sharra."

Hera casually turned to the statue and stroked the marble hair, her eyes never leaving Spider's face, whose expression ranged back and forth from furious to terrified.

"Don't call me by that name," hissed the creature. "I am not Sharra."

"But of course you are. Both of you are Sharra. It gave me great pleasure those years ago to split you into your good and evil sides. Granted, I did enhance your evil side by quite a bit."

"You promised me, Draukenberg," shrieked Spider, her front legs thrashing through the air in anger and frustration. "You promised me complete rule if we won and the destruction of that horrific statue."

Hera chuckled. "But you haven't won yet, although I'm beginning to believe that it is possible judging from the atrocious hordes of creatures you are bringing to help you. I have also brought you, my faithful soldiers, again, who will not remember anything after the battle. Don't forget, however, what will happen to you if you lose. The consequences...well, you know what they are. Oh, it will be an evening of fun, and I intend to see it all transpire from right here."

"What?" gasped Spider. "If you are seen, the members of the Olympus Council will know of your involvement and of all who have assisted you in this plot. They will destroy us all."

Hera gave a merry chuckle as her form began to alter and change, becoming something quite different and unexpected. "They won't know it is me, now will they?"

Spider seethed with hatred when she saw the result, but it wouldn't have mattered if she'd agreed or disagreed. One way or another, Hera would win no matter what side lost, and for the first time, Spider felt that her only role had been to come along for the ride.

Chapter Fifty-Two
Meetings In The Tunnels

Petre

Not far ahead of the others, creeping through the tunnel that was taking them past Kara's underground well, Petre and Yonnus kept close to the tunnel wall, staying alert for any sound that would herald danger. As soon as Petre received the message from Kara, he immediately sent one back to the others relating what she had said. Tovan sent back a quick reply telling him that they were on their way, and within minutes, the group rounded the corner of the tunnel.

"Watch your step," he warned, appearing to protect a section of the floor.

They moved forward more cautiously, but what they saw when they arrived caught them all off guard. Three mice, one brown and two white, were sitting at his feet and in front of the brown one was a message scratched in the dirt: *I have seed.*

"She can't speak properly and, of course, doesn't dare mind link," explained Petre, grinning broadly. "This is the best we could do."

Peter had been so relieved to meet back up with Kara that he had almost hugged her until the fear of squishing her had warned him off. He would never forget that Kara had saved his life after their arrival in Toria.

"Why, Kara," smiled Azmodeus bending down. "You look a bit different from the last time we met."

The little mouse could only squeak in response.

"Change her back, you can?" asked Bandi, who had returned to his normal size.

The wizard shook his head. "Only Spider can do that. If we fulfill the prophecy, all who have been altered might have a chance of changing, but we don't know that for sure."

A frown replaced the smiles on several faces.

"Does that mean there's a chance my sister and brother might always be goblins?" asked Tovan. "That Kara will always be a mouse?"

"I can't be certain," replied Azmodeus. "We can only hope."

Petre looked down at the little mouse and shook his head. What had Kara had to endure all this time alone in this horrible place? How had she possibly managed to survive? He had a feeling that the nervous, hand-twisting little girl who had had them ambushed at the creek so many days ago no longer existed, and the thought made him smile.

"What is your plan, Azmodeus?" asked Yonnus. "I have a feeling that that chamber is now full of our enemies, and their magic alone might overwhelm us. This group is not what you would call an army."

The wizard stroked his beard with two boney fingers. "Let us examine our resources," he replied. "You, Melisande, can talk to the fairies. Are there any in these caverns?"

The girl sent out mental feelers, and a smile lit up her face. "Rosamund," she cried. "She's in the mountain with her small army and brought the sprites."

A small cheer went up from the group.

"Excellent," grinned Azmodeus. "The dwarves are at this moment entering the Sanctuary along with the elves. Those Glockamarians who are capable of fighting will have joined them."

Kara went to work again. It was difficult for her, but she kept at it until another message appeared in the dirt.

trolls help me

"Now that's interesting," mused the old man. "Where is the seed now?"

under tree

Azmodeus chuckled. "The same thing would have happened if the seed had been around Spider's neck. The closer the seed comes to the tree, the less power she has over the trolls. We may have more on our side than we thought."

His expression became thoughtful. "However, her allies are still arriving in large numbers. We must not delay, and time is passing quickly. Mikel, you have the ability to guide your arrows but wish carefully so that they do not hit our own people. Jeremiah, can you contact any mountain wildlife that might help?"

Jeremiah closed his eyes and focused. It was several moments before he replied. "There are many mice in the deeper levels. They will most certainly help us because Spider and her cronies have been dining on their kind for weeks. That's why they went deeper into the mountain to hide."

Kara shivered. That was why the three of them had never found any other mice. She and her friends had obviously been lucky.

"Well, let us be off," stated Azmodeus straightening his shoulders. "It's time to take back Draukenberg."

The two groups parted and went their separate ways, Petre and Yonnus following the mice.

Jamie

"Where's Portia?" asked Tovan, looking around.

"That's strange," replied Melisande. "She was right behind me when we came into this grotto…at least, I thought she was."

"We must find…" began Azmodeus but stopped when the girl came around the corner looking even more disheveled than she had for the last part of the trip.

"I fell," was her sullen reply.

Jamie looked more closely at the other girl. Something was wrong, but she couldn't put her finger on it. Before she could say anything, Azmodeus strode down the tunnel, the rest following. As the others disappeared, leaving the two alone, Portia's face twisted into that of an evil leer. Transfixed by the horrible sight, Jamie gasped aloud as the girl's eyes glinted red, and she suddenly found herself unable to move. This was not Portia. This evil replacement was the work of Spider. Where was the real Portia?

The only thing that saved Jamie was her immunity to magic. The spell being cast by the creature was not affecting her. Her own terrified fear was keeping her in place, and that sudden realization sent her taking off at a run to catch up to the group.

"Azmodeus!" she shrieked as she ran.

The false Portia ran behind her, heavy steps echoing off the walls, and Jamie knew that if the creature caught her, she would never see the others again. Several times, she felt a tugging on her cape, which sent her flying even faster down the tunnel and into the hallway that would lead her to the main chamber. When the creature started to cackle with glee, Jamie spurted ahead and finally caught up with the group just as they entered a huge hall. The sight that greeted her shocked her to the point of forgetting to warn the others of the demon Portia.

The chamber was full of trolls and goblin-like brutes. Slimy, one-eyed monsters covered in mud, centaurs, imps, hairless croakings, and creatures that appeared to be made of rock were only a few of the different ghastly things that had come to join Spider's cause. Azmodeus was taken aback when he saw the swidgits roosting on various beams. Those appeared to concern him more than anything else. On a raised platform at the other end of the room were a ghastly spider-shaped creature and three witchy ones pulling off shreds of spider webbing from their clothing. Sitting at the end of the dais was the statue of a beautiful woman, pausing to look back at someone. What was a statue like that doing here, she briefly wondered. Jamie knew they were horribly outnumbered and suddenly felt her body turn to rubber and her heart begin to pound painfully in her chest. Never before had she felt so terrified.

"I think we're in trouble," muttered Jeremiah, his voice shaking.

Jamie was too frightened to reply.

"You have made a terrible mistake," shouted Spider from the other end of the room.

The hubbub in the room stopped as her creatures turned to stare silently at the small group. Their expressions were hostile and full of hate. Many gestured threateningly with their weapons, their message very clear.

"You and your little band of ghastly brats have no hope of stopping me," continued Spider. "You have rushed here only to face your own deaths."

Her minions began to edge closer to the group.

"Perhaps," replied the wizard calmly. "However, Sharra, someone had to try to stop you before you destroyed Draukenberg."

Spider screamed, the sound ricocheting around the room. "Don't call me by that name, wizard. I am no longer that person."

"Yes, you are," he bellowed back. "You have been enmeshed in evil for so long that you have forgotten your true self. We are here to help you find it, Sharra."

Again the creature shrieked as though in agony.

Out of the blue, the fake Portia began to laugh hysterically. The spider stopped shrieking and peered down the room, her eyes resting on the girl standing behind Jamie. She began to chuckle and then began to laugh as well. The creatures stopped advancing on the group and looked questioningly back at Spider, who was now shrieking with mirth. No one else seemed to understand the joke, including the three wicked sisters.

"You fool," Spider finally gasped. "Do you think for one minute that I would allow you to saunter in here and not attempt to stop you at all? Look at your triplets, old man. Look at the three who you have depended upon."

Jamie looked back at Portia, suddenly remembering the warning she had been too shocked to give. The others noticed her turn to look back and did the same. It was a horrifying sight. Portia's outline blurred and then settled into the shape of one of the most vicious imps to be found in The Hollows. There was a collective gasp around the hall, followed by a roaring cheer.

"Your quest is at an end, wizard," screamed the monster. "You no longer have six children. Nor do you have your important set of triplets. Attack them! Not one is to leave this room alive."

As her vile creatures began to move against them, Azmodeus shouted out a spell, and a wall of fire encircled the small group.

"Move forward with the flame," he shouted.

They did as they were told, moving further into the room surrounded by the fire. Jamie watched the wizard's beard, her heart sinking as it slowly grew shorter and shorter. He would not be able to keep this up for long and when his beard disappeared, so would his magic.

Chapter Fifty-Three
A Dangerous Path

Petre

Petre and Yonnus followed the three little mice into the tunnel, eventually leading them to the Laurel Tree. They moved with stealth, not wanting to alert anything that might have been lurking in the darkness. Not far down its length, Bandi stopped and gestured to Petre and Yonnus to move into the shadows.

"Something up there be," he whispered, pointing to a dark shape on the ground ahead of them.

"What do you think it is?" asked Petre.

"It could be anything or anyone," replied Yonnus. "It could be a trap."

"Look," said Petre. "Look at the mice. They seem to be gesturing to us to come."

Sure enough, the little mice were running toward them and then turning to run back to the shape. Yonnus held his sword in front of him and crept forward, Petre and Bandi following close behind. As they moved nearer, the shape began to appear to be a little figure hunched down on the ground. When they reached it, Yonnus gently jabbed at it with the tip of his sword. It didn't move. He jabbed a bit harder, and a small moan escaped from what appeared to be a bundle of rags. He bent down and stretched out his hand to touch the object. It groaned again. Slowly he lifted the bundle and turned it over.

"Portia!" gasped Petre. "But Portia's traveling with the group to the main chamber. I saw her."

"That was obviously not Portia," growled Yonnus. "The Spider has got her tentacles into a shapeshifter."

"But real Portia in the chamber must be," protested Bandi. "Fail will be the quest."

"I know," replied a grim-faced Yonnus. "Come on. We have several reasons to hurry now."

He picked up Portia, whose head lolled against his arm. Kara and her two friends took off at a faster pace, with Petre and Yonnus following close behind. They didn't try to keep quiet as they ran. They were running out of time, and speed was now more important than silence.

Their path ended on the balcony overlooking the chamber that Kara had discovered on the first day she had seen the three witch sisters. Petre could see the crowd of goblins and other creatures that had come to Spider's aid and sharply sucked in his breath when he saw the members of the small quest group seemingly trapped in the center of the hordes. They would have to get Portia down to them as quickly as possible but how. To the surprise of all three, Portia stopped them.

"I can't go any further. I think the demon did more to me than we realized."

"But quest fails, it will," protested Bandi.

Portia gave a strange smile.

"No. It will not. Azmodeus knows that I am not the third triplet."

"What?" cried Petre.

"I have always suspected that I was not one of the triplets. It never felt right or made sense. Jamie and Jeremiah told us of several dim memories of their parents, but I had none except those involving my own family. When Mikel received his riddle, I heard his thoughts for some reason; although he didn't, I understood the riddle. I know who the third triplet is, and it is not me. Now you must go. I will stay here and hope he finds out in time."

"Be safe, young Portia," replied Yonnus softly. "You are right. We must get to the Laurel Tree before the three get to the dais, or all will be lost. We will hope that you are correct and he realizes who he is in time."

"You know who it is."

"I do. Now let us hurry before it is too late."

They hurried down the steps and along the corridor that would take them to the tree. Thankfully, they met no one along the way and soon waited in the shadows a short distance from their goal. Kara had gone on ahead, ducking and darting around, constantly moving feet, each one capable of delivering death. Her desperate run to the rocks surrounding the Laurel Tree finally brought enormous sighs of relief from the three when she disappeared at last between the stones. However, when she tried to emerge a short time later, pushing the chain up the hole in front of her, her luck changed. The huge hunting birds loyal to Spider had seen her go in and were now pacing to and fro in front of the hole. Kara and the seed were trapped.

"I'm going to have to make a dash for it," said Petre. "I'll kick them aside and grab the chain."

However, before he could follow through with his plan, one of the birds caught sight of the chain glinting inside the hole. He pecked at it several times and then suddenly grabbed it and pulled. Kara's strength was no match for his, and he could wrench it away from her tiny claws. Spreading his wings, he lifted easily from the ground and landed on one of the dead branches above, the chain dangling from his beak. Yonnus yanked Petre back into the shadows as he darted out after the bird.

"Don't," he growled. "That would be suicide."

"Well, isn't it ironic…you telling me that," snapped Petre, wrenching his arm away from Yonnus' grasp. "I thought that was what I had been hired on to do."

There was an intake of breath from Bandi.

"I'm sorry," whispered the big man, and Petre nodded in acceptance, feeling slightly ashamed of his outburst.

Suddenly, he received a compelling message from Kara.

"The crystal containing the seed fell off when the bird was poking at the chain," he grinned. "Kara has it."

Yonnus sighed. "Someone must be looking after us. But you'll have to time it, boy. You can't reach the tree before the triplets reach the dais, and Spider is doing everything to make that impossible."

He pointed to the dais where the creature was wrapping and stinging everything in sight. There were also a number of stone statues scattered around the area that showed she had been busy. Azmodeus was battling up the steps toward her, but the three witches were not making it easy for him. Petre noticed that the old wizard had barely an inch of beard left, which was no good no matter how one looked at it. Blood was also running down his face from a nasty gash above the eyebrow.

"I the job does," stated Bandi. "Risk, not the boy."

Petre and Yonnus watched dumbfounded as Bandi's shape blurred and then evolved into that of a troll.

"Tell mouse not afraid to be."

With that, he sauntered out toward the tree, fiercely shaking his hands and shouting as Petre passed on the message to Kara. When Bandi bent down to retrieve the crystal, Petre had to do a great deal of convincing before the little mouse reluctantly placed the small crystal in the big hand. Bandi then stood and sauntered back into the shadows giving an amazed Petre the seed. No one except the bird had noticed a thing.

Chapter Fifty-Four
The Answer Revealed

The ring of fire suddenly spluttered and then died, leaving the little troupe exposed and vulnerable. They drew protectively in toward one another as the creatures advanced, enjoying the looks of terror on the faces of their victims.

Suddenly Spider shouted for her army to stop. It took a moment for her command to get through to all of them, resulting in a great deal of bumping, shoving and loud muttering. She continued once the grumbling stopped.

"Azmodeus," she said with a self-satisfied smirk. "I can't have you die without seeing this first. The bears and the dragon are almost in alignment."

The three witches raised their arms to the glass ceiling above the chamber, chanting loudly. It blurred and vanished, allowing everyone to see the natural sky above the mountain. As the night sky became visible, all eyes were turned to the millions of lights that appeared within its darkness. Although the Glockamarians did not recognize the three constellations, the five of the quest found them quite quickly, having had them described by Azmodeus. They were almost touching and were beginning to move into a clockwise rotation slowly. A ragged cheer went up from the monsters surrounding the group.

"What do we do?" whispered a terrified Tovan.

Azmodeus suddenly turned to Mikel, his eyes boring into the boy with a fierce intensity.

"Solve the riddle, Mikel," he demanded. "You must solve the riddle now, or we are all doomed."

The boy stared back at the wizard, and his gaze locked with his. He thought back to the mirror and the three figures staring back at him…Jeremiah, Jamie and himself. Portia and the others were not there. Jeremiah…Jamie…and…

What?" he gasped. "I'm the third triplet?"

"You are," yelled Azmodeus over the noise. "You were the one who assumed that Portia was the third triplet, but I never stated that. It was Willik who insisted that Portia be included in the quest for a reason that only she knows. Now we have to make certain that we complete this quest successfully."

He turned to the others, who were staring at Mikel in surprise.

"We must clear a way to get Jamie, Jeremiah and Mikel to the dais as quickly as possible. You three must position yourselves between Spider and the statue. Face Spider when you get there, hold hands and raise them in the air. Is that clear?"

They nodded as one. Suddenly, they were surrounded by chaos. The elves and dwarves had arrived along with the remaining Glockamarian refugees. Sparkles of light and the odd bee filled the air, and hovering above the entrance was Rosamund. From that point on, no one had time to think. Mice were everywhere. The battle had begun.

The group tried to move forward as one but soon became separated. Mikel, Jamie and Jeremiah lost sight of each other almost instantly and found themselves struggling forward on their own. Scurrying under legs and around bodies, Jamie dodged swords and spears aimed in her direction. Jeremiah was almost trounced upon by a troll, only to be kicked a moment later by another toward one of the pillars. He hit it with a crunching thud and cried out in pain. Fire shot up his left arm, and he knew without having to look that it was broken. He fought the sudden dizziness and nausea welling up inside him, conscious of one of the trolls turning in his direction. He tried to pull himself around to the other side of the pillar to avoid the monster's stare but, too late, realized that the creature was heading toward him. At the same time, Jamie found herself trapped in the middle of a group of dwarves battling a number of mudmen. It was an odd but terrifying fight. Every time one of the dwarves lopped off a mudman appendage, it simply grew back into place with a horrible slurping, sucking noise. No matter how hard she tried, she could not get through but remained hunched between the two groups, hoping she wouldn't be noticed. Azmodeus was popping out balls of flame and other magical wallops while Melisande and Tovan tried to find the triplets and not get killed at the same time. No one was making any progress, and the constellations were about to align.

High above on the balcony, Portia finally spotted Mikel, and the situation was far from good. The boy was defending himself as best he could against two heavily armed creatures by sweeping a sword he had found back and forth to keep the creatures at bay. The two squat figures with faces like wild pigs, complete with dangerous-looking tusks, were forcing him back against the wall. Another few steps and Mikel would have no place to go.

Suddenly, one of the creatures charged. Portia screamed as the creature's sword plunged into Mikel's side. A startled look crossed the boy's face, and he stumbled backward, collapsing against the wall. The creatures turned and ambled off, assuming their job was finished.

Portia stared down at her friend in horror. Mikel looked back up at her, an odd smile on his face.

Can you hear me? She cried. *Mikel, can you hear my thoughts?*

A look of surprise lit up Mikel's face.

I can.

His reply was faint. He sounded as if he was struggling to remain conscious.

Portia unclasped the bracelet from her wrist without a second thought.

I'm throwing you my bracelet, Mikel. The Willik said I could give it to someone who needed it, and you do.

I...I won't be able...I won't be able ...to catch it.

Wish for it to come to you. Wish hard.

I'll try.

Portia concentrated on throwing the bracelet with its precious stone directly at Mikel. For a moment, she lost confidence. She had never been good at accurately throwing things, and what if she missed at this most important of all times? Shaking thoughts of failure away and filled with renewed determination, she took careful aim and threw it as hard as she could. Mikel kept his eyes on it, wishing and willing it to come to him. It took every ounce of his strength, and even though it faltered once, it finally landed on his chest within easy reach of his hand. He grabbed at it, missing it the first time but succeeding the second.

Suddenly he was surrounded by a bright light that he had to shut his eyes. He had the sensation of being engulfed by white fire. The pain in his side eased and vanished as if it had never been there. He stumbled to his feet as the last beams of the light faded and then were gone. Looking up at the balcony, he waved at the girl beaming back at him. Portia was still beaming when the arrow came out of nowhere, striking her in the chest and sending her stumbling backward out of sight.

"Portia!" he cried out. "No! Portia!"

Several strange events suddenly occurred in sequence within the chamber. Rosamund appeared above the dais, waving her hands over the space beneath and chanting away the spider webs. At three different spots in the chamber, trolls converged on Jamie, Jeremiah and Mikel, lifted them gently in the air and lurched toward the dais. Trolls and Spider's Sanctuary goblins began to move in on Spider's allies from The Hollows, wrenching away their weapons and assisting elves, dwarves and humans alike in their battles. Some cleared a path between Petre and the Laurel Tree, and one gestured to him to come quickly. The triplets were placed on the dais, moving as fast as possible to stand between Spider and the statue. Jeremiah's skin was white, and his face was drained of color. His arm throbbed with pain, and perspiration beaded his forehead. Noticing that he was favoring his left side, the other two put him at the end of the row so he could raise his right arm. Petre saw his chance and raced toward the tree.

Draco and the Bears came into alignment.

The triplets raised their joined hands.

Petre leapt at the tree.

A violent roar rocked the chamber as the world suddenly shifted and darkness settled over all.

Silence permeated the space where the sounds of battle and the cries of challenge and pain had filled it such a short time before and remained that way for some time before Jamie began to stir. She had no idea how long she had been unconscious. The first of her senses to alert her to the fact that she was coming out of her stupor was hearing. She became aware of a wide assortment of sounds ranging from sobbing and wailing to shouts of joy. Opening her eyes and turning her head, she realized she was still on the dais, and Mikel and Jeremiah were lying on either side of her. Jeremiah was groaning, and she remembered that he had been injured during the fighting. Pulling herself into a sitting position, she shook her head to clear it and leaned over him.

"What's hurting?" she asked.

Either her tongue had swollen to twice its size, or her mouth was full of cotton wool. Her words sounded mumbled and garbled.

"My arm," gasped the boy. "I'm sure it's broken and hurts like the devil."

"We need help," she replied, looking around for Tovan.

The sight greeting her was welcome and sad beyond anything she had ever imagined. Spider and the statue had disappeared. There was no sign of the trolls, the witch sisters or any other creatures from The Hollows and Hag's Breath except those who had fallen during battle. The weird soldiers with strange dead-looking eyes were also gone. For as far as she could see, there were people, elves and dwarves helping those who were wounded or covering those who had died with cloaks. All the goblins had reverted to their human form, which brought a sigh of relief from her. Shouts of joy could be heard from those who had found friends or family alive and well. Others were crouched beside those who had fallen, some crying softly, others wailing with grief. Jamie hoped and prayed that none of her friends were suffering from losing family members.

Jamie turned to look on the other side of the dais and saw Tovan hugging an older boy and girl and laughing joyfully. She waved to her, but Tovan was so caught up in finding the other two she failed to notice. Luckily, the girl she was hugging saw Jamie's gesture and pointed it out to Tovan. All three came over to the dais and up the stairs.

"This is my sister and my brother, Jamie," laughed Tovan, looking happily up at the two smiling faces. "They were the other two mice. Oh, the adventures they've been having and…."

Jeremiah groaned, and Tovan cut off what she was going to say. She bent down over the boy. "What's wrong with him?" she asked.

"My arm," he moaned. "I think I've broken my arm."

Tovan placed her hand gently on his shoulder and the other on his wrist. "It is," she replied. "This is going to take a moment."

Maybell and Jon watched in amazement as their sister did the unthinkable and unimaginable.

"What is she doing?" gasped Jon. "Is she healing that boy? It's against the law. She'll be severely punished if the Council finds out."

"No, she won't be, Jon," said Mikel coming up to stand beside him. "Things have changed a whole bunch since you got taken by Spider. There isn't even a Council anymore."

As the three watched in astonishment as Tovan went about her business, Kara was on a search of her own.

"I've looked everywhere," said Kara to Azmodeus, "and I can't find Petre anywhere. He came toward the tree and disappeared."

The wizard took Kara's hand and led her to the Laurel Tree, which was now sprouting new leaves and blossoms in abundance.

"Kara," he said sadly, "we have all made sacrifices in this quest, but I'm afraid that Petre has made one of the greatest anyone can give. In order to bring the tree back to life and rescue the trolls from Spider's grip, he literally had to take the seed into the center of the tree. Petre has become one with the Laurel Tree."

Kara stared at the tree, a look of horror crossing her features. Imprinted on the trunk was the outline of a boy's face, its eyes closed as if in sleep.

"No!" she cried. "This cannot be!"

"I'm afraid it is," replied Azmodeus.

Kara pulled her hand from his and covered her face with both. "Oh Petre," she sobbed. "Oh, Petre. This is horrible."

On the dais, Mikel suddenly looked up at the balcony. "Portia!" he cried.

Leaping to his feet, he tore down the steps of the dais. Darting around the individuals who blocked his path, he reached the stairs and raced up their length two at a time. He burst onto the balcony and came to an abrupt halt.

Several people were seated or standing around a figure on the ground. He recognized Drogo, Portia's brother, tears rolling down his cheeks. The Willik was sitting beside the figure, holding the person's hand. A man he had never met, dressed in clothes that looked familiar, was standing quietly behind her. Mikel moved slowly forward, and several people blocking his path respectfully moved aside. He knew before he saw her that the person was Portia.

She was lying on her back with her hands clasped across her chest. There was no sign of the arrow, and her clothing showed no sign of damage or blood. Her eyes were closed as if she was asleep, and a peaceful expression was on her face. This was the girl he had hated so much not so long ago, and yet they had grown to become friends through the trials and tribulations of the quest. He fell to his knees, a harsh sob escaping from deep in his chest, and tears began to course down his cheeks. They all knew when they entered the quest that there was the possibility of one or more of them getting hurt or dying, but the reality was quite different from brave thoughts.

"The arrow pierced her heart," said the Willik quietly. "I told you all in the beginning that Portia held the destiny of the quest in her hands. Had she not thrown you the bracelet, Mikel, you most certainly would have died, and the triplets would never have become the trident. When you stood together and held your clasped hands high, you formed the shape of the trident, breaking Hera's spell."

"Did you know she would die?" asked Mikel, his voice shaking with emotion.

The Willik shook her head. "I cannot tell the future, Mikel. I did not know. I only knew that her presence here, at this time, was of great importance."

She made a gesture and called her elf maidens to her. Between them, they carried a litter and placed it beside Portia. Gently they moved her onto it and covered her with a light blanket.

"She will be taken to Donagal until it is time for her departure. I will go with them when they are ready."

Several people helped her to her feet, and for the first time, Mikel noticed that the strange man was no longer with them. Before he could ask who the stranger was, gasps could be heard from the people below the balcony…gasps and then silence. Mikel rubbed his eyes, took a deep breath to calm himself and went over to the railing to look down. Jeremiah, Tovan and Tovan's brother and sister were about to come down the steps of the dais, and Jeremiah was swinging his arm back and forth, looking very pleased with himself. Mikel hated the thought of having to tell them about Portia. After coming so far together, this news would be devastating for them. He was finding it difficult to keep it all together as it was. Azmodeus was comforting Kara for some reason, but a moment later, the wizard looked up at the dais and began to move toward it. There was no sign of Yonnus or Bandi.

He suddenly noticed Calliotrope pointing to a strange creature crouched at the end of the dais. All eyes were drawn to the larger-than-average goblin perched there for all to see.

"Why has it not been transformed back?" he asked.

"Because the original shape is not that of a human," replied the Willik softly, coming up beside him. "In fact, I think we're going to meet the villain of the piece finally, or should I say, villainess."

Chapter Fifty-Five
Consequences

Jamie

The creature's shape began to blur and then extend upwards. All watched in horrified fascination as just seconds later, a beautiful woman in a pale blue toga, her honey-coloured hair piled high on her head, stood before them. There was no mistaking the power that radiated from her.

"Hera," whispered Jamie.

The woman placed her hands on her hips and gazed imperiously around the vast chamber. "I am amazed, mortals. You succeeded where I thought for certain you would fail."

Her voice carried to all corners, and its tone was sarcastic and cruel. No one made a sound or moved except for those who were in too much pain to care.

"But I cannot accept this," she sneered down at them. "Io has once again been released from her prison to disrupt my life and…."

"You know that Sharra is not Io, Hera," shouted Azmodeus.

"Ah, Azmodeus," smiled Hera, gazing at him with a semblance of genuine affection. "Always interfering. You know she isn't but Zeus doesn't seem to want to believe it, so her existence is a major problem for me. I did like her so much better as Spider…such ugly, evil wonderfulness. Now, how am I going to correct this mess?"

"You have done enough, Hera," bellowed the wizard.

Shouts of agreement suddenly filled the chamber.

"We've had enough of your plots," shouted one.

"Go back to where you came from and stay there," cried another.

Hera shot her hands in the air and instantly a roaring wind blew through the chamber forcing most to hit the floor before they could be sucked away. It only lasted a second, but she had proven her point. Remaining silent might keep them alive.

"You immortals were not to interfere with the people of Draukenberg," continued Azmodeus, pulling himself to his feet. "That agreement was made when we all first came to this land."

"Agreements can change, little man," she sneered. "Do you have the power to stop me?"

The wizard stared at her for a moment and then lowered his head. Jamie stifled a sob. He had done all he could. She had beaten him. She had beaten all of them.

"I thought not," she laughed. "None of you can stop me."

Jamie's face flushed with anger as she marched over to stand in front of the goddess. "We might not have the power to stop you, but at least we know the difference between right and wrong and between goodness and evil. You're so old you probably don't remember what it was like to have a conscience. Do you not feel the least bit badly for being such a despicable creature who is despised by everyone?"

Hera appeared to be taken aback for a moment by Jamie's aggressive tone and unflattering description of her most enchanting self, and then she laughed. "Feel bad for what I have done? There is nothing more precious than a stupid, naïve child."

"Then finish me off and be done with it!" shouted a defiant voice.

From behind Jamie, a woman stepped out and walked purposely forward. Her head was held high, there was a determined set to her shoulders, and her steps were firm. In the years that followed, Jamie was to remember this moment with pride. This was her re-introduction to her mother.

"It's me you want, Hera," said Sharra, her green eyes blazing. "I don't know why you allowed me to hang around as that repulsive creature for so long. You should have destroyed me years ago. Well, goddess, here's your chance. Take me and leave the others alone."

Hera raised her hands and slowly clapped them together three times, the sound echoing through the chamber. The gesture and the smirk on her face clearly communicated to everyone how she felt about Sharra's little speech.

"Really, my dear. Do you think for one moment that I would make you a martyr in front of everyone? I don't want you to die. I want you to suffer. And I want all traces of magic or what you call gifts and talents to vanish from this world, except for The Hollows, of course, and I will make it so."

"You must not do that," shouted Sharra. "These races came to Eleusia to escape what was happening in Earth's dimension. Most are magical races. They cannot change who and what they are just because you don't happen to like it."

"They can and they will," replied Hera. "I don't care about the people of Eleusia. It is what I want that counts. As of this moment, there will be no magic in any form left on this world."

Cries of distress and disbelief went through the chamber.

"I can't feel anything!"

"My mind is…empty!"

Jamie watched in shock as the beard of Azmodeus disappeared in a flash. Melisande cried out that communications with the fairies had ceased, and Jeremiah found he could no longer speak with the mice.

"I can't link with any of you," gasped Mikel.

Hera laughed with pleasure.

"You will watch as I destroy each of your children, one by one, Sharra, beginning with this one."

She stretched out her hand, and Jamie was lifted off the ground as if someone had grabbed the front of her jerkin and yanked her up. Pain ripped through her from top to bottom. She screamed over and over, but still, waves of excruciating agony swept through her.

Suddenly, it was over, and she was sprawled face-first on the dais beneath. The pain was gone, but she felt like her body had been ripped to pieces and thrown back together again. Someone was trying to help her up into a sitting position, and she was vaguely aware of her mother holding her and a man she had never met trying to help her stand up. She turned her head and peered up at the goddess who was shielding her eyes from a bright light that had appeared in the chamber. What had stopped Hera from finishing the job?

A huge cloud radiating waves of white light was suspended in the air above them. A figure began to take shape in the center, the outline and features becoming more distinct with each passing moment. The figure was that of a man dressed in the toga clothing of an ancient Greek warrior. His body was muscular and had obviously been trained for battle. The black hair that fell to his shoulders was waved and styled in small curls around his face and a moustache and beard covered the lower half of his face. Nothing, however, could hide the blue radiance of his magnificent eyes or the burning rage and anger dominating them at that moment.

"Wife!" bellowed the figure. "You have much to answer for!"

"Zeus," whispered Jamie, her eyes wide with shock. "I'm looking at Zeus."

To Hera's credit, she did not cower in front of her husband but straightened her back and stood proudly in front of him.

"My affairs are not yours. I am equal in importance to you, Zeus, and hold equivalent power within the Olympian Council. You have no right to interfere."

"I have every right to interfere," bellowed the giant. "What you have done to these poor folk is atrocious. You have broken almost every agreement we made with the mortals, and you bring shame upon our council."

"I have done nothing wrong," replied the goddess, casually folding her arms across her chest. "These creatures have brought all of this down on their own heads. I simply came to see what was going on."

Jeremiah bounded forward and pointed an accusing finger at her. "That's a lie," he cried. "Hera has been responsible for everything. She kidnapped Sharra and changed her into both a statue and a monster. She forced six of us to go on a dangerous quest in order to get Sharra back and tricked us in the end."

Hera made an admirable job of looking shocked. "What quest? What statue?"

"She tried to murder us," added Jamie, joining the fray.

Hera tsked and shook her head. "My, my. I am not allowed to be involved in any mortal doings as the council and you well know, Zeus. They are making this up."

Kara had climbed the steps to the top of the dais, tears still rolling down her face, and now stood facing the goddess.

"She told Spider how to k…kill the Tree of Life in order to use the t…trolls. Someone had to jump into it with the seed. Petre did it. He's in the t…tree because of her."

Kara covered her face with her hands and sobbed as mutterings began to grow from the others standing in the cavern. Several dwarves took several threatening steps forward.

There was a gasp from the five others. They had known nothing of this, and they could only stare at the girl in shock. No wonder Petre had been so quiet back in Rosamund's glade.

Mikel turned back to Hera. "And because of her…."

He had to stop for a moment. He couldn't seem to keep his voice from cracking. "Because of her," he continued with more effort, "Portia was killed during the battle."

Cries of shock came from the group. Mikel had not yet had an opportunity to tell the others about Portia. Coming together, they wrapped their arms around each other, their heartbreaking sorrow at the losses of their friends who had gone through so much to help save Draukenberg, proving to be too much for most of the people in the chamber. Shouts and threats broke out as those still able to fight moved threateningly toward Hera.

"Stop," commanded Zeus, holding up an enormous hand. There was a reluctant silence, and all stopped where they were. That hand could have crushed them all with one swat.

"Listen to me, husband," pleaded Hera. "I don't know what these creatures are talking about. They are known for their lying. You…"

"Silence, wife," bellowed Zeus. "I have known of your horrific plots for some time. Mercury has been my watchdog ever since you made an attempt to destroy the elf messengers. Unfortunately for you, one of them made it through to us. Since then, Mercury has kept the council informed of all that has been taking place, and what he brought to our attention has been scandalous."

From within the cloud emerged a young man with wings on his hat and shoes. The last time he had been seen in Draukenberg, he had been dressed as a pirate and had held a meeting with Petre at the bottom of a river. Since that time, he had kept himself hidden, making certain that neither Hera nor her minions were aware of his presence.

"You have gone against our word," continued Zeus, "and have attempted to destroy these people for your own amusement. Some have died, and many have been injured as a result of your jealousy. You have been recalled to Olympia for trial."

"No!" shrieked Hera. "You have no right…"

"I certainly do," replied Zeus, giving her a dark smile. "Pray that your sentence will not be eternal banishment to the Seventh Dimension. Now be gone!"

Hera screamed with rage, but despite her best efforts, her outline began to blur and fade, and finally, she vanished from sight. All that could be heard was sobbing and the moaning of those who were grieving for lost ones. That included the group of five still on the dais.

Zeus cleared his throat. "I will not apologize for what my wife has done. We immortals never apologize. However, Mercury and I can assist with those who are injured. I cannot, however, bring back to life those who have died."

Kara pulled herself away from the group and nervously approached Zeus. "Can you help my friend?" she asked, pointing to the Laurel Tree. "Can you help Petre?"

Zeus looked at Mercury and nodded. Through her tears, Jamie watched in astonishment as Mercury flew over to the tree, with Kara quickly following behind. Surely one of the two who had given so much could be saved. Reaching toward the tree, she watched as Mercury's hands literally slid into the bark and seconds later, a very dopey and slightly green-tinged Petre emerged, looking only slightly the worse for wear. She gave a sigh of relief.

"Wh…where am I?" gasped the boy as Kara gave a squeal of delight and threw her arms around his neck.

Mercury laughed. "You're back with the living, boy."

Petre stared back at the young god, his eyes wide with wonder. "Who are you?" he asked.

"Perhaps you would remember me better in this form," replied Mercury.

In an instant, his shape and dress had altered. "The pirate!" gasped Petre. "You were the pirate."

Mercury laughed and changed back into his natural shape. With a slight bow, he lifted off the ground and flew back to Zeus.

"Why do you always have to play the part of a fool?" muttered Zeus. "Why can't you accomplish my tasks with more decorum? A pirate, no less. Now go help these poor people."

Mercury gave him a rakish grin and then flew down to help the others with their wounded.

Zeus turned his attention back to the crowd. "Never again will the Tree of Life be destroyed by a curse. If it must be restored for any reason, it will not be at the cost of anyone's life. Use your magic and be proud of your abilities. All those involved in Hera's schemes will pay a hefty price, and no one from The Hollows may go beyond its boundaries for at least one thousand years. So I have said, so it shall be."

Jamie gave a watery grin. Despite her relief that Zeus had arrived when he had, she couldn't help but think of him as a bit of a pompous buffoon. She also felt angry. If he had known all this time about Hera's plots, why had he waited until now to arrive? If he had stopped all of this earlier, Portia might still be alive.

Jamie was suddenly aware that Sharra was standing beside her, and at her side, with a hand on her shoulder, was the strange man that Mikel had seen on the balcony. She was suddenly struck by the strong resemblance the man bore to Yonnus. He was thinner, and his hair and beard were a rich red instead of pitch black, but the clothes looked like the ones Yonnus had been wearing. Zeus leaned down, his face only inches away from Sharra's.

"The years have been good to you, my beautiful one."

The man moved forward slightly as if attempting to protect her. "She is not yours, Zeus," he growled.

Sharra patted his hand. "It's alright, Nikolai. Move back for a moment and allow me to speak to Zeus alone."

Reluctantly, he stepped back and joined Jeremiah and Jamie who were both staring in wonder at the man. Was this Nikolai their father? Jamie knew that had been his name but if that was who he was, where had he been all this time? She turned their attention back to their mother who was speaking softly to the god who was listening intently to her. After several moments, to the surprise of all, he suddenly appeared to blush and to look incredibly embarrassed about something. She patted his large cheek and he withdrew from her, nodding determinedly and spouting, "I promise," several times. He and Mercury vanished into the depths of the large cloud and it disappeared from sight.

"What did you say to him?" asked Jamie.

"I simply reminded him that it was he who had started this terrible mess in the first place and that if he had behaved himself, Hera would never have reacted the way she had. He has promised never to let anyone interfere with us again. And speaking of us…"

She turned and looked at Jamie and Jeremiah standing in front of her, her smile fading and her eyes filling with tears.

"I will, however, never forgive him for taking your childhood away from me. You were babies when I last saw you, and now you are young adults. But you have helped keep them safe, dear one."

She smiled lovingly at Nikolai as Azmodeus joined them.

"But where is the third?" she asked.

"Here," came a voice from behind her.

She turned and held out her arms to Mikel, who awkwardly accepted the hug. He looked totally confused and very upset. Looking at Azmodeus, he gestured to King Nikolai.

"If this man is my father, who is Yonnus?"

Azmodeus looked over at Nikolai.

"Shall we?" asked the wizard.

Nikolai replied with a large grin.

The air shimmered around him as he transitioned from Mikel's new father to one that the boy and the other four instantly recognized.

"I told you, boy, not to touch my forge when I was gone."

"Father?" cried Mikel, his eyes wide with shock at seeing the big man standing in front of him.

"Yonnus?" squeaked some of the others.

Azmodeus began to laugh followed by a hearty one from Yonnus/Nikolai.

"I kept an eye on you and Jeremiah, Jamie," explained Azmodeus. "You were quite safe in the dimension of Earth with your new adopted families but I couldn't keep an eye on all three of you, so Nikolai and I concocted a plan to keep you, Mikel, here in Glockamar. In order to do that, we had to disguise Nikolai with a glamour so that no one would stumble upon his true identity. You were indeed raised by your natural father although, if you recall, he was absent quite often, leaving you in the hands of old Alga, the seamstress. Someone had to run the kingdom with our poor Sharra gone and a glamour can't remain in place for days on end."

On a signal from Nikolai, Azmodeus transitioned him back to his natural form.

"You will have to get used to me in this form, Mikel," said Nikolai, and then he turned to Jeremiah and Jamie. "Like your mother, I will always regret not seeing either of you grow up, but this was the best we could do at the time. Hera wanted the three of you dead and we could not let that happen. I hope you understand."

Jamie looked at Jeremiah and he looked back at her. This was not going to be easy for either of them and she knew it. She now had parents she did not know and their brother had been raised by one of them. She had developed strong feelings of friendship for both boys as a result of the quest but Jamie could not help but feel a bit of jealous of Mikel for his relationship with their father. It had been a shock to find out that he had been the third triplet and not Portia. Jamie had grown very used to the idea that Portia had been her sister and the two had finally grown close near the end of the quest. Tears came to her eyes at the thought of the girl and a death that never should have happened. Part of her would never lose the terrible feelings of loss when she thought of her friend.

"Come," said Sharra. "Come with me into the inner chambers. We have a great deal to discuss, including, from what I understand, plans for a very difficult departure."

It was a sad group that followed the king, queen and wizard out of the main chamber. Most of the wounded had been taken to the infirmary, but those who had died were slowly and carefully being removed on pallets. There would be many departure ceremonies taking place over the next few days, Jamie sadly concluded. They had won but at a heartbreaking cost.

Chapter Fifty-Six
A Moment For Portia

Jamie

On the morning of the ceremony, the group met with Azmodeus and the Willik in a room just off the main chamber where the battle had been fought. Drogo had been invited to join them. He had no one to help him through this except Portia's friends and he was surprised that they had actually wanted him there after all he'd put them through back in the village. Through a large open door, Jamie had a clear view of the Tree of Life and the procession of elves entering the chamber carrying a coffin between them. It had been decided that Portia would be placed beneath the tree in honour of the brave and critical role she had played during the battle.

The coffin was made of wood from the dark purplish trees that guarded Donagal. Intricate carvings of trees, flowers and forest animals had been worked into the sides, which in the light, appeared to be moving as if real. The elves placed it carefully on a stone platform that had been constructed to hold the coffin in place and then stepped back forming a line on each side.

"We will leave you now," said the Willik. "When Azmodeus and I reach the coffin and turn, we will gesture to those who are attending to enter. Once all have arrived, we will signal for you to come and stand beside the two of us."

Each nodded to her but no words were spoken. Azmodeus and the Willik walked through the door, the elf leaning heavily on the wizard's arm. Slowly they moved across the chamber and turned when they reached the others standing by the coffin. Azmodeus nodded and the mourners began to enter the room.

Jamie recognized most who entered. Calliotrope and King Reygould led in troupes of dwarves, and the Draukenbergians who followed were from all parts of the country. The elfin gryphon riders that had taken them to Aradell and back again quietly entered and Rosamund arrived with a very quiet, subdued group of fairies and sprites. Walking with her was a tall young man who she did not recognize, along with Bandi and Crooks. She was relieved to see that Bandi had taken on the shape of a human boy although it shifted precariously quite often. Bandi's mother and brother, now their regular sizes, walked quietly behind, attempting to keep similar shapes. To her surprise, three of the troll tree-keepers came through the doors and stopped as if guarding those attending the ceremony. As one, they bowed to Azmodeus and the Willik who acknowledged their sign of respect with a similar bow to them. When everyone took their places and silence filled the chamber, Azmodeus gestured to the six to enter. Petre had been allowed to remain behind in the room. He had not been on the quest with the others and after a quiet word with Azmodeus, had been granted his request to stay.

They walked in single file through the crowd, Jamie at the end, which parted quietly as they approached, allowing them to move to the front. When she reached Azmodeus and the Willik, she looked down at the coffin and tried not to gasp out loud. There was no lid on the coffin. Portia was lying on her back, her hands clasped together on her chest. She was dressed in a green gown that shimmered in the light like water flowing softly over the stones in a brook. Ribbons the same colour as her dress had been wound through her curls and slippers had been placed on her feet.

"She looks as if she's asleep," whispered Melisande, who was standing beside her.

"And peaceful," added Jamie quietly.

Drogo gave a small sob and she suddenly began to feel the effects of her own feelings of loss. Tears welled up in her eyes and her throat became tight as the Willik began to speak.

"We have come to celebrate the life of Portia dan Yoro, who deserves our respect and our love. As one of those who had to endure the trials and tribulations of a dangerous quest demanded by

Hera, she saw the journey through despite the personal battles that she herself had to fight. In the end, she willingly gave the gift of life to another before her own was taken from her. I ask that those who travelled with her and Drogo her brother, provide one remembrance of Portia to be shared with us now. Who will go first?”

Unexpected and unprepared, the individuals looked at one another in surprise. Why hadn’t the Willik warned them? Jamie looked over at the ancient elf woman and suddenly realized the reason. She had done this on purpose. This way, they would speak from the heart.

“I will go first,” she said, swallowing hard as she continued. “From the beginning, I was led to believe that Portia was my sister and despite a rough beginning, we grew close as the journey progressed. Even though…” she choked, “even though she was not my sister in reality, she will always be my sister in my heart.”

There was a moment of silence before Jeremiah spoke.

“I will always remember Portia for her courage. No matter what happened on the quest, she was never afraid to tackle the problem head-on. If we were reluctant to move forward, she would push us and challenge us to go on.”

Several gave watery smiles. Portia bullied them more than challenged them but as a result, they got the job done.

Drogo took a small step forward. “She always looked after me and made certain that I had everything I needed. She stood up to our father…

At that point, he broke down and stepped back. Melisande put an arm around him to comfort him. “At the beginning of our journey,” she said, “we didn’t know very much about each other, but by the end, Portia had become my friend. She was also the one who learned the secret of solving the riddles.”

Tovan was the next to step forward. An image of Portia suggesting they cover themselves in fairy wings at Rumplestiltskin’s bridge popped into her mind. Her suggestion had relieved some of the tension at that moment.

"Sometimes, when we were in trouble," she stated, "Portia could see the humour in something even though she didn't think she was funny. It helped us all be less frightened."

She stepped back, and Jamie turned to look at Mikel. The boy appeared to be struggling with what he was going to say. Finally, he stepped forward but moved instead toward the coffin. Leaning down, he placed something inside. When the others looked over, they realized that he had placed on Portia's dress the bracelet she had tossed to him. He turned to face the others and, with tears running down his cheeks, simply stated, "Portia saved my life."

There was silence in the chamber for a few moments and then the Willik raised her hands. A mist began to form around the coffin as she began to speak and those surrounding the coffin stepped back and watched in fascination as it began to thicken.

"Farewell, young child. From this day forward, we name you the 'Guardian of the Tree of Life'. The two of you together will protect our world and each other. Never again shall there be an opportunity for our tree-keepers to be used by evildoers for their own gain. Go with our blessings, Portia."

The coffin disappeared in a cloud of mist, which then began to dissipate. There were gasps and startled cries throughout the chamber as the coffin came back into view. A crystal lid covered in etchings that matched the sides of the coffin sealed the coffin permanently closed. The elves had designed it so that nothing could remove it from the base. It was also designed so that Portia's body was hidden from sight. When Jamie looked through the crystal, it appeared to her that the mist that had recently surrounded the coffin was now inside.

The Willik gestured to all to stand further away from the coffin and no one argued when the first strange noises drifted up into the air becoming louder by the minute. From the wooden sides, tendrils began to emerge and circle not only the coffin but the tree as well. The further they moved from the coffin, the larger they became, and leaves sharp and pointed like those on the trees around Donagal began to shoot out from the branches. When it was complete, both the coffin and the tree were encircled by leaves that would be deadly to anyone who attempted to remove them. Neither the coffin nor the tree could have received better protection.

"Snow White," whispered Jamie. "It's a combination of Snow White in the glass-covered coffin and the hedge in Sleeping Beauty."

"You're right," Jeremiah whispered back. "I was thinking the same thing."

"What's this Snow Beauty you're talking about?" asked Melisande.

"I'll explain later," replied Jamie.

Suddenly, low bellows booming out from the back of the room broke the silence. At first Jamie thought it was someone with a trombone playing one incredibly loud note. To her amazement, it was the trolls. Their faces were turned to the ceiling and the bellows were coming from their mouths.

"That is how the trolls celebrate their own departures," explained Azmodeus. "It is a great sign of respect to have three trolls contributing."

"Come," said the Willik, taking hold once again of the wizard's arm. "We must leave first. The others will not leave until we are gone. It has been a long morning, and there is still much to do."

The members of the small group, along with Drogo, remained for several minutes, their eyes on the coffin, their thoughts on Portia. Then as one, they turned and followed Azmodeus and the Willik into the room where Petre waited.

"Why weren't you at the ceremony, Petre?" asked Jamie.

Petre looked at her for a moment and then replied, "Azmodeus knows why." He turned abruptly and followed the others out of the room.

"I don't understand," she murmured.

"His last memory of Portia," said Azmodeus, coming up beside her, "was of her sending all of the Glockamarians to Spider to be possibly killed. He didn't have the chance to get to know her like you people did and he's angry. He can't forgive her yet for what she and Drogo did to all of them. He also blames her for the death of his friend, Crutchin, for some reason. It would have been hypocritical of him to attend and try to say a nice remembrance of her."

"Will he ever forgive her?"

"Possibly."

Jamie sighed, and the two left the room together. So Petre had lost a friend as well on his journey. It appeared that no-one had escaped suffering as a result of Hera's attempt at revenge.

"Poor Petre," she whispered to herself.

Chapter Fifty-Seven
Reunions

Jamie

The triplets had arrived with their parents at Magnigona Castle after the ceremony for Portia and were having an exciting time discovering the nooks and crannies of the fortress. Nothing had felt familiar until they entered the upper garden where Sharra had been kidnapped ten years before. The three stopped and looked around, slightly puzzled.

"We were playing here when it happened, weren't we?" asked Jamie looking around.

"That was a long time ago," replied Jeremiah. "It's hard to remember back that far. We were just little kids."

Mikel walked further into the garden and pointed to one of the trees. "I remember that swing. I think I was on it the day Hera kidnapped Sharra."

All three were finding it difficult to call their parents, mother and father. They had continued to refer to them as Sharra and Nikolai, which both parents accepted for now. It would take time, trust and love before that would change.

"Ah, I was hoping to find all of you here," smiled Sharra coming through the door into the garden. "I would like to speak with you before we join the rest outside the hall. Come and sit down."

She gestured to the benches, and all four took a seat.

"The new Council that your father and I have organized has invited guests from all the communities of Draukenberg. As you know, we have decided that all voices must be represented in the decisions we make in the future for our country. Many are going to expect to hear your actual names, not those that were given to you to hide your identities.”

The three shared puzzled looks with one another, and Sharra smiled gently. “I know that this has been a strange time for you. New information keeps coming at you from all directions and it has been, I’m quite certain, overwhelming.”

“What are our real names?” asked Jeremiah.

“You, Jamie, are named after my mother. Her name was Jasmina. Jeremiah, you are named after your uncle Jaxton and Mikel, you are Mikolai in honour of your father as you were born first.”

“Who was born second?” asked Jeremiah.

“Jasmina,” smiled his mother.

“That makes you the little baby brother,” teased Jamie, which resulted in a playful punch in the arm from Jeremiah.

“It is important that you know your real names as they will be used at all formal functions. Treat your current names as nicknames, used only when you are alone or with the others you journeyed with. Will that work for you?”

“I think so,” replied Mikel. “It will take some time.”

“I have a question,” said Jamie. “If we lived outside the mountain and Portia lived inside, how could she have looked so much like me and Jeremiah?”

Sharra thought for a moment before speaking.

“The people both inside the mountain and outside were all originally Atlantians. As we were the only human beings here, it was only natural that certain physical characteristics would follow through the generations. Red hair and green eyes were one of the dominant sets of characteristics. It wasn’t odd that there would be individuals in Glockamar who would resemble individuals outside.”

“But why Portia?” asked Jeremiah.

“That was the decision of the Willik. She knew that Portia was going to be a critical element in helping to beat Hera at her game. You and Jamie were safe in Earth’s dimension, but Mikel, who didn't resemble you two quite as much, was kept safe in Glockamar under your father's protection. What no one knew was that Nikolai was also watching over Portia. Her father was a dangerous man and there was always the worry that he would harm her as many believed he had done to his wife. When Nikolai as Yonnus kidnapped her, he may have saved her life. It was critical that Portia be protected because of her role during the battle."

"If the Willik knew what was going to happen during the battle," whispered Jamie, "then why couldn't she have predicted Portia's death?"

"Not everything can be revealed ahead of time," replied Sharra, gently. "We can only make decisions and choices on what we know or think we know. The rest is up to chance and hope. Even someone as powerful as the Willik could not have known. If she had, she would have done everything possible to stop such a tragedy. Now let us join the others. The meeting will be starting soon."

Jamie sighed in resignation. Her mother's explanation would have to do.

Outside the meeting chamber, the six of the quest greeted each other with enthusiasm. Even Petre made an effort to look happy. Bandi sat cheerfully on Mikel's shoulder as a parrot, trying very hard to sit still and not squirm with excitement.

"How great to see you all together," chuckled Azmodeus joining them. "I'm pleased that we can have one last gathering to say our farewells before we all separate."

It was true that they were all going to be going their separate ways, but they were looking forward to their next adventures. Jeremiah would be staying at Donagal working with several gryphon riders who could speak with animals. This would give him a chance to perfect his skills and learn to communicate with a wide variety of creatures. He was also going to be given the opportunity to remain with the dragons for a time, which was causing him great excitement. Melisande would be spending time with Rosamund, and Jamie and Kara were going to the new school at Citadel that Azmodeus and the Willik were establishing to help train young people who were demonstrating various skills and talents. Tovan would be returning to the Sanctuary to work with other healers in setting up a hospital and a school for healers. Bandi, of course, would be going with Mikel who would be training as a Magi with Azmodeus. Jamie had heard Azmodeus say that he was going to need more work than her brother which had caused her to chuckle.

"Where are you going to be going, Petre?" asked Melisande, but before he could answer, the door opened and in stepped the Willik on the arm of her assistant, her dark eyes twinkling merrily.

"Everyone is ready for you but before we continue, there is another who will be joining your group for today. Rosamund arrived with him just a moment ago. You may have seen him at Portia's Departure Ceremony."

"Adonis?" laughed Melisande getting to her feet.

Jamie gasped in surprise as a young man dressed in a tunic, leggings and boots walked through the entrance and made straight for Melisande. Black, curly hair fell to his shoulders and a bright smile beamed from his handsome, dark features.

"Adonis," whispered Melisande, looking up at the young man who now grasped both her hands in his. "Is it really you?"

"It is," he laughed. "When I was turned back to human form, and believe me, that was a wild story which I will tell you about some time, Cerce turned me back to the age I was when she originally made me a Minotaur. Ten. However, over the days following my change, I aged to my current age, which Rosamund and I believe is fifteen. I must apologize to you as well for my terrible behaviour while I was a Minotaur. It seems that I stayed ten as well in my head which didn't make me pleasant company."

"How wonderful," beamed Melisande.

'How crappy,' groaned Jeremiah. Jamie chuckled. He would never have a chance with Melisande now…not with Mr. Handsome around. Mikel looked as if he'd eaten something rotten.

The door to their chamber opened once again and Tovan's father entered the room dressed in the new formal robes of government. Tovan stared at her father in amazement.

"When did he become a government official?" she asked of Jamie.

"I guess just now," was her response.

"Would you all come in now?" smiled Talman dan Vay. "The Council awaits you."

He backed into the hallway and disappeared. The group got to their feet and followed Azmodeus and the Willik out of the room and into the chamber beyond.

The Council Chamber in Magnigona Castle was almost as large as the main chamber in the Sanctuary. Around the circumference were three tiers of seats now filled with representatives from every race in Draukenberg, excluding The Hollows. There were humans, elves, dwarves and trolls, the seats of the latter being quite a bit larger than the rest. The air was filled with fairies, sprites and pixies who took up their positions on the beams and wall fixtures. There were also many representatives of different races from places she did not know. Calliotrope was sitting with the other dwarves and waving frantically, ignoring the sour looks from Maxim, who was obviously wishing he would behave with more decorum. Queen Sharra and King Nikolai were seated on thrones at the top of one tier that also seemed to house important representatives dressed in robes similar to those of Tovan's father. Dragon and gryphon representatives were on the grounds outside the castle.

A buzz filled the chamber, and Talman dan Vay stood. Tovan hadn't noticed until that moment that her father was seated in the chair of the Chief Magistrate. He held up his hand and the talking ceased. Tovan stared at her father in amazement and it wasn't until Jamie nudged her in her ribs that she shut her mouth.

"We kept it a secret from you," she whispered, smiling broadly. "Your father was voted in yesterday afternoon. I didn't tell you earlier because I wanted it to be a surprise."

"Before we can begin our business," Talman began in serious tones, "we must deal with the prisoner. Bring him in."

To the surprise and astonishment of all, a decrepit creature was dragged kicking and yelling into the room. His clothes were dirty and torn, his hair hung in long, greasy strands, and he obviously hadn't seen soap in a very long time.

"It's Phineas," gasped Jamie. "It's Portia's father."

Boos and hisses rang through the chamber.

"Quiet!" bellowed Talman.

The chamber became silent, slowly and reluctantly.

"Phineas dan Yoro," continued Talman, "you conspired with Hera and Spider to capture Glockamarians and turn them into goblins."

Jamie gave her mother a quick glance. It must be a terrible thing to have been one of the most hated and feared creatures in Glockamar and to hear stories of what you did. Sharra looked far from comfortable.

"I was tricked," screamed Phineas. "The monster cursed me. She put a spell on me."

One of the trolls stood, and Talman nodded for him to speak.

"The trolls witnessed his evil doings," he stated in deep rolling tones. "He was not forced or put under a spell. He enjoyed what he was doing. He laughed often."

Other troll voices rumbled in agreement as he sat down.

"He lies," cried Phineas. "They are all lying."

"We have made our decision, Phineas," stated Talman. "Many witnessed your cruel acts and you need to pay the price. You are banished from Draukenberg and will be taken across the Faldor Passage and deposited on the shores of Hvedrung."

"They'll put me in the mines!" gasped Phineas, beginning to shake, his eyes rolling back in his head.

"Yes, they probably will," agreed Talman. "Take him away."

Phineas was dragged unceremoniously from the chamber.

"He survive not long," whispered Bandi to Mikel.

"I'm just thankful Portia wasn't here to see this," whispered Jamie on his other side.

Azmodeus moved into the center of the room, and the chamber became quiet.

"We have learned that we must work together in order to keep our land safe from peril. From this time forward, all races of Draukenberg, except for The Hollows, will be represented on this Council. Decisions for the good of our land will be made here by all those who will be affected by those decisions."

A tremendous cheer filled the room. The wizard raised his hands for quiet.

"We will also not turn our backs on the magical skills that many of our people possess. Instead, we are going to train those skills and develop those abilities that are still in infancy. To do that, we ask that you allow the Willik and I to take charge of a new school to be opened at Citadel on Fenwin Island. Children from all over Draukenberg and from all races will come to be trained properly. Please stand to demonstrate your agreement."

A buzz filled the chamber as representatives stood all around the chamber.

"What of the gryphons and dragons, Prince Jaxton?" asked Talman.

Jeremiah stood looking around happily at all those who had agreed.

Mikel nudged him in the back. "That's you, baby brother."

"What?"

"Do the gryphons and dragons agree?" he repeated for him.

We agree.

"They support the decision," Jeremiah/Jaxton blurted out.

He was never going to get his names right.

"Then the decision is unanimous," stated the Chief Magistrate.

Amid the cheering, Azmodeus shepherded the group out of the chamber and into the one they had previously occupied.

"They will be getting down to other business decisions, so you won't be needed. Now where is Petre?"

They looked around, but the boy was gone.

Kara sighed. "He hasn't been the same since he was pulled from the tree. I don't think he feels that he belongs to anyone or anything anymore."

"I wouldn't be too quick to judge," murmured the wizard. "No, not at all. Let us wait and see, shall we?"

Petre

Several days later, the object of their concern after having hitched a ride back to Toria in a farmer's cart, climbed the steps to the theatre. His feet dragged, and his hands in his pockets pulled his shoulders forward. He had left the group as soon as they had returned to the room beside the Council Chamber. Somehow he just couldn't be part of their company any longer and wanted desperately to return to his own sanctuary. For the hundredth time at least, he wished that Mercury had left him inside the laurel tree. When he'd pulled him out, something vital, some part of his soul, had been left behind, and he'd felt useless and empty ever since. The death of his father during the battle had added to his feelings of loss and loneliness. Perhaps he should leave Toria and head into the hills where he could be alone forever.

He opened the door and stepped into the blessed quiet of the theatre. Halfway down the aisle, he dropped into one of the seats and stared gloomily at the stage. Petre knew what the main problem was. He would never get over the loss of Crutchin. The Wildenchin had become as close to him as any father, brother, or friend could have, and he missed him terribly. Each day since he had moved into the theatre, he had spent most of his time sitting in this exact spot thinking of the little man and wondering what he could have done differently that might have saved the life of the Wildenchin.

"I spent all that time feeling sorry for myself," he snapped. "And yet, he knew for sure that he was going to die."

"Who was going to die?" came a voice from the shadows on the stage. "Is this a tragedy you're practicing for, boy?"

Petre stared at the stage, his eyes wide, his mouth open and his chin on his chest. Into the light stepped a figure that he would have known anywhere.

"Crutchin!" he shouted, leaping out of his seat and racing down the aisle. He jumped up onto the stage, tripped over the edge and fell flat on his face.

"Easy, boy," said Crutchin, bending down and hauling Petre to his feet.

Oblivious to his bleeding nose, Petre threw his arms around the Wildenchin and started to jump up and down.

"You're alive!" he shouted. "You're alive! You didn't die!"

"Hold it, boy," yelled Crutchin, grabbing hold of Petre's arms and holding him steady. Petre had forgotten how strong the little man was. "If you don't stop, I will die. You're knockin' the innards out of me."

"But you're alive," gasped Petre. "I saw you die."

"In a manner of speaking, I did," replied Crutchin. "As the trees died, so did I, but when you brought the Tree of Life back, you brought me back. I'm not human, boy. I'm a Wildenchin, one with the earth. We are not built like you, and we don't live and die by the same rules. Now, there is no need for this."

Petre was so filled with joy that tears were streaming down his cheeks.

"I can't help it. I'm so very glad to see you."

"And I am to see you."

He put an arm around Petre's shoulders and steered him off the stage.

"But we have work to do," he continued. "We're off to Findabair in the far north."

"Why?"

"Don't ask questions. We have a job to do, and you'll find out when we get there. First, we have to get you changed."

Petre looked down at his pants and jerkin.

"What's wrong with what I've got on?"

"If you're going to work with me and look like an actor…"

"Ah, Crutchin," groaned Petre. "Not the flooffy pants and the pink cape."

"I was thinking of the turquoise cape."

Petre groaned again, knowing full well that, in the end, he'd wear it.